Praise for *Sunshine Girl*:

"Nancy Townsley's debut is an elegy to community newspapers. Resonant and compelling, this multigenerational novel puts reporters on the page—their family dynamics and friendships, their misunderstandings and mistakes, and their absolute dedication to the profession."
—Laura Stanfill, publisher of Forest Avenue Press, Portland, OR

"A touching family saga of betrayal, loss, and forgiveness wrapped inside a cautionary tale about the decline of traditional community journalism. An important and timely debut."
—William Loving, author of *City of Angles*

"Such a vivid tour of the last half century in newsrooms, I can practically hear the keyboards firing through every era. A swift, affecting narrative against a backdrop that is equal parts alarm, nostalgia and homage for what newspaper journalism has lost, and still stands to gains."
—Lee van der Voo, author of *As the World Burns* and *The Fish Market*

"In this tender and intelligent debut novel, Nancy Townsley takes us on a family journey of loss and healing, framed by local and national news of over four decades. As Eliza, Martin and Mina report on the changing world, we come to love and care deeply about these journalists and the important work of truth-telling."
—Jackie Shannon Hollis, author of *This Particular Happiness: A Childless Love Story*

"Leveraging a multigenerational narrative frame and unforgettable characters, *Sunshine Girl* exhibits the rigor of true journalism through the lens of fiction to explore the implications of informational access, consumption trends, and the changing ways we understand—and misunderstand—our shared world."
—Jen Knox, author of *Chaos Magic* and *We Arrive Uninvited*

Sunshine Girl

A Novel

Nancy Townsley

 Heliotrope Books

New York

ISBN: 978-1-956474-56-5; eBook ISBN: 978-1-956474-57-2

Cover design by Gigi Little
Typeset Design by Heliotrope Books

For my dad, who always expected the best of me
and sometimes got it.

Elbows and shoulders jostle me as I walk briskly, staring down at my smartphone, my body ping-ponging left and right, my feet playing catch-up. Before the rally this morning I lingered in front of the bathroom mirror and carefully parted my hair down the back, separating it into two braids and securing each one with a black elastic band, like my friends advised me.

To contain the unruly red waves.

To give myself a sense of control.

For sure I need both.

People are already milling around when I get to the corner of First and Clay at 8:45 a.m. The message on the Facebook group, First Amendment Foo Fighters, said to gather one block east of the Marriott. We followed orders. There are so many of us that bodies are spilling over into the crosswalk. Shoving my phone in my pocket, I position myself at the front of the pack with a protest sign in one hand and an oversized bullhorn in the other. I know things could get ugly. All I really have is my voice.

My girlfriends said, "Eliza Donovan Dixon, if anyone can do this, you can," and I believed them, so here we are.

At 9:00 sharp I give the signal, moving everyone forward. As if it had been instructed to, the sky opens up and the rain starts to fall.

I lead the throng north, zigzagging through downtown. Water from a classic Portland downpour drips off the ends of my braids and onto my cardboard sign. It gets so soggy it reads We Are Not instead of We Are Not The Enemy. It rains two-thirds of the year in the Rose City. It ruins so many things.

The downtown streets are slick and dirty, the kind of cement-mix grit the Beaver State is famous for from November to May. Hardly the right day for a rally, but I pick up my pace and keep going anyway. We take a left on West Burnside and pass Voodoo Doughnut and Powell's City of Books. I think of ditching out into Powell's. I could use a good novel to get lost in.

But I need to stay the course, and I will.

I abandon my wet sign in a trash can right when the first alert beeps through. I can feel my cell phone vibrating inside my pocket. I fish it out and try to focus my eyes on its too-small screen. Every buzz confirms that something horrible has happened up in Alaska, where I used to live. I grip the phone tighter. Everyone's shoes, moving en masse, morph into a sad, disorienting muddle.

A stocky guy in a blue anorak comes up on my left and bumps into me, hard, knocking the wind out of me for a second. My legs feel numb, disembodied. A weird humidity rises from the street, a combination of the rain and so many bodies pressed together. There had been a few threats against the protesters on social media in the days leading up to the rally. The youngest, strongest marchers intentionally flank the group on the right and left, a ragged protective army. Two women dressed in matching tie-dyed T-shirts walk arm in arm, singing "We Shall Overcome" in a loose harmony. Others join in, evoking civil rights protests of the 1960s, long before I was born, though I learned about them in school and by reading a few volumes in my father's home library.

Two summers ago, racial justice protests in response to the murder of a Black man, George Floyd, in Minneapolis had turned the city into a battleground. The nightly skirmishes often ended with police declaring unlawful riots and arresting people for lighting fires, breaking down barricades, or just standing around in the wrong place at the wrong time.

Has any real progress been made in sixty years?

I shut my eyes to squeeze out the rainwater and try to banish the nagging doubts from my mind. The country has been through a hell of a time. More than a million people are dead from COVID-19, and forest fires have consumed thousands upon thousands of acres, on top of the indignities the last president inflicted on the press, the entire nation, and the world. With all the residual political division, can things ever really improve?

We need to be part of the solution, not part of the problem. To stand up and speak out, defend my chosen profession—well, my *former* profession and my father's and grandfather's. I left newspapers behind for good in 2020.

"Always forward, never backward," my dad used to say. My comrades and I have made it from the Park Blocks to the Willamette River waterfront south of the Hawthorne Bridge. My news feed is going crazy. Phones are chiming all around me. Mine is hot with notifications. Dozens of protesters reach for their devices simultaneously and start shuffling faster and faster, like they're trying to escape the Big One, the massive earthquake that's sure to hit Portland sometime during our lifetime, or so the seismologists say.

We're united in defending the First Amendment, which protects a free and independent press. We won't stand for all that "fake news" and "enemies of the people" crap anymore. We have to be the change.

My fingers are cold, but I can't put gloves on, what with the notifications and the bullhorn, so I scroll as fast as I can. CNN is reporting shots were fired inside a newsroom in southern Alaska, but that's all, nothing else. *Holy shit.* I swallow hard. My heart races. Where in Alaska? Such a vast state, bigger than California and Texas combined. *Tell me something, dammit.*

I scroll some more.

NPR breaks the news that people are dead in Juneau. At the *Juneau Tribune.* My old newsroom. The one that smelled of fast food and sweat and deadline angst. How many? And who? Is the shooter still active? It's completely unclear. I feel my body shudder, then straighten. I should be there, huddled under desks or behind doors with my colleagues. My *former* colleagues, anyway, the ones who let me down. Screw them.

Wait.

Stop.

I stumble toward the curb. Anxiety rises from my chest to my throat. My heart feels like it's in A-fib. Maybe my former coworkers already tackled the bad guy. Maybe they neutralized the situation. I can see Fletcher doing that. Mina too. Even Naomi might get in on that shit.

From AP: *At Least One Dead in Juneau Newsroom Incident.* Oh my God. It just can't be true!

In, out; in, out; in, out. Shuffle, shuffle, breathe.

Jesus F. Christ, when will they stop killing us? First *Charlie*

Hebdo, then the *Capital Gazette*, then Jamal Khashoggi, all in four years. Khashoggi couldn't have known what was coming when he walked through the doors of the Saudi Arabian embassy in Istanbul that day in 2018.

Ambushed.

Murdered.

Mutilated.

For what?

To control the message, that's what. To rattle journalists and scare them out of reporting the facts. To threaten them with prison, or worse.

And now it's happened at my own newspaper. My nerves snap and pop, my hands tremble to think of it. Staff members dead! Blood on the very walls that cocooned us, writers whose features had mirrored the community, reporters whose hard news stories had exposed graft and greed inside taxpayer-supported public agencies.

Thought fragments pinball inside my throbbing head: *Managing editor. Mina. Friend. Enemy. Story.* Ours is a complicated relationship.

Oh my God, Mina. Please be alive.

My Android is ancient, but my income has been pretty anemic lately, so I put off replacing it. Big mistake. People's voices are going in and out, muffled, like when I wear earbuds on my trail runs. The hood on my slicker shields me, but it can't protect me from the world. My skin turns clammy. I consider dropping out, as I did the year I registered for the Portland Marathon. *DNF: Did Not Finish.* That had been humiliating. I swear I'm not going to faint.

The tie-dyed T-shirt women stopped singing five or six blocks ago. Their groupies take up the slack, chanting a plucky slogan—"Hey hey! Ho ho! Journo hate has got to go!"—but lunchtime traffic along Southwest Second Avenue drowns out their efforts. Soon we'll all be back at the Marriott and the rally will be over. I hope we've attracted enough attention to make a difference.

We have to fight on for the cause, for the journalists, for the American people. We won't let the gaslighters and naysayers win. No one can shut me up. My dad never quit, and I won't either.

Mina?

A vision of her pops into my mind. Sitting at her desk. Straight back, salt-and-pepper hair, reading glasses low on her nose. My aging mentor, still beautiful. Still dedicated.

We're moving back toward Naito now. The smartphone pings keep coming. Someone should say what's happening, tell me what I need to know. We're getting the news in real time, as fast as technology can deliver it, but it isn't fast or thorough enough.

I doff my hood, raise the bullhorn, and clear my throat. "Not the enemy!" I hear myself shout, my voice strangling. Then, much louder: "Freedom of the press means freedom for all!"

The man in the blue anorak grunts out a wheezy "Yeah!" He leans his sign against a lamppost and sits down to rest. I recognize that post. Naito and Clay, where my dad and I watched the Rose Festival parade when I was a little kid. Perched high on his shoulders, I could see the themed floats and the cheering people in living color.

***

The sun is starting to go down. Rain is falling hard and fast. It's almost impossible to see my phone. I unzip my jacket and wipe the screen off with the front of my sweatshirt. No more news yet. I peer east toward the interstate. Blue and brown tarps bunch under the off-ramp, a hodgepodge village dissecting the urban landscape. Tunnel lights flicker on, illuminating old bicycles, shopping carts, and rudimentary stoves. Inside one tent a flame glows red-orange. I can make that out. Surely someone is crouching beside that fire, someone who could die if it gets out of hand. Homelessness has exploded on the east side. More poor souls are houseless (or unhoused?) than ever before. The local economy is in shambles as Delta and Omicron and all the other Greek-letter variants keep the coronavirus going. The anti-vaxxers are dug in. Schools are back to in-person learning, but for how long? Some folks are going out, but others aren't. It's confusing. The situation seems hopeless.

Goddamn disinformation. It's going to kill us. I blink the wet away. The sign against the lamppost says #JournalismSavesUs in bold letters, upper- and lowercase. Like a headline in the *New York Times*, only with a hashtag and no spaces between the words. There's no hashtag for what I wrote in all those journals I stashed away in dresser drawers over the years, my shattered heart on paper. About my dad, about Mina. About Mina and my dad. I'll keep them for always.

Water saturates my clothing. I'm soaked to the skin. Exhausted, freezing. What would my dad do? My left hand shoots up and makes a power fist. With my right, I raise the bullhorn once more.

"For the people!" I yell. "Never give up, never give in!"

The crowd echoes back in solidarity.

"For the people!"

"Never give up!"

"Never give in!"

Our entire group moves forward as one. These are my people. I feel it clean through to my bones. We're united in the fight to save journalism.

Part One

HEYDAY:
1968–1988

Chapter One
Martin Donovan Marries Judith Levy
March 23, 1968

Martin and Judith took the plunge during their senior year at Lewis & Clark College, on an early spring day two months after the beginning of the Tet Offensive. They made a handsome couple. His red hair and slight build. Her sturdily Rubenesque form, a crown of dark brown waves secured with pearl-and-abalone hairpins atop her head. The groom had chosen a charcoal suit, a purple tie—purple being Judith's favorite color—and had added a black armband with a white peace sign on his right sleeve to protest the Vietnam War. His twenty-one-year-old bride, nearly a year his junior, wore a tea-length dress with an antique lace bodice and a bleached satin skirt that flared on the sides. She carried a small bouquet of baby's breath and magnolias. Her face was radiant; her alabaster cheeks flushed with anticipation.

Martin's heart swelled when he saw her on her father's arm at the narthex door, as the first notes of Pachelbel's "Canon in D" rose from piano and cello. *So beautiful*, he thought, and at the time he thoroughly meant it.

The armband went wholly unappreciated by Judith's mother Sheila, who believed all young men eighteen and older were obligated to join the selective service and do their bit for the war effort, full-time students included. In her mind deferrals were for cowards. Martin did not share that sentiment and made sure to walk Judith back down the aisle with his left arm hooked inside her right, flashing the protest band at his new mother-in-law and winking as he did so.

Martin and Judith Donovan were young and in love and didn't have two nickels to rub together, just a couple of hippies from very different families whose matriarchs and patriarchs practiced quite separate religions, to the newlyweds' great chagrin. Judith smelled of musk and wore daisy chains in her dark, loosely plaited hair, and when she quoted Keats to Martin—his head nestled in her lap under the shade of a particular Norway maple near the center of campus, its dual trunks angled toward the sky—he gave himself completely over to her charms.

Whenever she recited "Ode to a Nightingale," typically with great flourish, they would sigh and swoon together, then retire to her off-campus bungalow to make love.

Adieu! adieu! thy plaintive anthem fades
Past the near meadows, over the still stream,
Up the hill-side; and now 'tis buried deep
In the next valley-glades:
Was it a vision, or a waking dream?
Fled is that music:—Do I wake or sleep?

***

Sheila Levy had agreed to attend the wedding, a small affair in the college chapel, in exchange for a promise that Judith and Martin would raise their future progeny in the Jewish tradition. They had made that pledge with fingers crossed behind their backs. Out of respect for his own mother, Martin continued to wear the silver Saint Christopher necklace she had given him upon his confirmation, though he considered himself a lapsed Catholic, drawn to the faith's scripture and structure but not given to confession or regular attendance at Mass. To keep peace between the families, the couple displayed both a crucifix and a Star of David in their living room, and during the high holidays they hosted an equal opportunity meal—rugelach and roast beef—with a range of alcohol choices.

Things went along fine for the better part of their inaugural year. Judith and Martin avoided most of the emotional traps set by family members, though their record was hardly perfect. That first Easter, they drove to Martin's parents' house in Laurelhurst for luncheon and an egg hunt on the Donovans' expansive front lawn. Their nephews sported neckties and worsted-wool jackets and their nieces wore frilly anklets and pastel pinafores.

They looked around and realized Judith's parents were nowhere to be seen.

"Where are Art and Sheila?" Martin inquired. His mother

balanced a tray of deviled eggs on white-gloved hands. He sampled one, too mustardy for his taste, and looked askance at the paprika sprinkled on top.

"I didn't invite them, of course," the senior Mrs. Donovan sniffed, a look of annoyance darkening her rouge-stained face. "They're Jewish, dear. They don't celebrate Easter. You know that."

Martin and Judith had been naïve to imagine their life together would remain unscathed by the religious and social eccentricities of their elders, three-meal Shabbat observances on one side and post–High Mass potlucks on the other, practiced more for show than salvation. Her parents' exclusion at the Easter gathering hurt Judith deeply, so much so that Martin felt compelled to sit for a man-to-man chat one evening at cocktail hour with his cerebrally oriented father, who sympathized but did not bend.

"You must be aware that I can't cross your mother," the venerable editor Colin Donovan said, emitting a small, nervous chuckle. He used a pair of stainless steel tongs to drop three ice cubes into his highball glass. "She'd have my head!"

In bed that night Martin pleaded with Judith to let it go.

"Controlling them is impossible, sweetheart," he said as they lay staring at the ceiling, arms crossed over their chests. "The best we can do is take charge of what happens in our own house." She regarded him with skepticism. He repeated the surety that his mother's arched eyebrows would remain a permanent fixture in their lives, no matter what they did or didn't do. There would be no opportunity for real compromise.

"In that case," Judith said, putting her size-five foot down, "next year we're having the holidays by ourselves!" Her velvety eyes went soft and she dissolved into tears. Martin slid his arm underneath her shoulders and drew her close. He kissed her, a gesture of solidarity.

"Fine by me," he agreed, his chest a perfect pillow for her head. He stroked her wet cheek. If his own father couldn't pierce the formidable wall of woman he encountered every morning at the breakfast table—when, by habit, he read her his column out loud— there was little chance Martin would be able to do so. But he could support Judith's vision for a quiet home and a comparatively tidy life, and he was wise enough to try.

Chapter Two
Judith, Martin Welcome Baby Eliza
December 13, 1974

There was frost on the windowpanes at Samaritan North Lincoln Hospital the morning Judith gave birth to her first child, a six-pound, fourteen-ounce girl, with Martin holding her hand as her labor transitioned, just as a new father should.

His vantage point was less than desirable. All he could see were Judith's bare knees, the hump of her tummy, and her toes gripping those awful chrome stirrups, as sterile and unforgiving a scene as he could imagine. But he said nothing. Appropriately, his wife was making all the noise, on cue and for good reason.

"Here she comes!" announced the obstetrician, his arms stretched out to receive the Donovans' bundle. "You have a daughter!" came a few moments later, a risible understatement to Martin's mind. Had he written the blessed event as an opinion-page headline, it would have read *Most Beautiful Baby in World Emerges at Oregon Coast.*

Martin had planned ahead. Along with Judith's small suitcase containing going-home clothes for her and their baby, he had packed the car with a cassette player and a mixtape of songs to buoy her through her labor. When the time for his departure came in 1972, Martin's father had played himself off the planet to strains of Bach—Concerto for Two Violins in D Minor—and the operatic overtures of "Nessun dorma." Martin thought it a fine idea to play little Eliza *onto* it. And so it was that when Judith gave one last Herculean push, releasing her burden along with her husband's hand, he reached up to press a button and the Beatles filled the room with cheerful, rollicking music.

A nurse suctioned the squalling child's nose, put drops in her eyes, and arranged her on her mother's chest. The newborn blinked and frowned up at the lights. Her daddy snapped a photo, then two. He was handed a pair of scissors and he did the honors, slicing the umbilical cord in two with one stroke and the precision of a surgeon.

"There you are, darling," he said to his daughter, who commenced crying. Judith looked on, sleepily, addled from the anesthesia, a cool cloth still covering her brow. "Daddy loves you, Sunshine."

***

The attending physician had called it absolutely correctly during that initial physical examination required by the health insurance company after Martin's hiring at the *Scanner*, a rural-toned rag that carried more op-eds than hard news, the way subscribers liked it. Dr. Fridley recognized the strange, jerky movements in his patient's face, neck, and arm for what they were, even though Martin had tried hard to conceal them as he traversed those early days in the newsroom. "Ipsilateral," Fridley dubbed the spasms, noting they were confined to Martin's "starboard side," a sailing enthusiast's joke that wasn't lost on the homunculus crinkling the exam-table paper.

The pain only got real bad when Martin was under extra stress, on deadline days for example, but he pushed through it with aspirin, favorite LPs spinning on his turntable, and mental fortitude.

"Dystonia," was the doctor's one-word pronouncement, after which he went into a long explanation about the cousin to Parkinson's disease "with a twist," another awkward attempt at humor Martin wasn't sure he appreciated. "Hemidystonia, to be exact," Fridley specified and delivered the bad news that it was a lifelong affliction and the better news that Martin's symptoms could mostly be controlled pharmaceutically, though he would have to make regular visits to a local clinic for monitoring and prescription refills. Within days, he was intimately familiar with the ins and outs of the neurology department at Samaritan North—he and all the other poor saps who spent time on the eighth floor, with its puke-yellow walls and barely muted beeps and whirrs coming from the inpatient rooms.

In Martin's opinion, the triage nurse was by far the best part about being there. She guided him to the same room every time, far corner, the one with the Van Gogh print above the double sink, *Starry Night*, the dark and the light. Sometimes he would grab a *Sports Illustrated* and flip through it while waiting for Dr. Fridley to arrive and commence prodding him, inquiring about any new twitches or uncontrollable movements. Martin didn't even like sports, but the articles were well done and decent distractions. Those magazine journos knew how to write a snappy first paragraph, and the page layouts were bold and colorful, just this side of sensational.

"Martin *DON-ovan!*" that wonderful nurse would call when it was his turn to stare at the Van Gogh, smiling and waving her clipboard in the air, its blue BIC pen suspended by a long red ribbon. Her voice was a high soprano, so very tuneful, one delight away from an aria.

"You're doin' so *well* Martin, aren't you, now!" she would singsong, the soles of her white Rockports squeaking as she crossed the linoleum floor, a black diamond pattern on cream. The name badge on her lapel was positioned just so beneath a round gold pin bearing the caduceus medical symbol, two snakes winding around a winged staff. Dierdre O'Shaughnessy, RN, was red-haired and quite thoroughly Irish. That was good enough for him.

It was the same barrage of questions every time: pain level on a zero-to-ten scale, any recent changes in his medications, did he feel at all depressed? Martin didn't mind because it was her doing the asking. They always nodded in tandem after that last one, since they both knew the answer. Who wouldn't be depressed if they had fucking dystonia?

Fridley would breeze in, check him over, and send him on his way with another prescription for carbidopa/levodopa, taken twice daily, each bottle of tablets lasting a full month.

The drugs functioned as birth control, so the timing of his treatments hadn't been ideal, given the way Judith continually gawked at all the young mothers and their little ones strolling in the sunshine on their neighborhood's sidewalked streets. Eliza was already three years old, which had been "more than enough time to make us wait for another grandchild," as Martin's mother had taken to interjecting into every conversation. Plus, Martin had always tried to give his wife what she wanted, as best he could. "I wish it could be different," he would acknowledge to Judith, then try to lighten things up with a quippy corollary. "Those little yellow tablets are way more effective than the Pill."

Martin spoke with a satisfied tone. He had never seen himself strapped down with a bunch of kids. Eliza was more than enough for him.

According to the good doctor, infertility was the medication's collateral damage, along with a bunch of other fun side effects like constipation and fatigue. Not to worry, he told Martin. "Have all the fun you want in the sack, if you can get it up, that is," he said. "Your little swimmers will be fried."

Judith remained unconvinced her dream was impossible. One of her colleagues had conceived after her husband had his vasectomy, after all.

"What if we didn't, you know, try to *prevent* it?" Judith asked Fridley, who blinked twice and assured her she could have all the sex she wanted, but a second pregnancy, he promised, "with Martin, anyway," would be tantamount to a medical miracle.

Funny guy, Doc Fridley, but Martin admired him for his diagnostic precision and appreciated him for improving the quality of his life, however much of it he had left. That was what he wanted most.

***

The initial months of parenting Eliza had been a complete blur, with one day running into the next. Judith and Martin were so consumed with feeding and diapering their daughter that if Martin hadn't had deadlines at the *Scanner* to adhere to, it wouldn't have mattered whether it was Saturday or Wednesday or Friday.

It was during that period that Martin, having grown quite disenchanted with life on the coast—the rain and gloom were more than he could take—started mailing out resumés. Ed McKee, publisher of the *Cascadian* in Yamhill, bit within weeks, and the Donovans were off on a brand-new adventure. Inland, but still rural. And definitely more sunshine. Judith secured a transfer to her computer company's sister office, a move she told Martin she didn't mind making, considering his new career opportunity. She recognized what a privilege it was for her as a woman to be able to move while keeping her job.

"I'm happy for you, dear," she said, then added, "I'm happy for all of us—the three of us, anyway," emphasizing the word *three*, reminding Martin of her enduring disappointment that for them, there would be no more children.

Chapter Three
News Editor Martin Writes Note to Readers
June 1, 1979

Dear friends:
My name is Martin Donovan, the new news editor of the Cascadian, *your hometown paper. I grew up in Portland, the son of a newspaperman, the late, great* Oregon Journal *columnist Colin Donovan. I often say I have ink in my blood. From my father I learned the value of the First Amendment and an abiding appreciation for the honorable and essential profession of community journalism. I think you'll find that the stories you read in the* Cascadian *are an apt reflection of the people and ideals of our community.*

We would be nothing without a free and independent press. I believe information in story form enriches us all.

Allow me to introduce myself and my little family. In my previous job I worked for the Lincoln City Scanner, *where I cut my journalistic teeth writing everything from obituaries to breaking news stories. My wife Judith and I are happy to be back in the Portland metropolitan area after six years on the Oregon Coast. Our daughter Eliza will enter kindergarten this fall, and we're looking forward to getting to know the other parents with children attending Rosario Gonzales Elementary School.*

I'm very excited that the Cascadian's *copublishers, Ed and LaVerna McKee, selected me as the paper's next news editor. We are in the process of hiring a reporter to cover sports and personality features. I plan to concentrate on the local economy, city hall, and the school district, serving as a dedicated government watchdog. Mr. McKee will continue to write opinion pieces and his popular upper right-hand corner column—with its tidbits about the comings and goings of your friends and neighbors—will continue to appear on the front page.*

Our staff will deliver the top news stories of the week to your door every Wednesday if you are a subscriber and to news racks all around the city if you wish to pick up a copy of the paper for fifty cents.

We appreciate each of you. We're happy you've chosen to stay informed by reading the Cascadian, *your leader in local news. Thank you for your support. If you'd like to stop by the office with a news tip, a word of encouragement, or just to chat, my door is always open. I look forward to meeting you.*

All best wishes,
Martin

Chapter Four
Chehalem Mountain Resident Succumbs to House Fire
November 14, 1979

The very first house on the very last road at the top of Chehalem Mountain was covered in English ivy. Even the windows of the two-story stone structure were largely obscured by a thick tangle of vines, having been left to their own devices for years or possibly decades. Peering into the windows beyond the half-drawn drapes, Martin had seen all the old newspapers with his own eyes, piles of them stacked up to the ceiling, right before they went up in flames, and poor Carson McClintock along with them.

He discovered all this quite by accident, after the bell on top of Yamhill City Hall shook him from sleep at four in the morning. The town had an all-volunteer fire department, a secretary being the only paid staffer, and no dedicated chief. Good-hearted helpers would leap from their beds, check their pagers for the location of the blaze, then drive there in their own vehicles, where they would meet the city's lone tanker engine and do what they could.

It was the consistent expectation of Martin's boss, Ed McKee, that he would chase that goddamn fire truck anywhere within the bounds of the *Cascadian's* coverage area, day or night. Ed was a quirky, bombastic fellow, but he possessed a keen intuition, and he'd had the good judgment to hire Martin in the first half hour after meeting him, when they had bonded over pulls of whiskey at a corner table inside one of two local watering holes. Ed had his way of looking at things, mostly through the bottom of a rocks glass, a view that often skewed reality. But Martin loved him anyway, regarding him with a mix of curiosity, affection and forbearance— as well as appreciation as the person who signed his twice-monthly paychecks.

Ed believed in Martin, and Martin needed that. Someone had to when he didn't believe in himself.

Martin was in his car by 4:15 a.m. Once he was off the highway he set his headlights on high beam, as no one else would be up that early, driving around the rural landscape in the pitch-black. There were no sidewalks or curb cuts here, not like in the big city. The road up the mountain was curvy and treacherous, particularly in the dark. It had no shoulder, so Martin crept along, hugging the center line to avoid plunging over the side. Any minute now a vehicle could come barreling back down the hill toward him, and what would he do then? These old roads were always last on the list for maintenance. His front tires kept dropping into potholes, and with each shudder of the vehicle, his hands returned to a death grip on the steering wheel. He was going to have to ask Ed to pay for a realignment—like that would ever happen.

When he arrived at 156 Mountain Top Lane, his nerves were still a bit jangly. The scene was chaotic, the fire licking the west side tree line, the residence fully involved. Men in turnouts and face shields filed back and forth between the water tender and the house, soldier ants on speed, one steadying the lower part of a ladder leaning against the gutters and another standing at the top, thrashing away at cedar roof shingles with an ax. A few tried looking in the windows for signs of life, but intense heat forced them back.

Martin tiptoed around to the north side of the property. That's where he spied the newspapers, rising to the rafters, flames licking headlines and melting them like wax. And for a surreal half second the homeowner's terrified face reflected in a black-laced window. Martin puzzled over why he hadn't tried to escape. A family photo album he had misplaced? A secret buried among the stacks, something he didn't want to get out? He made the sign of the cross for McClintock.

"Out of the way!" shouted a burly guy hefting a hose, water gushing ineffectively at the inferno. "This thing could blow any second!" The word *backdraft* throttled Martin's brain. He lurched away, the Canon AE-1 around his neck swinging on its strap. That camera was the best in the business, easy to operate and reliable. Always got good pictures if there was adequate light, sometimes even if there wasn't. Martin found a spot near the mailbox—C. McCLINTOCK, it said in peeling black decals—and opened the shutter wide, snapping away from a distance. The orange flames in the viewfinder would make for excellent shots. Front-page stuff. *If only we printed in color*, Martin thought, but that was expensive, something a paper operating on a shoestring never tried to manage, except in the most extraordinary circumstances.

It took several hours to completely extinguish the blaze. Part of the roof had collapsed into the living room, incinerating furniture, artwork, draperies, and all those stacks of newspapers. There was little doubt old man McClintock was a goner.

"That went up fast," the fire crew leader said to Martin, his face grimy with soot, his helmet in his hands. "No way to save him." He wiped something from his eye, a tear maybe, ash more likely. "Those infernal newspapers. Everyone knew he was a hoarder."

An ambulance ambled up the driveway, its tires crunching loose gravel, and came to a stop behind the perimeter. The paramedics were too late. It was the coroner's territory now.

The film wouldn't be needed at the *Cascadian* until midmorning, when the production crew got in, so Martin stayed on top of the mountain until well past sunrise. He waited to watch the mop-up, his back against a tree, a dew-coated bed of pine needles dampening the seat of his trousers. Smoke hung low, like whisper-thin clouds, around the charred shell of McClintock's house. It caught in Martin's throat. He coughed, then felt a sudden sharp twinge on the right side of his jaw. *Fuck, what was that?* Like a charley horse, only worse. Could it be back? The weakness, the pain, the vertigo? He massaged the muscle until the pain abated, then thought better of it. This time around, if he didn't aggravate it, maybe it would turn out to be nothing. He got back in his car and felt around under the driver's seat for the pint of whiskey he kept there for just such an emergency. He unscrewed the cap and took two long swallows from the bottle. He leaned back on the headrest and imagined Carson McClintock's final moments, how utterly alone he must have felt, facing the end with nothing around him but all those newspapers, all those stories, all that ink, flammable as hell.

Chapter Five
Return of Martin's Illness Thwarts Judith's Plans
July 5, 1980

Beyond the Donovans' cul-de-sac, the distant booms of leftover fireworks kept time with the tremors on the right side of Martin's body, which came and went but never disappeared completely. In the middle of the night, when he couldn't sleep, beset by worries over the state of his health and the health of his marriage, Martin's head echoed with his wife's pleadings for a second child, "sooner than later," her face bright with baby lust. Judith hadn't given up. She wanted both family and career on a preordained timeline.

Martin was grateful for the money she made. *Primary breadwinner* came to mind. Judith was a juggernaut. A workhorse. And a panoply of emotions.

"Let's make a brother or sister for Eliza," she cooed into Martin's ear one evening after tucking their five-year-old into bed and settling back down with him on their living room couch. She nuzzled his cheek and kissed his shoulder, inviting him to a session under the sheets. That same shoulder was aflame with what Martin could only describe as dozens of poker-hot pinpricks, dimming the prospect of successful coitus. He pushed Judith away and sat up. "It's useless. Please stop," he said, inching away from his wife.

He beheld her fallen face. God, what a cad he was! "Soon, sweetheart," he said from a comfortable distance away, genuinely sorry and thoroughly embarrassed. "We'll try again soon. I'll talk to the doctor. Maybe next year?" Judith pushed a button on the remote, producing their usual nighttime fare, *Three's Company*, two girls and a guy in the same living space. At least John Ritter made them laugh. During a commercial for Prell shampoo, Judith set her parameters.

"If we're not having another baby," she said in a punitive tone, "I'm going to put in for vice president at FasTrack. I think I can get it. No sense wasting the best years of my life." Martin pinched his lips together and pulled a knitted blanket more tightly around his torso. Sometimes Judith made him feel small.

The medication will keep Eliza an only child for always, he thought, but kept it to himself.

He got up and took the blanket with him. "Good night, Judith," he said. "I'm sorry you're married to a failed man."

***

Fall came, and to Martin it seemed like it had been two skips between Eliza's first words and first grade. She was reading short chapter books, her red curls—just like her daddy's—bobbing up and down as she turned the pages, her petite frame nearly swallowed up inside the big wingback chair in the sunniest corner of the Donovans' new house. Her teacher had nothing but praise for her academic efforts, marking *Exceeds* in every category on her semester report cards. Most impressive to Martin, though, were Miss Hill-Taylor's comments about his daughter's exemplary deportment.

Eliza is helpful and compassionate to all her friends at school, the teacher wrote in the margin of her spring report. *She is bright, pleasant, and a pleasure to have in class.*

Martin flinched. Perhaps he and Judith were raising their daughter to be too accommodating. Women had enough trouble making their voices heard. Hers needed to roar! He made a mental note to talk with Eliza about speaking her mind when she needed to.

***

Some days Judith left for work before seven, depositing a quick kiss on Eliza's ringleted head as she departed, and Martin would bring their daughter to the *Cascadian* until it was time to walk her to school.

The front desk ladies, Carla and Francine, made such a fuss over her, and who could blame them? Martin's Sunshine Girl—that was what he called her, *Sunshine Girl*—was a regular ray of light. Always curious, always smiling, always in a happy mood.

"Eliza darling, where's my squeeze?" Francine liked to teach Eliza jokes while Martin was busy typing up the first story of the day on his IBM Selectric, clacking away until he made a mistake and had to correct it with a couple well-placed strokes of Wite-Out.

"What's black and white and read . . . ?" she would start.

It was the riddle the youngster loved most.

"A newspaper!" Eliza would shriek, her eyes dancing, before Francine could say "all over."

Ten minutes before the school bell rang, Martin would help Eliza into her small coat, one wool sleeve and then the other, and she would button the front up herself. On the way she would collect fall leaves and tuck them into her pockets for show-and-tell.

"Aren't they gorgeous, Daddy?" she would say, and Martin's smile couldn't have been wider.

Thanks to the outsized influence of young Eliza Pearl, Judith and Martin found ways to stay in their parents' good graces, and though managing their own regrets was no summer picnic, they were a mostly solid team at home. And at the *Cascadian*, between interviews with city officials and celebratory end-of-day swigs of Irish whiskey, Eliza's antics gave her father joy.

Chapter Six
State Fair Offers Audience with Governor
August 3, 1980

The year Martin got promoted to editor at the *Cascadian*, Jimmy Carter was still holding on to his presidency, but barely. One last year for a good man with bad luck.

TV news footage did it: long lines at the gas station and American hostages in Iran, unsettling images flashing across living room screens every night. Voters had started to lust after a leader cut from a more dynamic bolt of suit-cloth. They didn't want the peanut farmer anymore. Didn't trust him. They wanted Ronald Reagan, the actor, with his Brylcreemed pompadour and his easygoing swagger. Someone to fix things, bring back the good old days.

Victor Atiyeh was governor of Oregon at the time, and he was enjoying immense popularity. Martin interviewed him at the Yamhill County Fair that summer, right in front of the 4-H sheep and goat pens, the animals chewing hay and paying them little mind.

Atiyeh was by accounts a smart, honest, and capable man. He was also someone who could keep his cool in a crisis, as Martin soon discovered. One of his black leather ankle boots wound up dead center in a fresh pile of goat poop when he stepped inside the pen to admire the blue-ribbon winner, a tan-and-white doe named Sadie Mae. Little brown marbles skittered everywhere, the softer stuff squishing up and over the top of the governor's boot, soiling his sock. He smiled, pet the goat, and shook the hand of the beaming boy who had raised her. He handed his aide his dirty boot and sock and, striding out of the pen with one foot bare and one foot shod, went over to a water spigot to nonchalantly wash off his appendage. He appeared nonplussed.

Atiyeh spoke Martin's name in a way that made him feel suddenly and exceedingly shy. The governor had an aw-shucks half grin on his face and maintained that look even as he pulled on a replacement sock and a newly clean boot. His family had come to Oregon from Syria. He and his brother were operating a rug company together when Vic won a seat as a state legislator, later rising to the top government job in the state.

"Knew your father from the *Oregon Journal*," he said to Martin, wiping his hands on a handkerchief. "Loved his writing. Great columns. Good man. Big loss for us all."

Then he added: "I'm looking forward to talking with you."

"Yes sir, Governor."

"Vic," he corrected, aw-shucks again. "Please. It's Vic."

Martin took out his notebook and clicked his pen open. It was his habit to lead with softball questions and up the ante from there. The Atiyeh interview was no exception. How was life in the governor's mansion treating him, and what were his priorities for the new legislative session? He moved on to tougher topics: Who did Atiyeh need to lobby to get the Columbia River Gorge designated as a preserved national scenic area? What was his strategy to win a second term? Vic responded to each query thoughtfully, measuring his words like a seasoned politician does. But there was an earnestness about him Martin found refreshing.

"What's the biggest obstacle to getting your food bank idea off the ground?" Martin asked. Vic paused, tapping his chin with his right index finger and thumb.

"My own party," he said finally, a revelation Martin found refreshingly candid. "Some of my Republican friends are pretty tight with the dollar."

"Fiscal responsibility and all that," Martin ventured.

Vic smiled a you-can't-kid-a-kidder smile.

"No," he said and leaned in. "Can we go off the record?"

Martin nodded an unequivocal yes.

"They've convinced themselves that these kinds of programs are giveaways to the lazy and unambitious. Not true, my boy," he insisted. "They're a way to lend a leg up to people who don't start out with all the advantages."

The governor frowned.

"You think politicians don't depend on the government for what we have in our bank accounts? Hogwash! I need to convince some of my more pigheaded colleagues that the New Deal is still a good deal. Our party platform should reflect that. It currently does not."

Atiyeh was talking about the modern welfare state. He slapped both hands on his knees and stood up. Their time together was over. But that was okay with Martin because he had what he needed for the paper, on top of the satisfaction of a fine afternoon at the fair.

***

Eliza bowled Martin over the second he came in the door, and he returned his daughter's affection, producing a stuffed Muppet knockoff from behind his back. A souvenir from the ring toss booth at the fair, where he had enjoyed a bit of success. Martin was always accurate.

"Grover!" Eliza yelped. "I love him, Daddy!"

Returning to the kitchen table, she set Grover up in a place of honor, overlooking her schoolwork. She pressed pencil to paper, practicing her cursive letters—the soaring loops of the *s* and the fancy curlicues of the *g*—her legs swinging, her feet barely skimming the floor.

"We have another writer in the family," Martin pronounced, turning Eliza's rosebud-lipped grin as wide as the sky. Judith glowered at him from her position at the counter, butt to Formica, and plunged a serving spoon into a ham-and-potato casserole.

"Chop-chop," she said to the two of them, turning on the heels of her pumps. "Supper's ready." Eliza started gathering up her things, but her daddy stepped in.

He held Eliza's paper up to Judith, who couldn't help but smile. Her husband smiled back. "Look at her go!" he exclaimed, putting the paper back down and turning to their daughter. "Practice makes perfect, Sunshine. Keep up the good work!"

Chapter Seven
Mina Breckenridge Joins the Cascadian *as Sports Editor*
November 6, 1980

Had she been told the grandstands would be packed with rabid fans—teens shaking pom-poms and adults screaming their heads off for the blue and gold—Mina wouldn't have believed it until she saw it. To her, the idea that folks were always there for each other—cheering each other on, fighting together to the bitter end—was fantasy. It just hadn't been her experience. When her mother lay dying in the den of her childhood home in Santa Barbara, California, used up and filled with regret, she gave Mina the most important advice of her life: *Don't look back. You're not going that way.*

Once she passed—"from a broken heart, mostly," according to Mina's aunt Carol, an uncanny combination of Anna Breckenridge's fine, dark hair and her daughter's heart-shaped face—Mina was alone. Her father had left them before she was two, and there were no siblings. Carol, her mom's only sister, lived five hours away in Walnut Creek, but she was the next thing to a recluse, so it seemed to a youthful Mina that staying in touch with her didn't serve much of a purpose.

"I'll see you," Mina told Carol during a quick hug after the memorial service, her aunt still smelling of the incense stick she had lit and placed in a box of sand near the casket. Sage, a favorite of Anna's. But Mina didn't actually think she would see Carol again, not for a very long time, anyway.

Her late mother's words remained a major theme for Mina through high school, the four years she was at college, and into her first full-time job as a reporter at the *Cascadian*, a small weekly newspaper in Yamhill County, Oregon. She puzzled over all those people in the bleachers. *Were they looking forward, not backward? Wouldn't they have had something better to do on a Friday night than stand in the rain, swooning over a bunch of jocks?* There was no clear gain in that. Still, as she navigated the mud on the sidelines at Yamhill-Carlton Field, she felt like a real journalist. On assignment at the end of her first week, she strained to hear the referees call the game above the din of the crowd. She scratched statistics into a rectangular reporter's notebook, holding it close to her slicker to keep it from getting wet.

What she felt most acutely—even as the cheerleaders jumped and gyrated, their pleated midthigh skirts flying high enough to expose more skin than some of them might have intended—was bemusement.

"Lean to the left! Lean to the right! Stand up, sit down, *fight fight fight!*"

Students in the stands obliged, leaping up and squatting down on cue. "Fight fight fight!" they thundered, their feet hitting the aluminum so hard it shook.

Mina tucked her pageboy behind her ears and leaned in. She was determined to get this right. Everything coming through the public address system sounded like gibberish, so she made up her own brand of shorthand.

First down, #23 to the 15, Donelson pass from Vandehey, short gain for offense. Next play, quarterback throws interception. Coach calls players back to huddle, bawls them out. Doesn't help. Tigers lose to crosstown rival, give up bragging rights for fifth straight year. Final score 45–7, not even close.

There were lots of hangdog heads in the postgame locker room. The players paid no attention to Mina as she walked by on her way to interview the coach. She felt sorry for the guys, most of them undersized, just four or five years younger than her. She was twenty-one and completely green as a reporter. She would have to find a way to write about another blowout without angering the hometown faithful. There was no chance any honest story could start with superlatives.

She found Coach Russ Hacker in the corner on a bench near the last bank of rusted gray lockers. She set her umbrella down, unzipped her coat, and took out her notebook.

"Coach?" She switched the pen to her left hand and extended her right. "I'm Mina Breckenridge. The *Cascadian*'s new sports reporter . . . I mean sports *editor*. Nice to meet you."

He sat up, his body unfolding into a ramrod straight ninety-degree angle.

"Got anything to say about the game? For the paper, I mean."

The coach blinked twice, looked Mina up and down before speaking. She set her jaw, gripped the pen tighter.

"A girl in the locker room. That's something new," he growled. "I'll say this for you, sweetheart, you've got balls."

There was no proper response for the misplaced metaphor. She wanted to interview him about the game, and he wanted to talk about her being female. Good God.

She waited. The coach yanked off his game shirt, saturated with sweat, and changed into a logo T-shirt. Mina looked down at her pen and pretended to scribble something in her notebook. She noticed her manicure could use some refreshing.

"Only good thing was that one TD in the second quarter, Vandehey to Donelson," he said finally. "Everything else went to shit. But of course, you can't write that."

He was right. She couldn't. This would be her first lesson in slanting the news while still telling the truth. She needed to keep her job.

"Say more?" she coaxed, locking horns with Coach Hacker's piss-poor attitude.

"Young lady," he sputtered. "In my locker room, you'll learn when to stop asking questions." He was like every other coach she had encountered so far in her lifetime, from cross-country in high school to Trampoline 101 in college. Looking her up and down, wanting her to shut up and perform. Her stomach burned.

***

The boss had taken a chance on Mina. Hired her right out of college, UC Berkeley on an academic scholarship, BS in technical journalism. Gave her the sports editor title, just like that. Amazing. What did she know about sports? Or editing? Her only credentials were occasional viewings of ABC's *Wide World of Sports* and that one Advanced Reporting class junior year, taught by the infamous Dietrich Schreima, a former correspondent for the Associated Press, whose thick black eyebrows did most of the talking during his two-hour lectures in Masterson Hall. The three of them—Mina, Mr. McKee, and Martin—had all laughed about her nonexistent bona fides during the interview, but in a way that made her feel more than, not less than. Better than she had felt about herself in a long time. In school, she had been too tall, too narrow in the hips, too studious to be popular. None of that mattered now. She was in.

No doubt Martin's endorsement put it over the line. Once she had decided to be a reporter, she paid attention to bylines, his in particular. She had read and respected his stories since before she applied at the *Cascadian*. Well written, concise, engaging. The big three. Exactly what she had learned in college. He was a master, the real deal. She would learn a lot from him.

Mina owed Martin big-time for taking her on, and she took advantage of a chance to thank him after the interview, following him down the hallway toward his office, her stride much longer than his. She nearly crashed into him when he braked suddenly at the water fountain.

"Whoops, sorry about that, Martin," Mina said, drawing back.

Martin turned around, swiping the corners of his mouth with a thumb and forefinger. She noticed the paleness of his lips, the pleasant curl of them. Two dimples, partially hidden by an untamed mustache. His tousled red hair. His blue eyes, looking right through her, piercing her armor. That gold band on his left hand's ring finger.

She wondered what his wife was like. She was probably a force of nature too.

She snapped out of her reverie when he spoke.

"No worries at all," Martin said. "It's definitely close quarters around here." Was that a flare of his nostrils, or was Mina imagining it? She produced a clunky run-on sentence.

"I'm so grateful for your support . . . thank you," she spluttered. "I don't know what I'd have done without this job . . . I feel like I'm meant to work at a newspaper!"

Martin nodded and smiled, a look of impish curiosity crossing his face, a look she would see a thousand times in the future.

"Glad to have you on board, Mina," he said, giving her shoulder a little squeeze, like a father might, only she had no reference point for that. "Let's get to work!"

He waved his hand toward her office. They parted ways.

***

Mina's starting salary would be $9,500 a year, enough for a studio apartment in a decent part of town. She could walk the two miles to the *Cascadian* on North Hemlock Street when she wanted, put gas in her VW Bug if it was near the beginning of the month. She got paid on the first and the fifteenth.

She also had her own office, right next to Martin's, the newsman known locally for his pep, his pipe, and his dark green fedora with a tattered press card tucked into its hatband. Mina's office had a big east side picture window that showcased five cherry trees planted in the common space paralleling the sidewalk. Ed told Mina they would blossom in late spring, like clockwork, pink and white. She found out the next April he was right. Whenever the breeze blew, flurries of little petals floated down onto her windowsill, a pretty sight, though she had little time for daydreaming. The job was busy and challenging all year long. Work went well into the evening two nights a week, Mondays and Wednesdays, parks board and city council, as she took some big things off Martin's too-full plate. Nice that the boss had enough faith in her already to assign her the extra gigs.

There was a surprising amount of news to cover in that small town, thanks in part to population growth, people flowing in from California as the cost of living trended upward down south. The "decade of greed," they called the '80s. For Mina it was the decade of leaving her past behind, striking out on her own, and establishing herself as an independent, professional woman. For opening her eyes to the way the world was, not the way she preferred it to be. She had read Friedan and Gurley Brown. When she was writing, she was skeptical but also hopeful, bordering on optimistic.

The city council president turned out to be a tough nut to crack. Took a while for Mina to recognize he had an agenda, with five people on the panel and three of them cronies. All in real estate, all voting lockstep on variance requests and zoning restrictions. Lots of ayes on the former and lots of nays on the latter. Lining their own pockets under the guise of magnanimity.

Folks in the know mostly looked the other way.

Council President Tooms sidled up to Mina after gaveling one meeting to a close, letting her know he was on the right side of that 4–1 vote on a strip mall going in on the city's west end. Setbacks of only ten feet, and business owners could waive permit fees if they paid a year's rent up front. The shopping center would sit smack-dab in the middle of a residential neighborhood, two blocks from the high school, with bus service both ways. An obvious win-win.

"Hope you can see your way clear to printing a positive story on the new development," he said from way too far inside Mina's personal space bubble with a wink of his left eye, the good one, the one not made of glass.

"News is neutral," she returned, remembering the ironclad caveat from J-school, smiling her most beguiling smile, tilting her head to determine which of his eyes to address. "You won't find any positive or negative in my stories."

Tooms took a step back. The wrinkles on his forehead went from friendly to frowning. "I've known your publisher a long time," he grunted, a definite edge to his voice. His good eye narrowed. "I'd sure hate to give him a bad report."

We'll see about that, Mina thought. No way Martin would dismiss an important story like this. At least she hoped not.

***

Mina ginned up the courage to talk to Martin about the whole affair the next morning, first thing. Two knocks on his doorframe and she was in.

"I just don't get it," she said. Martin's office was warm and inviting, with its space heater and blankets for winter and a big box fan for summer. She felt comfortable enough to sit sprawled on the expanse of his extra chair, the one he called his "interview chair," with real wood armrests and a floral-upholstered seat. She loved the way he stopped what he was doing in order to give her his full attention.

"We write the truth, don't we Martin, no matter what it is?"

Martin looked at her, glasses low on his nose. His hands, clad in fingerless gloves, were folded in his lap. His piercing blue eyes met her green ones.

"Of course we do," he said, then removed his glasses and turned his whole body toward her.

"Well," Mina started, resting a palm on the corner of Martin's desk. "I guess I'm confused about something. Maybe you can clear it up for me?" Her voice was one tick down from pissed. She shifted in the chair, hip bone to hip bone.

"I'll do what I can," Martin said. He locked eyes with Mina, inviting her to go on. "What's on your mind?"

She told him about the incident with Councilor Tooms, how he had pressured her and threatened her. She sat more rigidly in the interview chair, expecting Martin to confirm what she knew to be true, to back her up. Nothing less would do.

"So you can see why I'm upset," she said, leaning forward, her eyes meeting his.

"I do." Martin cleared his throat, ahemming his way out of Mina's gaze. "Been there many times. Sometimes you win, sometimes you lose."

Mina wrinkled her nose. "But this isn't right. It's never okay to intentionally skew the news. The people deserve to know. They'll be directly affected."

"I'll talk to McKee. But in this business, you've got to decide which hill you're willing to die on. This might not be that hill."

Mina wasn't sure she could accept that, but she would do her best. Of course Martin tried negotiating with the boss, but in the end Ed didn't budge.

"You understand my position," he said to Martin, and Martin did. Tooms owned Savvy Supply, downtown's most popular variety store and McKee's biggest advertiser. That money mattered—a lot—so Thursday's paper carried a milquetoast headline: *Development on Main Street Promises Business Boom.* Martin wasn't wild about it, and Mina was livid, but in the end she recognized the game, and Martin knew the score. At least they kept it below the fold, in a thirty-two-point lightface font. Mina spent the rest of the afternoon depressed to think about how many other small-town governments were railroading their constituents like this, with newspapers forced to choose their battles. It stung. It stunk.

Chapter Eight
Eliza Donovan a Chip off Dad's Reporter Block
May 7, 1981

Daddy had a big, old desk with a glass paperweight on it in his office at the newspaper. And a phone and two bookshelves. Plus a black-and-white poster of Kurt Vonnegut, the writer, on the wall. It's a funny name, Vonnegut, I thought at the time, but lots of writers have funny names. Daddy said the poster was an *illustration*. He taught me how to clap out the four syllables.

His typewriter was the old-fashioned kind, not like Mrs. Swanson's, the school secretary's, which plugged in. It used to belong to my grandfather, but everything else was kind of what you would expect. His desk was bigger than Mrs. Swanson's, but not as big as Mr. Duncan's, the attorney across the street. Daddy took me there once when he had to get something signed. To me, the things you couldn't see, things that weren't right out in the open, were always the most interesting. Daddy kept his pipe, his tobacco pouch, and a few bottles of pills in his desk drawer, the middle one on the right. I wasn't supposed to touch any of that stuff. Those were the rules.

When I went into Mina's office, I was allowed to touch anything I wanted. I loved it in there! Of course she had a typewriter and a phone and a desk, just like my dad did, but there was so much more. She had a shelving unit in one corner with a plant in a macramé hanger above it. Funny. My mom didn't like knickknacks, but Mina had all those things. She was tall, so she could water the plant without using a step stool. The top of my dad's head only reached up to her nose! A toy bear she called Teddy and a toy penguin named Wobbles were on the middle shelf, and an orangey-white candle in a ceramic dish sat right beside them. Mina said the name of the candle was Pumpkin Spice. When she lit it—she always did that, not me—it smelled so, so good, like pie at the holidays. "We have to be sure to blow it out when we leave," she told me, and sometimes I got to do that part. Mina said she lit the candle to remind her to do good in the world. It made me want to do that too.

"I know," I'd say, and "I will." My mom was usually too busy to sit and talk to me, but Mina really listened. Mom was always telling me to clean my room or eat my lunch or that it was time to wash my hair. I hated hair-wash day. But with Mina, I could just tell her things. I felt like we were already friends.

I added four words for good measure. "I love your candle."

Mina smiled at me when I said that. She walked over and gave me a hug. Her sweater was soft against my cheek. She had been growing her hair out, and that day she wore braids. When I touched them they felt bumpy and smooth at the same time. She wasn't afraid to try new things.

A bulletin board with lots of little pieces of paper thumbtacked to it hung on the wall by Mina's desk. "Reminders," she called them. Below that was a framed diploma from the school she went to, where she got her journalism degree. Her name was printed out in big capital letters: MINA FAITH BRECKENRIDGE.

"That diploma means everything to me," she told me once, when just the two of us were in her office. "I worked hard so I could be a reporter."

Mina took the diploma off the wall and let me hold it. I ran my fingers around the frame, tracing the gold rectangle inside the black. I was careful not to smudge the glass.

"You must be really smart," I said, pointing to a word I didn't know, *technical*. Of course I recognized the word *journalism*.

For a second it looked like Mina might cry, but she didn't. Then she said something that sounded important, like it was a secret. "College wasn't always in the cards for me. It costs a lot of money. My aunt Carol made it happen, though, and I'm really grateful to her for that."

Even then, I already knew I was going to go to college. I wasn't exactly sure what I would be when I grew up—maybe a numbers person like my mom, but that seemed kind of boring. Maybe a newspaper reporter like my dad and Mina. I wanted my family to be proud of me, and I wanted Mina to be proud of me too.

Chapter Nine
Real Estate Section Introduces "Advertorial" Content
August 12, 1981

"I've got an idea for boosting the bottom line." Ed had called an all-staff meeting, which meant him, Mina, Martin, Ed Jr., and LaVerna. He didn't dare leave his better half out of the equation. He would pay big-time for that. "Houses are selling like hotcakes right now, and realtors are getting pretty greedy. I think we can talk them out of some of that profit."

He called his plan for a new special section—trading agents' advertising dollars for increased visibility in the community and its surrounds—"inspired," and he did it with a eureka-level grin. Not only would regular subscribers get the section inside their weekly paper, delivered right to their doorsteps, but it would also go to every household within a five-mile radius of the city limits—"complimentary," Ed made sure to point out, though everyone knew that wasn't exactly the case. Ed worked angles like a mathematician works theories.

Mina was curious whether Ed had a role related to the project in mind for her. Short of proofreading copy, she couldn't imagine what that might be.

"You and Martin will do all the writing," the boss had said, making it clear that participation was mandatory. "There'll be a small bonus in it for you, but you might have to lower your standards a little bit."

She found out what he meant by that even sooner than she expected.

"It's a new type of product," he said and leaned back in his leather chair. "A special section. It pairs ad revenue with puff pieces that make businesses look good. Isn't that brilliant? Even the *Oregonian* is doing it."

Martin's eyes telegraphed skepticism. Mina was itching to jump in, but he tackled the elephant in the room first.

"I hear you, boss, but how do we maintain our credibility if we editorialize our news content?"

He paused for Ed's answer. Mina thought he looked a little nervous.

"That's the beauty of it, Martin." Ed didn't miss a single beat. "It's not news. It's advertorial." He drew out that last word: *ad-ver-to-ri-al.*

Mina put two and two together and offered an observation. Even as it fell from her lips, she knew it smacked of impertinence. "So what you're saying is, we're going to trade our integrity for ad dollars."

Ed was not amused. He wove his chubby fingers together and clamped them to his chest. The big vein in his forehead got bigger. He waited two whole seconds to let her have it, and when he did, it was as if a dam had burst.

"I'm keeping you both employed!" he bellowed, grabbing a printout from his front drawer and slapping it on top of his desk. "See these figures? They're not all that rosy, I can tell you that much. We have to go with a new print product if we're going to survive."

Mina wanted to say something about the spanking new Ford truck parked at the curb, the one with the vanity plate that said PBLSHR. She wanted to ask about the manicures LaVerna indulged in each week, not just regular nails but press-ons at twenty-five dollars a pop. She wanted to point out that Ed Jr. regularly showed up late, and in a sleep-deprived haze, to deliver papers out of the back of the slick black 280Z gifted to him on his sixteenth birthday. Plus, she was sure he got more per hour than she did. Maybe more than Martin.

But Mina stayed silent, leaving it up to her news editor to deliver a robust rebuttal. Instead, Martin the diplomat showed up to save the day, a little too feeble for Mina's liking.

"More money in my pocket sounds great, boss," he began,

and Mina pushed down her doubts. "But here's the thing. As journalists, our bylines are the only real currency we have. When people read our news stories, they expect unbiased reporting. I'm not about to give them anything else. For me, and for Mina, that's nonnegotiable."

The boss frowned but fanned his hand Martin's way, giving him permission to continue.

"I also understand that for you, as the man holding the purse strings and all the responsibility for making this operation go, special sections look like a godsend, a way out. You have to do it. I get that."

It seemed like Martin was admitting defeat in the face of the cards stacked against them. Mina gave him a withering look.

"Yes . . ." the boss encouraged.

"I propose a compromise," said Martin, brightening considerably. "We grit our teeth and write the stories, do our best to make your advertisers shine. They like it, and the paper gets more revenue.

"But keep our bylines out of it," he added and meant it. "It could read 'staff report, the *Cascadian*' instead, or something like that."

He leaned forward. "Deal?" he said and reached out his hand. The boss leaned forward too.

"Deal. Good suggestion, Martin. I like the way your mind works."

***

A livid Patrick Dorsey burst in and let the door slam shut behind him. He yanked a copy of the *Cascadian* from the foyer rack, stomped into Mina's office, and planted himself in front of her desk, blocking the cooling air of her fan on a hot August afternoon, the day after the paper came out.

"YOU!" he boomed. "You got something against my agency?" He was winded and purple-faced, his voice an excruciating baritone whine. That final word, *agency*, was so loud it rang in Mina's ears.

Her first inclination was to apologize and dissolve into tears. Big, fat, female tears. But she didn't. She held it together.

Dorsey inhaled deeply, then exhaled his exasperation directly into her face. His breath stank of cigarettes and the faint suggestion of orange Tic Tacs.

"Your story. The one about all the realtors in the area?" He shoved the not-yet-paid-for paper into Mina's hands and jabbed his index finger at a particular paragraph. "I'm listed third. Third! It's outrageous. Dorsey is the biggest name in real estate in this whole dad-blamed county! Everybody knows that."

Mina felt her face muscles go slack, then tighten. How could this guy talk to her that way? She pushed her chair back, stood, and extended her hand.

"Mina Breckenridge, Mr. Dorsey. Don't think I've had the pleasure?"

Dorsey took her hand and shook it unconvincingly. He wasn't about to let his righteous anger go unanswered.

Mina was sure Martin was listening in the next room. She gave her accuser a clear accounting of her decision-making process, alphabetized and annotated.

"Abbott comes before Bauman, which comes before Dorsey," she said, expecting him to chew on the information. "That's why you're listed third. No other reason."

Dorsey frowned and straightened the knot in his tie.

"There are ten agencies in our coverage area. You're up pretty high, and you're not on the jump page," Mina pointed out, and the main art on the section cover included an illustration of his building, front and center.

She tried diffusing things with a joke. "Lucky your last name begins with a *d*, I guess."

He wasn't having it. He pursed his lips in surly defiance.

"I'm pulling my ads from this rag right now," Dorsey said and stomped off down the hallway toward Ed's office. "You'll regret what you did, young lady. You'll see!"

Mina didn't have the heart to yell after him that the boss was at lunch. She sat down, rolled her chair toward the north wall, lowered her head, and peered through the rectangular hole in the heavily stuccoed wall between Martin's office and hers.

"Did you hear all that?"

"Yeah. You handled yourself perfectly."

"You think so? That guy's intimidating. Not sure who he thinks he is, anyway. The nerve!"

Martin gave her a thumbs-up and a grin before turning back around.

The problem of Patrick Dorsey wasn't going away anytime soon. But it could wait until midafternoon, when Ed returned from lunch and put in a call to him, talking him down from his very high horse. With any luck, he would report a change of heart on Dorsey's part by the end of the day. A vindication for Mina and a reportorial victory, however small.

Chapter Ten
Martin Tries Grandmother's Cure-All Recipe
February 7, 1982

Roger ran the printing press in the back of the building, eight o'clock to five o'clock Monday to Friday, never a minute more or less. No one had a clue what he did on his days off, because Roger never said. He was a sad, sorry sack, and Martin felt for him.

"Hey dude," he would say to Roger, producing a thumbs-up whenever they ran into each other between the metal door marked with a Vondracek Printing placard and the coffee nook at the back of the building, two separate spaces, one shared by all. Roger would lift his chin in response, sometimes emitting a growly "Hey yourself," but the late-middle-aged bachelor—six foot three, with hands as big as small boulders—rarely engaged beyond that. He was intensely private, and Martin's gut warned him to steer clear, except when Roger appeared genuinely ill, which he frequently did. In those instances, Martin's gut took a back seat to the do-unto-others training he'd absorbed as a child.

"Can I help?" he might say, to which Roger would respond with a shy grin, wipe his too-large proboscis with a grimy handkerchief, and disappear inside the print shop without so much as a by-your-leave. Completing print jobs was hard work, and tedious. All day long Roger walked a circle around the gigantic black machine, feeding it paper on one end and grabbing the finished product from the other, practically wearing a rut in the floor. He would squint at a sample to make sure the colors came out right and nothing was blurry, and if it didn't meet muster, swear words often escaped his lips. Roger hated wasting paper, but even more, he hated losing money.

When Martin passed the front desk, Carla, who heard pretty much everything that went on in the office, gave him an I-told-you-so look. They each raised an eyebrow and went back to what they had been doing, filing and writing, writing and filing.

***

Martin would have liked to figure Roger out, but he had his own problems, health-wise. He was trying to perfect a recipe for homemade elderberry syrup that had been his maternal grandmother's answer to every physical ill: the common cold, various flu viruses, rheumatoid arthritis, gout. "The substance," Nana Emma had called it, coaxing sips from him whenever he had so much as a sniffle. In her telling it was a magic elixir with the power to make everything better in a matter of hours, or certainly overnight. She had written the recipe out for Martin sometime in her later years, the ingredients and the directions in her distinctive cursive, loops on her lowercase *y*'s and *b*'s and *d*'s. She even drew a little syrup jar in one corner of the card, a reminder of her offbeat sense of humor. That was part of the reason Martin loved the recipe, but the substance had also served him well. Whenever he felt a cold coming on, or his head was pounding, or his digestion wasn't quite right, he would whip up a batch of his grandmother's syrup and supercharge his immune system. It never failed him, the substance.

It wasn't explicitly his doctor's recommendation, but lately Martin's dystonia—the dizziness, the ringing in his ears, the muddled brain—had led him to branch out into elderberry tea, a soothing adaptation he was sure Nana Emma would have approved of. He was making some one Monday when Mina walked to the back of the building to get a second cup of joe. Martin, observant journalist that he was, knew just how she liked it: strong, no sugar, with two shakes of Coffee-Mate. He had turned the coffee nook into a factory assembly line of sorts, with dried elderberries and cinnamon and turmeric powders separated into little plastic cups and a squeeze bottle of honey on the side. All of it took up too much space, but Martin persevered in moving them around like chess pieces, this way and that, lining them up in a perfect row.

A control thing, Judith would say, but this was his kitchen. He enjoyed the freedom of doing what he liked.

Martin detected Mina's presence before she appeared, her perfume spicing the air as she drew up beside him and started pouring. She put the carafe back on the Mr. Coffee hot plate and glanced at him sideways, curious-like. He knew an explanation was in order.

"You smell nice," Martin said. The words settled without response.

"I'm making tea," he announced then, an attempt to change the subject. "It's my nana's recipe." He stirred the contents of the saucepan, perched on a single plug-in burner, clockwise then counterclockwise. The nook offered a few other accoutrements, a small microwave and a mini fridge the boss brought from home, but that was about it. Mina nodded her acknowledgement.

"Special recipe," Martin said, by way of elucidation. "Ever tasted elderberries?"

"No," she said. Her back was stiff. She was slow to get going in the morning. Martin went on about the fruit's natural healing properties, how it could start out sort of bitter but if you added a teaspoon of honey and a dash of lemon juice, it was actually pretty delicious. "Good and good for you," he declared, filling the quiet space where he wished she would speak.

"If you say so." Mina sipped her coffee, warming her hands on the ceramic mug she had grabbed from the dish rack under the Clean sign, the one with the Sandra Boynton cat on the side. It had to be LaVerna's mug. She was the only person in the office who drank coffee and also liked cats.

Martin watched Mina walk down the assembly line and mess with his cups, turning them, picking them up, setting them back down. She used a paper towel to wipe a smear of her lipstick from the mug. "Tell me more," she said, and Martin smiled.

"If you're trying to get the recipe out of me, it's top secret," he teased. "I'd ask my nana's permission, but she's been dead for years."

The elderberries were already simmering. Martin dumped the turmeric and cinnamon into the pan and stirred again, then lowered the heat to nearly off. "You don't want to overcook it," he said professorially. "If you do, you have to start over."

"Can I give it a try?" Mina took hold of the spoon handle without waiting for an answer. Martin let go and it flipped up, sending a sticky stream of syrup across the counter and onto the floor.

Mina performed an exaggerated shrug.

Martin retrieved the spoon, grabbed a wad of paper towels, and started wiping up the mess. Down on all fours, he mumbled expletives he was glad she didn't hear.

"So sorry!" Mina said, meaning it and not meaning it at the same time. "Clumsy me." He heard her suck syrup from her fingers as he blotted the floor with more paper towels.

Just then Roger ambled up, sleepy-eyed and disheveled, one of his overalls straps unbuttoned and hanging down his back past his knee. He drew a bead on Mina, cocked his head, and homed in on the Mr. Coffee.

"Morning Roger. You after some java?" Mina said, turning around, offering him the carafe. Martin took two steps to the side so Roger could stand between them. Roger sniffed a bigger sniff than usual, taking in Mina's scent. His stuffy nose was legendary around the office. He was always leaving used tissues on the nook counter and near the sink in the restroom. He stifled a sneeze with the back of his hand.

"Allergies," he said, shooting a hole in Martin's unspoken theory that he might be into cocaine, as cockamamie as that was. No one could afford that habit on newspaper wages.

Roger sniffed again, doctored his coffee, and went back to the print shop, Martin trailing along behind him. When they were alone, he pitched the merits of elderberry tea, offering Roger the cup he had just made. He certainly needed it more than Martin did.

"Really does wonders if you'd care to give it a chance." Martin heard his nana's voice inside his head.

Sniff. Cough. Wheeze.

"I'm all right. Just a little congested," Roger insisted. "Forgot to use my damn inhaler this morning." He pulled a rag from his back pocket and rubbed fresh grease off one of the ink rollers. He snorted twice and didn't turn around, leaving Martin with the cup in his hands and his mouth open in disbelief.

Roger wasn't one for pleasantries. "Thanks anyway, dude," was the best he could do.

***

The midmorning sun was filtering in through the window blinds in Mina's office when Martin returned with his lukewarm tea and his wounded pride.

"He didn't want any of the substance," Martin said. He stared into his half-empty mug, set it down on Mina's desk, and plopped down in the same chair Pat Dorsey had ignored the previous summer, opting to stand while he shouted.

Mina put her elbows on her desk and rested her chin in her hands, her brown eyes wide. Rings made of silver and turquoise on all but four fingers. She waggled them at Martin, opening them like flowers, closing them into fists.

"Yeah," she said. "Hard to tell what Roger's thinking."

"He doesn't let people in easily," Martin agreed.

Mina drummed her fingers on her desk blotter. Her rings clinked together, tinkling pleasantly, like little bells. Martin thought he should probably leave before hanging out in her office became awkward. The bells stopped tinkling. He looked up to meet her gaze.

"Being misunderstood isn't easy," she said finally. Her voice sounded flat, even distant. "Never has been for me, anyway."

Chapter Eleven
Cub Reporter Eliza Goes on Real Interview
December 20, 1982

With only five days to go until Christmas, I was really excited. Even more excited than I had been for my birthday on December 13. After I turned eight my parents let me read in bed until I got sleepy.

All I wanted for Christmas that year was my very own kitten, black and gray, but I didn't actually think I would get it because Mom was allergic, just like Mina. Daddy said she could take shots for that, but she didn't want to. She hated needles. "Mama gets to decide," my dad said, but I knew he was on my side because he wrinkled his nose.

Ed and LaVerna were different. They loved cats. They had six of them at their house. That was a lot of cats but not too many. Daddy and Mama wanted me to call Daddy's bosses *Mr. and Mrs. McKee*, but the McKees asked me to use their first names instead, so that's what I did.

On the last day of school before winter break, my class had a party. I got a present from my Secret Santa, one of the older girls, because second graders traded with fifth graders. My Secret Santa gave me a journal with a reindeer on the cover. I loved petting the soft felt on that reindeer. My Secret Santa buddy was Maria. She was tall and dark. I gave her a bottle of red fingernail polish with sparkles. Mama took me shopping for it. I hoped Maria liked it. Mama made me write a thank-you note for the reindeer journal so Maria would know how much I loved it.

There was a Christmas tree on the front counter at the *Cascadian*, one of those tiny ones meant to sit on a table, and it was covered in tinsel and decorated with plastic ornaments from Fennell's drugstore. My favorite one was Santa riding on a motorcycle with miniature newspapers peeking out over the top of his pack. He had a dimple in his cheek, like mine and my dad's.

Daddy wasn't thinking about Christmas just yet. He was working on a story about homeless people who were camping out near the cement plant. He was doing a phone interview with the mayor, Joe

Sharkey. He didn't sound like the daddy I had at home. His voice was a lot more serious.

"Where will they go after the police clear them out?" he said. "If the main shelter isn't open anymore, I mean?"

He had his pipe between his teeth, and the air above his head was a big puff of smoke. The receiver was scrunched between his ear and his shoulder, and the cord was knotted up.

When Daddy saw me, he smiled out of the corner of his mouth without the pipe. He kept talking to the mayor, who I guess said something he didn't like.

"Really, Joe? Off to McMinnville, just like that?" He sounded kind of mad. "Is that a direct quote? Just checking."

Sometimes when Daddy took me to Meier & Frank in downtown Portland, we would see the homeless people, three or four of them in front of the Methodist church where they could get a free lunch. They all looked kind of like the picture of Jesus inside the front door, which was always open.

I didn't understand everything about how Daddy did his job, but I could tell he was good at it. He had a bunch of awards piled up against the bookshelves in his office, maybe five or six of them. Also a blue paperweight from the Yamhill Chamber of Commerce, right next to his stapler.

It was a big day. Daddy said Mina was taking me on an assignment! She was writing about a club called Kiwanis that was doing a service project. What a funny word, Kiwanis. They were chopping wood to give to people so they could stay warm over the winter. Mina said I could use my reindeer notebook when we went. Since I was eight, I had more responsibilities.

***

It was cold out on the morning of the assignment. Mama told me to wear my warm coat, but I was afraid it would cover up my name badge, the one Mina asked Francine to make for me. It was white with a red line around it, and it said ELIZA DONOVAN, CUB REPORTER in capital letters. I got to take it home with me if I remembered to bring it back.

Mama waved from the front door as I climbed into the front seat of Daddy's car. "Be careful!" she called. All the way to the office Daddy talked to me about newspapers, how my grandfather liked to write just like we did.

"Your grandpa Colin would be so proud of you, Eliza, seeing you go on your first assignment," he said and nudged my arm. "I sure wish he could have known you. I bet he'd have written about you in his column."

Daddy had a meeting with his boss first thing about a change from typewriters to computers in the office. It sounded important. I was going to miss his typewriter, and I told him that, but he said not to worry, that he would keep it after his computer arrived.

"You'll still be able to use the black monster, Sunshine." He smiled that daddy smile. "I'll be handing it down to you someday anyway. I'll set it up for you somewhere in the office and we can write stories together when you're here."

My heart was full to bursting thinking about that.

It was eleven o'clock, time to leave for the interview. I peeled the backing off my name badge and stuck it to the front of my coat. I wanted it perfect. What I really cared about was that my name badge showed. My first time practicing being a journalist.

Daddy brushed past us on his way to his meeting. Brushed past Mina, anyway, and I saw their hands touch. I felt a little shiver go up my back.

When we got to the armory, some men in blue vests with the letter *k* on them were standing in the parking lot near a truck with a big pile of wood in the back. Mina pulled out her reporter's notebook, and I pulled out my journal.

She asked one of the men some questions about where the wood came from and how many houses they would deliver to. She scribbled his answers down. I tried to do the same thing, but it was hard to keep up with Mina. She wrote really fast.

"We've been proud to help our neighbors in need for more than five years now." The man puffed out his chest. "We believe our efforts save lives during the winter."

He got closer to Mina and looked over her shoulder at her notebook to see if she wrote down exactly what he said.

"Did you get all that, miss?"

"Got it," Mina said, but I wasn't sure she meant it. She stopped writing and snapped her notebook shut. "Let's go, kiddo," she said. It felt like she was trying to teach me something.

"We've got our story, so we're done," she explained. We said our goodbyes and left.

At the paper things looked different than they had that morning. So cool! Someone, probably Carla, had strung a tissue paper garland from the ceiling—red and white in the shape of Santa hats. There was mistletoe Scotch taped to the top of the doorframe in Mina's office, and the tree on Francine's desk had green paper tags on it, with a number and a few words written on each one.

Age ten, pink scarf, said the tag I read first. *Age four, wooden puzzle,* said the second one. I made Francine promise to take me to buy the scarf and the puzzle, if Daddy would give me the money. I didn't want those kids to be disappointed.

"Of course I will," Francine said and hugged me tight. "You bet." I kept looking at the tags, wondering what a girl my age might be asking for.

Daddy came out of his office and announced that in honor of Christmas, LaVerna had put foil-wrapped chocolate Santas on Ed's desk instead of the usual boring peppermints. I could have some, "but don't spoil your supper," he said, mussing my hair. His smile was wide, and his dimples danced on both sides of his face. His beard was trimmed shorter than normal.

"What are you waiting for?" Daddy laughed his chipmunk laugh and shooed me down the hall.

When I got back to the front of the office, Mina had taken off her winter coat. She was wearing a shiny green blouse and a black skirt. She usually wore sweaters and pants. She looked really pretty, like a model. She and Daddy were standing under the mistletoe. They didn't see me. They giggled, and their faces got close. I saw their lips touch! Daddy stepped away from Mina, quickly, like she was a hot stove. I breathed in but didn't make any noise. I tiptoed back to Ed's office and hid behind his desk. The drawer handle poked me in the back, but I still stayed quiet. My whole body trembled, like that time I fell off my bike and busted my lip. I took my reindeer journal out of my coat pocket and slid the pencil out of the spiral. I felt a little guilty writing what I did, but I didn't think I would get in trouble. Daddy and Mina both taught me that if you wanted to be a good reporter, you had to watch and listen and write things down. And you had to tell the truth.

Chapter Twelve
Publisher Calls Mina His "Little Sports Gal"
June 15, 1983

It was the middle of June, and with school out for summer, Mina was finally getting a break from covering prep sports. She looked forward to the weekend stretched out in front of her, unagendized and promising peace. She practically whistled as she typed up a few last interview notes before heading home.

Ed the son was just leaving to make his afternoon newspaper deliveries when Ed the boss returned from lunch, an hour late. He grabbed at the wrought iron railing as he struggled up the office steps, hand over hand, like a child traversing the monkey bars on a playground. The brass bell above the door heralded his sloppy entrance. Mina's office, the first one on the left, provided him a haven from Francine's and Carla's disapproving glares.

Mina was good at pretending to ignore the boss's behavior, for his sake and also hers. If she didn't let on, he wouldn't bug her. Generally but not always, and not today.

Ed Sr. stood there, wobbling and panting, one shoulder pressed against the wall across from Mina's desk. He smiled a ridiculous smile.

"Mina Breck-en-ridge," he said, drawing out the three syllables of her last name. "How's my little sports gal?"

She stopped typing. She looked up from her notebook and beheld his ruddy, smirking face. He slurped spittle back inside his small mouth and wiped his lower lip with the back of his left hand, which clutched a white cocktail napkin.

"I'm just fine, boss," she said, her fingers poised on the space bar. "What's up?"

Ed stared at Mina's face, at her hands, at his napkin. Brought it all the way up to his eyes and back down and out ten inches or so in an effort to focus.

He slurred his words. What Mina got was "lunch" and "AD" and "story tip." He wadded the napkin up and thrust it her way, but it missed and landed at her feet. Her mouth puckered as she realized he expected her to pick it up, as he was in no shape to do it himself. She looked at the napkin, then at Ed, and waited for him to bend down and fetch it, a feat he managed to complete only after a considerable dose of grunting and swearing. Once upright, he slammed it on her desk in disgust.

She smoothed the napkin out with both hands and tried to read his chicken scratchings. A water ring blurred the writing, but she could make some of it out.

Garrett. Senior. Falcner's fav. Title matereal. Ed had misspelled "material" and "Falconer," but she understood. Coach Falconer thought this lean, sinewy kid, last name Garrett, had what it took to win a state cross-country championship. The day-drinking high school athletic director wanted Mina to write a feature about him in the preseason.

Which wasn't until fall, two whole months away. Yamhill was really big into cross-country.

"You got it, boss." Mina pressed the *on* button at the front of her Compaq Portable and inserted a floppy disk. The screen lit up slowly, going dark for a moment, and then reassuringly brightened. "I'm all over it."

Ed blinked twice and waggled five napkinless fingers at her as he started to leave her office, tripping on the threshold as he did so. He lurched around and leaned back in.

"You didn't see that," he managed, a glow of affection relaxing his brow. "My little sports gal."

No way he could take the words back. It wasn't something Mina had ever expected to hear in a professional setting, or a personal setting either, especially directed toward her, and particularly from someone a generation older, someone who ought to know better.

But there it was, out in the open, slipped from the booze-loosened lips of her employer, copublisher of the town's only newspaper, whose origins could be traced as far back as 1888, during the western expansion.

The *Cascadian* was an independently owned business, and it was Ed and LaVerna's favorite child, Ed Jr. notwithstanding. They did with it what they wanted, a gamble that had generally turned out well. This latest thing with Ed was over the line, though.

"Excuse me, sir?" Mina began, one eyelid twitching involuntarily. "I did not go to college and graduate magna cum laude, Phi Beta Kappa no less, only to have you address me as your 'little sports gal.'"

She returned to typing. She didn't even wait for him to respond. He wouldn't remember the incident anyway.

***

By the time Martin got in, Mina had spiraled into an indignant lather. Ed's words were hurtful and wrong. Manipulative, too, as in girl Friday, the ubiquitous junior office worker who brought coffee and made twice-a-day runs to the corner post office. Women were supposed to be equal to men nowadays, weren't they? It wasn't the '50s anymore. Martin understood these things. He was an ally to women and was going to hear about this, right now.

As soon as she heard the wheels of his swivel chair squeak, Mina was in his office. She started with a note of appreciation.

"Thank you for never calling me your 'little sports gal,' Martin." He whirled around in his chair.

"What?" he said. "Mina! What kind of claptrap is that?" He had been practicing not using profanity in front of Eliza.

"Ed called me that, in my office, not more than an hour ago. 'Little sports gal.' Can you believe it?"

Martin sat mute. While Mina fumed, a few choice adjectives galloped through her mind: *derogatory, dismissive, dumb-as-fuck.* Ed's comment to her was all that and more.

It took her a few seconds to catch her breath. She was so riled up her nostrils flared. Delicate, expressive nostrils, like an Arabian horse's, Martin thought. She wasn't finished.

Martin sat back in his chair. "Did you just say what I think you said?" He half grinned.

She narrowed her eyes at him.

"I'm listening," he said. "I hear you, and I certainly agree with you. I love the way you're expressing yourself. The boss acted like a jackass."

Mina's body jerked. Her hands went to her hips. She wanted to be angry, but she smiled. "Thank you for seeing it my way. Today's woman doesn't want to be called any dumb pet names."

Martin wasn't so sure. He told Mina a story about his first date with Judith in the late 1960s, how he held the car door open for her and called her "sweetheart" for good measure, insurance to get her to go out with him again.

"And did it work?" Mina pressed in a sarcastic voice, more challenge than question.

"Well, *duh.*" A playful smile sent his message home. "We got married, after all."

"I mean, did it work for her when you kept on calling her 'sweetheart'? Does she call you 'baby' or something like that?" She really hoped Martin would say no. Even though it was wrong and went against all the feminist ideology she had ever held, she kind of wanted to imagine him calling her, not Judith, *baby.* With those twinkling blue eyes. She knew their conversation had crossed a boundary, but Mina couldn't help herself. She felt the heat rise up in her the same way it did when he had nearly kissed her under the mistletoe.

"Actually . . ."

"I don't want to know," she said, even though she did.

The two of them talked through it, how women had been through so much, how they had spent decades—millennia, even—smilingly deferring to men, how they were finally starting to get their due, nudging the patriarchy ever so slightly off the stage.

For the first time in what seemed like forever, Mina felt understood by a man. By Martin. It was a nice feeling, and she didn't want to lose it.

"You're right to expect respect around here." Martin struck a match to light his pipe. "Your work ethic and professionalism are rock solid. You deserve it."

Mina appreciated Martin's words, she truly did, but it took a while for her to calm down. Whether or not Martin went to bat for her, she would stay mum in front of the boss. Nothing would be gained by making a fuss. She would acquiesce, and though she hated doing that, the potential for misunderstanding or conflict with Ed just wasn't worth it. As Councilor Tooms had so indelicately pointed out, she really did need this job. So long as she had people around her who understood, like Martin, she would be okay.

Chapter Thirteen
La Verna Adopts "Office Cat" Miss Molly from Shelter
February 25, 1984

"*What?* You don't like *cats?*" The boss's wife was incredulous. "That's the silliest thing I've ever heard. I'm taking you down to the adoption shelter. Right now, today. You'll see. They're the most adorable creatures. Besides, you can do a story. They have a new volunteer for you to write about."

Mina's eyes begged LaVerna for a rain check. "I'm allergic," she ventured, expecting her words to sink in, hoping that would be that. "And besides, I have an interview with the JV basketball coach at ten." She checked her watch. Just thinking about cats made her skin crawl.

"Car, Mina. Let's go!" LaVerna opened the office door and wedged her penny-loafered foot into the breach, letting the cold air in. Mina asked Francine to make excuses to the coach. She grabbed her bag and a notebook and off they went.

***

LaVerna Austin McKee, five foot one with a face as weathered as a dock foreman's, poked two thick fingers through the bars of the metal cage. She cooed at the very large tabby crouched in the far corner, snapping its tail from side to side and purring loudly. Mina took that to mean the animal did not wish to be disturbed. The women were deep inside the bowels of the Sherwood Cat Adoption Team headquarters—SCAT for short—and Mina still wasn't sure how she had let LaVerna talk her into going there.

Right. A story. At least the day wouldn't be a complete loss, if she didn't wind up in the ER from an asthma attack.

LaVerna was trying her darnedest to bond with the angry-eyed ball of fur, whose back was now arched in a decidedly defensive posture.

Mina sneezed and rubbed her nose. The dander was already getting to her.

"Kitty, kitty, kitty . . . come here, you sweet thing," LaVerna cooed, her fingers stretched to their physical limit. "Mama's got a treat for you in her purse." The cat kept on purring and her tail kept on snapping. Her whiskers twitched a warning. Her front paws wore snow-white socks.

LaVerna kept at it, making smacking noises with her lips until a SCAT volunteer with *Alice* on her nametag stopped by to see how things were progressing.

"That one's a baffler," said Alice, hooking her thumbs inside a wide nylon duty belt and rocking back on her heels, then forward to her toes. SCAT volunteers all wore beige uniforms with badges above the shirt pockets. "Came in over the weekend. Stray, no tags. A bit cranky, but probably just scared. Don't think she'll bite."

Mina very much doubted that.

"You mean she's feral?" she said, rummaging in her bag for a tissue. Finding none, she ripped a piece of paper out of her reporter's notebook and blew her nose into it with a honk. "How can you adopt out a feral cat?"

Alice raised unkempt eyebrows and her mouth clapped shut. She wasn't keen on the question. A sympathetic look crossed LaVerna's face. Mina rolled her eyes behind both their backs. LaVerna was always trying to rescue things, particularly her husband Ed, but also cats, especially cats. The McKees had a bunch of them roaming around their house already. Litter boxes figured prominently in the spare bedroom, downstairs bathroom, laundry room, and garage.

Mina had been at the McKee residence once for cake and coffee and took mental notes during the brief tour provided by Ed.

"But none of them qualify as office cats," LaVerna had reasoned before dragging Mina off to the shelter. "They don't have the right temperament. I want an office cat. Don't you think that'd be nice?"

No. No, Mina didn't. Whenever she was even in the same room with a cat, her throat got dry and scratchy and her eyes itched and swelled. And on the few occasions she had been careless enough to pet one, she had gotten hives for her trouble. Besides, they were sneaky and self-absorbed and just plain mean. Most cats would sooner claw your forearm bloody than nap contentedly in your lap. They were nothing like Mina's old beagle, Randall. Now *that* was an animal. Friendly and sweet-natured, loyal to a fault. Randall had lived until he was seventeen, ancient for a dog. She still missed that pup.

But Mina knew better than to say any of that to LaVerna. She'd had to scrounge for coins to pay all of last month's rent. She literally couldn't afford to disagree.

"I'm more of a dog person," she said instead. LaVerna looked wounded.

"Nonsense," she said flatly. "Cats are the best! I'm going to win this one over, you'll see. I've already named her Miss Molly. As in, 'good golly,' get it? Let's fill out the paperwork, and we'll stop at the vet after I pay." She turned around to see Miss Molly stretch in that drawn-out, look-at-me way cats do, shaking one front leg and then the other. She sauntered toward the front of the cage.

"Off we go then, darling." LaVerna's voice had changed. So soft and reassuring Mina wasn't sure if she was talking to her or the cat. "We're going to be just fine."

Mina sneezed in violent succession as they made their way out the door and across the parking lot. She would need to powder her nose when they got back to the office. On top of her misery, she hadn't even gotten a story. "I'm not one for publicity," Alice had said, declining an interview, picking up the white longhair runway walking the front counter and stroking its back. "The cats are the only stars here!"

"Complete waste of an afternoon," Mina mumbled, grabbing

more tissues from the middle console of LaVerna's gold-toned Buick LeSabre. "I'm dying here," she continued, but LaVerna was humming loudly to Elton John's new single on KGON 92.3, Portland's classic rock radio station. Mina's appeal for sympathy was a total no go.

Chapter Fourteen
Yamhill Siblings Perish in Leaf Pile Accident
October 30, 1985

What Mina remembered about that day lived on in parts of her body that didn't want to feel anything, parts which, at her still-youthful age, should have been showing themselves off in living color. But instead they were muted. Grayscale. Because of what had happened, a calamity that would stay with her forever.

She couldn't shake the memory of that terrible day, of the story she and Martin had been compelled to cover together, him poring through police reports and her speaking to the family. Division of labor. Tag teaming, he called it. He had the easier assignment, interviewing the cops, though he said they weren't too forthcoming with details.

But how do you ask questions of someone awash in fresh grief? *Intrusive* wasn't the word for it. It made Mina doubt herself. It made her think of quitting.

Sitting with the father, between moments of ashen-faced stoicism and jags of uncontrollable weeping, Mina pieced together precisely what had taken place.

The day before Halloween, two young children had been playing in a leaf pile across the street from their home on Belvedere Avenue, making the most of a clear, crisp autumn afternoon. Their father ducked back into the house to get his camera, intending to capture his kids' mischievous smiles as they peeked out from under the fallen maple and oak leaves, like E.T. in the closet in the movie.

Shannon Doyle was gone for two minutes. Within those 120

seconds, the unimaginable occurred.

His daughter and son had submersed themselves in the giant leaf pile, waiting to pop up and surprise their dad. A car came by, its occupants deciding in a single fateful moment to swerve into the leaves neatly piled at the curb and send them flying into the air. A fall frivolity, a lark.

The two kids were giggling, and the joyriders were laughing. The car's front tires hit a bump. The leaves flew. The father's precious children, only six and eight years old, were killed in a single surreal instant. His camera slipped from his hands and fell to the pavement. He did not get his picture.

"I should have protected them," he said to Mina in his living room the next afternoon, bereft, his eyes bloodshot and sunken. He lifted his unshaven face to meet her gaze. "I should have been able to do that, right? Why did I go inside?"

She wanted to put her arms around him. She steadied herself and held pen to paper instead.

"It wasn't your fault," she consoled, breaking her journalistic persona. "It was just an awful accident." The word *just* sounded so trite she wanted to apologize, but she didn't. After what he had been through, what he was going through now, it wouldn't have mattered at all.

Five minutes into the interview the phone jangled on the kitchen wall, and the man excused himself. When he came back, he told Mina it had been the funeral home on the line.

"I'm sorry, but I'm going to have to leave now," he said, his voice straining to rise above a whisper. "They need me to come down and pick out caskets for my babies."

It was all Mina could do not to rush over and embrace him. Tell him a lie, that things would be all right. She flipped her notebook shut and stood up. The man gestured toward the door and said thank you. She shook his hand. She said she was so very sorry. She promised to be in touch.

"Pink," he said, starting to cry. "Lauren's will be pink." Liam's would be yellow, he added, "his favorite color."

***

When Martin returned from the police station with a sheaf of papers under one arm, he was visibly shaken. "It could've been Eliza," he stammered as he hung up his coat, sat down, and commenced typing. "Just as easily could have been her."

The city's public works department had begun a leaf pickup program several years before, to keep tree debris from clogging up storm drains and causing high-water issues in the streets. Belvedere Avenue hadn't been on the service rotation the last week of the month, and that was where Mina thought Martin's story would start: at the beginning with raw facts, like most news stories do. She would fold in the personal part about the Doyle children later on—their divorced truck-driver dad, where they went to school, their hobbies and hopes and dreams—but she soon learned how completely wrong she was. When Martin handed her his draft several hours later, as he routinely did in an effort to help her learn, Mina's eyes welled up as she read, her tears turning the pages to mush.

Two young Yamhill siblings lost their lives last Wednesday, Oct. 30, when they were hit by a passing car while hiding in a pile of autumn leaves. Their father, Shannon Doyle, 36, said he had gone into their house on Belvedere Avenue to retrieve a camera when his children, Lauren, 8, and Liam, 6, were struck and killed. The driver of the car, 27-year-old Abel Branham, remained at the scene and is cooperating with police. An investigation is ongoing.

How does he do it? Mina thought to herself. How does he distill a story this horrific into a single nut graph, giving his readers the most critical information in fewer than a hundred emotion-laden words? She was in awe. She dabbed at her eyes with a tissue and read on.

Police confirmed that the leaf pile obscuring the Doyle children had been awaiting the city's regular pickup service, scheduled for Nov. 6 along Belvedere Avenue. As of last Friday, neither Branham nor his passenger, 26-year-old Lena Metzger, have been charged with a crime, though they have been ordered not to leave Yamhill County and to be available for continued questioning by local and state authorities.

"The circumstances that came together to produce this tragedy are indeed unfortunate," Chief Alan Womack said in a press release. "We

join the Doyle family and our entire community in mourning the loss of Lauren and Liam."

Mina walked into Martin's office and sat down. Everyone else had gone home. He stopped writing. She touched his arm.

"Oh my God, Martin," she said admiringly. "Your story." He looked at her hand, then stared into her face, still streaked with tears.

There was so much to say.

"I usually have plenty of words," Martin said. "I think I used them all up already."

"It's all right," Mina said, an attempt to soothe him. "I know how you feel."

He took her hands in his. They sat for the longest time with only silence between them, the *what ifs* and *could have beens* hanging in the air like ellipses.

Mina spoke first.

"I wouldn't ever want you to lose Eliza," she said.

Martin's eyes softened at the edges and turned an even more remarkable shade of blue. "I need to make sure I never do."

Those eight words blunted some of the sorrow and uncertainty of what lay ahead. Mina picked strands of damp hair from the side of her face and stood up. Martin went back to his writing.

***

Composing a headline for a story you never wanted to write in the first place was an excruciating thing, Mina thought. It's impossible to capture, in five or six Times New Roman words, the essence of a family ripped apart by sudden death. Mina knew whatever she wrote would be too much and also not nearly enough. Yet that was her task the week after the Doyle children died, when the *Cascadian* went to press, when the city's gargantuan leaf-collection machine rolled down Belvedere Avenue and sucked up the remaining piles, when she went to visit Shannon Doyle and saw yards of yellow caution tape suspended between two trees across the street from his house, flapping in the breeze.

Like he did with so many other things, Martin mentored Mina in headline writing, and he did not back away from that commitment, even in the present circumstance. It fell to Mina to write the saddest six words she had ever written, words that would lead readers into an agonizing story they would consume at breakfast the following morning along with their eggs, toast, and juice. She did her job—*Yamhill Siblings Die in Leaf Pile*—and as soon as Martin signed off on it, she drove over to Shannon Doyle's house to tell him how the story had turned out before he had to discover it himself, all alone at his kitchen table.

***

She made one quick detour on the way to Shannon's place. She didn't want to walk in empty-handed. There was a small flower shop on Main Street that sold really nice bouquets. Mums were popular that time of year, but Mina selected three roses instead, white and pink and yellow, in a tall, clear glass vase in the refrigerator case. When she told the florist she was going to visit the Doyle home, she looked at Mina with sympathetic eyes and added a wide grosgrain bow, "no charge," and some fern and baby's breath. News traveled fast in a small town.

"For you," Mina said when Shannon answered the doorbell. "For you and your family, I mean. Again, Mr. Doyle, I'm so very sorry."

Shannon motioned toward the living room and invited Mina to sit down in the same chair she had sat in five days before, the day after Lauren and Liam died. It was upholstered in blue, with fabric-covered buttons on the seat and the ends of the armrests. Shannon placed the vase on the coffee table between them, turning it so the bow faced Mina. An agonized groan came out of him, a noise she was sure he hadn't intended to make, and he leaned forward to rest his elbows on his thighs, one large, rough hand cupping the other. He rocked back and forth to mute the sound of his grief.

"I'm sorry," he said. "It's just that . . ."

"Please don't apologize," Mina said, reaching toward his hands but drawing back before she touched them. "I must be a terrible reminder for you. We can put this off if you want."

Shannon asked her to stay. He was clear about it. He had some things he wanted to tell her, about his girls, about their lives and their futures, things that maybe she could put in another article, if she planned to write one.

"I definitely would like to do a follow-up story," Mina reassured him. "I'm sure our readers would be very interested in knowing your children better."

He looked relieved. She said she was glad to have more information. That's what reporters do—gather facts, give them context. She opened her notebook and took the cap off her pen, ready to ask him more questions.

But Shannon had a question for her instead.

"Can you please not write that my little ones died?" he asked, haltingly, and his face turned somber and serious, as if he had thought a long time about how to make his request. He settled his hips more deeply in his chair and sat up straight. His chest was wide and well-muscled. A heavy silver cross hung from a box chain around his neck, above the first button on his plaid flannel shirt. "When that car hit them, they went straight up to heaven. No doubt." He tilted his head toward the ceiling and got a faraway look in his eyes.

"Liam and Lauren will live forever," he said, "in the loving arms of Jesus."

Chapter Fifteen
Martin's Idea Addresses Bereaved Father's Request
November 4, 1985

No way.

Martin was going to lay it right on the line as soon as Mina got back from her latest interview with Shannon Doyle, the young father who didn't want her to say in the paper that his kids had died, who wanted her to say they had "gone to heaven" instead.

There was no freaking way they were going to write *Liam Doyle, 6, and Lauren Doyle, 8, went to heaven on Oct. 30, 1985.* They would write exactly what had happened, that the children had been hit by a car. That they died. They couldn't tiptoe around that. Martin felt very strongly about it, stubborn even. When he thought about it, he could feel the heat rise up from his chest to his neck and face, which looked far too red to be normal when he caught a glimpse of himself in the hall mirror between Ed's office and his.

Mina parked outside the *Cascadian* at 3:05 p.m. She had barely set her backpack down before he busted into her office with a preemptive strike.

"We just can't say the heaven thing, Mina," he said and gave her a bunch of reasons why, as if he should need to. They couldn't afford to alienate any of their readers. He had a list ready of the kinds of subscribers who might object to such language: "People who aren't religious. People who might think we're a conservative publication, which we most certainly aren't," he said, holding his fingers up one by one. "People who would just think it was weird that we wrote it that way."

He paused to catch his breath, to give the lump in his throat a chance to subside.

"We can't even say passed away," Martin reminded her. "You know that. It's against journalistic norms."

Mina frowned at him, then raised a challenge of an eyebrow. She notched her hair behind her ears so her peace-sign earrings showed. "Can't we make an exception? Just this one time?"

Her deep-set eyes were fiery with the potential to knock Martin off-balance. He couldn't let that happen.

"Tell Doyle to buy a display ad," he spat, immediately embarrassed by his outburst. "Then he can say whatever the hell he likes. He can say his kids were abducted by aliens if he wants to."

Mina sat back, hard, as if he had slapped her. She nodded curtly. "I get it, boss. No heaven. You don't have to hit me over the head twice." She scrunched her forehead in a way that marred her pretty face.

She rose up again, her tone sharper than before. "But come on, Martin. Isn't there some way we can respond with compassion to a man who just lost his entire world?"

God, sometimes Mina could be a pain in the butt. It was a good question, and Martin knew the answer, but he wasn't ready to concede. He went outside and walked around the block a couple of times. In the space of fifteen minutes, he saw Ben Pollock walking Dixie, his miniature schnauzer, who barked at him like usual. He passed Saul Hersher on his daily noontime trip from Valley Baptist to the post office, a stack of newsletters in his hands, stamped and ready for mailing.

He figured out what had been eating at him.

Mina was standing when Martin returned, her A-line skirt skimming her hips, its hem an enticing five inches above her knees. She was sprinkling the spider fern in the green macramé hanger in one corner of her office. She put the watering can down and sat, extending her long legs and then pulling them in, crossing them at the knees. She pulled at her fingers and smiled a smile that was nervous and defiant at the same time.

"Here's the thing," Martin said, as serious as he had ever been. "If Shannon Doyle wants to say his kids went to heaven, we can quote him that way. 'My children went to heaven.' Literal quotation marks around those words. Make it unmistakably clear they're his, not ours."

He crossed his arms, raising the volume of his body language a couple of levels. "Does that work for you?"

Mina relaxed a little and uncrossed her legs. The frown melted away. Her pretty face was back, and that made Martin feel slightly better.

"Don't know why I didn't think of that before," he said, even though he *did* know why. He needed to be in charge somewhere, somehow, and that somewhere and somehow had become here, at the office, even if it meant getting his way in a disagreement about how the paper should report a devastating story.

Martin read Mina's expression like tea leaves. He decided she was satisfied.

"Fair enough," she said as he exited her office, "I can live with that. Thanks, Martin."

She returned to her fern, plucking off the dead parts with renewed enthusiasm. Martin went back to typing, but also back to peering at Mina through the slot between their offices. He felt his body responding to the glory of her legs. He wondered how he was going to deal with the emotional complexities eating away at him: the growing ambivalence he felt toward his wife and the maddening unpredictability of his ailment—the two most pressing impediments in his life.

***

"How're you feeling about today's edition overall?"

It was evening. Martin had switched off the light in his office, put on his trench coat, and pushed his fedora down low on his forehead, perfecting its jaunty angle with a tap of his thumb. The keys to his ancient station wagon dangled from his fingers.

"All right. You know." Mina shuffled papers, stuffed some of them into her messenger bag. "I would've preferred to have kept faith with Shannon Doyle."

"I know," Martin said, leaning on the doorjamb. "We do what we can. There's always the op-ed page. And there's always next week."

Something in him shifted. His blue eyes twinkled, full of mischief.

"I'll ask the boss to send us to Mama Cass's Big Blast next year. They're billing it as a second freaking Woodstock. At the campsites, near the county line."

Martin reached into his desk drawer and pulled out a bright pink Post-it note. He wrote his request down, deposited it in McKee's office, and reemerged triumphant, smelling of mint and sugar.

LaVerna came in every Friday to collect tear sheets for advertisers, who wanted to see proof of what their money had bought. She kept the bowl on Ed's desk stocked with round red-and-white peppermints, the cheap kind wrapped in cellophane.

"Something for us to look forward to," Martin said, making smacking noises. His left cheek twitched. "We'll go out into the field for a change. Take a break from night meetings."

Martin looked tired. His shaggy head wobbled beneath his hat. "Bluegrass music, lots of pot, naked people, fireworks if the cops don't show up. That should give us plenty to write about."

"No kidding. Naked people?" Mina said, more statement than question. She was learning a ton thanks to Martin. Not just the mechanics of community journalism, but how to draw someone in and then draw them out. Ways to get to the heart of things, stories about life, about what it meant to be fully human.

Chapter Sixteen
Newspaper Staff Witnesses Space Shuttle
Explosion on Live TV
January 28, 1986

It was a tight squeeze for everyone to fit inside Ed's office on that midwinter morning, first at his invitation, then at his insistence. He had brought in a TV set from home, wrestling it out of his car trunk, up three concrete steps, and in the front door.

"First teacher in space!" he called down the hallway. "Come on—show's about to start!" He hooked the set up to an antenna and bungee corded it to a high shelf in the corner so everyone had a good view.

Morning agendas had gone by the wayside in order to humor him. Watching the spectacle on television had nothing to do with anyone's responsibilities at the newspaper.

"We'll get back to it as soon as it's over," Ed had said the day prior. "But this is big. The whole staff should see it together."

Cable News Network, Ted Turner's fledgling twenty-four-hour news channel, was broadcasting the launch live. "Exclusive rights," Ed noted as he tweaked the volume. The audio feed from Florida's Kennedy Space Center crackled.

Martin walked in fashionably late and spied Mina in the far corner. She lifted her chin to acknowledge him, then looked straight ahead at Ed. Martin wove his way through the scrum of bodies, scouting around for an empty seat. He didn't want to stand—this could take a while and the medications were making him feel a bit unsteady. Roger, Francine, and Carla stood shoulder to shoulder behind Ed's desk, like good soldiers. LaVerna and Ed Jr. sat in folding chairs. LaVerna looked at Martin and patted the seat of a chair next to her, so he sat too.

Electricity mingled with what little oxygen was left in the room as all of them awaited the launch of the space shuttle *Challenger* and its crew, including Christa McAuliffe, a social studies teacher from New Hampshire. Everyone at the *Cascadian* counted down along with the rest of the world, then *bam*—the spacecraft lifted off from the platform inside a giant cloud of smoke. Roger pumped his fist a few times as the shuttle rose against a bright blue sky off the Atlantic Coast.

"Whoo!" Francine yelled, cheering with the thunderous sound of engines straining.

"History in the making," LaVerna said in an exaggeratedly hushed tone. In her lap she held Miss Molly, who had, to almost everyone's surprise, become a decently well-behaved office cat. "It's marvelous, just marvelous. We're all going to remember this day!"

The *Challenger* kept going—up, up, up—but seventy-three seconds in, without warning, it exploded in a ball of fire. Terrible white plumes flew left and right, like alien antennae.

Martin's mouth fell open. His brain did not compute what his eyes were seeing. He glanced sideways at Mina. Her lips were pale, pressed together in a tight, straight line.

"Obviously a major malfunction," came a shaky voice from mission control, and then they all knew. The shuttle had broken apart, killing everyone on board. The room inhaled a collective gasp. Some of the staff bowed their heads.

"Land sakes," breathed LaVerna, bringing her hands to her cheeks. Miss Molly jumped down and scampered out the office door.

Ed reached up and switched off the TV. There would be no watching the talking heads after the fact. It was the day before deadline, after all. He took off his glasses and wiped his eyes with his handkerchief.

Before the *Challenger* disaster, no one at the *Cascadian* knew much about the state of the US space program. Even fewer were familiar with the thinking of pundits on CNN. Over the next several weeks they learned a lot about engineering mistakes and O-ring seals and the human propensity for pointing fingers. One of Martin's aunts, who came over for a roast beef dinner the next night along with his mother, shook her head and pursed her lips, tsk-tsking five words: "We must affix the blame."

The whole crew filed back to their desks in silence, each pondering in their own way the enormity of what they had witnessed in real time: the indelible image of the explosion. The loss of seven lives in a split second. The surprise of Ed's tears.

When she finally spoke, Mina succinctly summed up the experience. "Well, that was depressing," she said and went outside for a walk.

Martin's office suddenly felt very empty to him, even with his beloved books on the shelves—organized into journalism, music, and philosophy sections—and the usual framed photos on his desk, five of them placed just so, two family pictures in front. Miss Molly sauntered in, rubbed against his leg, and began purring loudly. His eyes filled and spilled over as he stared at the pictures.

One was of Eliza at around age five, playing with a puppy in a neighbor's backyard. The dusky summer sun backlit the image, making her round face into a silhouette, her small nose upturned, her mouth open and laughing. The other photo had been taken aboard a boat on Judith and Martin's honeymoon in Alaska's Kenai fjords. He couldn't remember why, but he was standing, leaning on a railing above Judith, who was sitting on a bench seat on the vessel's starboard side. They looked a little like the farmer couple in that famous American Gothic painting, without the shovel and pitchfork. Judith stared up at Martin, his right arm draped around her slim shoulder and her left arm encircling his waist. Two of her fingers were tucked inside his wide belt loop, for safety, as if he might fall overboard. They looked more like brother and sister than husband and wife, but Judith had gifted the photo to him on their first wedding anniversary, so there it was.

Long after Dr. Fridley diagnosed his dystonia, and in the years since he met and nurtured a congenial and collaborative relationship with Edwin "Doc" Ralston of Yamhill, Martin continued his habit of researching how the body responds to grief, because that was how it felt. Like grief, like loss. When his mind was occupied by a book, he could avoid the dark places he didn't want to visit. Looking things up helped him reclaim a sense of control, wobbly though it was. He pretended he was fact-checking a news story, only the story wasn't news. The story was about him.

He learned stomach cramps and night sweats were physical manifestations of grief-related stress. Same with fatigue and dizziness. His heart literally ached, as if someone had ripped open his rib cage and pummeled his insides. It took a lot of concentration for him to stay focused and grounded, to remember that his affliction and his anguish were separate things. He and Judith would treat the former with medicine and hope. Martin would have to learn to live with the latter.

***

The bell on the office door signaled Mina's return. Martin knew it was her and not someone else by the sound of her footsteps on the vinyl floor, soft yet purposeful. "I'm back," she said through the opening in the wall between their offices. The staccato sound of her typewriter pierced the quiet.

He wondered what Judith would say at the end of the day, after he told her the space shuttle catastrophe was hitting him hard, that it was connecting with raw emotions about the failure of his body to protect him from invaders, about the overwhelm of adult life, about a future that could not be known.

"Martin dear," he imagined her saying, half listening, pencil in hand, poring over data on spreadsheets. "It was just an awful accident, nothing more. It's not about you. You have to let it go."

***

When he walked through the door between the carport and the kitchen, Judith was indeed working. In the nook, her back to him, on a phone call. The cord was stretched between the kitchen and her desk. He heard a low rumbling, the kind of noise that indicated things weren't going well.

"I haven't the foggiest what the second-quarter books mean for the bottom line," Judith said, all impatience, irritation, and bluster. "I'm a software developer, Al, not an economist."

She didn't hear Martin come in until after she hung up. He was rummaging around in the cupboard for a tall glass. He needed a beer. She looked surprised to see him. It was only four fifteen. She still had work to do.

"Oh!" she said, clasping both hands to her chest. "You startled me, Martin. You're home early."

"Judith," he said, but she interrupted.

"I mopped the floors." Her voice was strained and monotone. She took two tablets from the aspirin bottle on the counter, washed them down with a single gulp from Martin's glass, and pointed at his feet.

"Please take your shoes off before you walk through the house," she said, wiping her lips with the back of her hand. "Eliza's doing homework in her room, and supper's in the oven. I'm going to finish this report and take a bath. We'll eat at six."

Martin yanked off his loafers and started down the hall. Eliza's door was open a crack. He looked in to see her hunched over a workbook from school. "Hiya!" she said brightly. She turned serious at the sight of his fallen face. "What's wrong, Daddy? Tell me."

There was no hiding from Eliza. She always knew when he wasn't okay. Martin hoped she hadn't heard about the *Challenger* disaster yet, that her teacher wouldn't have had the TV on in their classroom.

"I had a tough day, Sunshine." He sat beside her on her bed. "How was yours?" She put one hand on his shoulder and narrowed her clear green eyes, as if trying to see inside him. She turned the workbook around so he could read what she had written.

To the McAuliffe family:

I am so sad about the terrible space shuttle accident. Christa was very brave to go into space. I know you're going to miss her a lot, and I will be thinking of you.

Sincerely yours,

Eliza Donovan

Chapter Seventeen
Mina, Martin Venture into Woods for Concert
June 28, 1986

Summer couldn't have come quickly enough for Mina and, along with it, a day of adventuring in the woods. A welcome break from city council and parks board meetings, and definitely better than covering recreational baseball. Martin would pick her up at noon the first Saturday after the solstice. They would be at the Blast by two o'clock or so, spend a few hours mingling, get what they needed, and head back to town. That was the plan, enough for a double truck photo montage in the following week's paper, along with a catchy art headline and some long, detailed cutlines. Or maybe a short feature, if they stumbled across something interesting.

When Martin pulled up outside Mina's place at 12:05, she was ready. "Hey," she said as she opened the door, ducked her head, and slid in, smelling of citrus.

"Hi yourself," said Martin, who had been up early that morning tending to a family obligation.

"I had to make breakfast for Eliza and her friend Skyler," he explained. "She slept over, Skyler I mean. Judith's been at her mother's since before the girls were up. They'll be at it all day, making food for Shavuot."

Mina regarded him quizzically. She wondered why he was talking so funny, and she wanted to know what Shavuot was. She was pretty sure it was part of the Jewish calendar, not nearly as important as Yom Kippur, but she didn't bring it up until they were buckled in, out of the neighborhood, and well on their way.

"Don't worry," Martin said, as if Mina was. He checked the rearview and the side mirrors before inserting the key and turning the engine over. "I dropped Skyler off at her house, and Eliza's with her mom and her bubbe. We're good to go now."

There were mud boots on the floor in front of the passenger seat. Mina nudged them over with her left foot. She felt a little silly about bringing her slicker and hat along—the clouds were threateningly gray and she thought it might rain—but Martin's boots made her feel better about her clothing choices.

"It's gonna be cold up in the woods," he said as they tooled along past the city limits and into more rural country, the car's trusty heater blasting warm air on their ungloved hands. "I'm hoping we can hold our interviews inside one of the cabins." He was all business, not quite what Mina was hoping for, but not unlike him either. He got laser focused when there was newspaper work to be done. She took out her notebook and wrote *the Blast, East Yamhill County.*

"So, Shavuot," she said while scrawling. "Say more about that."

***

Growing up, Mina's experience with religion had been spotty at best. Her family hadn't been atheists, exactly—more like incurious agnostics, a constant bone of contention between her mother and her mother's mother. Grandma Sue, a staunch Missouri Synod Lutheran, had made it her habit to agonize out loud about Anna Breckenridge's salvation, a scary thing for a preteen to hear, especially one predisposed to lolling in the sun at Bethesda Beach, nurturing the darkest of tans. One who wasn't into contemplating whether her mom was going to heaven or hell.

"It's beyond me how I raised a daughter who doesn't interpret the Bible literally," Grandma Sue had said to Mina's mother more than once, when she thought Mina was out of earshot. "Better start paying attention if you want eternal salvation, missy."

Anna always had some kind of retort that displeased Grandma Sue, like she didn't believe in either ascendancy or descendancy when it came to the afterlife. "I'll be fine, Mother. I'm a good human. You don't have to fret about me," she would say in a singsongy voice, earning either a sidelong glance or a steely-eyed stare depending on Grandma's mood and a sad shake of her silvery hair clipped into a severe, short bob.

The Breckenridges were what Grandma Sue called, with unbridled disdain, "chreasters," people who only went to church twice a year, on Christmas Eve and Easter Sunday, to appease the pious faction of the family. That was due to the influence of Mina's alcoholic father, "the heathen" as Sue sometimes called him, even to his face.

"That man's no good for nobody, and he never will be," Sue often said, until she didn't have to anymore.

***

The long drive to the festival seemed the perfect time to bring up the topic of Judith's fealty to her cultural roots. The car rumbled along, the ride silent except for the *whoosh* of the wind through an inch of rolled-down window.

"Tell me about Judith's faith," Mina asked again as she fiddled with the radio dial, AM to FM and back again. She finally settled on a soft rock station, figuring Martin wouldn't object too much. "Is Shavuot like Purim? I've heard about that." She batted her eyelashes instinctively, then wished she hadn't.

Martin's cheek flinched at the unexpected question, as though she had bumped up against a hurt place in his life. Or maybe it was her eyelashes. He sipped in some breath and attempted an answer.

"It's part of what comes after Passover," he said, checking to see if Mina recognized the significance. She nodded. "And Passover's a really big deal to Judith."

Martin had made no bones about his on-again, off-again relationship with Catholicism, although he was well past his altar-boy days. At the office he and Mina shared self-deprecating jokes about the "smells and bells" that had defined the occasional Lutheran service of her youth and the regular Mass attendance of his. She could recite the Nicene Creed from memory, though she hadn't been inside a church since Grandma Sue's funeral at Our Redeemer, a packed-sanctuary affair back in 1976. She liked the creed's last line best, the part that said people could look forward to the life of the world to come. Better than the one they were in now, not all milk and honey for sure. That futuristic idea comforted her somehow.

Martin mused out loud about the appeal of an afternoon of apron-clad time in the kitchen, trying to lighten the mood. "I figure there's a whole lot of fancy bread-baking going on at Judith's mother's house right now," he said. "Eliza must be having fun tossing all that flour around."

***

Across the Ross Island Bridge in one of East Portland's most well-appointed kitchens, Eliza and her mother were deep into making challah. Eliza stood over a large bowl and worked the dough, laboring over Judith's special recipe, accompanied by lively commentary from Bubbe Levy.

"Mind the salt," Bubbe instructed as she glided across the floor to "Sunrise, Sunset" from *Fiddler on the Roof.* "Only a pinch extra, and only while the loaf's still hot."

Eliza and her mama looked at each other knowingly and, after depositing the baking sheet in the oven, joined Bubbe in her happy dance. It took the full five minutes of cooking time to finish the song, with all three of them drawing out the last word for effect.

"Tearrrrsssss!" the trio crescendoed, then broke into simultaneous peals of laughter.

Out popped the braided bread, browned and glistening. It was time for cleanup as Bubbe rested in her bedroom.

"I've had such a good afternoon, Mama," Eliza said, giving Judith a hug. "I think I know your recipe by heart. Like I do your matzah. Let's make them together every year."

***

Mina fiddled with her seat belt, thinking her own thoughts. They were deep into the woods now, and getting deeper. Martin piped up.

"It's so good to be out here in nature with Saint Francis of Assisi," he said, his hands thumping the wheel to the beat of the music.

What he didn't say was *out here in nature, with you,* which was probably for the best. Mina wanted to know so much more about Judith's allegiance to her faith—how much it informed her worldview and her morals, how closely she and Martin planned to adhere to its tenets in raising their daughter—but decided she shouldn't push it. She changed the subject to something they both embraced: their deep, unwavering devotion to journalism, the patron saint of curiosity.

"What story are we going for, exactly?" Mina's words caught in a scratchy throat. She had been fighting a bug for a week but hadn't let on because she didn't want Martin to call off the trip. She reached into her pocket for a box of lozenges. She offered one to Martin, and he took it.

"I'm figuring on a human-interest piece about the kinds of people who travel around the country to attend these events." He sucked loudly on the cherry-flavored disc while deftly playing the steering wheel around tight curves in the road. "Sort of a where-do-they-go-and-why-do-they-go-there piece. Should be some interesting folks out there in the woods. Hope you don't mind weird." She assured him she didn't but at the same time wondered what they were getting themselves into. She was content to see what might develop.

They talked shop for the next twenty miles, chattering away about deadlines and bad print jobs and Ed and LaVerna's office fights. They passed through several bump-in-the-road towns—Dundee, Dayton, Whiteson—each of them smaller than the one before, all of them fading like shooting stars in the side-view mirror. Martin kept his eyes on the road and Mina noticed every little thing. The birches and maples were beginning to show off for the season, plumping out with wide, green leaves. Kids without helmets rode in bike lanes paralleling the highway, something she had never seen when she lived in the big city where everything was more carefully curated. Eventually, Martin turned onto a two-lane road that led them deep into the forest between Amity and Hopewell, tall stands of conifers forming a mind-spinning mass as they whizzed along.

He returned to the topic of their story, a quirky, photo-heavy feature for the front page. "We'll have to see if anyone's up for talking to us, let alone getting their picture taken," he said. "Music festivals in the woods tend to attract folks who'd rather stay anonymous."

The pavement ran out and the road got curvier and even more rural, opening up to a dirt trail that was barely passable by car. The station wagon's tires followed the zigs and zags of deep, muddy ruts, its front end squeaking like an accordion as they bumped along over tree roots and rocks.

Martin reached behind the driver's seat and handed Mina a *Thomas Guide*. "Can you look up what comes after Route 154?" he said, looking a bit worried, like they might be lost. She flipped through the spiral-bound pages to find their location and hoped they weren't. Then again, what if they were?

"I think we're getting close," Mina said, pointing to a jagged yellow line, but she actually didn't have a clue.

They drove a bit more, the ruts getting deeper, the outside temperature falling. Mina was glad she had worn layers under her rain jacket after all. Rounding another bend, they approached the back end of the first car they had seen in miles, then another, and another. Suddenly it was bumper-to-bumper along the lane, a line of trucks and vans stretching a good half mile in front of them. The Blast was just up ahead.

Martin pretended to lose control of the car, just for fun. "Whoa, this whole thing better be worth it," he said, making exaggerated motions with the wheel, cranking it left and right. "Could very well be our last hurrah."

They rolled up to a wide clearing. Suddenly they were in the midst of the gathering, a throwback to a more innocent time, a time of turning on, tuning in, dropping out. Martin smiled his trademark smile—teeth showing, mustache dancing, blue eyes flashing and full of life. "Look at all the free spirits," he gushed, gesturing toward a couple holding hands, their bare backsides mooning the crowd as they disappeared behind a clump of Douglas firs.

"Counterculture hippies," Mina corrected, feeling her eyes widen. She rolled her window down a few more inches to see if she could hear music. Guitar riffs and the merry vibrations of strumming banjos echoed not far away.

"Bluegrass," she said and beamed at Martin. "That's your kind of music, right?"

They parked, set up folding chairs on the perimeter of camp and dragged the cooler out of the back seat. They wanted to sit close enough to the action to get the flavor of it, for the sake of accurate reporting, but they needed to blend in too. Mina exchanged her slicker and hat for a fleece jacket and cap she had stuffed into her backpack. Martin fetched a wool blanket from the trunk and spread it across their laps, wedging his reporter's notebook between his knees. He reached into the cooler and produced two beers and a bottle opener.

"Cheers," he said as the caps flew off. They clinked their bottles together.

Mina felt the weight of the blanket on top of her legs, the cool of the bottle against her palm. People milled around in the darkness, backlit by the fire, many of them sans clothing, getting high and swaying to the music. Some took the hands of a partner and performed loose swing dances, while others stood and oscillated, their faces turned toward the night sky.

It was like Mina and Martin were inside a dream, one that would end with something tangible.

The Rolling River Boys played on and on, well past nightfall. Songs of yearning, of hitting the road, of heartbreak, of unrequited love. The whole scene was surreal and gorgeous: supple fingers plucking stringed instruments, the stage a natural backdrop for flickering campfires and pine-scented woods.

"This is the life," Martin said, leaning back in his chair.

"Agreed," said Mina, following his lead. "Gotta love the music and the atmosphere." He winked at her, like he always had since she met him. *And the company*, she thought of adding but didn't.

A litany of questions flashed through her mind. What were they thinking, staying out in the woods together until the morning side of night? What would Martin tell Judith? How would it feel to be in the office together on Monday?

She let the questions flit through her brain and settle like embers at the bottom of a fire. Her body was deliciously warm, and she felt as carefree as a schoolgirl. It was all so intoxicating. Martin kept time to the music with one mud-booted foot. Mina let her head fall back. She stared up at a hologram of stars and constellations, and her heart wandered, unfettered, into the unknown.

***

Mina's reverie broke when the naked couple returned from behind the tree line and stood right in front of her.

"Hello there!" said the man, his groin at eye level. Mina managed not to stare. "I'm Adam, and this is Eve. Where're you two from?"

Martin saved Mina from stammering out a reply.

"Hi, yourselves!" he said and stood to shake Adam's hand. "My name's Martin, and this is my friend Mina. We're from the local newspaper, just stopping by to see what the Blast is all about. You two look like you're enjoying yourselves!"

Smooth, thought Mina. Vintage Martin, entering an interview sideways.

Eve glanced at Adam, who squeezed her hand reassuringly.

"We really are, man. This whole scene is where it's at. The weed's glorious, the music's fine, and the people are totally cool. You can quote me on that."

Martin flipped his notebook open to a fresh page and nudged Mina with his left heel.

"Uh, nice to meet you, Adam and Eve. Mind doing a quick interview?" She straightened up and pointed to the sky, which had started to produce some moisture. "Over there in cabin B?" Her mind raced to the obvious reportage problem. She had to get permission to use their real names for the story. But first things first.

"I'm a wannabe flower child from way back," Mina said, the words flowing from her mouth like water. She smiled at Eve, and Eve smiled back. "Joni Mitchell and the Mamas & the Papas were all my mom played when I was growing up."

"Me too," said Eve, pushing damp, ringleted hair away from her eyes. "You're a California girl, I can tell."

The four of them headed for the cabin and settled in around a table and chairs in the back. Seated was much better than standing. Less skin meant more revelation. The interview went for hours.

Chapter Eighteen
Martin Reckons with Judith After Night with Mina
June 29, 1986

"Thanks so much for your time, both of you," Martin said when his end of the conversation with Eve and Adam ebbed around two in the morning. Adam leaned forward, wanting to continue. He had much more to say about his love for his lady, strings music, and quality reefer—not necessarily in that order—but Martin had stopped writing almost an hour earlier, leaving the note-taking exclusively to Mina, who looked at him with exhausted, imploring eyes. *Get me out of here*, they said.

"Yes, we really appreciate you telling us your story," Mina added, raising her notebook in the air and closing the cover for emphasis' sake. She slipped it into her backpack, precious cargo she couldn't afford to misplace. She was already formulating a headline and lede in her mind about the most carefree of couples and the groupie lifestyle that had taken them from the Everglades of Florida to the forests of Northwest Oregon—but both could keep until Monday.

Eve smiled a weary, wasted smile and gave her interviewer a hug.

"This has been so cool!" She clasped Mina's hands in hers. "I didn't know reporters could be so nice. It's like we're soul sisters or something."

Martin dropped Mina off at her place. They were both still energized by the events of the evening. She walked around to the driver's side door, leaned down, and rested both hands on the open windowsill.

"Thanks for an awesome night," she said, and Martin couldn't disagree. She had lit a fire inside him, a fire he wasn't sure he wished to quell.

"You're welcome, Mina," he returned, his mind a delightful blur of kaleidoscopic images. "It was pretty extraordinary."

***

A faint feeling of dread thumped in Martin's chest as he navigated the few miles home. He remembered the last argument he'd had with Judith, a doozy about parenting styles. He had let Eliza spend the night with one of her friends from school on a weekend when Judith was out of town.

"I don't even know that family!" Judith had exclaimed when she returned from her business trip. "How did you know the situation was safe? You're completely spoiling her."

She also used words like *indulgent* and *reckless* as the big vein on the side of her neck got bigger. She even hinted that Martin had offloaded Eliza for another reason, one that involved spending more time with Mina, the accusation so outlandish that he walked out of the room and refused to reengage after Eliza went to bed.

"You need to fight fair, my dear, or we won't fight at all," he had insisted, so they didn't continue. Judith retreated to their bedroom, reemerging only to hand her husband a blanket and pillow for the couch.

***

It was nearly dawn when he pulled into his driveway, cutting the headlights as the car came to a stop. The light above the kitchen sink was on and he could see Judith moving about inside the house.

"Here we go," he said to no one but himself, "reckoning time." He shut off the motor, climbed out, and shoved the keys into his pants pocket. Pain radiated down his right arm as his fingers turned the doorknob.

A bustling, ponytailed Judith was never a good sign, especially so early on a Sunday. She didn't look at Martin when he walked in; instead, she snapped a dish towel from her shoulder and tossed it his way. "You might as well get busy," she said and handed him a dripping dinner plate left over from the night before. "Eliza's still asleep. We have some talking to do. I think you know about what."

Martin narrowed bleary eyes at the back of his wife and went for it. "If you want to discuss my relationship with Mina, this isn't the time." He swiped the plate once and set it down on the counter. What came next was as unavoidable as it was predictable.

"This is *exactly* the right time," Judith barked, turning off the faucet with a single strike of her palm to the handle and doing a 180 to face him. "Actually, there is no other time. You've been out all night with another woman. I have a right to know what's going on between you two!"

Martin felt everything in him shut down. His words, his explanations, any inclination to appease his partner. "There's nothing going on between us," he said, not even believing it himself, "except what you're making up in your own suspicious mind."

Chapter Nineteen
Undercover Operation Yields No Gambling Evidence
August 15, 1987

The air inside the Do Drop Inn was thick with cigarette smoke and the sticky-sweet aroma of cheap beer flowing from a long row of taps behind the bar. It was dark inside, flashlight dark, and it took a minute for Martin's pupils to fully dilate so he could locate the bartender, a diminutive man leaning against the back wall beneath a large oblong mirror and wiping a glass out with a rag. Mina followed along behind her colleague, grasping his elbow for guidance as they approached the bartender, whose small, deep-set eyes finally came into focus. Shaggy black brows hung above them like fringe on a lampshade. He jerked a sparsely whiskered chin their way to acknowledge their presence, then kept on wiping.

"Howdy folks," he said, as if they were actors in a B-grade Western. He set the glass down, tucked the rag inside his waistband, and extended his hand. "Name's Jim. The regulars call me Jimbo."

Martin reached his right hand across the bar, holding on to Mina's with his left. "Howdy yourself. We're new to the Do Drop, Jimbo. Appreciate it if you'd hook us up."

Ed had sent the two of them there on a night assignment to check out a rumor that the place might be hosting illegal video poker. There hadn't been any reports of gambling in town, not that

Martin had heard anyway, and he kept in close touch with the cops. The boss was quirky like that, asking Mina and Martin to chase down random tips he heard on the street, usually about allegedly illegal activity. In this case Martin didn't mind—it sounded like fun, and he could do with a bit of adventure. Besides, what if Ed was right?

Ed was all in. That afternoon, he did something he rarely did. He took out his wallet and handed Martin twenty bucks.

"For drinks. For the both of you," he said, grinning. "Think of it as a one-time expense account." Martin thanked him and stuffed the money in his jacket pocket. It was only one evening—how bad could it be? But he also knew he would have to talk fast to convince Judith.

She was in the den reading *Madame Bovary* for the umpteenth time, her slippered feet perched on the edge of the ottoman, when he told her about the assignment. Eliza was at the nook table, finishing a bowl of ice cream.

"You're going to a bar in Dundee? Tonight? With Mina?" Judith said, her jaw turning rigid.

Eliza's spoon dropped into her bowl, making a clanging sound.

"Isn't this just another one of Ed's weird whims?" Judith asked.

Of course it was, Martin admitted. No doubt about it. But Ed was the boss, after all, so he had to go.

"Why don't you and Roger go instead?" Judith suggested, then piled on. "Mina's barely old enough to be in a bar," she said, her voice dripping with sarcasm.

Martin didn't let Judith's jabs get to him. This was work. He had accepted the assignment, and that was that. He put on his hat. "I'll be back before Dan Rather signs off for the night," he promised, scooping up his car keys.

Judith took Eliza by the hand and led her down the hall toward her bedroom. "Make sure you are," she barked over her shoulder as mother and daughter disappeared around the corner.

***

Martin and Mina took Mina's car because hers was less conspicuous than his, with its faux wood paneling and Support Your Local Newspaper bumper sticker. They left their press credentials behind.

It was a Friday, payday, and the Do Drop Inn was packed. Martin smelled trouble from the get-go.

"Gin and tonic," he said to Jimbo. "Twist of lime, heavy on the gin." He reminded himself Ed had generously paid for a double.

The barkeep turned to Mina.

"White Russian, please."

Jimbo smiled, nodded, and got to work, whistling as he did so. Martin gave Mina a quizzical look. "Odd choice," he said, tossing her a cocktail napkin printed with the words "Do Drop Inn, Est. 1979, Where friends meet to drink." *Or play video poker*, he thought with proper reporter's skepticism, though at first glance he didn't detect any brightly colored machines.

Mina's lips curled up in a mischievous grin. "Seems appropriate for what we're doing," she said in a low voice. "You know, Russian spies and the like." Jimbo slid her drink across the bar. She picked it up and rattled the ice in the glass.

It was all fun and games inside Dundee's seediest watering hole, at least until it wasn't. The Do Drop was two miles away from Martin's neighborhood, as the crow flies, and less than a mile from the front door of the newspaper. He and Mina were there to conduct an undercover operation, and both of them took that seriously, though they had agreed on the way over that they didn't expect to find anything big going on. They got up from their barstools one at a time, trying not to arouse suspicion, as each of them snooped around for a locked door or a back room behind a curtain, like in the movies. They checked out suspects as they came and went: to the bathroom, back to their seats, their shoes sticking to the booze-soaked floor as they walked.

Mina's impassivity game was far better than Martin's. She nursed her drink and rotated her body ever so slightly on her barstool, scanning the room for evidence of graft.

"Mmm," she said and winked Jimbo's way. The vodka was starting to go to her head. Maybe Jim had tipped a bit extra into her glass. That, or Mina was quite the lightweight.

"I'm sure no one will figure out what you're doing," Martin teased.

Mina frowned, then smiled. "Hey! Let's pretend we're in a real-life game of Clue," she suggested, poking him in the side. "You're Professor Plum, in the kitchen. And I'm Miss Scarlett, in the library, of course."

Martin was so bemused by this new version of Mina, this Mina with a buzz on, that for a moment or two he forgot what they were doing there, at a dive bar, after dark. A sudden jerk of his arm broke the spell. He clasped his elbow to his side until the pain abated.

"C'mon Mina, let's focus on why we're here," he said unconvincingly.

"Oh sure, Martin, no problem," she returned, but he didn't think for a minute she meant it.

From the back of the room, a rough-looking dude in stonewashed Levi's and black cowboy boots sauntered up and positioned himself to Martin's left at the end of the bar. He pulled a Winston out of the pack in his front pocket, lit up, wagged two fingers the bartender's way, and pointed to his can of Coors.

"I'll have another," he said and slapped down three bucks. "Keep the change." Martin was glad to be wedged between the cowboy dude and Mina. He turned his back to the man in a protective stance.

"You got it, Harley," Jimbo said, and Harley flexed his biceps under rolled-up sleeves. He was fiftyish, way too old for Mina, and a burly six feet tall to Martin's wiry five foot nine. Martin needed him to stay in his own lane.

Harley glanced past him toward Mina. His heavy mustache quivered, and his eyes were bloodshot but determined. He touched the felted rim of his Stetson with a thumb and forefinger, nodded her way, and produced a broad, crooked-toothed smile.

Martin felt every muscle in his body stiffen as he waited for the guy to address Mina.

"Hello there, beautiful," he finally said, leaning forward to make eye contact, as if Martin wasn't there. "Buy you another?" He pointed to her tumbler, its contents drained, the ice nearly melted.

Mina hadn't been listening to anything except the music bleating from a cheap set of speakers perched on shelves above the bar. Her head bobbed to drum rhythms in the latest Stevie Wonder hit. Her eyes were dewy, her heart-shaped face open and vulnerable. She rolled the remaining slivers of ice around in the bottom of her glass, then swallowed their remnants and parried the stranger's advances by sitting back, out of his line of sight.

"'Part Time Lover,'" she said to Martin, wiping her mouth with the napkin. "I love that song."

He had underestimated Mina again. She could take care of herself. He glanced at his watch. After two drinks and an order of wings, he had five dollars left in his wallet. It was already nine forty-five. There was no chance they were getting what they came for, a serious news story.

It was time to go home. Fifteen minutes to make good on his promise to Judith.

"What do you say we get out of here?" Martin tapped Mina on the arm, got up, and started putting on his jacket.

Marlboro man looked at him and scowled, then gave Mina a final, resigned glance. He drained his beer and lumbered away. Mina sniffed, smiled, and fixed her gaze on Martin.

"Geez, boss. Don't be a spoilsport," she said. "They're playing Journey now." She grabbed the sides of her barstool to steady herself. Her eyes flickered with pleasure. Martin sat back down, called Jimbo over, and ordered another gin and tonic.

"That'll be four bucks," he said as he put down the drink.

Martin handed him the five. "Keep the change, buddy, and thanks."

**

Five hangers-on, plus Jimbo, closed the bar down in the wee hours. Mina was in no condition to drive, so Martin, who could hold his liquor, got behind the wheel. Lucky for him there were no cops patrolling the streets that night. He dropped her off at her place and told her he would bring her car to the office Monday morning.

"You can ride your bike to work and pick it up there," he said, a bit patriarchal for Mina's taste. She displayed a wobbly wave and a comely, inebriated grin, then tripped through the door into her apartment.

Martin sat weighing his options. Should he or shouldn't he? All the signs were there. He got out of the car, climbed the steps, and let himself in, locking the door behind him. The word *wantonness* played inside his head, reaching all the way down into the rest of him.

A coquettish voice floated toward him from a back bedroom. "Are you here, Martin?"

"I am. Is that all right?"

"Of course. Yes. At least I think so."

Martin entered the room, undressed, and laid down beside her, his chest to hers. He smelled her hair, its notes of cinnamon so enticing, the curve of her hip so fetching. He didn't have to wonder what he should do next for very long.

"Do you have protection?"

Martin's answer was immediate. "No need. My treatments took care of that."

"Ah, right. Good then." Mina shifted on the bed and pressed her lips to Martin's. "I need you," she purred, all the encouragement he required. He answered that need until almost daylight.

***

Judith was at the nook table working on a different kind of spreadsheet, one that wasn't related to work.

"We're running pretty close to red this month," she said to Martin, who had put a record on the turntable, intending to while away his Sunday afternoon reading with a little Coltrane in the background. "I'm not sure how we're going to make the electric bill."

Martin lifted the needle and placed the tonearm back in the notch.

"It's that bad?" Judith handled the budget—not his bailiwick.

He got up, walked over, and placed a tremoring hand on her shoulder.

Judith shrank back, shrugging his hand away.

"You know I said summer would be tight," she hissed. "That little trip into the woods you made didn't help, with gas prices so high. It's going to be rough finding the money for Eliza's soccer camp."

Here we go again, thought Martin. He was so tired of the blaming and shaming. Couldn't Judith tap into that sacred cow of a savings account of hers, just for once? Still, he knew he needed to throw her a bone.

"I turned in a couple expense vouchers to Ed," Martin said. "He'll pay them soon. That should give us an extra hundred or so. Will that suffice?"

Judith scratched out a few more figures—hard. Her mechanical pencil lead broke. Martin felt the chill in the air as Judith rose to get more lead from the junk drawer.

"It'll help," she said through clenched teeth after a few ticks of the clock. Though he couldn't see it, Martin knew she was scowling.

"But it won't be enough. Not for me, not for our daughter. Not after your foolish full night with Mina. What were you thinking?"

Martin snatched the needle from the turntable, scratching the record. He stalked through the house to the backyard. "Not enough," he said to himself, to the blue jay above his head in the old oak tree. "It never is."

***

Things between Mina and Martin had felt odd and unnatural the Monday after the Do Drop Inn assignment when they went back to just being coworkers, as if they could have expected anything else. Martin kept to himself far more than usual and took the long way around the building in order to avoid Mina. He stayed away from the coffee nook and responded to her questions about deadlines and stories with a simple yes or no when she encountered him in the hallway. She was afraid she had ruined their friendship.

"I feel better than I have in years," he said to her one morning shortly after their liaison, when she cornered him outside his office. He pushed his sleeves up past his elbows and stretched his left arm across his chest, as if to demonstrate his renewed vigor. "How about you?" Mina passed it off as a backhanded compliment. It wasn't in Martin's nature to be cruel.

"I'm okay," she said. Curtly, flatly. "I mean, I'll be all right." She leaned in and spoke to Martin in a low whisper. "But you and I both know it can't happen again."

"Right." Martin stumbled on his words. "No, it can't," he said, recovering the advantage. He reached for a handshake. "No harm done, right? Still friends?"

Chapter Twenty
Inaugural Newspaper Potluck Features Food, Feud
November 23, 1987

Even if the food had been made of plastic and wax, the first annual office potluck still would have been a study in requisite collegiality. At Ed's request Roger hauled out a long rectangular table and folding chairs from the back of the print shop and set things up in the foyer. LaVerna came in early and unfurled a blue checkered tablecloth with great flourish, tossing it into the air and letting it float down onto the tabletop, smoothing it in place with freshly manicured hands. She set down a pair of matching silver-edged bowls filled with pillow-shaped pastel butter mints, the kind popular at wedding receptions.

LaVerna turned the bowls this way and that to achieve maximum effect. "Family heirlooms," she said, puffing up, making sure everyone understood. "Noritake china."

There were two main dishes, a chicken casserole from Carla—"the secret ingredient is the water chestnuts!"—and barbecued meatballs from Francine. Bags of Ruffles, along with onion and clam dip, came from production; and a wilted spinach salad arrived with Martin, who had gone home midmorning to toss the greens with shallots, sun-dried tomatoes, and pine nuts in a savory dressing.

Mina brought a pie from Albertsons. Pumpkin, in keeping with the theme of the season.

"Looks delicious," Carla said admiringly as she placed a gravy boat and ladle next to her creation. "I can never get my crust right. Can't wait to try it!" Mina didn't let on that the pie wasn't homemade.

Martin had been angling to get the gang together for a while—an effort to promote camaraderie and teamwork "in lieu of annual raises," he had said, waggishly, causing Francine to purse her lips. The jury had been out on the question of whether to include significant others, until the boss's wife weighed in.

"Well, I'm coming for sure," LaVerna told her husband, according to the office rumor mill. "And we have to have Judith and that sweet little girl." While she couldn't be bothered to remember Eliza's name, she was definitely on top of those mint-bearing Noritake dishes.

Mina wore a plaid shift to the event, its hem falling just below her knees, and tan faux-leather flats. Most of the attendees were singles—Francine was a widow from way back, and Carla was a confirmed bachelorette, a stay-at-home-on-Friday-night-washing-her-hair type of woman. Roger and his part-time assistant Ted spent their weekends drinking beer and watching TV football, eschewing the dating scene out of fear of rejection, Mina supposed, or because of broken hearts that had not yet fully mended. Mina had very little interest in marriage at this point in her life. Ever since high school graduation, men had been trouble for her, dishing out uncomplimentary insinuations about her height which, at five foot ten, she regarded as neither an anomaly nor a deal-breaker. In college the frat boys down the street dubbed her "Mina Mountain," a distraction from the real work of midterms and pulling all-nighters during finals week. But Mina was all about academics, about getting ahead, so she trained herself to ignore their boorish behavior.

Now she had a job—maybe even a career—in journalism, her chosen field. Lucky her. The wheels were turning inside her head.

"Try the meatballs yet?" Judith had sidled up to Mina, her long crepe skirt making a swishing sound and her chandelier earrings tinkling like wind chimes. She was holding a cup filled with toothpicks dressed in frilly red cellophane curls in one hand and a tray of Francine's meatballs in the other. "They're pretty spicy, if you're into that," Judith confided, her back turned toward the chef.

She stabbed a meatball and offered it to Mina over a cocktail napkin left over from Christmas. Greasy juice dripped onto the holly leaves and berries.

"Hadn't yet," Mina said, "but sure." She accepted the toothpick and popped the hot morsel into her mouth, blotting her lipstick with a corner of the napkin. "Mmm, good."

It was the first time Judith had initiated an actual conversation with Mina or even spoken a full sentence in her presence. She felt an obligatory twinge, a nudge to keep things going, but had no words or desire to do so. The two women stood by the buffet in silence, save for the chewing and the hum of an oscillating fan, until Martin crossed the room and attempted a rescue.

"Ladies!" he said as he approached, sporting a Glen plaid shirt and bow tie. Strange, because Martin never dressed up. "What's happening over here?"

Judith looked at Martin, then at Mina, then back at Martin, her earrings tinkling.

"Nothing much," she said, moving a section of hair behind her ear so they jangled a bit more. "We were just sampling Francine's delicious meatballs."

"Ah, I see. Good, then." Martin took two steps forward to stand between them. "I can tell you the chicken casserole is excellent." He had a dab of everything on his plate and an urgent question on his mind.

"Can you pick Eliza up at three and bring her over here?" he said to Judith. "I think she'd like to eat potluck with us. I haven't planned dinner at home."

She curled her lip at him, then forced her face to relax. "I can do that. Mina, are you staying for a while?" she said, touching her on her arm.

Roger appeared out of nowhere, his plate heavy with Carla's casserole. "It's so good," he said, slurping an egg noodle. "Have you tried it, Mina?"

"I have," she said to Roger, then turned to Judith. "And yes, I am."

Roger's eyes said he was glad Mina would be staying. Judith's said she wasn't. Martin's said he was fine either way. It was all too much to take. Mina grabbed her store-bought pie off the table and shoved it toward Martin's belt buckle. Hunks of crust and glops of orangey filling fell to the floor.

"Oops!" she sang, cocking her head and licking canned pumpkin from her fingers. Her hand dropped down to her too-full belly, and she winced at a sudden cramp. "Roger, be an angel and fetch me a broom and a dustpan?"

Chapter Twenty-One
Martin Wrestles with Effects of Dystonia, Wife's Wrath
January 20, 1988

Martin's right hand cramped, spasmed, and twisted inward, three of his fingers bending grotesquely toward his wrist. He was finding it impossible to hit any of the keys on the home row anymore. He left the office early and went directly to the emergency room in search of painkillers first and an answer second.

"Tylenol with codeine," the nurse manager said, handing him a prescription, a Band-Aid that would see him through the weekend. The next week he saw the resident orthopedist at the local clinic. He wanted a new prognosis. He wanted to know what was going on, yet he also didn't.

"It's keeping me from doing my work," he said to Judith when he got home, his wrist trussed up in a brace to immobilize the joint. Even with the medicine on board it still coursed with pain. "I don't know what to do, Judith. I've got to confide in Ed. I've got to do something." Judith regarded him sympathetically but persevered with her task, studying a pair of Microsoft Excel spreadsheets that took up the entire kitchen table.

"Let's talk when I'm finished here," she said, her mechanical pencil poised, her voice a measured monotone. Martin wandered down the hallway into their bedroom to rest.

"Sure thing, sweetheart," he sighed to himself. "When you're finished."

***

The waiting room at the clinic wasn't ideal for a heart-to-heart. It was chilly in there and not particularly private. But Judith had insisted that what she had to say to Martin couldn't wait another minute, let alone another day. She was meeting with her company's HR team and would be a little late getting there. He should go to the clinic without her and check in. They could talk while Martin waited for the doctor. That seemed strange, not their usual habit, and it made Martin nervous. He thought maybe the admitting desk representative could tell, but she didn't let on.

When Judith arrived she dragged a folding chair over to where her husband was seated and set down her valise. "Martin, dear," she began, "I'd like you to read something our daughter wrote." She opened the latch and produced Eliza's reindeer journal. He hadn't seen it in almost a year. She shoved it into his hands.

Daddy and Mina kissed at the office, Eliza had written in perfect cursive. *They were under the mistletoe. It might have been an accident, but I'm not sure. I hope everything will be all right.*

It was a Friday. Martin felt the double whammy of deadline fatigue and insomnia, but there was no arguing with Judith about Eliza's wistful words, her eight-year-old heart on paper. He didn't know whether to feel proud of her or angry at her. He decided neither.

Tears streaked Judith's face and fell from her chin, making small wet marks on her white muslin blouse. She dabbed at her cheeks with tissues from the box on the arm of Martin's chair. Her next seven words changed everything between them.

"I feel like I can't trust you," she said, strong and staccato, as if each syllable had a period after it, making them all weigh the same. She looked suddenly older and unbearably sad. "Our life together, our marriage vows. They were supposed to be forever."

The hush between them grew louder.

"There's nothing going on between Mina and me," Martin whispered, barely believing it himself. "Not anymore, anyway." They had shared important, intimate conversations, the kind that can turn into more, the kind that *had* turned into more. He had betrayed his own code. He felt himself to be deeply, irretrievably defective.

He had no denials in him.

"You're my person, sweetheart," he said, his upturned eyes begging Judith for clemency. "I'm so sorry you had to read that."

Judith was sorry that her husband had done what he did. She tucked Eliza's journal back into her bag and rose. She had never seemed more determined.

"We should keep Eliza out of this. She doesn't need to know about you and Mina."

Martin felt the blood drain from his face—from embarrassment, from self-loathing, from confusion, from the cursed luck of recurring illness. From his keen awareness that Western medicine wasn't working at all.

He told his wife what was on his mind, if not everything that was in his heart.

"This is my last chance, Judith," he said between deep breaths. "You and I both know it is." His words tumbled out: Herbal remedies. Shamanic healing. Mexico. "I've been looking at options, reading about where I could go for help. There's a place near Tulum, a long-term residential center. I have to try it. I'll talk to Eliza about it."

Judith's sunken eyes filled again.

"You're going away. For good. I can feel it," she said, pressing another tissue to her face. Martin was grateful she didn't use the term *abandonment*. The moment needed to end, but he couldn't make that happen by himself.

Judith blew her nose and stuffed the tissue into her bag. She stepped into the breach but not in the way Martin hoped.

"So you're leaving us to go to Mexico, just like that!" she accused, her voice rising. She set her jaw. "Well, we'll be better off without you, especially with that bastard kid of yours on the way!" Her face contorted into something Martin had never seen in all the years he had known Judith. He felt his mouth fall open.

What the hell? A baby? Mina would have told him! Wouldn't she?

Judith smiled a wicked smile.

"I can see you're surprised. Guess your lover hasn't said anything? Well, women just know these things. You can count on that, Martin."

Count on that. God. Martin would be only too happy to get away from here, away from his troubles, from all this strife. He wasn't sneaking away. He was doing what made sense to him. He couldn't work, so he couldn't provide for Judith and Eliza. He was unworthy of their affection. His guilt over the affair with Mina was giant, all-encompassing. It was eating him alive. And now she was having his baby?

Judith had regained her comportment.

"All right, Martin," she said, sniffing. "You win. Eliza and I will adjust. We'll get along fine. I won't say a bad thing to her about you. Not ever."

He glimpsed his reflection in the window overlooking the highway. It was certain death.

"Thank you, Judith. I appreciate that," he said. He straightened and added, "I love you, you know."

"I love you too, Martin. Always will. But we won't be sleeping together anymore."

There was that boundary again, the kind Judith was famous for, direct and deserved. Martin nodded his agreement. Starting that night, they would retire to separate rooms.

Chapter Twenty-Two
Eliza Learns of Mina's Move to California
February 25, 1988

My school friend Skyler came with me to my dad's newspaper office two days a week after school, Tuesdays and Thursdays, before band practice. The bus dropped us off across the street, and we raced each other to the front door. We usually tied.

Ninth grade was harder for me than eighth grade, but Skyler made it better. She was in my math group, the intermediate one, and we were starting to learn geometry. Algebra had been bad enough. Me and Skyler would trade math class for English any day, but we had to take math. We made a pact not to talk about it during lunch, so instead we talked about how we would never like boys as much as we liked animals, especially cats.

It was Tuesday, a *Cascadian* day, so Dad would give Skyler a ride to band after he was done working. She played the clarinet. It was neat that our families carpooled together.

Skyler had met Mina, but I wasn't sure she liked her. She said Mina had big feet and a too-loud voice. I didn't agree with either of those things. She thought my dad was funny, though, and that was definitely true.

"Girls are supposed to be quiet and soft," Skyler said one day at lunch. "My mom says it's nicer that way." I told her my mom had never said anything like that, and to me it sounded weird. Girls could be any way they wanted to be. That was when she said the thing about Mina's feet. I asked her what difference it made what size a person's feet were.

"All I know is, if you're a girl it's better if you wear small shoes," Skyler said. "Otherwise the boys might call you names, like bigfoot. That would be so embarrassing."

One Tuesday when we walked into the *Cascadian*, I could tell things were different. I heard my dad typing away in his office, but it was after three in the afternoon, and it wasn't even deadline day. We poked our heads around the corner. He stopped typing and stood up. He gave me a hug and Skyler a high five. His face looked thinner and redder than usual, like something hurt inside.

I felt a little worried. "You okay, Dad?" I said and followed him out of his office.

"I'm fine, Sunshine," he said near the front desk where Carla and Francine sat. "But there's something I have to tell you."

I knew something was wrong. Skyler went to the back of the building to use the bathroom. She did that a lot. She had her period already, but I didn't have mine yet. I wondered when I would.

My dad nudged me inside Mina's office. What had happened? It wasn't there anymore. I mean, Mina's things weren't there—not her big brown purse with the leather fringe, not her stuffed animals, not the typewriter she brought with her when she came to the paper. Only her press pass, right in the middle of her desk, all by itself. I picked it up and ran my thumb over her laminated face smiling back at me. I slipped it into my pocket, tucking the red lanyard inside. Dad didn't stop me.

Her office walls were bare except for a few picture hangers still sticking out. The diploma Mina showed me the first time I met her was missing. She was really proud of that.

"I bet you'll go to college someday, Eliza," she had said. "Maybe you'll be a journalist like your dad and me."

I couldn't even smell the scented candle Mina always kept on the bookshelf in the corner. I couldn't smell it because it was gone.

I asked Dad to tell me why Mina's office was empty. He was leaning against the wall next to the window that looked out onto School Street.

"She got a new job in California," he said, but that was all, no other details. He crossed his arms over his chest. "She won't be working at the *Cascadian* anymore."

I felt my lower lip start to shake and my mouth make an upside-down U.

"Wait! When did that happen?" That's all I could think to say. What I really wanted to know was if Mina had quit because of what I wrote down in my reindeer journal years ago, but neither one of them could know about that. No way.

I felt like someone had socked me in the stomach.

"Why did Mina leave?" I said, half sad and half mad at her.

Dad lowered himself into the chair that went with Mina's old desk and reached out his arms to me. I put my hands inside his and looked at him square. His face said he wasn't all right.

He sighed two deep sighs. "It was time for Mina to go. She needed a new challenge. That's all there is to it," he said, but somehow I knew it wasn't. He spoke more slowly than he usually did. I felt like he was being careful, like he was trying to protect me. I didn't know whether to be upset with him or not. This wasn't the way I wanted things to turn out.

"Mina has always wanted to live in California. She has family there—an aunt, I think." Dad kept on trying to explain, but he was wringing his hands like he might be hiding something. "She told me she was resigning a few weeks ago, but she stayed around for two more deadlines. That was nice of her, not to leave me hanging, doing all the work myself."

He smiled, but it was not his usual smile. There were no dimples, and his mouth turned into a flat line across his face. I was pretty sure Mina moving away would be good news for my mom, maybe the best news she could get. I had seen the way Mom looked at Mina, probably because of the way Mina used to look at Dad sometimes. All of this was really weird. Adult stuff, probably not even my business. But the news about Mina leaving didn't make me happy. I was going to miss her. She had already taught me a lot.

The more my dad talked, the more he sounded like he did when he gave the eulogy at my grandma's funeral. Someone recorded it and he let me listen to the tape once, since I hadn't gone. His voice was all squiggly.

"I'm so sorry, Sunshine," Dad said finally. It seemed like he had been practicing all day what to tell me. "Mina was a good reporter and a wonderful lady. We'll wish her well, won't we? I know she's going to miss you."

***

When Skyler got back from the bathroom, Dad motioned both of us into his office and pushed two folding chairs up beside his so we had a good view of his keyboard. "Time for a typing lesson!" he said, more cheerful than before.

We dropped our backpacks in the corner. Skyler checked her watch. She wanted to be on time for band.

"Let's work on the home row today," Dad suggested and started winding a piece of paper into the carriage. It made a *whirr-click* sound, like a camera shutter. "Which one of you wants to go first?"

I didn't say anything. I was still thinking about the other thing he told me when Skyler was out of the room, that Ed hadn't hired anyone to take Mina's place. Dad was going to be working harder than ever, but I didn't think he would mind. When he was at home, he and Mom argued a lot, and sometimes their voices got real loud. I could hear them in the living room, down the hall from my bedroom, after they thought I had gone to sleep. I would get out of bed and creep down the hallway so I could hear what they were saying. I needed to know the truth.

"It'll never be the same between us," I heard Mom say to Dad. "You can't expect me to just forget about something like that."

"I'm not asking you to forget," Dad answered. "But maybe you could try to forgive me, for Eliza's sake."

I didn't like to take sides, but I could see why my mom was upset. If you were married, you weren't supposed to like someone else. Maybe Mina liked Dad more than he liked her. That might help Mom be less sad, if she knew Dad loved her best.

"I'm done with the home row!" Skyler was finished with her lesson. "I'll make a great secretary someday!" she beamed. We exchanged chairs. Dad put his arms around me and placed his hands on top of mine, guiding me.

"You're not going to be the secretary," he whispered into my right ear. "You're going to be the writer."

Chapter Twenty-Three
Martin Laments Mina's Loss as Colleague
March 1, 1988

After she got the job offer to become a features writer at a much bigger paper in the Bay Area, Mina hadn't decided what to do right away. She wrestled with whether to stay or go. She didn't talk to Martin about it ahead of time because she needed to make up her own mind, without his input, so when she finally told him that she had accepted the position, it came as a shock. He hadn't seen that curveball coming.

Even now, he could hardly believe she was gone.

"It's the next logical step for me, Martin," Mina had said the week before she left, as if that was all there was to it, her eyes not meeting his, her hands in her lap. "I've learned everything I can here. But I want you to know it's not going to be easy leaving the *Cascadian.*"

What he wanted her to say was that it wouldn't be easy leaving *him.*

"Okay then," he said and shrugged his shoulders up and down in time to the syllables. "If you're sure. We all want what's best for you, Mina, me included." He wished he'd said more in their last conversation. There was nothing to be done about it now, though.

It was after hours, and Martin was alone in the building. He peeked around the corner at the beanbag chair and the books littering Mina's former office. Soon there would be another reporter in there. That needed to happen. He wasn't doing well handling the entire news operation himself. His hand, arm, and shoulder pain had gotten worse since Mina left. He wandered into Ed's office and opened the middle drawer of the oak filing cabinet, thumbed through the personnel folders. He found Mina's employment record. She had been on staff at the *Cascadian* for seven years, ten months, and fourteen days—an eternity in the community newspaper business. He sat with her file open and thought about her contributions to the paper. There had been so many. What were some adjectives to describe her work as a reporter? *Solid. Driven.*

Focused. And as a person? *Bright, resilient, loyal.*

She had filed her last story—a piece about the old paper mill shutting down—on a Tuesday afternoon, then stayed late to pack up. Martin had already gone home. He wasn't there to help her.

He sighed, regretting that.

When Ed hired Mina, Martin figured she would be around for a year, two at the most, jobs at small papers being what they were—stepping stones to better things. Dailies or big-deal papers back east. Even then he could see she had talent that would find its high-water mark somewhere else down the line.

"I'm going to be here forever, though," Martin had joked to her at the time, only half kidding. Judith's career would keep them in the area, and Eliza loved her school and her friends. Plus there was something about his father's career at the *Journal* that felt like a legacy to Martin, whatever that meant. It held weight for him. A gravitational pull.

Martin put Mina's file back in the drawer, under *B* between *A* and *C*. It was thinner than some of the others, people who had been at the paper for decades. He told himself he had contributed to Mina's career path, been a springboard for her growth and aspirations. Still, she didn't have the responsibilities and pressures he did: a wife, a child, and an affliction that was rotting him from the inside out.

What's going to happen to me? The question was for him alone.

He shook his head. His right cheek tightened, sending the masseter muscle into spasm. He brought his hand to his face and massaged the pain away. He wondered how long it would be before he wouldn't be able to visibly express emotion at all.

His body wasn't even responding to his granny's substance anymore. Nana Emma would not have been pleased.

Chapter Twenty-Four
East County Register Gives Mina Fresh Start
March 15, 1988

Mina pulled a handful of paper towels from the dispenser in the ladies' room at her new office. The *East County Register* occupied the entire third floor of an ancient brick building, space the company had leased in the middle of a gentrified neighborhood. Its tree-heavy streetscape and striped awnings obscured decades of façade decay. There were some nice amenities—a community kitchen, showers and lockers, a room for nursing mothers. In many ways the office was ahead of its time.

As she stood there drying her hands, Mina looked left and caught a glimpse of her profile in the big mirror.

There was no denying it now. She was way, way too far in to back out.

"Jesus F. Christ," she muttered, alone in the lavatory, her words echoing off the walls. "You've really done it this time, Breckenridge."

The bathroom door swung open and Charlotte appeared, disrupting Mina's epiphany. Charlotte was Mina's new deskmate and was in her third week on the job as a general assignment reporter. She was smart, bespectacled, Audrey Hepburn–lovely, and younger than Mina by at least five years. She whistled while she worked, an eccentricity Mina found unnerving.

At the *Register* the newsroom was organized into pods, sports reporters in one area, news reporters in another, and photographers walled off from everyone else. Mina shared a desk with Charlotte because that's the way things were set up, two computers and two phones on either end of a six-foot expanse of oak veneer, three drawers per person for files and personal items. So different from the *Cascadian*, with its three separate offices and a dedicated reception area. Old-school, the way Mina liked it.

Charlotte broke the silence inside the ladies' room with a whine that rivaled the roar of commercial jets taking off from San Francisco International, a daily cacophony as the *Register* sat directly below the airport's flight path.

"Sweet little baby Jesus!" she exclaimed, untucking her blouse and jerking her skirt up past her pelvis on her mad dash to the toilet. "That meeting with the legal department took *forever!*"

Then, from inside the stall: "I swear I thought I'd pee my pants."

Next came a gush of water and a deep moan of relief. Not at all what Mina would have expected from Charlotte, given first impressions, but then again nothing in the last many months had turned out quite like she'd anticipated.

She took one last glance in the mirror and grimaced, adjusting her mustard-colored sweater, a caftan style that extended past her hips and covered her tummy. She had taken to wearing a lot of layers lately in the chilly confines of the office, a habit that offered her options when her body temperature took its wild swings. The associate publisher liked to keep things right around sixty-five degrees. A no-nonsense note Scotch taped to the thermostat in the main hall directed employees to refrain from messing with the mechanism. *Do not touch the dial or else*, it said, followed by *trust me, you don't want to find out what else*. Classic ass-pub humor.

Charlotte was whistling now, a version of "Too Ra Loo Ra Loo Ral," the Irish lullaby, the same tune Martin used to hum to himself in the old office when he thought no one was listening. But Mina always was. Listening and learning new things about him. Now she was in Northern California, a news editor sharing a desk with Charlotte the tuneful reporter. The new title, she thought, didn't justify the agony.

"See you back at the ranch," Mina said to the door behind which her coworker squatted.

Charlotte grunted in an unbecoming way. "You bet. See you," she replied. The *whoosh-gurgle* of the autoflush commode echoed around the room, drowning out her voice. Mina thought she heard, "As soon as I can," but she couldn't be sure.

***

For quite a while, by forcing her mindfulness game, Mina had mostly been able to ignore the sea changes inside her body, going about her days as if things would magically return to normal. She didn't feel nauseous or overly tired, like some expectant women do, and her appetite was as it always had been: moderate and without cravings. The image in the bathroom mirror at the *Register* turned out to be a game changer, though. This couldn't be wished away any more than she could erase her memories of the *Cascadian*, mostly good but also some bad, though on balance there had been very few of those. One or two maybe. Mainly just the one, that time she and Martin had gone to the Do Drop Inn on that crazy evening assignment from Ed. She had still been warbling a Journey song when Martin dropped her off. She had opened the car door, stumbled up the steps to her apartment, and waved, though it wouldn't be the last time she saw him that night, not by a long shot.

***

She could have dealt with it in the beginning, in the early weeks, but some part of her must have wanted to keep Martin's baby. She hadn't told anyone at the *Cascadian* about her pregnancy—she was leaving, so what would have been the point?—and wasn't inclined to inform the father. His life was complicated enough. Judith's suspicions, his health issues. Now it was too late to do anything about it. She was in it for the duration. Knowing a tiny person was growing inside her was really starting to freak her out. A human who, in just a few months, would emerge as a real, live baby demanding care around the clock. A helpless, mewling, kitten-like creature, sapping her energy and stealing what little was left of her youth.

Mina had serious doubts she was up to the task.

On the weekends she spent whole afternoons loitering in the parenting section at the public library in downtown Walnut Creek, five miles from where she shared a bungalow in the foothills with her aunt Carol out of the goodness of her mother's sister's heart. Carol was a spinster with a geriatric beagle named Champ and a limp from an auto accident that put her on permanent disability. Mina told Carol about going to the library but not about the books she checked out, every title a pregnant woman's distress flare. The only other reference point she had for successful parenting was Judith and Martin's example, but it wasn't like she could call them up and ask for advice, so she hid the books in her bag on her way back to Carol's and stuffed them between the mattress and box springs in her room. Carol had made it clear her free-rent offer would never expire as long as Mina did her own laundry, emptied her own trash cans, paid her portion of the phone bill, and bought her own food. "There are limits to my generosity," she said with a laugh when Mina moved in, a laugh that wasn't kidding.

Mina had a few manipulations of her own in mind.

"So, Carol," she ventured one evening, after a dinner of angel-hair pasta and marinara sauce—jarred, not homemade. "How about a little *Magnum P.I.*?"

That did the trick. Threw her aunt off the scent for a while, anyway. Carol loved that show starring macho, mustachioed Tom Selleck. It was pure escapist fantasy, and Champ didn't mind it either, the old boy twitching and chasing rabbits through the entire forty-eight minutes.

Mina felt the baby move, mostly at night and away from the office, the workaday grind, and Charlotte's infernal whistling. She was grateful to be living with Carol and Champ until she could afford an apartment of her own—the cost of living in Northern California had come with a fair amount of sticker shock—and get back on her feet. But those same feet were achy and swollen and getting harder and harder to locate as her belly protruded ever outward, stretching her blue-veined skin and her ability to see things clearly. She played with her new outie as she lay in bed trying to figure out her future.

She was in her sixth month. She had found a doula in the classifieds who agreed to come to Carol's whenever Mina's labor began—barring complications, that is—but that was as far as she had gotten in terms of planning.

"You can stay here as long as you need to," Carol reaffirmed one evening, after *Baywatch* but before bedtime, shifting in her recliner to quell the pang radiating down her right leg. "Seriously, Mina, I'm happy to have your company."

She leaned over to stroke Champ's silky head, and he went back to his habit of light snoring. Things were all right, Mina thought, for the time being.

***

The pay at the *Cascadian* had been abysmal and the hours ungodly. Because of the high school sports gig, Mina hadn't had more than a half dozen weekends off the whole time she worked there. Martin had gotten lucky the day Ed hired her. He was grateful for her work ethic, her service to the town, her stories—which were brilliant—and he had often told her so.

He also couldn't have been sorrier that she moved away, she liked to think anyway, words he hadn't actually said but words she was sure he'd have meant, if he had given it any thought at all.

***

Mina had made love with Martin only once, a fact she still regarded as a triumph of forbearance on her part and maybe his as well. She couldn't be sure.

"It's now or never," Martin had said to her at the Do Drop Inn, keys out, hands on his hips, a mix of intrigue and exasperation on his face. "If you want a ride home, I mean." He knew Judith would be waiting for him, whether it was ten at night or two in the morning, not a good thing either way.

He hesitated and gave Mina one last chance.

Her eyes beheld a blurry Martin, a blurry bar, a blurry Jimbo behind it. She wobbled a little on her stool, lowered herself down, and let Martin escort her to his car.

Martin had taken care of her in all the ways she wanted that night. Theirs was an intoxicatingly sweet interlude, slow and satisfying. The two of them slept until daybreak, their bodies spooned together, their legs entwined under a cornflower-blue coverlet, its wide satin binding soft against their faces. In her hypnopompic state, Mina felt Martin's mustache brushing the back of her neck, his warm arms around her waist, his hands clasped together against her navel. She wondered what he would walk into when he got home, but did not let it ruin her bliss, the rhythm of his breathing and the soft tick of his watch lulling her back to sleep.

"You're amazing, Martin," she murmured into his left ear. "I hope you know that."

***

Now she was carrying his child. Her carelessness, her problem was the way she saw it. Not an enlightened viewpoint, but one that aligned with what she had always been taught: if something good happened, it was probably a fluke, but if something bad happened, it was 100 percent her fault.

Two weeks after the line on her pregnancy test stick turned an unequivocal bright blue, Mina turned in her resignation at the *Cascadian*. That very weekend, she turned the page and drove to California.

She tried to work, and she tried to sleep.

"Damn you, Martin Donovan," she said to a framed black-and-white photo of the entire *Cascadian* staff she kept on her bedside stand, she and Martin in the second row and the rest of the gang behind, almost everyone smiling wide, except Ed, who stood in front like the Godfather, arms crossed over his chest, eyes shifty and stupefied, his mouth a thin-lipped smirk.

"Damn you all to hell," she snapped, turning the picture over and slamming it onto the nightstand so hard she had to check and see if she had shattered the glass.

It seemed like two lifetimes ago. Tears pooled on Mina's cheeks and the baby kicked her innards hard, bringing her back to the present, to her impossible situation, to her growing existential dilemma.

"What're we going to do now?" she said, first to her belly and then to the photo, as if either could give her any insight. She ran a hand across her girth, pressing the baby's knee back in with her palm. "Can you tell me, little one?"

The baby gave her another sharp jab. She set the picture back down in its place. And just like that, she had the answer, one piece of the puzzle that had become her life.

The wall phone in the Donovans' kitchen nook rang with a persistence that couldn't be ignored. Judith heard Martin pick up the call on the extension in the next room.

"Hello? Yes?" The volume of his voice dropped precipitously, sounding every one of her emotional alarms. She carefully lifted the receiver so she could listen in. Her Playtex Living Gloves dripped soapy water onto the linoleum floor. She tossed a rag down with her free hand and sopped up the mess with the toe of her shoe.

Her eyes lit on the sink full of pans and plates and bowls. Martin had been on dish duty the night before but had managed to shirk his responsibility.

A woman's high alto on the other end of the line took Judith back to moments she would rather not remember.

"How are you?" Mina asked, to which Martin responded, "Fine," and "what's up?" in as neutral a tone as Judith had ever known. It was unusual for anyone to call the house on a Saturday morning and totally weird that Mina would call on *any* morning, since she'd up and moved to California. Last Judith had heard, Mina was living with an aunt in the Bay Area, but that was about all she knew or wanted to know.

Judith wedged the receiver between her left ear and her shoulder and peeled off the rubber gloves. Slowly, silently. She couldn't let them know she was listening in.

"Anything new with your health?" Mina inquired. "I mean, are you well?"

Martin spoke in clips: "I'm about the same. Maybe slightly worse. Thanks for asking."

There was a pause on the line. Judith's stomach did a little flip.

"I'm pregnant," Mina blurted. "I'm due in a month."

Martin was so quiet Judith thought he might have fainted. She felt like she might.

"Martin, it's yours."

"How?" he managed. "I mean, when?"

He sensed Mina's exasperation from 535 miles away.

"You know very well *when*," she snarled. "Does the Do Drop Inn ring any bells?"

The Do Drop Inn? That undercover assignment? So that was it! Judith nearly dropped the phone.

"Holy shit," Martin breathed. He didn't dare question the truth of what Mina was telling him. "Is there something you need? Financial support, maybe, or a box of Eliza's old baby clothes?"

Eliza. She couldn't find out about this.

"Not a thing, Martin. I'm going to be fine. I mean *we* are, me and the baby. I just thought you should know you weren't shooting blanks." Judith felt an odd mix of anger and empathy welling up inside her. Mina was having the baby she herself had wanted! She would have to dig deep to forgive her husband. She wouldn't be ready for that for a while, maybe ever.

Martin had nothing more to offer Mina. "Good luck to you then," he stammered and placed the receiver back in its cradle. He went into the hall bathroom and splashed water on his face. Four words played over and over inside his head: *Judith's gonna kill me.*

***

The late-summer sun was already baking the clay soil inside Judith's garden boxes, the spinach and carrots requiring multiple dousings from a watering can she kept by the back door. When she returned to the house, she swept through the kitchen in scorched silence.

She found Martin sitting on the side of the bed in the guest room, struggling with his socks, his right hand in spasm. He would have to make his morning mug of tea for himself, British Breakfast, when he got to the kitchen. Judith hadn't made him tea in months, and she definitely wasn't going to start now.

"Who was that on the phone?" she said to him, feigning ignorance. "You got to it before I could."

Martin blinked and rubbed moistureless eyes, a side effect of the drugs. The painkillers hadn't kicked in yet. It wasn't even eight. Another long day stretched ahead.

He decided to tell it to Judith straight.

"It was Mina," he said, getting up to shut the door, bumping Judith's gardening hat from its hook beside the closet.

"Really?" Judith said coolly. "What did she want? If it's about her new job, or anything else in her life, I'm not sure I care to hear it."

"She's expecting," Martin said, monitoring Judith's response through a rapid eye tic, new to his constellation of symptoms.

His wife plopped down on her mother's old velvet settee.

"It's yours, isn't it?" she said, not really asking. "What are you going to do about it?"

There was only one answer that made sense.

"Nothing," Martin said. "Mina doesn't want anything from me."

"She didn't say if she's keeping the baby?"

"No."

Martin said he hoped Eliza didn't have to know. "Please," he said to Judith, twitching again.

It took a long two seconds for her to agree.

"I won't say a word," she said, then wagged her finger. "But that's for Eliza's sake, Martin, not yours."

***

Summer had turned to fall by the time Judith discovered the letter, tucked between the pages of Kerouac's *On the Road*. A missive from Martin to Mina, one he never sent, penned during what must have been her eighth month.

Judith hadn't meant to find it. She was dusting the house, doing a better job than usual, when she lifted the book off a high shelf and the paper fell from its hiding place, floating like a feather onto the desk below.

I hope this finds you well, the letter began, *and the baby, too*, it continued. Martin again offered Mina support of an unspecified nature, a matter Judith had regarded as dead and buried. He laid out the most pressing issues of his life:

I'm finding it a greater strain than I can handle to contend with my health here in Oregon. I hurt all the time. I can't type, so I can't work, and you know how much my work means to me.

I'm going to a healing center in Mexico. I'll tell Eliza soon. I don't know how long I'll be there. I hope it helps.

On another topic, Judith and I are still in the house together, but we're in the process of getting a divorce. Our troubles are not your fault. I want you to be clear about that.

He told her to take care. He said he would be in touch. He signed the letter *Always, Martin.*

Judith felt herself splitting in two, separating from her husband in new, more permanent ways. She cried for a long time, tears of sorrow and relief and regret. She permitted herself to wonder why she was feeling sorry for Martin when she was the one who had been hurt.

Part Two

PAYDAY:

1988–2005

Chapter Twenty-Six
Mina Writes to Martin about Future
May 10, 1988

Mina started her note in the middle of the story, the only place it could have begun.

Dear Martin:

There are only a few weeks to go until my due date. I'm feeling up to the task of giving birth. My midwife expects an uncomplicated delivery.

Who knew our one night together would result in pregnancy? You promised me that couldn't happen, and if I'm honest, I'm still pretty mad about that. But it's water under the bridge.

I want to release you from any obligation you may feel toward me or this baby. I've arranged for her adoption by a family here in the Bay Area. The social worker told me they live in Lafayette and that they are stable and lovely. They'll be good parents to our daughter. I wish things were different, but I don't have the emotional or financial wherewithal to raise a child as a single mother.

You don't need to keep in touch with me. In fact, I wish you wouldn't. Both of us need to move on.

I've asked Judith to forward this letter if you've already left for Mexico. I hope it finds you in better health and in good spirits. I wish you well, Martin.

Give Eliza my love. I can't believe she'll have a half sister soon.

Always,

Mina

She sat back, her watermelon belly still grazing the keyboard, read and reread the document. She pressed a button to print it out.

"That'll do." Mina licked the back of a Love stamp with a pink rose on it. She addressed the envelope to Judith and slid the twice-folded paper into it. Chances were almost zero that Eliza would recognize her handwriting.

Chapter Twenty-Seven
Mina Delivers Daughter at Aunt's House
May 24, 1988

The exam room at the clinic smelled of antiseptic and latex, a combination that nearly gave Mina the vapors. It stung her nose and caught in her throat. This was where she would meet the midwife who would deliver her baby when the time came, in a few short weeks if all went according to plan, though Mina understood that babies had their own way about such things.

Her baby, no one else's. She felt quite completely alone.

It was 12:05 p.m., Mina's lunch hour, and her practitioner was already five minutes late. She perched uncomfortably on the white butcher paper–covered table, the thin cotton gown handed to her by the medical assistant barely covering her girl parts, with a single snap in front and two ties on the side. She lifted her chest in an attempt to create more room for her lungs to expand, crowded as they were by her burgeoning uterus, which sometimes felt as if it had pushed all her other organs up and out of the way. She heard someone lift a clipboard from the hard plastic sleeve on the outside of the door, then an officious rustling as the person—her doctor, she hoped—skim read her chart. "Breckenridge," the muted voice said, then "right!" and "ah."

The knob turned and the door squeaked open. "Hi there! Good morning! How are we?" A small, spritely woman entered the room with a flourish, wafting in on notes of eucalyptus and verve, a springy cascade of glistening curls barely contained by a colorful headband, yellow wildflowers on a background of black. She looked her new patient in the eyes—directly, expectantly—and smiled a bronzed, full-lipped smile. Her eyebrows lifted, revealing powder-blue eyeshadow with dark eyeliner winging upward at the corners.

This person was not at all what Mina had pictured when she spoke to Erica-Lee Merchant, certified nurse midwife, by phone the month before. That woman had an obvious New Jersey accent and a no-nonsense attitude that made Mina feel confident she would be in good and capable hands during labor and delivery, even without the presence of the father, as if she would have invited him. She had imagined the woman on the call—who asked all sorts of questions Mina was glad to answer, stopping short of probing the details of the baby's paternity—as tall, young, and take-charge. She was wrong on two out of three, but totally right on that last one. Erica-Lee was a ball of fire, her authority clear, her enthusiasm contagious.

"Will there be a birth support person here with you on the big day?" she wanted to know, adding "other than me, of course!" with a throaty, robust laugh Mina very much enjoyed. She gravitated toward people with signature laughs, though there were always exceptions, like Roger's low buzzy rumble, a laugh she could never be sure of. The chipmunk chortle of her former news editor crossed her mind. Martin Donovan was the one man who had always given it to her straight, except for that one time when he said they didn't need a rubber.

The woman in front of her, with skin the color of Baltic amber, was an even more pleasing version of the one she met on the phone. Oregon had been so thoroughly and disappointingly white-bread, and California—at least Walnut Creek—had turned out to be no more diverse, possibly less. The midwife was fiftyish and wizened, her lovely visage a welcome contrast to the sterile environment in which she worked, not so different from Mina's current newspaper, which was a study in homogeneity. *There isn't one employee of color in the entire* Register *organization, including the newsroom, quotas be damned*, she thought as she leaned back on her palms, the exam-table paper crackling as she did.

"Just the two of us," Mina chirped, the shaky timbre of her voice a surprise to them both. "Or three, if you count the baby, which we should." She took in the dewy glow of Erica-Lee's cheeks and the parade of freckles marching across the bridge of her nose. Her multicolored socks rose like aspen shoots above brown Birkenstocks, and she wore pedal pushers beneath a pleated gray smock.

"It's so good to meet you in person!" Mina said, and her tinkling ringed fingers moved, involuntarily, to her navel. The baby responded with a small jab.

The midwife approached the exam table and placed her right hand on Mina's. "Isn't it exciting?" she said, patting the hand with gusto. "It looks like a baby girl's on the way! Nothing sweeter in this wide world, is what I say."

She stepped a half pace back, gauging Mina's comfort level with her touch. "May I call you Mina? I'd love for you to call me Erica-Lee," said Erica-Lee, pointing to a badge with her first name only, a rainbow peace sign sticker affixed to it. "That is, if it's all right with you."

It was, Mina nodded, feeling good about their initial exchange. After a little more chitchat—the first day of her last menstrual period, when she first felt the baby move, whether she'd had any spotting or pelvic pain up to now—Erica-Lee invited Mina to lie all the way back on the table and guided her feet into the padded stirrups.

"Let's see where we're at with this little firecracker," Erica-Lee said and commenced with her exam, pushing and prodding Mina's abdomen, using a small measuring tape to determine the distance from her pubic bone to her fundus. "Mm-hmm," she said, and "oh, yes." Mina intuited her murmurings as positive news but still wondered exactly what they meant. Erica-Lee helped her back up to a sitting position, nudged her legs off the side of the table, and sat down beside her on a swivel stool. She jotted a few notes on her chart. She flashed an ambrosial smile, minty, with a dash of honey.

"Everything looks fantastic. Head's down low in your pelvis, and baby's face down. She's growing along just fine, and you're right on schedule," she said, showing Mina the notes as she rearranged her gown. "How do you feel about delivering at home?"

Erica-Lee circled a date in red on a cardboard calendar—June 1, only a week away—and handed it to Mina along with several pamphlets and a prescription for prenatal vitamins.

"I'll see you real soon!" she sang. "I want you to take those supplements every day. And don't hesitate to call me if you have any questions." She clicked her pen two times.

Mina leaned away from Erica-Lee. "I'd really like a home birth," she said after a pause, "if you think it's safe."

Her midwife said yes, particularly with a hospital situated so close to where Mina lived, just in case. Carol could be her emotional support person, Mina told her after reconsidering.

There was one more thing.

"I'm not planning to keep the baby," Mina said, matter-of-factly and intentionally expressionless. She worked hard to hide a cyclone of mixed emotions. She hurried her next words to get it over with.

"I've been in contact with an agency in San Francisco that will take the baby as soon as it's cleared, health-wise. The couple wants a closed adoption. I'm fine with that."

Mina dropped back on her elbows and waited for a response. A few seconds ticked by. Erica-Lee stood up and faced her, woman to woman, human to human.

"Thank you for telling me," she said, kindness opening her face up like a flower. She placed a hand on Mina's shoulder.

"Those are hard decisions. I'm not here to judge you. I'm here to help you along between now and that baby's birthday. Everything after that is completely up to you."

***

It took five hours of labor for Mina to bring her daughter into the world. The baby emerged with a full head of auburn hair and a howl that pierced the air in the living room of Carol's house in the hills. Carol steadied Mina's quaking legs while Erica-Lee wiped away the vernix caseosa still clinging to the baby's face after thirty-nine weeks on the inside. The gooey white substance of gestation. The protective coating. Mina was barely aware the baby was out before the midwife placed her on her chest, the umbilical cord still attached. She breathed shallow, contented breaths, sighed sweet newborn sighs. Her body was curled up, knees to stomach, fetal. She slumbered, skin to skin, as if the events of the day had been routine.

"She looks like you," Carol said admiringly, stroking the child's tiny back with two fingers. "All that dark hair."

"Your baby is beautiful," Erica-Lee observed to both of them. "You did good, mama. Rest while I check her over. I'll tend to you in a jiffy."

Seven pounds, two ounces, nineteen inches long "and a tidge more" were the stats, according to the midwife, as she lifted the baby off the scale and swaddled her in a cotton wrap. The newborn responded with another little yelp, not as strident this time.

"She's okay then?" a worn-out Mina asked, her eyes beginning to close.

"Better than that," whispered Erica-Lee, tucking the baby under her mother's arm. "She's magnificent."

***

Mina bit the inside of her lip and maintained her composure when she placed her daughter—blue eyes, button nose, ten tiny perfect fingers, all wrapped up in a pink-and-white receiving blanket, a gift from Carol—into the arms of the intake person at Caring Connections. She gave the baby her bravest, truest smile. The last thing she saw before they took her away was the telltale dimple on her cherubic face. Mina would never meet the adoptive parents. She would never see her child again.

She had already determined she was done with San Francisco, with sponging off of Carol, with the job at the *Register*, as unfulfilling as it had turned out to be. Not the paper's fault, not completely. The complications of her own life had intervened in huge ways. Mina had hidden her pregnancy at work until she could no longer do so. Her supervisor, Hugo—young, single, and without kids—had reluctantly signed her maternity leave paperwork. Mina knew her future at the newspaper would be shaky after those six weeks were up. Hugo did her a solid, laying her off so she could collect unemployment. He'd long had an up-and-comer in mind, Mina knew, so she didn't feel too bad about it.

She made herself thumb through the Help Wanted ads and found one for a seasoned reporter, West Coast. In Alaska, as far north as she could go without immigrating to Canada.

Everything felt perfunctory and final. As she exited the building, Mina's stomach hurt, and she dabbed her eyes with a tissue from the restroom. On the Bay Area Rapid Transit train she willed herself not to open the envelope in her lap. If she read the paperwork, she would break down. There would be no baby book, no journal entries describing her daughter's delicate, shell-pink fingers or the way she startled at the faintest noise. Recording the details of her child's newest newborn days and keeping them for posterity would have wrecked Mina forever. Of that she was most definitely sure.

The infant's new parents would undoubtedly change her name, but Mina would remember her as Greta Hope for the rest of her life. She had already christened her in her heart.

Chapter Twenty-Eight
Eliza Hears Dad Is Going Away to Heal
October 15, 1988

Mom's oldest brother died a long time ago, when he was a teenager. She hardly ever talked about it because it made her sad. His name was Stuart and he was riding in the front seat of a car that got into an accident one night. He was with his friends, but he wasn't driving. His friend Brad was. Stuart and Brad died right there on the highway, but the three people in the back seat lived. Mom's face still got scrunchy whenever anyone mentioned Stuart. I guess they were really close.

I don't know what it would have been like to have a brother or a sister, since I am an only child. But some of my high school friends had siblings, and when they talked about them, it helped me understand how it must have been for my mom to have a brother and then all of a sudden not to have one.

I've thought about how Stuart lived only half as long as my dad, so far, anyway. That's a pretty weird thing to think about. The doctors have said Dad probably won't get better, that his disease is "chronic" and "progressive," but they just have to be wrong. They don't know everything, right? My dad's strong, and he wants to live. He has a lot more things to do in his life, and I really need him.

"I'm going to walk you down the aisle someday, Sunshine," he has said to me about a hundred times. "We're going to dance a jig together at your wedding."

I believed him when he said that. There were a lot of medical people trying to make him well with all kinds of medicine, pills that tired him out. He was getting shots, too, to control his spasms. I watched the doctors' eyes when they came in to ask him questions and when the nurse checked his vitals. They scribbled mysterious words on their clipboards and smiled the way people did when they were nervous.

The doctors knew a lot of things. They had been to college. But they didn't know my dad like I did.

"Dad's going to get over his dystonia, isn't he?" Mom did not like that question. She smiled, just a little smile, and gave my shoulder a squeeze. She didn't answer me exactly.

Even with Stuart gone, Mom still had two sisters and one brother. She said it had been way too soon for Stuart to die and that she missed him—his practical jokes and the way he kept his sideburns long even after that sort of thing went out of style. "Chicks dig it," he would say and then laugh like a donkey, throwing his head back with his mouth wide open. That's one story Mama told me about Stuart.

Aunt Midge and I walked through the revolving door at the inpatient rehabilitation center, down the long hallways toward my dad's room. Midge was Mama's sister who was twins with Uncle Stuart—whom, of course, I had never met. She lived just one town over from us on a farm in McMinnville. There was also Aunt Zelda and Uncle Ari, but they lived on the East Coast, so we didn't really see them, except maybe once a year at the holidays.

Mom said Dad came to the rehab center because the doctors at the hospital couldn't do anything more for him, and maybe he would do better there. The halls at the center were wide and beige, with dusty rose diamond shapes on the floors shiny with wax.

My Oregon aunt's real name was Marlene, but we called her Midge for short. Mom said she's petite and that's why. *Midge* was kind of like *smidge*. I thought her nickname was cool. It fit her. I liked the way she smiled at me, and how we had fun when we were together. Her personality was a lot like Dad's. She wasn't like my mom at all.

A lot of Dad's friends had already visited him. Midge told me the names she could remember, some of them from all the way back when he was in high school, and a few from Grandpa Donovan's newspaper. Dad had been off work for several weeks. Some of the people from the *Cascadian*—Ed and LaVerna and Francine and Carla—had already been to see him. I wished Mina had too.

When we finally got to room 55 the door was open a crack. If a nurse or doctor was in there, we never interrupted. But it was only Mom sitting beside Dad's bed, so we went in. Mom turned around when she heard our footsteps. I stood on the other side of the bed so I could talk to Dad. Midge came up behind Mom and hugged her tight. Mom leaned back against Midge's chest and her face did the scrunchy thing.

Dad looked small in the bed, with its metal guardrails and plastic headboard. His left arm was on top of the covers. There were tubes sticking out of it. I felt bigger than him, like I was the grown-up and he was the kid. His eyes were closed at first, but he opened them when Mom told him I was there. "Say hi to Eliza," she said and patted his hand. I smiled at him, and he smiled back with only one side of his mouth, not the big smile I was used to.

"Sunshine," he said, and I looked up.

I said the first thing that popped into my brain. "I'm here, Dad," and kissed the top of his head. His hair was messy, sticking out everywhere. I tried to smooth it down, but it didn't stay. It smelled like him but also like medicine. I loved my dad's red hair. It laid flat when I put my face on top of his head and sprang back when I took my face away.

"You're my favorite," he said to me. It seemed to take all of his energy to say those three words.

Dad was trying some new therapies for his spasms, which were happening more and more often. Someone had shaved off his mustache since the last time I was there. Mom said one of the nurses did it so he could get more oxygen through those little tubes in his nose. His lungs weren't working too well, a side effect of the medicine. But I had never seen my dad without his mustache before. His upper lip was whiter than the rest of his face. It was kind of funny. I thought he looked handsome when I imagined him without the tubes.

Dad was staring at my face, like he was memorizing it. I stared back because I didn't want to forget his face either. His skin was a weird blue gray. I looked at my mom. She knew what I was thinking.

"The oxygen should help with that," she said, in a hopeful way.

Dad's voice was soft, and he didn't laugh. I really missed his laugh.

"Are you happy, Dad?" I asked.

He turned toward me and looked me straight in the eyes. "I'm happy with you, Sunshine." I knew that was true. I tried not to cry, but I felt tears behind my eyes wanting to come out.

A nurse came in. She checked all the monitors, turned a dial on one of the machines, and wrote something down on Dad's chart, finishing with a sharp dot of her pen. She looked at us and smiled a sad kind of smile.

"Is there anything I can get you?" she asked Mom and Midge. They shook their heads no.

The nurse turned to me. "How about you, young lady?" she said.

"No, thank you," I said.

I held Dad's hand for a while. I wanted to rub it, to comfort him, but the needle was there, so I didn't. My fingers tapped the palm of his hand, like Morse code. What I meant to tell him was *I love you, I love you, I love you*. He was lying on his back now, and his eyes were closed. He smiled underneath the oxygen tubes. His breaths were tiny puffs. I'm sure he understood what I was saying.

My aunt went to the cafeteria to get Mom some tea. She didn't want to bother the nurse for it. A few minutes later Midge brought it back in a white Styrofoam cup and set it down on the table beside Dad's bed. Steam rose from the cup, and a little string hung down the side with a tag attached to the end. *Lipton*, it said. *Direct from the tea gardens to the teapot.* Midge clutched her handbag strap and leaned over to whisper something in Dad's ear.

Mom sipped her tea and watched me watching my dad. His breathing slowed down. He had fallen asleep. Mom's face was sad and tired, crumpled like a wadded-up piece of paper.

Dad stirred and motioned to Mom. "Get the thing," he said, so she reached into a drawer in the bedside table and took out a little box.

"Eliza," Dad said then, "I want you to have this." Mom handed me the box. "I love you very much."

The box was dimpled and white with a pink bow glued to the lid. Mom held on to the bottom of the box so I could pry the lid off.

The gift was a beautiful locket. It was round and made of real gold, with a picture of the sun engraved on top. I lifted it from its bed of cotton and felt it between my fingers, the bumpiness of the sun, the smooth gloss of the gold. I turned it over and read the inscription on the back. You Are My Sunshine, it said.

I stared at the necklace in my palm. "Thank you, Dad," I said and gave him a kiss.

I tried opening the locket. It was kind of tricky, but I got my fingernails under the clasp and it popped open. Mom and Midge leaned in to see. There was a tiny picture of me and Dad inside, one from my fifth birthday. I recognized it because there was a Christmas tree in the background between our heads. We had the exact same smiles and the exact same dimples.

"I love it," I said to all three of them. I lifted my hair off my neck and Aunt Midge helped me fasten the necklace. The chain hung down long enough so the locket sat high on my chest, Dad near my heart. I was never going to take it off.

***

Back at the rehab center the next day, my mom stood instead of sitting. I sat in her usual chair. We had reversed positions, and her hands skimmed my shoulders. Dad was awake, sipping tea, so Mom left the room to give us a moment. He looked up at me and grinned, seeing the necklace. He raised his right hand and touched the locket.

"We need to talk, Eliza," he said then. "The people here have done everything they can for me." He had that no-nonsense look on his face, the one that didn't show up very often, and even then he usually smiled afterward. Not now. He shifted in the bed.

"I have to go away for a while," he told me. "I need to go to a place where I can get better. Where I can rest and heal, where I can keep on living."

My whole body went numb. Dad was leaving? For how long?

"Where are you going?" I tried not to whine. "And when?"

He took my hand and kissed it.

"Somewhere beautiful," he said, "and soon." He took my other hand and held both of them in a way that showed me he still had strength. And determination, like when he was chasing a story at the newspaper.

Dad turned quieter. "This isn't the end, Sunshine," he said. "I'll be back for you." It was a promise I knew he wouldn't break.

***

Mom insisted to my aunt, who insisted to me, that Dad should not see grim faces, that we should smile and tell stories, so I told him the ones I knew he would like best—about family, and newspapers, and Mina.

"Remember when she took me on that firewood donation assignment?" I sat up straight. "To the Kiwanis club?"

"I do, Sunshine." Dad nodded and adjusted his oxygen. He was home now, so there was a tank in our living room beside his chair. "That was a lot of fun."

Now it was his turn.

"Tell me about Grandpa Donovan."

He smiled a Daddy smile.

"What do you want to know?"

"Tell me about Mill Ends Park. About the leprechauns."

Dad closed his eyes and leaned back against the headrest. "Of course, sweetheart," he said. "That's a very happy story."

With his words, he took me to a place that existed only in tales about my grandfather, the Irishman, the editor, the family member I always wished I could have met but never did. It was a place "made from magic and memories and love," my dad told me once, a place where "one man's imagination transformed an idea into a real city park, the world's smallest park, smack in the middle of a major thoroughfare in downtown Portland," a park my grandpa wrote about in his column each week. Over the years Mill Ends Park hosted tiny Christmas trees with light strings, flower gardens, American flags, and a miniature swimming pool with a diving board. In Granddaddy's writings, it was home to an invisible clan of leprechauns who carried on with their merry- and mischief-making through floods, wars, Rose Festival parades, protests, and his own early death ten years before I was born.

"Those stories were beautiful gifts, meant to be opened again and again," Dad said to me, his voice barely above a whisper. "Treasure for his readers. For me, too, and for you."

Chapter Twenty-Nine
Martin, Judith Part Ways
October 5, 1989

After the rehab center and before Tulum—around the time Judith promised herself she would forgive Martin's peccadillos—came the business at hand. Eliza was nearly fifteen, only three years away from college, so the stakes were higher, financially and otherwise. Judith and Martin had kitchen-table worries, debts and assets, which they possessed in unequal measures. A thirty-year mortgage, a small savings account, a modest 401(k), a reliable and paid-for car.

Martin had begun to pack before the ink was dry on the divorce papers. There were only a few small wrinkles in the area of shared possessions yet to be ironed out. Martin cared little about their stuff. It was easy to turn over the wedding china and stainless to Judith. He wouldn't need it where he was headed.

All he cared about was the fact that as a teenager, and a female one to boot, Eliza had questions and concerns he couldn't adequately address. After he was gone, she would need her mother more than ever.

***

"Hand-stitched queen-size quilt in tulip pattern?" Judith's lawyer stared at them impatiently over the top of her glasses.

"Your grandmother's, Martin," Judith said, and the quilt moved into his column. Same for the cello his niece had given him before she went to Europe, a move that demonstrated her distaste for American capitalism. But what was he going to do with that?

"Three-by-six chest?" The lawyer set her pen down, awaiting their decision. The cedar hope chest her parents had given them, gathering dust in a corner of their living room, felt to Martin like an exceedingly cruel irony. He had no idea what Judith had stored in there, but he was sure none of it mattered to him.

"You take it, Judith," he said. The attorney picked up her pen and scribbled a note. "Hope is something I'm happy to give you."

Chapter Thirty
Martin Arrives at Mexican Retreat Center
February 14, 1990

Martin's right arm had a mind of its own, a mind that couldn't be controlled. Doc Ralston's longtime patient was about to travel south of the border, so he recommended one last therapy, a series of botulinum neurotoxin injections, a temporary fix at best.

The doctor deployed a sports metaphor, knowing Martin wasn't at all interested in athletics. "Think of it as a boxing match. You're already bruised and bloodied, so the next round is going to be the hardest," he said, removing his glasses and putting them back on, twice, cleaning them with a handkerchief in between. "There's no perfect answer, I'm afraid."

Martin and Judith had never seen Ralston so flummoxed. "Let's get you on the radiation schedule, then follow up with the injectables," he said with a pessimistic-sounding exhale.

"No to radiation," Martin said, drawing a line in the sand. "But yes to injectables."

The doctor blinked at both of them and cleared his throat.

"I need to be clear," he said, his voice trailing off. "If you're entertaining the idea of a second child, you know the drill." Martin tittered, though nothing about what they were discussing was funny. He was stuck on Dr. Ralston's use of the word *perfect*, knowing that absolutely nothing was.

It had been fifteen years since Judith was pregnant with Eliza. Was this some kind of joke?

"You've got to be kidding," she said to the back of the doctor's lab coat as he exited the room. "Definitely no more kids for us." Ralston had no idea Judith's almost ex-husband could still impregnate someone. He had no idea about Mina.

She took Martin's hand and patted it a bit too hard.

Martin was older. His body carried more scars. In the coming days he would need every ounce of energy he could muster. As he rose to leave, his right arm contracted and convulsed, and he cried out in pain. Judith helped him with his coat, left arm through the left sleeve, leaving the right sleeve to dangle.

"Let's get you home and resting," she said, a last-ditch look on her face.

Martin went on redirect. "Home isn't home anymore, Judith," he said matter-of-factly. "I've booked my ticket to Tulum."

***

Reclining on a chaise lounge beneath giraffe-necked palm trees, mere feet from the warm rectangular pool at the Holistic Healing & Wellness Retreat, it would have been easy for Martin to believe he might actually be cured someday.

"¿Jugo de naranja, Señor Donovan?" Pedro Morales inquired. That's what it said on the plastic nametag safety-pinned to his black cotton vest: *Pedro Morales*. Though it was early in the morning, his crisp white shirt already showed signs of heat-induced perspiration. He stood stock-still, his brown skin gleaming in the sun, ready to help. Martin felt a bit awkward. He had never needed a servant before.

Pedro was the person who had made it his mission to keep his Oregon guest hydrated and comfortable, with a fresh pillow daily and a light blanket for his legs. Good man, Pedro. He got it, knew what was important. The other orderly, Juana Vasquez, was more concerned with the status of Martin's room—clean bedsheets, emptied waste cans, a sparkling sink. Juana was a very nice woman, if not a tad too pragmatic.

Martin nodded yes to the offer of orange juice from behind the cover of Joe McGinniss's excellent book *The Selling of the President 1968* and a pair of outsized aviators. It occurred to him that he must have appeared disgustingly arrogant, the ultimate ugly American, but it didn't seem to matter to Pedro. He spun around on hemp-sandaled heels and, with a quick nod and an "en siguida," trotted back toward the building and into the cafeteria to fresh-squeeze Martin another tall glass of liquid citrus hope.

"Muchas gracias, amigo," Martin said when his assistant returned, but there was no way he could have adequately expressed his appreciation for the way Pedro was making what everyone expected to be Martin's final weeks on Earth not only tolerable but joyous. Martin truly hoped Pedro knew how grateful he was for his dedication. He believed he did. In passing exchanges at first, and later during long sessions of deep listening on days when Pedro was off the clock, they developed a close friendship, or amistad, the two of them enjoying conversations about life and work and family, what it meant to live in an imperfect and unpredictable world. About Pedro's esposa hermosa, Gabriela, who had died during childbirth decades before. Her departure had left a persistent ache in his heart. About Mina, about Martin's ex-wife Judith, and about their daughter Eliza, whom he missed every day.

About why Martin had done what he did, leaving her behind in Portland.

"Those doctors—they were frauds in white coats," he said to Pedro, his forehead folding into a freckled frown. "I wasn't getting any better. They were giving up on me, so I decided to get out of there. ¿Tu comprendes, sí?"

"A veces, los abrigos blancos son malos," his friend responded, with more than a hint of indignation. "At times, the white coats are bad."

"I had to do what I did. For myself but also for Eliza," Martin continued, the story starting to fill itself in. "Did I take the coward's way out? Or did I do the right thing?"

"Sí, señor," Pedro said, nodding understanding and absolution. "Lo correcto. No te preocupes."

Martin grasped Pedro's bony shoulder. "But that kind of longing, that kind of regret," he said, his face turning sorrowful again, "never goes away."

Martin had prepaid his time at the retreat, eighteen months' worth to start, thanks to the sizeable chunk of bull market money his father had left him, securing a favorable deal in the bargain. He tipped Pedro quite well and also put a few pesos a day in the office slot marked Juana for the services she rendered with remarkable attention to detail. But Martin knew the bonus money he gave Pedro could never repay him for his kindness and compassion. They were such different people, after all, from completely different backgrounds. Yet Pedro was able to bridge it all.

"I owe you mi vida," Martin said to Pedro on more than one occasion, a tribute to their bond. "Nunca te olvides," he added. "I'll never forget you, even after I go."

***

An observation by the early twentieth-century journalist A.J. Liebling had always stuck with Martin: "There's nothing crummier than a one-paper town." Martin felt this down to his socks because he regularly imagined it might happen—newsroom staffs dwindling, finances tanking, entire newspaper companies shutting down, citizens losing fact-based printed records of their communities. It was, to him, an unfathomable thing, a prescient fear.

The son of a wealthy Manhattan businessman, Liebling was a Dartmouth dropout and Columbia University journalism school student who sailed across the ocean after graduation to study French and, upon his return to the US, joined the staff of the *New Yorker* in 1935. By reputation he was an egocentric, bombastic man who earned the right to his opinions during World War II when—as a young reporter doing his newsgathering in battlefield trenches across Europe—he made his professional mark.

Martin supposed he might die young, like Liebling did at fifty-nine and change, but he hoped to do it quietly, without much fanfare. He had no real illusions otherwise, orange juice and towels and extra pillows notwithstanding. It turned out that Liebling's musings accurately foreshadowed the demise of the American newspaper, as tragic a tale as was ever told. Someone, Martin couldn't recall who, remarked that on his deathbed Liebling confessed his myopia, his short-sightedness, all the ways he had focused on things he considered, at the time, to be all-encompassing but that turned out in the end not to be important in the least—things like overwork and the push to get ahead and the sumptuous buffets that were undoubtedly part of his undoing. Before he drew his last breath, Martin intended to think about three people: his daughter, his father, and Mina, each of them having taught him, in their own way, about love. Thank God the columnist Colin Donovan was already gone when the *Oregon Journal* went out of business in 1982, a victim of greed and overreach by wretched, hoary men who knew not what they did. Had he thought he could save the *Journal*, Colin would have thrown himself on top of the offset press and refused to yield until the great grasping cylinders swallowed him whole and turned his bones to dust, happy to go out that way, a martyr for a noble cause.

***

Martin sometimes thought the way he came to be a patient, or "residente" as the staff referred to gringos at the HHWR, would have made a great story. Pedro called it *HHWR* for short, or sometimes *La Retirada* when he was feeling cheeky. It was a sad story to people on the outside looking in, but to Martin it was about fate, missteps, reclamation, and redemption. He vowed to write it someday for Eliza.

***

Martin and Pedro stood at the end of a narrow dirt road staring at a dilapidated trailer dwarfed by massive Mexican Weeping Pine trees. Martin was agog at the outside, never mind the inside. "Es viejo, pero es hogar," Pedro said in a soft apology. "It's old, but it's home," he repeated in English, but there was no need. Martin had learned a fair bit of Spanish over the length of his time in Mexico. The screen door on the left side of the trailer hung by two rusty hinges. Pedro swiped the air with his hand, giving Martin permission to enter, and he did so carefully, his good arm leading the way so as not to completely dislodge the door. They were greeted by a pair of mangy, swaggering cats purring and rubbing against Pedro's legs and then Martin's, content after their overtures to escape the trailer and go out hunting.

Past the parquet square of an entrance was the kitchen. Pedro had installed the cabinets himself, using scrap wood from a pile outside the lumberyard on the north side of town. Pedro made sure Martin understood that anyone could take it. "Yo nunca robaría nadie," he said, worriedly, but Martin assured his friend he knew he wouldn't think of stealing.

The double sink was shiny and clean, as was the broom-swept vinyl floor, a happy abstract of red, orange, and yellow geometric shapes. The compact living room boasted a small TV, an upholstered couch, and a card table. The bedroom looked homey, appointed with a pair of twin beds in mismatched coverlets and a double chest of drawers. An airplane bathroom–size loo lurked behind a door in the hallway between the living room and the bedroom, sink and toilet only. "¿Dónde te bañas?" Martin asked, carefully, as he did not wish to insult his amigo. Pedro flashed a smile that said he was glad Martin asked and led him outside, to the back of the house where he had constructed a handsome open-air shower, an al fresco oasis with a bent-wood bench on one side and a flourishing *Vinca major* arbor that twined across its intricately latticed roof. A towel bar and two hooks for clothing completed the room, which faced a small grouping of pine trees under which the cats were now lolling, the sizzle of the afternoon sun having lured them back into the shade.

Pedro smiled. "Es la mejor parte de mi casa," he said to Martin. He cranked the hot and cold handles, producing an impressive cascade of water from the showerhead.

Pedro had come to regard Martin not only as a good friend but also as a brother. "Somos hermanos," he said, looking hopefully at the American for signs he might accept his offer to live together after Martin's discharge from the retreat, two viejos contentos swapping stories about what was and what might have been. Also, what could be.

Martin felt the same way. Not just friends but brothers, for the rest of their lives. But he couldn't stay, not forever. There had to be something better for him back home. He had to return to the states and reconnect with Eliza. He had to get to know her as an adult.

"Lo siento, hermano," he said, sincerely sorry to decline Pedro's overwhelming generosity. Pedro shook his left hand, understanding. Martin's right hand, weakened and withered, hung uselessly by his side.

***

Though the spasms still took hold from time to time, it was remarkable how Martin's physical discomfort all but melted away in Mexico. If he was sweating, it wasn't the affliction but the atmosphere, sixty percent humidity or higher being the norm. He mostly stayed in the shade when he went outdoors—strolling beneath the swaying mangroves—or in his room, where a rattan ceiling fan provided a consistently satisfying flow of hibiscus-tinged air. The four-color brochures had talked Tulum up as a hidden gem midway down the Yucatán Peninsula, largely undiscovered by the typical tropics-enthralled tourist. The people who ventured there were drawn to the town's rich history, its Mayan port-city ruins, partial walls of handwrought stone providing a time-travel portal to the thirteenth century. Tulum's white-sand beaches and cerulean waters weren't too shabby either, but Martin was there to get better and, barring that, to spend the last phase of his life in a place of unspoiled beauty, where he could purge himself of the soul-crushing sense of discomfiture that had permeated his final years as a newspaperman in the Pacific Northwest. The years when he felt the most sorry for himself, when he had flown too close to the sun, when he paid far too little attention to the four last things: death, judgment, heaven, and hell.

***

Mail from Martin arrived at Judith's house in early December, two weeks before Eliza's birthday, in the form of a greeting card with a galloping palomino on the front and a crisp ten-dollar bill tucked inside, currency her father had procured at the local exchange in Tulum. Eliza had checked the mail that day and decided not to tell her mother about the correspondence. She took the steps two at a time up to her room and ripped the envelope open.

No horsin' around, cowgirl! the front of the card read. *Lasso yourself a very happy birthday.* The joke made Eliza laugh, and cry, and long for her father all the more.

Chapter Thirty-One
Judith Meets Harold in Multnomah Village Art Class
March 26, 1990

Six of them sat in metal folding chairs around a long rectangular table in room 101 at the community arts center, waiting for the teacher to arrive for their first class of spring term. The brochure had promised Watercolor Painting for Beginners would provide students with "a fun, fearless introduction to a classic medium" and, once enlightened and empowered, Judith planned to specialize in country landscapes. As the minutes ticked by, though, her resolve wavered. The magnificence of daffodils sprouting from window boxes just outside tempted her to get up and abandon all hope of adopting a new and preferred pastime. No way she would ever get their bright faces right, let alone the milky magic of their stamens and stems.

But leaving had never been her inclination, so she made herself look away from the flowers and stay put. She shifted in her seat, straightened her back, and stretched her arms—elbow pressed to chest, one then the other. She played around with her paint set, flipping the little round discs out with her index fingernail and putting them back in, reorganizing them into primary, secondary, and tertiary color families. Reds with reds, blues with blues, yellows with yellows first; then oranges, greens, and violets.

When she looked up, he was directly across from her, smiling shyly through a neatly trimmed salt-and-pepper beard.

"Hello there," said the man who would become her second husband.

The instructor sashayed in at exactly five minutes past the hour.

"Good morning, lovely people!" Susan Goldfarb yodeled, removing a flamingo-pink visor and releasing a wild mane of gray-blond hair. She dropped her large macramé bag onto the desk with a thump, its contents spilling out willy-nilly. Car keys, a pack of paintbrushes, breath mints, Kleenex. Ms. Goldfarb, a veteran of the art center, was fiftyish, stout of frame, and boisterously loud compared to the pin-drop silence that had preceded her tardy entry. She wore neon green socks above high-top sneakers and a gingham apron over a plain blue housedress. A peace-sign mandala hung from a thick strand of black leather lace between her unbuttressed breasts, which swayed when she took a breath and burst forth with an initial challenge to the class: "Are you ready to create some timeless beauty?"

The teacher's ear-to-ear grin illustrated her enthusiasm for art, whimsy, and creativity. Within minutes, her students were painting.

***

It wasn't that Judith hadn't enjoyed a robust sex life with Martin, at first anyway, in their younger days at college. Before their wedding, before Eliza, before he got sick. Martin had picked opportune times to surprise her with his talent for yogic Tantra. She had felt deliciously wicked at times.

"My lover," Martin had said to her then, and she believed him. That was long before Mina, wayback history now. Judith had let it go and even indulged pleasant memories of Martin from time to time. She was happy with that.

She had no conscious intent to marry again. Not now, not ever. But there was something about the man at the watercolor table— his name was Harold Dixon, he told her after class before inquiring after hers—that put Judith's mind at ease. His wide-open face, his strong jawline, his aquiline nose. His eyes, worldly and serious but also curious and kindly.

Nothing like Martin's, nothing to fear.

He announced his intentions on their third date. What was the point of a long courtship at their age? Judith could almost hear him thinking it. She tended to agree.

"My people live in Alaska," Harold said between sips of espresso and bites of biscotti, chocolate almond, and took her hands in his across the expanse of the burl wood table. "I've been in Portland nine months. My leave's almost over. They'll be expecting me back."

Something shifted inside her lonely, skeptical heart.

"I'm ready to go home, Judith. I'd love for you to come with me, and Eliza too."

Judith felt the milk froth in her mouth evaporate, the bubbles going *pop-pop-pop*. She let the proposal sink in.

"If you'll have me, of course," he added, all earnest eyes and propitious grin.

Harold let go of her fingers and set his cup and saucer to the side. He motioned to the waitress, who hustled over.

"Check please, young lady," he said, dipping a paper napkin into his water glass, twisting the end into a point and dabbing at his beard, taking care of the chocolate. "Thank you for everything."

Then, to Judith: "I know it's sudden, my dear. You'll need time to think about it. Talk it over with your daughter."

The three-block walk to the car was quiet, her arm in the crook of Harold's, his black-gloved hand on hers. "Alaska," Judith breathed, trying on the silliness, the spontaneity. She was fortysomething now, desirous of companionship, not necessarily more. Harold was older than she, not May-December older, but affable and intriguing. Their kisses, so far, had been affectionate and sweet, lips touching but avoiding entanglement. Cautious, respectful, platonic.

They stopped at a corner as the traffic signal blinked red.

"Harold," said Judith, and his rugged face inclined toward hers. She pressed her body upward into his, the fullness of her breasts stirring him to erection. He kissed her, deeply this time, sucking in her bottom lip and sweeping his tongue into her mouth. She felt her mound turn warm and wet. They didn't wait for the green. Harold pulled her across the street and into the car, taking her in the back seat, her hands pressed against the window, moans of ecstasy filling the vacuum.

Alaska, Judith mused as Harold held her afterward. What an adventure that would be! Fuck Martin and his mistress and their baby. It was time for her to live life on her own terms.

***

They appeared before the justice of the peace on a Tuesday, by themselves. No guests, no cake, no music—only the officiant behind an old wooden desk, a candle lit on each end. Harold had gone to the barbershop on the way. He tugged at the starched white shirt collar, trying to get at the leftover hairs still tickling his neck.

Judith held a nosegay in her right hand. She was resplendent in lavender chiffon.

"You're my dream come true," Harold said, giving his collar a final swipe and pecking his bride on the cheek.

Judith giggled like a schoolgirl.

"We're the only ones in the building," she teased, elbowing her groom in the ribs. "Serves us right."

Harold and Judith promised to love and cherish but not to obey. They slipped simple white gold bands onto each other's fingers before departing the courthouse, going home to make the requisite phone calls.

They hadn't consulted Eliza beforehand, but their marriage didn't surprise her in the least.

*****

There would be other mail from Martin to Eliza at selected junctures—birthdays, Christmas, Rosh Hashanah, Easter, and during the Rose Festival—*occasional*, as Judith had proscribed, though Martin convinced himself that connecting with Eliza more often, and surreptitiously, was not only permissible but essential. So he kept up with her on the sly.

"I'm no good for her," he lamented to his ex-wife over the phone in an effort to cover his tracks. "I can't bring myself to face her with my misdeeds. I'm sorry I gave up on us, Judith. Maybe you could remember me fondly to her?"

Judith chose not to engage with the entreaty in Martin's call. To her, the forced infrequency of his communications with their daughter seemed like just desserts. Meanwhile, however, Eliza enjoyed semimonthly missives from her dad, along with clippings of various articles from *La Jornada*, a newspaper in Mexico City. It pleased her to know what her dad was doing, that he was thinking of her. Eliza had convinced her mom that retrieving the mail six days a week was one small way she could contribute to the household. For a time Judith was none the wiser.

Chapter Thirty-Two
Eliza Moves to Alaska with Judith, Harold
September 23, 1990

I had to give Harold credit. He tried to get to know me better by inviting me to do things, watch him paint or come along on walks in the countryside.

One time he came up with an idea to take me fishing. Mom insisted I go even though she knew fishing was the last thing I would ever want to do, especially on a weekend morning in summer.

"It'd make Harold feel good," she said, which made me want to go even less. "And you might actually enjoy it."

I was still curled up in bed when Harold knocked on my bedroom door at six in the morning. When I opened it he had two poles in one hand and a metal tackle box in the other. He looked so hopeful that I got up, got dressed, grabbed a banana, and climbed into his truck. I would go, but I didn't have to like it.

We sat on the bank off Eagle Beach. Harold baited my hook. We tossed in our lines and waited.

"Nice day," Harold said to stagnant air. He adjusted the brim of his fishing cap, all kinds of dumb-looking lures sticking out of it. His face turned redder and redder as the sun got hot. I slathered my nose with zinc oxide and covered my head with a wide-brimmed hat. I might have to sit there with Harold, without my books, for an entire half day, but there was no way I was going to let myself get sunburned.

"How about a little music?" Harold snapped on his portable radio, a General Electric job from RadioShack. Garth Brooks was singing "Friends in Low Places" on the country station. My face must've looked pained because he changed the dial to KRCK, Juneau's best rock. "Welcome to the Jungle" by Guns N' Roses, more my style.

"That's better," I said, throwing him a bone.

"Well, good," he replied. "I can dig what you kids are listening to."

At least the sound of the radio kept us from having to talk. At lunchtime we shared the food Harold packed: tuna fish sandwiches, apples, a bag of chips, Oreos, and Diet Pepsi. I didn't have any luck, fish-wise, but he caught a walleye and a couple small bass. "Your mom will fry them up for supper," he said and smacked his lips.

Couldn't help it. I stuck out my tongue. "Gross," I said. Harold never invited me to go fishing again.

***

We lived in a rented condominium in East Portland for a while after Dad went away, to be near family, Aunt Midge and the rest. I made sure Dad had our condo address. I knew Mom wouldn't think about it. I looked forward to his letters more than almost anything. I had just gotten used to the postal carrier's delivery times, between one and three o'clock in the afternoon, mostly in the middle around two o'clock, when things changed again.

The way Mom informed me she was taking me to Alaska and moving in with Harold was by saying she needed to get away from our life in Oregon, from "all those difficult reminders," and that it would help me, too, but that was hard for me to understand. She knew I loved my memories of our life in Oregon. Most of them were about my dad or the *Cascadian*, topics she never brought up. Sometimes I felt left out of what was really going on with her. Ever since she took up with Harold, I had been trying to figure that out.

About him: Harold Quane Dixon. He was a nice enough guy, I supposed, but it was weird how they got together before Dad had been away for even six months. She decided to take Harold's last name even before they got married. I hated thinking about that, how quickly Mom forgot about Dad. And I didn't get a say in whether we moved or not. I had to go because I was still a minor and that's how it was. I blamed my mom for forgetting my dad, but I didn't blame her for hanging out with Harold. She deserved a good life.

I wanted to stay a Donovan. I definitely looked like one with my freckled cheeks and red hair, Irish all the way. I wondered how Dad would feel if he knew Mom had changed her last name to Dixon. She went to the county courthouse to make it legal. I guess it was important for her to get rid of the Donovan name for good. I didn't throw it in Harold's face, not exactly, but every school semester when it was time to make covers for my new textbooks out of paper bags, I would write *Eliza P. Donovan* in the corner with permanent marker and leave them in the den near his reading chair, where he would be sure to see them. Was that bad?

If I became a Dixon I would feel awful, like I was being disloyal to my dad. Maybe someday. Not now.

***

It was cold in my room in the attic. It had electric heat, but Mom said it was expensive to use so I didn't turn it on very often. I overheard Harold worrying about the insulation, that maybe there wasn't enough of it behind the wall across from my daybed. That wall had the prettiest wallpaper, so I hoped he didn't decide to tear it apart and fix it. I didn't mind bundling up. I wore flannel nightgowns and left my socks on when I went to bed. I didn't tell my mom because it would make her feel bad. She and Harold didn't have a lot of money. He was older than her, a widower who never had any kids. He got a pension from Fishers United because he had been a commercial fisherman for a lot of years before he got arthritis in his hips and gave it up. Mom was still working for her computer chip company, at the Juneau FasTrack branch, but she said supporting a family of three on one income was tough. Harold sold his landscape paintings sometimes for extra cash. They were pretty good, actually. He said he had learned a lot in that watercolor class. He also tinkered with woodworking. The Fergusons down the street had him replace the faces on their kitchen cabinets.

"We get by," Harold said, smiling, and Mom agreed. She liked agreeing with him. She wasn't painting anymore, but she handled the budget.

Reading was the best thing in my life, hands down. I could exchange three books for new ones every week at my new high school, which was a bonus considering the library at my old school had been pretty puny—not much to choose from. I wrote my name on the checkout cards in cursive, and the librarian stamped them and smiled. Most of the other students printed their names, but I liked cursive. Mrs. Sheppard handed over the titles I picked out. Some of my favorites were *Jacob Have I Loved, Tiger Eyes, and My Side of the Mountain.* I also liked *A Tree Grows in Brooklyn.* It was about looking for truth and beauty in an ugly world. I could relate to that.

Sometimes when I was reading I got so involved in the characters' lives that I forgot to eat. My mom would send Harold upstairs to fetch me at dinnertime. I wished she would come instead.

That's what I called him, Harold. I was so relieved he never asked me to call him Dad.

"I swear, Eliza, you'd waste away to nothing if we let you," Mom teased as she pried the latest book from my hands. She had a rule about no books at the table, and Harold went along with it. Mom called their relationship "egalitarian." I was happy she was happy, at least most days, but I didn't care if Harold was happy or not. I guess I felt pretty neutral about it. I didn't hate him, but I didn't love him either.

***

The three of us filled up every part of that drafty old house. Mom and Harold were in the only actual bedroom. That's why I had the attic space. They made it nice with colorful pillows and a desk where I could do my homework. I spent a lot of time there by myself, reading and writing my own stories. It drove my mom crazy. I figured it reminded her of the way Dad was, his "head always in the clouds," as she used to say, but I never thought so.

"What'll you do with all these notebooks someday?" she asked me more than once. "When you grow up and move away, I mean?"

I didn't have an answer for that. But I knew I was going to keep them. They meant everything to me. They had a lot of stories about Dad in them.

I missed the smell of his pipe and all the books in his library under the stairs at our old house in Yamhill County. His "Superman cranny," he used to call it, six shelves in a right-triangle shape and a long piece of oak he hammered into a desk. He made the whole thing himself. He was comfortable in small spaces, part of the Irish in him.

From my new bedroom window I could see the stained glass windows of the Episcopal church on Gastineau Peak after dusk. The light made them look like the inside of a kaleidoscope. They were so pretty and shimmery. Sometimes, at just the right moment, the colors settled on my tall stack of notebooks, like rainbows from heaven. When I got done writing for the night, they went right back under my bed. I tucked all my letters from Dad underneath their cardboard covers, one letter for each cover. For safekeeping. For always.

***

My mom wasn't home when I got my first menstrual period. It happened after school. I knew what was happening because of those films we saw in sex-ed class, so I went into the master bathroom to find some maxi pads. Stayfree, the kind with wings. I had seen a commercial about them on TV.

It wasn't fair, but in a way I kind of enjoyed how clueless Mom was. Payback for putting almost all of her energy into Harold and her job. And for erasing our life in Oregon.

My dad still thought about it. He told me so. He wouldn't forget.

"Everything okay with you, honey?" Mom breezed in from work way past six and poked her head through my bedroom door. I thought maybe she had discovered that some of her pads were missing, but I didn't tell her my news right away.

"Sure, Mom," I said. "I'm fine."

"Just wanted to make sure. You've been pretty quiet lately."

Yes, I had been. Nice of her to notice.

Mom looked nervous. I felt sorry for her. I gave in.

"I got my period today." Her hands went up to her face. For a second I thought she might cry. She came in and sat down beside me on my bed. Her eyes did that dewy thing where all her feelings are there at once, ready to burst out.

She started smoothing my hair. "Oh, Eliza!" she exclaimed. "That's wonderful! Can I get you anything? A hot water bottle, or some aspirin?"

My cramps weren't bad and I didn't need any aspirin. "Just stay here with me for a while," I heard myself saying. "I miss you, Mama."

Chapter Thirty-Three
Martin Buys One-Way Ticket Back to Oregon
May 23, 1993

The way Martin left things when he went to Mexico in 1990 was, in a word, unsettled. He paid the final invoice from his divorce attorney the same week he took off for Tulum, relegating the notarized papers to the top drawer of his desk. At the time Eliza indicated little awareness of her parents' marital devolution, save an inquisitive eyebrow here and there when she heard them arguing, and Judith and Martin were determined to keep it that way. As far as they were concerned, Eliza knew only that her dad had gone somewhere to get better and that he would be back home when he was.

In those early days Judith and Eliza went over everything: how Martin had gotten sick in the first place (his pipe habit had likely triggered the dystonia), why he had been able to recover his health once but not twice (again, the pipe), and the things that meant the most to him in life (Eliza, and newspapers, and his pipe).

They never, ever talked about Mina.

***

Martin's black canvas backpack, now faded to charcoal, had been around a long time, given its mended zipper and frayed front pocket, into which he slipped his one-way ticket back to Portland. He believed in accessibility and also in order, and he demonstrated both in the way he organized his luggage, pants and shorts rolled up in hay-bale coils, T-shirts with the sleeves tucked back in two crisp creases, tidy as could be. He folded the last of his Hawaiian shirts—his favorite featuring smiling hula girls in coconut bras and palm-frond skirts on a sea-green background—and set it on top of the others, a quick change upon arrival at Portland International Airport, when his travel clothes would be wrinkled and smelling of stale, recirculated air.

The last things he added were the bottles of supplements he started taking at the retreat center, at Pedro's suggestion. He would need the rose hips and turmeric on the plane to ward off inflammation. It would be a long flight. He latched the bag and stepped back to admire it. He felt accomplished. Someday he would be six feet under, just like everyone else, but today was not that day.

After his time in Tulum Martin wasn't whole, but he was somewhat improved. He had accepted his body's deficits as permanent: the shriveled arm, the stilted gait, the shortness of breath, the occasional pronounced stutter. He was going home to Oregon, though he didn't know exactly where home would be.

He was glad Judith had softened when it came to him communicating with their daughter. "Once a month and no more," she told Martin, but he had the feeling that her rock-solid wall was more porous than before. He would write more often, and there would be no trouble. Getting together with Harold must have done that, smoothed the rough edges of Judith's attitude. Bully for them.

"Go ahead and write her," Judith had said the last time they talked. "I know I can't stop you anyway." It made him wonder how many letters she had intercepted, whether she smiled when she did so, whether she steamed open the envelopes and read them. No matter. At least Judith seemed more relaxed. She even gave him their address, hers and Harold's and Eliza's. It sounded like a nice place, Juneau, but what would have possessed Judith to move up to Alaska, a place with even less sunshine than Oregon? Eliza would hate that.

Martin wasn't wild about flying alone. He was superstitious enough to send preflight postcards back to the states from the Cancún airport in case he didn't make it, if something unforeseen were to occur—a loose bolt on the airplane engine or a rental car crash, even a last-minute capitulation on his part, though that was unlikely, as there was nowhere he wanted to be except back in Portland.

He would work on a plan to see Eliza once he was settled. Juneau was only a car, airplane, and ferry trip away.

***

Martin paid the woman behind the convenience store's cash register for three postcards, found a table out in the concourse, and sat down to write. He pulled the first postcard from his bag—one with a photo of a fiery Mexican sunset—and scribbled *Dear Ronny* on the back. The postcard would go to his brother in Pennsylvania who had headed east after high school in pursuit of a girl and hadn't attended college, both choices nearly sending their mother around the bend. Ronny was Jane and Colin Donovan's youngest. Their mom had been particularly attached to him, for no good reason according to their aunt Constance, other than the fact that he was her sister's bittiest baby.

"Coddled and swaddled in cotton from the day he was born," Constance had observed at more than one big family dinner, the words flowing from her mouth unedited after several gin gimlets.

Jane Donovan's proclivities were evident from the early years forward. "Ronny dear, you look a bit peaked—perhaps you should stay home," she might say at the beginning of a new school week. "Be a love and fetch Mommy her knitting," she would add as Martin gathered his schoolbooks. She clearly preferred Ronny's company to his and to another day by herself in the family's ordered and extraordinary house in the suburbs. Ronny would stay, and Ronny would fetch, and Ronny would sit in a corner of the den at his mother's feet, playing with his train set as Martin went out the door, walking the one city block to the school bus stop by himself.

"Be a good boy, won't you, Marty? And be on time getting home," Jane would call after him. "Ronny and I will be waiting." No mention of their father, who often stayed late at the office, seeing another edition of the *Journal* off to the press and starting on his next column, chock-full of mischievous leprechaun adventures. Colin loved working at the office in the quiet of the evening rather than from his home on Maple Street. His dinner would be warming in the oven when he came in the door. He would eat it by himself at the kitchen table, chewing each bite with the same sense of purpose he brought to his writerly musings. He would remove his loafers at the foot of the stairs, go up, and look in on his boys long after they had drifted off to sleep in their shared bedroom, down the hall from their parents' suite, stylishly appointed with velveteen drapes and a lamp on each side of the queen-size bed, half of its chenille bedspread turned down in a triangle, awaiting Mr. Donovan's late arrival.

Jane was often asleep with a book on her chest. Colin would turn off her lamp before putting on his pajamas and getting into bed, brushing aside any fleeting inclination to kiss his wife goodnight, as he did not wish to wake her. She would repay him in the morning with sausage slightly undercooked and eggs slightly overdone, offering him the newspaper and her cheek instead of her lips as he sat down to breakfast.

"How was your night, dear?" Colin would inquire, to which Jane would answer "just fine" before turning to the boys and handing them their brown bags.

"Ronny, be sure to wear your warm jacket," she would say if the weather was below sixty, and "Martin, save a seat on the bus for your brother." Two hugs—the longer one for Ronny—and all three of them were off, Colin's head already at the newspaper, anticipating typewriter keys pressing the ink ribbon against the paper bail roller, "the best sound in all the world," he often said to Martin, who paid rapt attention to such pronouncements from his father, the wisest man he knew.

***

Martin took a drink of water, licked the back of a stamp, and pasted it on the corner of the postcard as squarely as he could. He addressed it to Ronny Irving Donovan in Hershey, Pennsylvania, using neat block letters. On the left side Martin wrote about his two big dystonia flares and how, now that he was "at least somewhat improved," he hoped to see Ronny again. Fifteen years was too long. A meeting needn't happen right away, but sometime soon, he wrote and signed it, *Your older brother, Martin.* He also drew a smiley face with curly hair and freckles, so Ronny would know it was really him, whether or not news of Martin's illness had previously reached him.

Maybe there would be a reunion, an end to their estrangement, and that would be grand. It was high time Martin tried to make amends for his behavior, omissions and commissions both, things he had neglected to bring to the confessional booth in Oregon or in Mexico. He had lost faith. Not so much in the big-*G* God of his childhood, the one he studied as a catechumen, but in himself, having broken his marriage vow of fidelity to Judith, having so badly tarnished his reputation with their daughter.

If Martin still believed in a supreme being, and most days he wasn't at all certain he did, it was a small-*g* god, a much more New Testament than Old Testament version, one who could forgo punishing Martin for his failures. He was only human, after all, and he quite disliked the idea of burning in hades for all eternity. But he could not figure out how to forgive himself.

***

The next postcard had a picture of a newspaper reporter on it. A female reporter at her desk, green eyes wide with determination, hands poised on the keyboard. And—incredibly—a black-and-brown pipe in her mouth. As soon as he saw it on the store display rack, Martin knew he had to buy it.

A postcard meant only for Eliza. One he knew she would be happy to receive up in Juneau.

He penned a brief note, left-handed, as he had taught himself to do.

Te quiero, mi hija, Martin wrote—*I love you, my daughter* in Spanish. *Wishing you days of leprechaun capers and nights filled with happy dreams.* He laid the postcard on top of his suitcase, along with Ronny's, and affixed the proper postage.

After three years it was time to leave Pedro and the Holistic Healing & Wellness Retreat behind. It was time to get back to Eliza.

Chapter Thirty-Four
Channel Tempest Heralds Email Message from Martin
October 22, 1994

The morning was wet, the heavy bank of clouds over the western horizon a menacing gray. Taku winds gusted across the Gastineau Channel at forty miles per hour, according to the television news, bending black spruce and paper birch to their will and scattering leaves in all directions. The anchorman looked as if he might blow over himself, his yellow slicker and hat providing little protection from the tempest.

Judith switched off the set and stared out the tall bay windows in her front room. The view rarely failed to inspire her, but today wasn't a typical day. She walked over to the desk Harold had made her from the decades-old stand of cottonwoods ringing the perimeter of their property, a third wedding anniversary present, and turned her computer on. A bit of milk skin clung to her upper lip as she took a sip of coffee, now gone cold. She opened her work email to see what was happening at the office—*ugh, a dozen new messages!*—and made good use of the trash icon. Delete, delete, delete. Ninety percent of it was garbage. Her eyes lit on a message from AOL, heralded by the familiar cheerful announcement: "You've got mail!" Most people used Yahoo now, but Judith kept her AOL account for purely nostalgic reasons. She licked away the coffee-milk residue, wiped her lips dry with the paper doily beneath her mug, and clicked to view the sender.

Judith had to blink twice to believe what she was seeing: a message from Martin. Her heart thumped against her rib cage and her face flashed with irritation. Her first instinct was to drag his message to the trash unread. They had promised not to bother each other after he left on his journey. Over the years, whenever he crossed her mind, she wondered if his health had improved or declined, whether he was still with them, with the world's "sinners and saints," as he used to say, without betraying a preference for either category. She would push her curiosity aside—"compartmentalization," her therapist called the technique—and go on with her day. But now here he was, in her personal inbox, obliterating every boundary they had set that long-ago day at the rehab center. It was so wrong of Martin to write. What on earth would he have to say to her?

She moved her mouse until the cursor hovered over his message, steeled herself, and opened it.

Dear Judith, it began. *How have you been?*

Her hand knocked the mouse away. Clumsy, maybe. Or not.

I'm pretty sure you didn't expect to hear from me, the email continued. *Surprise!*

Judith blanched. *Goddamn you and your playfulness, Martin Donovan. You were supposed to leave me alone.* Then: *Wait, you're alive. You're better. You did it!* She felt her scalp prickle and her hands go damp, then endured a full body sweat from her toes to her head, a premenopausal rash of remorse. What had they been thinking, shielding Eliza from her father's moral failings, only a meager trove of letters maintaining their tie?

She sat back, forcing herself to focus on all the reasons: Martin and Mina's affair. Mina's pregnancy. Judith's struggle to forgive. The flare of his affliction. His insistence that he had to leave. Her pride. All that and so much more.

None of it mattered as she read his words, words out of the blue, words that had circumvented the grave.

Before you delete this note (I know you've already thought about it), I'm writing to you for two reasons. Firstly, I'm still earth-side—let's hear it for alternative medicine!—and secondly, I'm back in Portland. My bad hand can't type, so I can't work in journalism anymore. The very kind Mrs. Pratt at the Multnomah County Library transcribed this email for me. Basically, I'm broke. But I'm staying with Roger for a bit—remember him? Sniffly Roger?—and I've applied for disability and subsidized housing. Fingers crossed.

I'm going to be all right. Don't feel sorry for me, Judith. I don't deserve to live any other way.

Leave it to Martin to adopt a completely different lifestyle than the one we shared. Sponging off poor Roger. Ridiculous! Judith shook her head from side to side, as if she could rid herself of all thoughts of him, a fruitless endeavor.

Wait, did Mina keep the baby? She needed to know. She would never stop thinking about that until the day the question was resolved.

Judith continued reading. It was a lengthy email.

The thing I want most is to see Eliza. My heart has pined for her every single day over all this time. She's nearly twenty by now—our little girl, all grown up! Maybe it's better for her to live her life without me, I don't know, though I continue to write to her from time to time. I wanted to be so much more, Judith, but I failed, and I'll never be able make it up to the two of you. I went my own way. I can't come back from that.

No, you can't, you bastard. Stay away from us.

I wanted you to know I made it, if you can call it that. Please hug our daughter for me. I look forward to the day when I can get up to Alaska. Or perhaps she could meet me halfway? Thank you for taking such good care of her, Judith. Be well.

Right. Be well. As if the last many years hadn't been a steel-toed boot to her gut. *Screw you, Martin,* she seethed. *It would be easier if you actually were dead.*

She felt crazy, talking to her ghost of a former husband like that. How was it that he still held so much sway over her emotions? Martin had powers no other man possessed.

Irish powers. Catholic powers. Irish Catholic superpowers.

The screen door creaked open, releasing her from her reverie. A key in the lock, the turn of the knob, footsteps over the threshold. She exited out of AOL just as Harold walked in, brushing snow from his coat in the entryway. Thank God she hadn't told him her password. The email from Martin—the old Martin, the cheating Martin, the titan of self-absorption and self-blame—would stay safe for another day.

Later, as she made preparations for dinner—chopping carrots, potatoes, and leeks for vegetable soup and setting the oven to 325 degrees for sourdough biscuits—she recalled her ex's obsession with James Joyce. The story went like this:

One hot, do-nothing afternoon the summer before his senior year, a seventeen-year-old Martin stopped by the air-conditioned nirvana of Downriver Books on the Willamette River's west side and picked up a used hardcover copy of Joyce's *A Portrait of the Artist as a Young Man*, which beckoned him from the classics section up front. The book had been around for five decades— hardly an accurate reflection of the complexities of modern life, Martin mused as he flipped through its yellowed pages. But something about the scuffed and faded brown cover drew him in and wouldn't let him go. He ran his fingers over the gilt letters of the title on the spine as he handed the bookseller a fifty-dollar bill and got a quarter back in change, "no sales tax," she pointed out, an attempt to convey he had stumbled upon a rare bargain. It was all the money he earned from an entire month painting houses in his father's geographic area of influence, manual labor he had detested from the start, having already decided he was someone who aspired to a higher rung on the ladder. Whenever he wasn't working or sleeping, he was immersed in the tortured world of Joyce's protagonist, Stephen Dedalus, emerging from his bedroom only to eat and go on errands, jaunts to the pharmacy or grocery he was obliged by his mother to complete each day.

Joyce, the twentieth-century Irish writer and teacher, had consigned to the literary opus in *Portrait* a serpentine story of a doubt-ridden seeker whose surrender to seduction and outsized propensity for self-flagellation strongly resonated with the anxious and impressionable Martin. The fictional Dedalus's very personal war with Roman Catholic repression had rung lastingly true for the real-life newspaperman's son, who absorbed and internalized its unfortunate truths.

"You made me confess the fears that I have," he had read to Judith, early in their marriage, from a section in chapter five. "But I will tell you also what I do not fear. I do not fear to be alone or to be spurned for another or to leave whatever I have to leave. And I am not afraid to make a mistake, even a great mistake, a lifelong mistake and perhaps as long as eternity too." At the time, though the idea made her feel quite nervous and perplexingly sad, it occurred to Judith that Martin had identified his psychospiritual touchstone, using it as a long lash across his own tender back.

"An honest and authentic person always stops to consider what part he may have played in a relationship that goes badly in the end," Martin had said then, his expression indicating he was committed to such an exploration, sounding like Dedalus but also like the man Judith was trying hard to love, a man she sometimes couldn't reach, no matter the degree of intention she put to the task.

***

Judith thought about all of this as she worked on the evening meal, a hearty soup from a recipe handed down by Harold's grandmother, his baba on his father's side. Into a broth seasoned with thyme, coriander, white pepper, and a pinch of sea salt went stewed tomatoes, the leeks and carrots, and the potatoes, parboiled and diced. She set down the spoon and wiped her hands on a tea towel. If only she could have relieved Martin of his tendency to punish himself for every small failing, each time he veered from the impossibly narrow path he carved for himself out of his own misguided zeal.

If only he could have forgone mentoring Mina, as innocent as that enterprise may have been in the beginning. If only Mina's carelessness in circling too close to Martin during her years at the *Cascadian* hadn't wrecked his sense of who he was, of who he and Judith had been together.

Chapter Thirty-Five
Judith Spies Mina's Byline in Juneau Paper
January 15, 1996

Boo strained at the leather leash as Judith made her way up the last knoll leading to the wetlands. She knew they would find the usual sandpipers and dunlins there and, if luck was on their side, a short-billed dowitcher or two foraging for food in the silt near the shore. She leaned down and spoke into the dog's perked-up ear, alert to every cracking twig.

"No growling," she said, patting the thick fur along his spine, his ribs expanding and contracting with each electrified breath. "Be a good boy. We don't want to scare off the wildlife."

Boo's soft black muzzle was dotted with dew from tall grass that lined the zig-zagging pathway down to Mendenhall Lake. Even though it made her daughter bristle, Judith sometimes referred to him as a "rescue," not because Eliza had found him at an animal shelter but because she left him with her mom and Harold when she went off to her initial term at City University at age twenty— "better late than never," Harold had chuckled, an observation Eliza found unfunny. Still, Judith felt it was a good trade for her daughter's agreement to start a two-year degree program and jump-start her life.

"Yeah, such a deal," Eliza had snapped back one day when she was in a particularly churlish mood. "It saved my social life, anyway," she admitted. The dorms didn't take dogs.

***

Judith brought Boo up short and brushed the snow off a large, flat rock so she could rest. She sat, and the dog did too, regarding her with one sapphire-blue eye and one brown, cocking his head as if to ask her, Why the delay? His nostrils puffed little white clouds into the frigid air. "Just for a minute," Judith said to him, and Boo laid down at her feet with an audible grumble. "We'll go soon, I promise. I know you want to see the birds."

159

As she sat, something yanked at her. Something deep inside, where the real wanting lived. That something was actually a *someone*, and he had a name: Martin.

Judith worried about Eliza missing her father. Not just missing him but possibly disappearing into the abyss his long absence had left. There was no way Harold, as sweet and patient as he was, could make up for that. As much as she hated acknowledging it, Judith knew Martin wasn't easy to forget.

***

The phone rang two seconds after Judith arrived home, Boo leaping through the doorway ahead of her and shaking water off his fur all over the entryway rug.

"Mom!" Eliza said excitedly. "Glad you picked up. I snagged three tickets to graduation this spring! For you and Harold and a plus-one. You'll get to see them hand me my associate's certificate. For real."

Judith knew intuitively Eliza wanted the plus-one to be her dad whether or not it was feasible. She coiled up Boo's leash and set it on the kitchen table, where Harold had left that day's edition of the *Juneau Tribune*, Alaska's second-largest daily newspaper. As she reached up to untie her headscarf and finger comb her hair, her eyes fell not on one particular headline but on a particular byline, déjà vu–familiar.

By MINA BRECKENRIDGE, the byline read in bold capital letters.

Chapter Thirty-Six
Eliza Gets Package from Judith Before Finals Week
March 20, 1996

Mail call in Miller Hall was at four o'clock on Wednesdays, when Cecily the resident assistant shouted a handful of names down the hallway in a voice that needed no amplification. She knocked on dorm doors with the energy and verve of a navy SEAL. "Sam Harding! David O'Neill! Sarah Bernard!" Those three got a crazy amount of mail, the most on the third floor by far, from who knew who—aunts or cousins, maybe. Dave tended to get boxes containing homemade sweetbreads and cookies. Sam and Sarah got manila envelopes or long rectangular white ones, stuffed with notes from home, magazine clippings from their mothers, and bad poetry by former high school friends. I hung back inside my room, pretending I didn't hear their names being called, that I didn't mind batting zero in the someone-cares department.

Which is why, on that one hump day when the RA bellowed my name, it didn't register for the longest time. "Dixon! You have a package!" Cecily yelled, adding an unnecessarily embarrassing "from your mom!" I didn't flinch at first, didn't get up from the bottom bunk where I was vegging in the far corner with a used romance novel, a bag of chips, a can of Diet Coke, and my favorite tasseled pillow pressed against my chest.

It took a second callout, with first-syllable emphasis—"*DIX*on! *PACK*-age!"—to jolt me into dashing out the door and into the hall, practically tackling poor Cecily around her fanny pack–adorned waist. She turned around just in time to avoid a calamitous body slam and stood there, rock-solid and unsmiling. She shoved a twelve-by-sixteen-inch box into my spaghetti-noodle arms before trudging off, shaking her head and muttering something about the unfortunates who hardly ever got mail, who apparently weren't well enough connected to their families to know what they would want if they *were* to get mail.

But that wasn't the case with me. My family and I were doing fine. And anyway, why would I want mail from my mom? I had pretty much everything I needed, and she knew that, so if she sent something it would be totally self-serving. A dress she bought at the mall I would never wear, a book she picked up at Walmart I would never read. Maybe she had knitted me something—she had recently taken up the hobby—but if she did, it would be hideous for sure, something I would hate but would have to say I loved, like a hat I would only wear when I went home for a visit. Our tastes were so far apart they weren't even in the same galaxy.

"Wait! Can I do a return to sender?" I called after Cecily, but she was already in the elevator, headed for street level in front of Miller. "Why would she do this to me?"

All of that ran through my head, and most of it out my mouth, in the time it took me to nearly mow Cecily down and return to my room, a distance of eight and a half feet, give or take. I flopped down on my bunk and held the parcel aloft. It was longer than it was wide. Maybe a shirt? I turned it over and noted the return address: Judith Donovan Dixon of Chilkat Road in Juneau. "Judith Donovan Dixon. For God's sake, Mom," I said to myself, my voice echoing against the walls. "So formal. And you added your last name from when you were married to Dad. What will poor Harold think?"

My roommate Ivy—the same Ivy I had known in high school—had gone on a study date to the library. "Until late, so don't bother waiting up," she had said, so it could be morning before I saw her again. Ivy didn't get much mail either. Her family had moved to California—out of sight, out of mind. Too bad for her. As for me, I felt like throwing my package on the floor. Stomp on it, shove it under the bed, or light it on fire.

Then again, it was a box. An actual, physical box from home! Not for Sarah, or Sam, or David. For *me*. I took it in both my hands and shook it. Nothing inside it moved. I took the butcher paper off, used scissors on the tape, and opened the top. There were layers of white tissue paper inside, cushioning the contents, and in the very middle was a framed copy of "Desiderata." My favorite poem since forever. I mean, Max Ehrmann's prose. Life-changing. Everyone loved "Desiderata," especially me.

My last finals week was approaching. I would be out of there soon, a college graduate. And Mom had sent me a package to celebrate. I put everything back in the box and hugged it close. "Thanks Mom," I whispered and kissed it. "Really. Thank you."

***

Dad was in a testy mood when he caught me between an all-nighter and my first cup of French roast.

"Living here is becoming impossible," he complained when I answered, blotting coffee off my *History of Modern Journalism* textbook. The phone's shrill ring had made me jump, thus the coffee blotting, but it was my dad, so of course I picked up. I wouldn't have answered if it had been Jimmy Bledsoe in room 217, that fifth-year senior with the bad teeth and receding hairline who thought he had a chance with me. Thank God for caller ID.

Roger was a worse slob than he had been at the *Cascadian*, Dad said. "I hate calling him a hoarder, but I'm afraid it's true." Dirty laundry everywhere, dishes piled high in the sink, stacks of random papers in every corner, no place to go that wasn't chaos. It reminded him of Carson McClintock, the sorry sot who died in the Chehalem Mountain fire way back when, a victim of his own compulsions. It was straining my dad's last nerve. I could hear the frontal lobe of his brain, the part that demanded order, short-circuiting.

"And the cats," Dad growled. "So many goddamn cats!" Their multiple food dishes contained half-eaten portions of damp kibble rotting in the sunlight, attracting flies. Roger had taken in three of Ed and LaVerna's cats when they downsized from their big house in the country to a condo, easier to take care of in their older age. The McKees kept Miss Molly, "the best one," Roger told Martin with regret, but the others had taken over. Litter boxes in the laundry and the living room, even in the shower. He had to move it before he turned on the water. The clay bits felt like gravel under his feet.

"It literally stinks here," Martin said to Eliza. "And I can't get away from them. They're always purring and rubbing against my legs when I'm trying to relax."

There was one more big reason he was about to do a runner.

"Roger's entire house is a freaking pharmacy," Dad's voice had grown tense and hoarse. "Pill bottles everywhere. Not just the medicine cabinet—the kitchen and living room too. I'm not talking over-the-counter meds. I'm talking prescription painkillers! And some of the caps are missing! It's nuts, Eliza."

I covered the receiver and yawned a somnolent yawn. "Are you worried Roger is addicted?"

Or what if Dad is? I thought but stayed silent.

"Not really," he answered. "I mean, I never actually see him taking any. I talked to him, but he seemed pretty lackadaisical about it. Guess it's my problem, not his. I need to get out of here, though. The whole thing makes me nervous."

It should. For someone with dystonia, those pills could be tempting.

"What's the status of your subsidized housing application, Dad?" I was fully awake now. "And are your disability checks coming in regularly?"

No word yet on housing, he told me—women and children always took precedence, way ahead of veterans and men in the queue—but the checks were arriving each month on schedule. A shade under $350, enough for a Section 8 studio apartment if one ever opened up.

"Lots of red tape," Dad said. "Got to go pay the feds another visit." He sounded tired and frustrated. I felt sorry for him, but I knew he wouldn't want that, so I turned the sparkle in my voice up a notch.

"It'll happen soon, Dad," I said, only half believing my words. "Those Housing and Urban Development folks won't be able to resist your charming personality."

"Thanks, Sunshine," he replied. "Love you to the moon."

"And back," I said as he hung up.

***

Once he left Roger's place, Martin could breathe again. He had made peace with his decision to stay in the decades-old black Chrysler his buddy gave him—"Don't need it anymore," Roger had insisted with a loud honk of his nose, his tossed-away tissue missing the trash by two feet—as well as a cell phone with prepaid minutes. Roger was a mess, but he was a munificent mess. It made Martin happy that they parted on good terms and even happier to have the Crown Imperial, a land boat with dual rear tailfins. Very cool, very retro. Ample floor space for his meager belongings and a roomy back seat to sleep in. The registration was up to date, and less-traveled side streets, off the cop shop's radar, were plentiful in Portland. It was a short-term accommodation, one Martin planned to fashion into a novel adventure. He would flex his formerly robust reporter muscles, atrophied as they were. Put them back into circulation. Use them to look after his basic needs. He would get by.

Martin used to write stories about people like the man he had become. People on the periphery, people on the down-and-out. *Bums*, his mother would have called them.

"Now I'm that guy." He waited for Eliza's response during a Saturday phone chat. He tried to laugh it off, though his daughter—burning his minutes from Alaska to Oregon—didn't find his comment funny. Martin wasn't sure he could handle falling from the pedestal Eliza had set him on.

"I can't stand that you're living in a car," she said instead. Then, with her voice betraying a hint of exasperation, "You could come up to Juneau, Dad. Stay with me."

That wouldn't work for either of them, Martin knew. He was too needy, and she was too independent. He ignored the suggestion.

"When can I see you, Dad?" Eliza persisted. "If you won't move up here with me, I mean. Maybe Mom would spot me the money to fly down to Portland . . ."

All of Martin's nerves flared at once. She couldn't see him like this!

"Soon, Sunshine," he hedged, masking his emotions as best he could. "Or I could drive up," he false promised, stalling her off. *She'd have a hard time recognizing me with this potbelly and bald spot, not to mention my gimpy arm*, he thought. *And the Chrysler probably wouldn't make it past Spokane.* But those were just excuses, false pride, not his real reason for putting her off. His head hurt as their conversation ended. His arm and face spasmed. It was asking far too much for Eliza to accept him for the person he had become.

***

Martin sniffed the pits of a black KISS T-shirt, put it on, and checked the time. Twenty minutes to get to his meeting at Saint Andrews. Adult Children of Alcoholics was spiritual, not religious, in its focus. Buddha, not shoulda. He looked forward to seeing Becky there. Single-mom Becky, with a six-year-old son and a transdermal patch. They had begun a habit of sitting next to each other in the circle.

Today, Martin planned to tell his story.

***

It was Pedro who first introduced Martin to the twelve steps at a session in Rancho Viejo, not far from Tulum. "Come with me, amigo," he had said, brown eyes searching and kind. His uncle Jorge had lived at the anexo adjacent to Maria de Gracia until he got sober and stopped hitting his tía Consuela. She took him back *con brazos abiertos*, Pedro said, "un milagro en mi familia." Anyone could change for the better. Whatever problem a person had, the program could help. "I understand my family better now and also myself," Pedro told Martin. "I am a new man." Martin wanted to be a new man, too, so he went to Rancho Viejo. And kept going to meetings after he returned to the States, though it had been years since he touched a drop.

Chapter Thirty-Seven
Eliza Searches for Mina in Contacts
May 24, 1997

That byline thing really got to my mom. She had mentioned it a bunch of times, on the phone first, then in person when I came home that Memorial Day weekend, five days after commencement.

"What do you think of this?" she said to me in the kitchen, pointing to the newspaper. She saved the front page and circled Mina's name in red pencil. She looked at me more carefully than she had in a very long time, to see how I felt about it.

"Interesting," I replied, not wanting to give Mom the satisfaction, not knowing what I *really* thought about it, except that it brought back memories.

It irked my mom that Mina was in Juneau, and to be honest, it kind of bugged me too. Maybe she followed us up here, chasing after my dad.

The lines on Mom's forehead were deeper now. I could tell she was weighing whether to say what was on her mind.

"You aren't thinking of applying for a job at the *Juneau Tribune*, are you?" she said, anxiety in her voice. She pulled at her fingers as she spoke.

I couldn't resist the urge to hector her. "I might," I said, all devil-may-care, all try-me. "Would it bother you if I did?" I added, though I knew the answer.

Mom pursed her lips and sucked in air. The forehead lines got deeper, if that was even possible. "I just hope you think about what's best for you," she said, her countenance suddenly smaller. She steeled herself. "And I don't think what's best for you is being around Mina every day."

***

I should get out of the house and do something—"anything," Mom said to me as she put on her coat and tugged on her galoshes for a walk with "the boys," as she called them, the canine and human varieties both. I was messing with my flip phone, but out of the corner of my eye I saw Mom clip a new leash to Boo's collar. One of those retractable jobs, totally unnecessary. She called Harold from the next room, then turned to me. "You've been staring out that window so long I'm afraid you'll go snow-blind." Her face was a canvas of black-and-white disapproval. I pressed more buttons and gave her a look.

My eyes are just fine, I groused to myself. *I can roll them behind your back, no problem. Do you think I'm still five? I'm twenty-two now. I can spend my time however I wish. You're the one who dragged me up to this godforsaken wilderness in the first place. It's so unfair.*

I watched her finish bundling up: hat, earmuffs, mittens, wool scarf, gaiters. The whole process exhausted me. I turned back toward the window as Harold appeared. He had been in his study. Reading, no doubt, because he still had magnifiers perched on his nose. God, those history books. Books on the fishing industry, the Alaskan wilderness, pioneers. I had gone through them all. One time I rearranged them behind his back when he wasn't home. They were nothing like what had been in Dad's collection, a mix of fiction and nonfiction, a literary homage to the Beat Generation's Burroughs, Ginsberg, and Cassady, not to mention Kerouac, hands-down his favorite.

I played a bad joke on Harold one boring, uneventful day, but predictably, he didn't say a word.

"Who put *Working on the Edge* next to *Two in the Far North*?" he called from behind the afternoon shadow darkening his study's doorway. "They're from two different genres!" He laughed a lusty, blameless laugh. Oh, Harold. How he could spend so many hours in that mess I would never understand.

"Your boots and hat are ready for you," Mom said to him, "all warmed up by the fire." I gave her solicitous behavior an Olympic-champion eyeroll. *See? No worries, Mom. I can still move my eyes. Go on your walk already, you and the abominable snowman.*

Boo whined and danced from one paw to the other while Harold wrestled his boots on. He lifted the orange whistle from the hanger by the door, looped the lanyard around his neck, tucked it under his anorak, and patted the spot.

"In case we get lost," he said, like always. "You can hear this thing a mile away."

I should be so lucky.

I wasn't proud of the way I felt about Harold, or even Mom sometimes. She was trying, I knew, and Harold wasn't such a bad guy. He had his own way about things, and that was his right. It was his state, his house, his book collection. It wasn't like I wished him dead or anything. I just wished him away. Not from my mom—not exactly—but definitely from me. He tried to care for me, tried to get close. He had always wanted his own kids, according to Mom, but "life just didn't go that way," meaning his long-dead wife had been against the idea.

Mom wasn't one to say bad things about the departed, but I knew she felt sad for Harold that he didn't get to be a father. Maybe I should have felt bad about it too. I hoped it was good enough that he had a stepdaughter, even though I hardly ever accepted his invitations to go along on their walks.

"It's fine." Harold let me off the hook. "But you're always welcome to come if you want."

Harold tried. He did. But he wasn't my dad, not that he ever actually tried to be. I gave him props for that. He was smart enough to know the score.

I fluttered my fingers at them as they left. "Toodle-oo!" I called, not caring if they heard the mockery in my voice. Mom opened the door, and like always, Boo bounded out first. Harold latched the door behind them, "to keep the boogie man away," and that was something. I felt a tiny bit guilty, watching as they made their way down the driveway, a tall figure and a shorter one, ambling like old people, the snow up past their ankles. They looked kind of comical but also fragile. I hoped one of them didn't fall, because the other one would go down too.

I should have been walking Boo myself now that I was back with Mom and Harold, now that I had my sheepskin from City. But he seemed more like their dog than mine now. And what the hell was I going to do with an associate's degree in communications? It wasn't my fault. Mom pushed me to go there.

God, it was cold in the house. There was a definite chill from the crack under the door. I grabbed another blanket from the basket next to the sofa. Its fringe caught on the side. I yanked it free and checked for damage. Oregon was so much warmer than this, so much better. Give me a Douglas fir landscape over western hemlock anytime, and definitely rain over snow and ice. I was happy in my home state, once upon a time. I still remembered even if they didn't.

I hated to admit my mom was right, but she was. It was time I made a change. I was getting nowhere fast. I shifted onto my side and fished my phone out of my sweatpants pocket, started scrolling through my contacts in the newspaper world. There weren't many left: Carla, Ed Jr., Francine, LaVerna. No way I would ring Roger the druggie up.

When I got to *m*, there it was. Or rather, there *she* was: Mina.

Chapter Thirty-Eight
Voice from Past Reaches Mina at Millennium
January 3, 2000

The impending start of a new millennium had a lot of people spooked, Mina included. Before the end of the last work week of 1999, she went through her files and saved the critical ones on floppy disks. She really didn't believe that all the world's computers would shut down at midnight, but she wasn't going to take any chances either.

When morning dawned on January 1, after the ball dropped in Times Square like it always had, the *Juneau Tribune* building was still standing and Mina's faith that the apocalypse would wait for another day remained intact. At the office the following Monday, she smiled and shoved the floppy disks into the back of her desk drawer. She felt lighter than she had in weeks.

The reception desk phone rang with a synthesizer sound. Louise checked the In and Out Board, scanning the rows of names until she found Mina's hot pink magnet in the Out column. Mina wasn't in the office, Louise told the caller, but she expected her soon.

"Around one o'clock," Louise said. "She's usually pretty prompt."

So it was that Eliza Donovan Dixon left her old friend Mina a voicemail, a long-winded, stream-of-consciousness message, one with specific intent.

***

Mina returned from lunch to a flashing light and hit Play and Speakerphone on her machine. The sound of Eliza's voice sent a tingle up Mina's spine. She quickly picked up the receiver so the whole office wouldn't hear. She went back to the start of the voicemail and listened twice, just to be sure.

"Hello, Ms. Breckenridge . . . I mean Mina. This is Eliza, Martin Donovan's daughter," the recording began. "I'm not sure if you remember me—I hope so, because I most definitely remember you."

Twelve years. Practically a lifetime ago. That's how long it had been since Mina had seen Eliza Pearl Donovan, her young friend, her protégé, whom she deserted. The daughter of her beloved boss.

***

It was clear to Mina she had to call Eliza back, and soon. It was also clear to her, by the sound of Eliza's voice, that there was no animosity on her end. But what to say?

Telling her about Martin and the baby was out of the question.

Maybe she would one day.

For five years Mina had managed to avoid running into Martin's daughter. His *older* daughter, anyway. She had heard from Francine that Judith had moved to Alaska and remarried, but Juneau was a big city, and she and Judith had never traveled in the same circles.

Now her luck had run out. She picked up the receiver and dialed the number at the top of the call history.

Maybe Eliza wouldn't answer. Maybe Mina could leave a voicemail.

"Hello?" a hopeful voice said after just one ring. *Shit*, Mina thought, but she stayed professional.

"Eliza." She wanted to sound cool but also caring. "It's good to hear from you. How have you been?"

She had been just fine, Eliza said, her voice more mature than Mina remembered. Finished her degree, took jobs at a coffee shop and a motel, "stepping stones to something better." Was living with her mom and stepfather for the time being.

"Ah," Mina said, nothing further. She knew Eliza would step into the breach.

"I'm meant to be a journalist, Mina," she said, "just like you and my dad." Eliza's speech was optimistic and pressured, both. "Is there a position for me at the paper?"

There it was, the question that had been at the back of Mina's mind ever since she came to Alaska, a state that wasn't easy to access except by plane or a road trip through Canada. Would she and Eliza ever work together? Good Lord, what were the chances that both of Martin's favorite women could wind up in the same 3,255 square miles?

Mina drew in a breath. "It's been really nice to catch up," she said flatly, "but there are no openings in the newsroom right now."

She could feel Eliza's disappointment through the telephone line.

"Oh," Eliza said, and "thank you," and "some other time."

"Yes, some other time," Mina responded. "Send me a resumé," she blurted. An olive branch and a placeholder.

Chapter Thirty-Nine
Martin Checks On Subsidized Housing Application
January 10, 2000

Car-dwelling had been miserable in winter. Snow flurries were hitting Portland not just once, but two or three times during the dark months. Martin hated the cold. It made his symptoms worse. Back in Mexico, he hadn't hurt. Not physically. Not like this. He woke in the back seat for the umpteenth time. Flocculent pillow and down sleeping bag aside, he knew he had to take action if he was serious about changing his fortune. It struck him as ironic that he and Eliza were in similar places in their lives. She needed a job and a place to live, and he needed a place to live and something purposeful to do.

Martin sloughed off a thick layer of blankets, then folded and stacked them. He pulled on his best pants, a pair of chinos that hung loosely on his hips, given the weight loss. The rearview mirror didn't lie about his balding pate and the bags under his eyes. "No hair on top means more hair on the sides," he said to himself, stuffing his thinning, graying strawberry blond waves into the collar of his jacket for extra warmth. He steeled himself for the six long blocks to the HUD office on Southwest Third Avenue.

It was 8:05 a.m., an hour past dawn. As he walked, the dull sunless sky kept Martin's mood subdued and his hopes in check. He gave the handle on the glass double doors a pull. They felt heavier than the last time.

"Paperwork's in the bins on the wall," the woman at the first window told him before he could explain he had been there many times before. She pointed over his shoulder and handed him a clipboard. "Fill out the forms and get back in line over there." She pointed again.

The second line already had twenty people in it, a winding procession of rascals. Several men in wheelchairs took up more room than others. The veterans, Martin supposed.

So this is how my conscientious objection is coming home to roost, he thought as he offered to push a one-legged fellow's chair forward, keeping the line moving. *But that was thirty years ago! Isn't there a statute of limitations on begging off?*

Apparently there was not. Martin had been informed by functionaries, more times than he could recall, that military vets superseded civilians when it came to Section 8 assignments. "You serve, you deserve," was the way one of them put it.

The man with one leg wheeled himself away from the counter, nodding his appreciation. Martin stood up straighter, ready to take his place.

"Number eighty-nine!" the second-queue clerk barked. Martin's number. He stepped to the window and handed over his forms. Again. He didn't think it prudent to mention he had stopped counting go-rounds. He wouldn't take any chances. He would keep coming, no matter how long it took.

But damn, it had been so long already. Women and kids at the top, then veterans. *Two- to five-year wait* echoed in his head.

"Where am I in the system?" he inquired, pleasant as could be. He slid his papers toward the middle-aged woman with the permanent frown lines, who stared at her computer screen and tapped the keyboard with her right pointer finger.

"Not much higher, I'm afraid," she told Martin. "Lots of folks still ahead of you." Her frown lines softened slightly as she gave him unsolicited advice, advice he could hardly stomach. "Paperwork and patience is the way it works around here!"

The clerk stamped his papers. "We'll call you, since you don't have an address," she said unceremoniously. "You should hear something from us within six weeks." She sniffed and stared past him. "If not, come on back."

Come on back. *Right*, thought Martin. The cards were stacked against him. He would never be able to afford housing in this economy unless he got a voucher. Apartments cost a thousand a month.

He sat back down, processing. Free of papers, wracked with pain, full of pessimism. He read the room, all those defeated-looking folks in folding chairs with clipboards in their laps, and his mood got gloomier. How had he wound up here, endlessly reapplying for government housing? No profession, no wife, no daughter, no identity? How was he part of this ragtag group doing the same?

He knew the how, but mostly avoided the why. He tried to focus on the who and the what: himself and survival.

"This chair taken?" A shabby-looking man pointed to the one next to Martin and pulled at his earlobe, anxious-like.

"It's all yours, buddy," Martin answered, moving his car keys and wallet so the man could sit down. His new companion smiled through unkempt facial hair and settled into his seat.

"What're you in for?"

Martin took the man's humor as a positive sign. "Trying to improve my situation," Martin said. "Been staying in my car. Long time now. How about you?"

"Same," the man replied. "Not a car, though. A tent on Sunderland Avenue." He fake-shivered and sent another smile Martin's way.

Ever the reporter, Martin noticed skull tattoos on both the man's hands. Biker gang, a commitment to ride until death.

"Name's Pete."

Pete held out his right hand, and Martin shook it with his left. Touched the tattoo.

"Hey. I'm Martin," Martin said. "Former journalist. Current failure."

The words were out of his mouth before he could sip them back in. He looked at Pete with please-don't-shiv-me eyes.

"Whaddya mean, 'failure'?" Pete asked, making Martin feel unreservedly listened to for the first time since Pedro.

He gulped and began. He told Pete about his former life. Judith, their daughter. His affliction. About Mina and their affair. About

175

the baby. About everything.

The pain welled up behind his eyes. He thought he might cry. He thought Pete might too.

"I couldn't work in my chosen field anymore. I couldn't make things right. I was sick and I was desperate. I went to Mexico, left everything behind." Martin was on a roll. "I screwed up big-time. Now I'm paying for it."

Martin sat back, drained. A pen marked Affordable Homes for All escaped Pete's fingers and clattered to the floor. Pete leaned down to pick it up. When he was upright, he scribbled something on a business card and pressed it into Martin's palm.

"Call me if you need someone to talk to," Pete said. "Number's right there."

**

Weeks in the Crown Imperial had stretched into months, and months had morphed into years in Martin's fend-for-yourself world. He had made friends with most of the neighborhood patrol officers, who seemed to cycle through the Portland Police Bureau as fast as it burned through police chiefs. Charles Moose lasted six years. Lynnae Berg made it six months as an interim. Mark Kroeker arrived at the millennium and was hanging in there, so far, but the way political protests were heating up downtown, Martin figured it wouldn't be long before City Council gave him the boot too.

The cops generally left him alone. He was a good citizen, picking up trash in parks, steering clear of trouble, moving along when he was told. Martin loved learning. He appreciated experiences he hadn't known before. He had his routine for rest and food down pat, and he had located all the best porta-potties. One day was never like the last, a journalist's dream. From Buckman to Lents, car living was an observational Candy Land.

"Eye-opening," he often told Eliza, reassuring her that he was okay. "I like that I'm the captain of my own destiny." But she didn't buy it, not completely anyway.

**

Of all the steps in the program, Martin was most closely aligned with number nine, making direct amends to people he had harmed. He had never been much of a drinker, and he gave up his pipe when he went to Mexico as the retreat center didn't allow smoking.

He was, however, more repentant than on any of the evenings he had sat adjacent to Father Richards in the booth of his youth, occasions numbering as few as his family had allowed.

"I seek forgiveness from Judith, Mina, and especially Eliza," he confessed during circle time at Saint Andrews, while Becky held his hand, her boy River sitting cross-legged on the chair beside her, a coloring book in his lap. "I was a self-centered asshole. A workaholic. I learned that from my father." It felt like betrayal, speaking the truth—one of the truths—about Colin Donovan for the first time.

The late nights at the office. The empty booze tumblers clinking together as his mother collected them in the morning. God, that had been awful. Colin's shame became his son's.

Martin's admission started Becky's tears flowing. Her friend was a good man. Eager to do better, like her. He was trying, and she hated to see him struggle. Sipping a soft drink after the meeting, still holding his hand, she offered him an out. "I'm in a subsidized apartment, Martin," she said. "It isn't much, one bedroom, but we could share. It would get you off the streets. You'll be waiting forever otherwise. My only request is that you pick River up from school on days when I work."

***

Back at his car, Martin remembered Pete's card at the bottom of his pocket. He pulled it out, along with a bit of tan-colored lint.

PETE THE ROADIE, it said in all caps. *Doctor in another life.* And below: *Retired to Dignity Village. If I can help, I will.*

A doctor? Martin wondered what had happened to Pete. Malpractice lawsuit, maybe. Or a drug habit? Doctors were famous for dipping into the pharmaceutical stash. He held Pete's card in his good hand and committed the phone number to memory.

It occurred to him that Pete got around, knew folks in the area. Something that could come in handy in the future.

Chapter Forty
Mina Hires Eliza to Write Obits at Juneau Tribune
February 4, 2000

Housekeeping at the local motel hadn't done it for me—all those sex-stained sheets, all those wastebaskets overflowing with used tissues—and slinging coffee drinks for minimum wage plus tips wasn't my cup of tea, either. I needed to move out of Mom and Harold's house for good. One morning at breakfast, between bites of toast, my eyes fell on a Help Wanted ad in the *Juneau Tribune* for a general assignment reporter, "competitive salary, good opportunity for a self-starter." I knew intuitively it was the right time to jump. Well, not exactly. I knew it because the ad directed applicants to contact one Mina Breckenridge, former news reporter for the *Cascadian* and now managing editor for the *Juneau Tribune* Mina Breckenridge, the same Mina who had turned me down when I asked her for a job three weeks before.

The same Mina who had up and moved to California all those years ago without even saying goodbye.

I printed out my resumé and put it in the mail, along with a cover letter and a fresh headshot. I followed up with a phone call, counting on Mina to reconsider. She just had to.

***

"I don't have a journalism degree, but I have a journalism pedigree," I said during the interview, which seemed to amuse the panel of four inquisitors across the table from me in the enormous boardroom lined with crystal clear, floor-to-ceiling windows, much nicer digs than at the *Cascadian*. I prattled on about my father, the former editor, and my long-gone grandfather, the columnist, how I had ink in my blood and totally understood the significance of the First Amendment and the sacred role newspapers played in society, bringing readers critical information about their communities, fully fact-checked and unvarnished.

All of that was absolutely true. If they could overlook that big-deal college, official journalism degree thing, we would be golden. Maybe my associate's certificate would be close enough.

"We appreciate your coming in, Ms. Dixon. We'll be in touch," the man in the brown tweed jacket said, very noncommittal, but he shook my hand in a way that gave me hope, and by the following Monday, I was on staff at the *Juneau Tribune.* I squealed for a minute straight after I got the green light and celebrated with friends all weekend, taking care not to close the bar down either evening. I couldn't risk a hangover on my first day. When Sunday night rolled around, I hardly slept a wink. I held a picture of Dad in my hands as I lay there, inert and nervous. *I'll make you proud, Daddy.* I blew the photo a kiss and put it back on my dresser. I thanked the goddesses, especially Mina, for believing in me.

***

It would be a huge understatement to say my mom was unhappy that I had landed a job at the *Juneau Tribune.* I had to tell her, even though I knew she might blow a gasket. She would find out sooner or later.

"You're kidding," were her exact words, not three seconds after my announcement.

Her next words were even more pointed, ominous even.

"Don't follow in your father's footsteps, Eliza," she pleaded, "and especially not in Mina's."

Mom had more. So much more. About how she wanted better for me, about my various talents, "for more than just journalism," and how a career in newspapers could set me up for financial ruin.

"The most your dad ever made was fifteen dollars an hour," she said, stone-faced, accusatory. "And with you being single . . ."

It was all I could take. I wouldn't let her insinuate that I needed a man to support me. I loved my mom, but she couldn't tell me how to live my life.

"I'm doing this. I'm taking the job, and there's nothing you can do about it."

Mom glowered, then softened, and looked like she might cry. I didn't let up.

"You've got to get over the Mina thing."

***

I rushed out of my apartment with my phone in one hand and Dad's leather briefcase in the other, its brass clasp engraved with the letters MJD, for Martin James Donovan, way better initials than RID for his brother, Ronny Irving Donovan. The plan was for Mina to meet me outside the building at eight o'clock.

The two of us showed up at once, 7:59 a.m. on the dot. Though she didn't need to, Mina ducked under the doorway. Still tall, still compensating. This was Mina plus a few decades, the same woman I had known since childhood. Suddenly I was eight again, a name badge stuck to my coat, ready to go on assignment with her.

"Glad to have you on board, Dixon!" Mina's chin-length bob danced as she spoke. Her hair was an attractive salt-and-pepper combo, the bottom of her bangs skimming a pair of rectangular eyeglasses in plastic leopard-print frames.

She looked the same as she used to, but also different. We were both more worldly.

"It's a learning curve for sure, but you'll be all right," Mina said then, her fingers gripping a thick manila file folder. "You've got the chops for this, Eliza. You had them even as a kid." She wore a gold cardigan with fake pearl buttons over a white collared blouse. A silver charm bracelet jangled on her right wrist. And she still had all those rings! So many of them, I couldn't fathom how she worked her keyboard. Her impeccably groomed eyebrows looked like caterpillars reclining on her forehead. There were two deep vertical creases in the skin between those eyebrows, just above the horizontal line of her glasses.

"Elevens," my friend Ivy, who studied to be an aesthetician, had called those face caterpillars back in college. "All women over a certain age get them."

We paused at Mina's desk. It was lined with knickknacks that could use a good dusting: A small pink teddy bear with one eye missing and a fuzzy red heart sewn into the middle of its chest. Two melamine awards for reporting, one from 1995 and one from 1998. A coffee cup that said Will Edit for Food on the side, holding an assortment of pens from Sitka Springs Art Center, Juneau Light & Power, Marie's Home Cooking, and the Do Drop Inn. That last one sounded familiar somehow. I let the thought go and moved on to other things.

***

The interview. Thank God that was over. I must have been laser-focused on the three men asking me questions, giving them the answers I thought they wanted, an embarrassing development. Mina was clearly the paper's most seasoned reporter, and anyone would be fortunate to have her as a mentor, like I did back at the *Cascadian*, albeit as a young girl. My memory of the interview was a little foggy, but I think Mina was scribbling in her reporter's notebook the whole time. I probably spaced it out because I was worried about what she was putting down in there. Shades of my reindeer journal. I wondered if she remembered that.

I thought about how nice it was of her to welcome me so warmly to the *Juneau Tribune*, which would please my dad, no doubt. I would have to tell him all about it.

Mina's desk was all the way up front, in the cubicle closest to the publisher's office. She had a functional swivel chair, and her filing cabinets didn't have any dents. My workstation was in the back, near the employee bathrooms, where the ambience didn't always inspire creativity. My chair's seat was patched with gray duct tape and my desk was built for someone left-handed, which I was not, but I would adjust. It was like when people visited the United Kingdom and had to get used to driving on the opposite side of the road.

Max sat right in the middle of the newsroom, one row behind Mina and one ahead of me. I could swear that guy had eyes in the back of his head. Just about every time I stopped typing, I heard him walk past my desk toward the men's room. He was either spying on me or he had a serious issue with digestion. One day he up and told me, out of the clear blue, that his father had been an alcoholic, "a mean drunk, and abusive," he added while wincing. That explained a lot of things.

I figured my spot in the newsroom was the proper place for a newbie, especially one who had faked her way into the job. I'd had it with working two or three part-time gigs. It was time I used my skills.

***

Mina was a neatnik and pretty old-school. Besides the teddy bear, the awards, and the mug of pens, she kept just one photo of her family—her mom and her aunt—in a round frame to the left of her phone. Her screen saver was a lone white tennis ball that bounced across her monitor whenever it went idle. She used black plastic stacking trays for sorting snail mail. It was kind of funny that she still got actual mail, with postage stamps in the corners of the envelopes, but she did.

She wasn't above pitching a righteous fit when certain circumstances called for it, just like in the old days.

"Jiles! My email account's down again!" she yelled to Mr. Ogles one day on deadline. She threw her hands in the air above the cubicle divider and muttered something I couldn't make out. If she walked back my way and didn't seem too awfully out of sorts, I might decide to ask her what her priorities were for me, for the first week, anyway. I wanted to find out if there was a juicy assignment for me inside that manila folder. I couldn't wait to get started.

***

It was wending its way into my dreams, this obsession to become the ultimate lady newshound. Like Lois Lane chasing stories, only more modern and sophisticated and with better hair. I set aside the fact that for the time being, I was on the obit desk. It wouldn't last forever, Mina assured me when we happened to be in the ladies room together. She was pacing back and forth, probably not the best time for me to pester her. But she seemed okay with it. "Don't worry, Eliza," Mina said, watching for the next open stall. "It won't be long before you're covering city council."

I chose a brown long-sleeved top, a tan blazer, rust-colored corduroys, and fleece-lined Uggs for my second-day outfit; wound my red curls into a loose chignon; and secured the whole shebang with bobby pins, neat and professional but not too boring. I checked myself in the big mirror by the door, noticed a few stray hairs, and tucked them in. I swept my keys from the kitchen counter in apartment J-206, humming on my way out. Tuned my car radio to the local station, KTOO, in case there was breaking news. I had to be on top of that stuff.

When I arrived Mina was already there, circling things with a red marker. The newest issue of the *Juneau Tribune* was open on her desk to a double truck feature on pages eight and nine. I flashed back to my dad's small office at the *Cascadian*. He had gone through the same process every Thursday after the paper came out. "We need to find the stars and the scars," he had said, meaning the best and worst things about each week's effort, in order to learn from them. A star might be an exemplary lede or a hard-hitting quote. Misspelled names and errors in photo cutlines were scars. It wasn't the most elegant way to assess performance, but Dad thought it was effective, so he persevered.

***

Mina's morning included a budget update with the publisher followed by a staff meeting, scheduled for nine o'clock on the hallway calendar.

"You coming?" she asked me as she gathered up her things, as if I should've known I was invited. Why would a lowly obituary writer get to huddle with real reporters?

"Oh, sure," I responded, blunting my excitement, happy to be included. "Anything I should bring?"

"Just yourself and a notebook." She handed me a big stack of them. "You'll be surprised how many of these babies you burn through in a month." It made me think Mina might have something more for me, something beyond inquiries to the mortuary. I would kill for that.

"Wait," Mina said, and I turned around. "Don't forget this."

She tossed me a press pass, strung on a burgundy lanyard. *Eliza D. Dixon, reporter, the* Juneau Tribune.

My own press pass! I almost skipped to the back of the office, back to my workspace. A potent sense of déjà vu came over me, and I smiled a Donovan smile.

Someone had put the latest edition of the paper on my desk blotter, squared up below a picture of my family of origin, taken on a trip to the Oregon coast in 1988. In it, Dad had a camera around his neck, as he always did. I was wearing a cropped white sweatshirt with a lion on it. My mom had on something similar, but her smile seemed tenuous and bewildered, bordering on grim. *I look like her mini-me*, I thought, *except my hair is even shorter than hers*, a pixie cut I had asked for and later wished I hadn't. The sky behind us, beyond Haystack Rock, was dark and overcast. All of us had our hands in our pants pockets.

I swigged my hours-old coffee and brought myself back to reality. I stared at the front page and scanned the headlines: *Juneau Expects Warm, Slushy Week*; *Assembly Scraps Illegal Junkyard*; *Coast Guard Secures Runaway Tugboat to City Dock*. I considered how I might have written those headlines myself if I hadn't been stuck on the obit desk.

My work appeared on page A21, in neat single columns, the CliffsNotes of all the lives most recently lost in the local area: *Maude L. Mundinger, 77; Lester R. Chambers, 96; Andrew M. "Andy" Klein, 41*. Forty-one? That was way too young.

I could write obituaries in my sleep. Learned the formula a long time ago. Birthplace, parents, childhood, college, career, hobbies, survivors. Whether they had been burned or buried. Nothing to it. But also everything: people cut them out of the paper, stuck them under fridge magnets, tucked them between pages in the family Bible. Records of peoples' lives, memorials made of faded newsprint.

***

The news meeting wouldn't start for another half hour. I read the particulars of the staff box, then the bylines, memorizing the names of the people I worked with, reporters and editors with actual beats. Naomi Waltz—I loved her name; it was so lyrical—covered education and wrote features. Fletcher M. Ferguson covered city hall. Mina Breckenridge, managing editor, covered the county. Assistant editor Max Medlin covered cops and courts. Thomas Stanley Harwood II wrote sports.

Thomas went by Tommy in real life, Fletch had already told me. In the paper his name took up two whole lines of print. *THOMAS STANLEY HARWOOD II*. Boldface, twelve point. Ridiculous. I couldn't wait to meet this guy. And I would in just a little while.

When I had a page-one story, my byline would say *ELIZA D. DIXON*. I liked that—it was kind of mysterious. No one would know what the middle initial stood for, except Mina, but I couldn't be Eliza Donovan Dixon because it was too long. I didn't want to be pretentious like Tommy.

***

Everyone was assembled when I walked in at 9:02, fashionably late, and took the seat to Mina's left. It wasn't hard to match names to bylines. They were so obvious. Naomi, short gray hair, peaceful-looking, middle-aged. Fletcher, even older, face pitted with acne scars, gentle smile. Max looked like every other midcareer cops reporter I had ever seen, a bit paler maybe, with small, shifty eyes. Tommy was iron jawed and magazine-model attractive, twenty-five if that, the quintessential sports guy. He gave me a curt nod when Mina did the introductions. "Good to see you," he said, as if I was only a visitor, and folded his hands on top of the table. He was missing part of the middle finger on his right hand, the section above the first knuckle. I wondered how it happened. It explained the adaptive keyboard. Nothing like that was available when Dad was having his troubles with dystonia. If there had been, maybe he wouldn't have had to leave journalism.

"School board meets tonight. I'm sure we're all over that," Mina said, checking the master calendar. She turned to Naomi. "We're expecting some fireworks from the abstinence crowd, right?"

Naomi shifted in her chair. "Another glorious evening listening to folks fight over sex ed," she said, pretend-wincing. "Should be all kinds of fun!"

Tommy had basketball previews to offer, Fletcher a piece on the new city administrator.

Mina fixed her eyes on Max. He met her gaze with a haughty stare.

"Let's talk about the police department story." Mina tapped her fingers on the table, one, two, three. "I think you buried the lede."

Max opened his mouth and started to speak. He stiffened, lowered his hands to his lap. "How so?"

"Officer Haas's official misconduct is the whole reason for the story. I don't see his name in there until the third paragraph."

Mina was unrelenting but managed to avoid condescension. "I've got a suggestion for your opening."

Max leaned forward, his face stop-sign red. "Okay, shoot, boss. I'm all ears."

Mina's tone turned professorial. "Sergeant Wayne Haas ended nearly two decades of service with the Juneau Police Department this week when he resigned rather than face an internal investigation into alleged sexual harassment. While his departure was technically voluntary, several of his colleagues told the *Juneau Tribune* that Haas had received an unmistakable shove out the door.

"Next time," Mina insisted, "we're gonna need 'sexual harassment' somewhere in the first few sentences."

The five of us breezed through Mina's agenda. In less than twenty minutes she had a list of what everyone was working on and a plan for the next day's front page. "I just need to check with Kirk about art," she said and noted my confusion. "He's our staff photographer." The meeting broke up and everyone scattered. I was the last one out. I wanted to savor the vibe of my first official newsroom mixer. Mostly business, some sarcasm.

When I emerged, Max and Tommy were hanging out in the main hallway near the In and Out Board. Louise hated it when people didn't move their color-coded magnets into the column that matched their whereabouts. Mina made sure to warn me about that. The board was next to the nice bathrooms, the ones the visitors used, not far from the lunchroom. I was still clutching my coffee mug when I saw Tommy and Max. I didn't think I would look conspicuous if I loitered there a minute. I flipped my notebook open to look busy.

"Jeez, what's going on with Mina?" I heard Max say. He removed his glasses, cleaning them with the hem of his T-shirt. His eyes were even smaller than I thought they were.

Tommy tried to look sympathetic, but he couldn't quite pull it off. "I know, man. It's not her usual thing to call one of us out."

"I just mean, it's a bit much the way she's so obsessed with sexual harassment lately."

"Wonder what that's about."

Max heaved a long, loud sigh. He moved closer to Tommy. "I'll tell you the truth," he said in a sulky tone. "I feel a little bit sorry for Sergeant Haas. It's getting so a guy can't have any fun anymore."

My coffee had gone cold, but not as cold as my gut reaction to their exchange. It was just guy talk, I told myself. Water cooler bravado, nothing I needed to worry about.

Chapter Forty-One
Eliza Stands Up to Judith
March 5, 2000

Four weeks. That's how much time went by between the day I went to work for the *Juneau Tribune* and the day my mom took me to task for it. To be honest, I expected her to come unglued way before she did. She hated Mina with a white-hot hate, and in some ways I understood that. But this was *my* life, not hers. I was a grown-up now, and I got to choose.

Mina told me about the phone call, how upset Mom had been that she hired me.

"I don't want to come between the two of you," Mina said, "but I'm really happy with the job you're doing, and I'd love for you to stay. I hope you and your mom can work things out."

It wasn't that Mina hadn't done anything wrong. Not exactly. I knew she had flirted with my dad back in the day—I couldn't forget their mistletoe moment—and that hadn't been okay. But Mom wasn't innocent, either. She was a hard woman to live with. Stones at glass houses and all that.

Mom and Harold showed up at my apartment one Friday, right when I was getting ready to go out. The doorbell rang and there they were, their Mukluk-covered feet planted on my *As for Me and My House, We Will Serve Mega Pints of Beer* doormat.

Not even a warning call. Rude.

Harold looked sheepish. Mom looked determined. She had a full head of steam going.

I started with "I'm meeting my friends—can we do this later?" but it went nowhere.

"We're having this conversation NOW, young lady!" Mom said, bracing the door with a fleece-jacketed arm. She stepped forward, her winter boots leaving mud marks on my entryway rug. Dad would have paid for that for days.

Harold followed her in, still sheepish. He took off his hat and boots. "Nice doormat," he said and gave me a little wink.

Mom was in no mood for chitchat. "You could work at any

number of other papers around here if you're bent on going into journalism," she said, as if she knew the market. "I want you to resign from the *Tribune*."

That wasn't happening, I told her and mumbled "when hell freezes over" for good measure.

"What did you say?"

"I said 'when hell freezes over,' Mom. I like my job! I like working with Mina, and I'm not quitting."

Harold interjected, trying to help. "Is there a way we could compromise, somehow?" he ventured. "Like maybe you could arrange for a different supervisor?"

Mom wasn't having it. Neither was I.

It was never easy crossing my mother. She was one of those black-and-white people, not a stitch of gray. Her way of looking at things was always the right way. Nothing like Mina. Not unlike Max. I steeled myself for her ultimatum.

"If you stay there . . . if you work with that woman, it's going to be a while before the two of us speak again," Mom stuttered, her eyes narrowed and unrepentant.

I couldn't resist calling her bluff. "Fine by me. Sorry you feel that way, Mom, but I'm staying."

It would be a cold day in Mexico before I changed my mind.

Chapter Forty-Two
9/11 Nightmare Precedes Bus Barn Interview
September 11, 2001

The morning sky was cloudless and serene, as though nothing could permeate the stillness. It had been chilly when I left home for my interview, but it turned out my cardigan didn't suffice. I held the clutch in, popped the stick shift on my geriatric Volkswagen Beetle out of gear to keep the engine idling, and put the heater on. It made the inside smell funny, like burned tires, like the first time you turned the furnace on in winter. This was my second VW. The first one gave up the ghost at 230,000 miles. They were dependable and uncomplicated, the way I wanted to live my life. Also, the windows rolled down manually, a quaint feature that hinted at control. The clock on the dash was hard to read because of condensation. I wiped it with a Kleenex. It said 8:55 a.m.

I was parked in front of the Juneau School District bus barn, way out in the boondocks, waiting for Dr. Dennis Andrews—a PhD, not a medical doctor. I was lucky to get this interview. Administrator types could be pretty elusive. I was going to ask him why the district was bent on retrofitting the bus fleet with a gadget that reduced diesel emissions. I wanted to know whether the end justified the financial means. It would cost at least $750,000, a pretty penny for a small school district. How could they spend that kind of money when the school board laid off ten teachers in the last budget cycle? Andrews would probably consider it a gotcha question, but I was going to ask it anyway.

Naomi had gone home to Nebraska to care for her mother who had late-stage cancer, so I was covering the education beat for a month. I wanted to show her, and also Mina, what I was made of. I had been up since six. Andrews was late. I thought maybe he had stood me up—but my story was due that afternoon. While I waited I flipped through radio stations to catch the news.

"It's 9:01 Alaska standard time on September 11, 2001, and this is the news," said a voice from the local NPR affiliate. The reporter spoke in a strange, clipped monotone. "Four hours ago, a passenger plane crashed into the World Trade Center in New York City, followed by another one a short time later." He stammered out an editorialized corollary: "We're hearing the north and south towers are on fire. We don't know what happened, but it looks pretty bad."

Good Lord, is it al-Qaeda?

I didn't have time to keep listening. My interview rolled in and parked his big-ass SUV to my left. I cranked my window open and held my notebook up, signaling I was who he was supposed to meet. The SUV's exhaust choked me, and I coughed, not that he cared. I noted Dr. Andrews's dark blue suit, his solid red tie, the American flag pin on his lapel. He pushed a button to lower his passenger-side window. "Morning, young lady," he said and gave me a little salute. Sort of funny for an administrator. *He has no idea*, I thought, *about the towers, about the airplanes.* Or maybe he was just that stoic. He might have been in the military. Iran–Iraq War, by the looks of him. Anyone could do more than one thing in a lifetime.

"The White House press secretary just said this is most likely a terrorist attack. We will bring you updates as they come in." I snapped the radio off and put up my window. Both of us got out of our cars and stood about five feet apart. My eyes and Dr. Andrews's eyes met. He broke the silence first.

"I guess we should get on with it," he said and motioned me toward the door at the front of the bus barn. "After you, Ms. Dixon."

Inside, we sat at a card table, wobbly and small. Andrews produced a thick set of papers that explained his best thinking about the diesel retrofit project. It had an index and pages marked Proposal and Timeline and Cost/Benefit, along with component drawings and a glossary at the end. The front of the bundle was stamped with MEDIA COPY in red, all caps.

"So you see," Dr. Andrews said after a while, "the district wants to get this done by spring at the latest." I stayed silent, my mind elsewhere, far away on the East Coast, where the first tower had fallen and the second one had been hit, but there we were, talking about balance sheets and the aging Juneau bus fleet and the sin of knowingly exposing students to dirty particulate matter. I tried to get my head back in the game. *Children are more susceptible to air pollution than healthy adults because their respiratory systems are still developing and they have faster breathing rates*, I read on page five, under Overview. *Asthma is the most common long-term childhood disease in America, making cleaner buses an urgent priority*, it said on page fifteen, under Conclusion.

Dr. Andrews leaned back in his chair. "Student safety is our number-one concern," he intoned with a buttoned-down grin and steepled fingers.

We stood up and shook hands. I crammed the media copy into my bag. I switched the radio back on as soon as the engine on my Beetle turned over.

I waited through a too-long Nordstrom Rack spot for more coverage. I wondered if Dad had heard the terrible news. I wondered what he thought about it, how he would write the story if he still could.

A scary image struck me like a thunderbolt: *My dad's on the street! Living in a car, still waiting to get into subsidized housing. There are hundreds of homeless folks in New York. Did they all die when the planes hit the buildings, snuffed out by fire and smoke?* All I wanted was to be near my dad. To know he was safe.

I grabbed my phone and dialed my mother, ending our stupid estrangement.

"Mom!" I shouted as soon as she picked up, to radio silence. She was still upset about me working with Mina. "Mom!" I said again. "C'mon, this is important! It's about Dad."

***

"Hijackers have flown passenger jets into both of the Twin Towers in the heart of Lower Manhattan," the reporter said, still in his monotone. "A third plane has crashed near the Pentagon and a fourth near Shanksville, Pennsylvania. The World Trade Center's South Tower has collapsed."

There were no commercials that morning. I imagined President Bush in the Situation Room, huddled with his cabinet. I didn't know he was at an elementary school, like the one I planned to visit the next day in Naomi's stead, reading a picture book to children sitting in a circle on the floor, when an aide whispered in his ear that America was under attack.

It occurred to me I never did ask Dr. Andrews my question about expenditures and laid-off teachers. People were jumping from the inferno when I made that omission.

Chapter Forty-Three

Serial Killer Case Gives Reporter National Exposure
December 1, 2001

The AP dateline on the bottom of the front page sent chills up my spine, the headline grabbing my attention like very few others. *Police Apprehend Serial Murderer.* I speed-read the first couple of paragraphs. I could hardly believe it: Gary Leon Ridgway had been arrested at a truck factory in Seattle, Washington. They finally got that son of a bitch, the Green River Killer.

I had been following the story for a long time—a macabre curiosity about that awful case, I guess. A reporter I knew at the *Seattle Times*, Stephanie Sands, had been in close contact with the King County authorities, checking in with them every week, but new information had been hard to come by, privacy rules and all that. Apparently they applied to everyone, even murderers. Ridgway's run-ins with the law dated back to the early 1980s, when the cops named him as a suspect in the disappearance of dozens of teenage girls and young women, but he had only just recently become a household name. In the newspaper photo of him at the downtown precinct, he wore handcuffs and an eerie I'll-never-tell slip of a smile.

Stephanie's story included some gut-churning nuggets. Arresting officers charged Ridgway with the strangulation deaths of forty-eight women, many of them sex workers or runaways. He tossed some of their bodies into the Green River south of Route 60 and dumped others in wooded areas near Seattle and Tacoma. He'd even engaged in necrophilia with some of their corpses. Could it get much worse?

"*Allegedly*, of course," Max said with a know-it-all smirk, looking up from the office copy of the *Seattle Times*. "Her story says *allegedly*, as it should." Sometimes he really gave me the creeps.

Turned out that Ted Bundy—yes, *that* Ted Bundy—had given interviews to investigators before his execution in a Florida electric chair in 1989. He had actually helped them nail Ridgway by describing the mindset of a serial killer, something Bundy knew from experience. He suggested that the cops stake out the shallow graves where some of Ridgway's victims were buried, in case he returned to the scene of the crime, which he had often done. One rapist and murderer fingering another. Unbelievable.

***

The *Times* switchboard put me through to my friend. The line beeped three times, an annoying fragmented whine, then clicked open.

"Stephanie! Holy cow! Look at you, girl—you're *famous!*" I shrieked into the receiver, covering it with my hand so I sounded a little less crazy.

Max turned halfway around and gave me a weird two-fingered wave. I ducked below my cubicle partition and kept talking to Stephanie.

"Yeah, can you even believe it?" Stephanie squealed, like she used to do when we sat next to each other in Media and Society at City University. "I swear I'm still pinching myself!"

We went on like that for almost a minute, me insisting she could win a Pulitzer, she *no-way*ing me back. Even as I praised her, I felt the dichotomy: part of me was delighted for Stephanie, another part was so jealous I could spit—the bigger part. I mean, I was the one who had kept our group projects on track when we were in college, tinkering with term paper manuscripts into the night, copyediting them into pristine shape to beat each deadline. Stephanie had been too busy flirting with our wavy-haired rogue of a professor to be bothered, finding flimsy excuses to hang out with him after class. The dude had zeroed in on Stephanie from day one, while I did all the heavy academic lifting. But Steph always had a way of rationalizing things, wheedling her way back into my good graces.

"Eliza, don't be such a drag," she would say before pulling another brilliant idea out of her perfect, step aerobics–sculpted ass, something that tied the whole assignment together and guaranteed us an A. Later on, of course, she turned into the crackerjack reporter she was today. Was it her or was it the professor? A combination, I supposed. Somewhere along the line, Stephanie could have learned something about journalism through osmosis. I know I did, thanks to my dad—and yeah, thanks to Mina.

***

Years of confinement could give a person a whole new perspective and sometimes a whole new life. That had been the case for Martin before he finally, at long last, got the go-ahead to move into a HUD-sponsored Section 8 apartment. The break came as a relief to both him and his friend Becky. She quoted "Free Bird" to him when they said their so longs, flicking her ashes onto the asphalt as he loaded his suitcase into the Chrysler. River, who was in middle school and no longer needed rides to and from classes, high-fived Martin at the door. Their social exchange had run its course.

Martin sold Roger's car the very next weekend and used some of the money to buy a couple funky lamps and a pair of used hiking boots at a secondhand store off McLoughlin in Sellwood, on the TriMet line. His well-worn apartment was barely there—a bathroom, a kitchen, and a Murphy bed in a ten-by-ten living room—but it had a patio out back where he could sit, watch the birds, read, and daydream. And it was a pleasant, walkable neighborhood. To Martin, it all added up to heaven on earth.

Chapter Forty-Four
Mina Mentors Eliza with Mind on Greta
June 9, 2003

School was out for summer. As Mina walked past Juneau's largest community pool, a gargantuan facility that took up a whole city block, she could hear whoops of delight echoing out the doors. Through the open side she glimpsed the teenage lifeguard in his high perch, overseeing the children as they splashed and played. It was the best job a kid could get in July and August, she had thought long ago, growing up in California.

She had so loved swimming then. She thought of her daughter, now fifteen years old. *Did she have lots of friends? Was she happy? Did she love swimming too?* Maybe she was at her neighborhood pool down south at that very moment, doing cannonballs off the diving board. Mina hurried up Dimond Park Loop on her way to the *Tribune*, her heart full of wonderings, her mind locked on the day ahead.

***

"I think you're going to like this one!" Eliza presented Mina with her newest story list before she had time to sit down. "Three hard news stories and a personality feature. Bam!"

Mina let an armload of books and papers drop to her desk. She took the list from Eliza and scanned it. She gave her what she hoped was an appreciative look.

"Nicely done," Mina said, still a bit breathless after her brisk trot uphill. "Thanks for following up on the nurses' strike. You're really getting into the groove, Dixon." She handed the list back, sat down with a plop, and smoothed an errant piece of hair into place.

Eliza was still standing there.

"Anything else you need?" Mina picked up the phone, peering over the tops of her glasses.

Her protégé was waiting for something.

"What?" Mina said, her throat feeling suddenly rashy. "Tell me."
Eliza took a step back but stood her ground.

"I need to take a day off," she said. Each word was equally weighted and unequivocal. "I've been working for three weeks straight, weekends included, without a break."

The I-deserve-it look on Eliza's face sent Mina right over the edge.

"You of all people should know this business isn't for slackers," she said, setting her jaw. "When I was starting out I worked fifty-to sixty-hour weeks." She depended on Eliza—reliable, ambitious Eliza—not to pull a Tommy or a Max, to understand that self-care and a career in journalism were mutually exclusive.

She couldn't be with her own daughter, helping her with her homework, guiding her into her future. But she sure as shit could shape Eliza into the reporter she knew she could be. She wasn't about to let her off the hook.

"I'm only asking for one day," Eliza said. Then, "I'll front-load my stories so the workflow won't be affected. I need this, Mina."

In that moment Mina remembered how Eliza had stood up to her own mother, how she had chosen her job at the *Juneau Tribune* even in the face of Judith's wrath. Eliza and her mom hadn't spoken for a while after that.

Mina felt embarrassed. How could she have doubted Eliza's dedication to her profession, or to her?

"One day," Eliza persisted. "To go to the fjords, to clear my head." She would get to Tracy Arm by boat. She had saved up for it. She would be out on a Friday and back the next Monday, ready to go.

Mina not only relented but apologized. She opened her wallet and handed Eliza two twenties and a five. Pulled an Ed McKee. "For lunch," she smiled. "On me. Have a good time."

Chapter Forty-Five
Martin Accepts Help from Eliza
July 20, 2003

Pete the Roadie returned to the housing office every fiscal quarter, just as Martin had done for so many years before his luck changed. To see if anything had come open, anything for someone like him. His record, a record Martin didn't have, was working against him.

"You'll get there, Pete. I'm sure," Martin encouraged his friend from his first-floor studio across the Morrison Bridge from the housing office, not far from Rimsky-Korsakoffee House. That spooky old place had been around since the '80s and was still serving up classical music, ginger cake, and Portland weirdness. Sometimes on sultry nights, if he kept his window open, Martin could hear strains of Stravinsky from there.

"They won't make it easy for you, though," Martin said. "It's that background check thing. But one day it'll happen." He could hear the defeat in Pete's voice and the regret in his tone.

Pete had gotten pinched a decade back for possession, not intent to distribute—a misdemeanor. Marijuana in a baggie. "That security guard was a fucking rent-a-cop," he said to Martin. "No honesty in that guy."

Now Pete was feeling his age even more than his rage. As much as he had gone on about the freedoms and fellowship of Dignity Village—"self-regulation with benefits," he called it—his old bones weren't happy with tent living anymore. So every twelve weeks, on a Tuesday before lunch, he showed up in front of the HUD clerk and handed her new paperwork, as was required. "There you go, Zelda dear," he would say with a gleam in his eye. Not expecting anything but hoping for something and dreaming of everything.

***

When Martin was in college, it wasn't unusual for his father to slip a twenty-dollar bill into his shirt pocket, patting it afterward as if it might fly back out, whenever he and Martin's mother visited campus. "I'm sure you'll find a good use for it," Colin Donovan would say as his wife looked away, pretending not to notice his openhandedness. And likewise, when Eliza was growing up in Yamhill, Martin might press a couple quarters into her hand for Jolly Ranchers at Fennell's or give her extra lunch money to buy chocolate milk instead of plain.

Now it was Martin's turn to accept what Eliza called *assistance* but he called *charity*, something his Catholic parents had extended not only to him but to their less well-off neighbors on the outskirts of Laurelhurst—even the vagrants in the parking lot behind their church when the family left Mass on weeknights. "Do unto others," his mother often said, his father issuing a tractable smile. Young Martin had taken their example to heart, but older, world-weary Martin couldn't help thinking of it as welfare.

Eliza's caller ID popped up on the front of Martin's cell phone.

"Dad, are you getting enough to eat?" she said from far away in Juneau. It was a plain question that demanded a plain answer, one Martin couldn't deny his daughter. "Pete says you're not. Seriously, I'm worried."

"I'm working on it," Martin said, certain that if Eliza saw him, she would know he wasn't making nutrition a priority. "Clay at Rimsky saves me day-old pie. And whenever I see Pete the Roadie outside HUD, he always has an extra slice of pizza for me."

He could barely make his rent, let alone eat properly. Eliza couldn't leave things alone. "Dad!" she exclaimed. "Pizza's fine, but you need vegetables! And greens. I'm going to make sure you have them." She had heard about a community supported agriculture garden called Southeast CSA, a small plot around the corner from Martin's apartment. "Convenient," she said, and she would pay for it.

She hurried through something about a cost-of-living raise, leaving out the part where she still only made fourteen dollars an hour.

"I'll get in touch with the CSA person right away," she said confidently. "I got you, Dad."

Martin didn't argue with her.

Eliza wasn't sure how to make the exchange work. But she would find a way.

***

On her trip to the fjords, Eliza had time to think. And read, but mostly think. Her musings took her back to the *Cascadian*, to her first experience in a newsroom, when everything seemed possible. And to her dad. Which brought her back to her current newsroom and Mina, who had given her something else to think about while she was away: a chance to attend a professional seminar in Seattle, an opportunity to add to her résumé.

"The topic's investigative reporting," Mina had fairly sung, knowing Eliza was more than a tad envious of her reporter friend Stephanie. "Three days of intensives. Cream of the crop instructors. And two nights at an Airbnb on Queen Anne hill, courtesy of the boss. Maybe you could even get together with Stephanie."

The idea intrigued Eliza. "I can't afford the airfare, though," she said without a shred of confidence that Mina would counter.

"That's the best part, Dixon! Fletcher was on board, but he dropped out—oral surgery or some such—and his ticket's transferable. All I need from you is seventy-five bucks for the seminar itself. That's doable, isn't it? You really ought to take advantage of this."

Mina beamed, but Eliza demurred. Her last paycheck was already spoken for. And then there was the puzzle of how to help her dad. "How about I let you know Monday?" she said, and she was out the door.

***

A hundred and fifty bucks. "Could you spot me that much for the seminar, Mom?" Eliza asked Judith, in person, knowing her request was unusual, that it was cover for helping her dad. "I can pay you back the middle of next month."

Judith wanted to ask questions before letting go of the money. Where were Eliza's paychecks going? Had her landlord raised the rent? Was she spending too much eating out with her friends? Instead, at her kitchen table she reached into her purse, unzipped her wallet, and produced five crisp twenties and five tens.

"Been to the bank today," she said and smiled at her daughter.

Her fears about Eliza working next to Mina had mostly melted away. Nothing awful had come of it so far. And now Mina was giving Eliza a chance for professional advancement. Judith could appreciate that.

"You deserve this," she said, holding out the money. Eliza accepted it with a thank-you, a hug for Judith, and a look that said she was grateful, knowing her mom and Harold weren't rolling in it.

"Harold's been getting new woodworking customers," her mother said brightly, her body elongated, her expression one of pride. "The extra money's been nice. We're able to put more away—savings for retirement or a rainy day. I don't mind helping you."

***

Judith discovered the truth by accident while thumbing through a pile of mail near the wall-mounted phone. Seventy-five dollars to the Society of Professional Journalists, state of Washington chapter, 2003 Seminar, the letter said and PAID, according to a red ink stamp on the invoice stapled to the receipt.

Judith had a lightbulb moment. Seventy-five dollars? Eliza had asked for twice that amount! Judith saw red. She would talk to Eliza that night when she came over for dinner. Shepherd's pie, her favorite.

"He's not eating, Mom," Eliza wailed when Judith confronted her, defiance on her face, culpability in her voice. She wasn't proud of lying, but she had convinced herself it was a white lie for a righteous cause. Harold excused himself to the bathroom. Mother and daughter were by themselves to sort things out.

Judith took the first shot. "Who's not eating? Some boyfriend of yours?"

"No! Not some boyfriend. It's Dad, down in Portland."

Judith's eyes went deer in the headlights. Eliza went fully on the offensive.

"I can't let him go hungry in that crummy apartment, all alone!" she cried, tears flowing. "He's suffering! I can hear it during our phone calls. I figured it out. He won't agree to see me because he's ashamed, Mom. He's ashamed!"

***

It hadn't taken long for Judith to respond to her daughter's tearful entreaty regarding her father's well-being. Only part of an afternoon, and then she visited Eliza at her place—strewn with unlaundered clothes and dusty bric-a-brac, a fetid odor immediately sending her hand to her nose.

Judith opened a window. *My word, who taught you to keep house this way? Your bubbe would be appalled!* whistled through her head. But witnessing Eliza's genuine pain softened Judith, blurred the lines between what she wanted and what her child needed, assurance her dad would be all right.

"Mom, we have to help him!" Eliza stood still and choked out her plea. "He won't tell me how he's really doing, but I know things are bad. Couldn't we find a way . . ."

Judith passed Eliza a cotton handkerchief and sighed.

"What's your best guess about what he needs? Per month, I mean."

Her daughter wiped her nose and snuffled, looking up at Judith, feeling some solidarity with her for the first time in a long while. "A hundred dollars, maybe? That would keep him on decent food, anyway. I could give twenty-five or so . . ."

"And you think I could spring for seventy-five." Judith was going to make Eliza work for it.

"Well, if there's any way you could, Mom. I know you and Harold are in your retirement years."

Harold. Judith blanched. He couldn't find out!

She made Eliza agree that if the two of them helped Martin, her husband needed to be left out of the equation. For now. "Seventy-five a month. Fine," she said, then tossed in a stunner. "And Eliza, should I predecease your dad, you're to keep on giving it to him. I'll create a trust in my will. Harold's so easygoing. Once I'm gone, I don't think he'll mind."

They both broke down and fell into each other's arms. No more words needed to pass between them.

Chapter Forty-Six
Greta Endures Parents' Anti-Muslim Rhetoric
September 11, 2003

Two years after the Twin Towers fell, Greta's parents still believed in George W. Bush's explanation that extremist terrorists had carried out the attacks. But they did not accept the administration's later insistence that the suicide bombers' actions were unrelated to Islamic teachings.

Darla Sloan deemed the first part of the president's statement "gospel." Yet she agreed with her husband that anyone who worshipped Allah was suspect, even now.

"Outsiders with an ax to grind," Reg Sloan declared at dinner on the second anniversary of the tragedy as Greta was passing the peas. He pounded one fist on the table, rattling the stainless steel utensils. "We have to remain vigilant against al-Qaeda," he added, failing to differentiate between regular Muslims and the murderous, militant kind.

Greta flinched and set the bowl down hard.

"Come on, Dad," she said, knowing she was bucking him, willing to pay the price. "My friend Aisha is Muslim. So are her parents. And they're not terrorists." Greta had stayed overnight at Aisha's house the weekend before with her mother's permission.

"Is she the girl who wears a headscarf?" Darla wanted to know.

"It's called a hijab, Mom. And yes."

Darla wrinkled her nose in an isn't-that-cute sort of way and turned toward Reg. "She's very nice. I met her family in the market," she said. "Before Greta ever went over there."

Reg looked unconvinced.

"They didn't seem at all dangerous," his wife continued, digging herself in deeper.

Greta gaped at both of them, then began a full-throated defense of Aisha. "She's the first friend I had freshman year. We were in orchestra together, remember? I was first-chair flute and she was second chair. You couldn't find a better or kinder person," she said. "I don't care that she's Muslim. She knows we're Christian, and she still hangs out with me. Can't we give her the same courtesy?"

Reg stayed mum. Darla smiled a coy smile and changed the subject.

"Flute lessons were perfect for you, Greta. You're quite talented, as everyone knows," she said, her grin giving way to a surprising accommodation. "Of course we'll give your friend a chance, sweetie," she said. "Youth group is next Wednesday. Why don't you ask Aisha to come along?"

***

Holy Shepherd was the perfect excuse, and the perfect venue, for Darla to make good on her promise to her daughter, and Reg hadn't overtly objected. Aisha's parents dropped her off at six thirty. Youth group started at seven. In between, the girls practiced their instruments in Greta's room.

"Let's go back to that first movement," Aisha suggested, flipping through the pages on the music stand. She had played a sour note, messing up the fingering for Allegro maestoso, Mozart's Flute Concerto no. 1 in G Major. Greta had noticed but hadn't said anything, not wanting to hurt her friend's feelings. The girls sat more rigidly in their straight-backed chairs and went at it again, this time performing a perfectly phrased rendition of the piece, right down to the trills.

Aisha's face beamed. She looked for affirmation that the orchestra director would appreciate their efforts.

"Old man Riler's going to love it," Greta said, raising her instrument in the air in a celebratory salute. "You definitely rocked it that time."

***

"Thank you for giving me a ride, Mrs. Sloan," Aisha said from the back seat of the Sloan family minivan. She tapped Greta's shoulder. "And thanks for inviting me, Grets."

Grets. The moniker grated on Darla as the trio neared the church. She and Reg had kept the name Greta's birth mom had given her, out of respect for her selflessness. Darla wasn't keen on nicknames. Aisha was different, that was for sure. Darla sincerely hoped she wouldn't return their gesture and invite Greta to her mosque. For now, she said nothing.

Chapter Forty-Seven
Greta's Sixteenth Birthday Holds Surprise from Bio Dad
May 27, 2004

Upstairs in her bedroom at 3525 Shenandoah Lane, Greta Sloan was primping. It was the afternoon of her sixteenth birthday, and her friends—three boys and five girls from Holy Shepherd High— were due to arrive in less than an hour.

Her mom and dad had said a reluctant yes to her request for a coed party, the first one ever in her life, even though Reg and Darla had known the families for years. They lived in a small community.

"Only if we talk to their parents beforehand," Darla Sloan had said. "And only if the party ends before ten o'clock." There would be cake, presents, and a movie—Greta chose *Raise Your Voice*, rated PG, with Hilary Duff and John Corbett—but no party games. Reg thought games inappropriate for a girl her age.

Greta released the hissing curling iron blades from her long auburn hair and stood back to assess her appearance. "Not bad," she said to herself, but her next thought was *not great, either*.

The fact that she was adopted had never been hidden from Greta, not since she was old enough to grasp the concept. Reg and Darla wished to be forthright with their daughter, a value their minister had encouraged during couples counseling sessions in his office at the church.

"It's up to you when you think the time is right," Pastor Don had said, "but a child of five can understand the loving sacrifice you made to become her forever family."

They had explained to Greta that Mina, the woman who gave birth to her, had been unable to provide her a proper home. They skipped over the father part of the equation. The word *biological* surely would have been over their kindergartner's head. What the child knew was that a lady named Mina had brought her into the world, but the Sloans had given her a stable place in that world, an upbringing that would lead to "life everlasting," Darla had said, as if the girl could make any sense of the concept.

The name *Mina* floated through Greta's head the day she turned sixteen, then floated right back out.

***

Martin stepped to the front of the line at the Portland Greyhound depot. It had not been too long of a wait, thanks to the bustling efficiency of the uniformed man taking reservations. The rumble of diesel engines and the *whoosh* of bus doors opening and closing filled the cavernous room, distracting Martin from the noise inside his head.

He felt torn. He was going to visit his secondborn—taking pains to do it—while continuing to refuse overtures from his firstborn for an in-person reunion. He and Eliza had their phone calls. He wasn't ready to see her. Just days ago, he had put her off yet again.

"Daddy, please," she said, and "don't make me beg," exasperation and resignation twinned in her voice.

Martin's heart felt small, saying no, hard as a pebble on the beach in Lincoln City. He hated hurting Eliza, but what else could he do? She had known him when he was whole.

Greta didn't know what he had been like in the past—the responsible, motivated, self-actualized Martin. He had nothing to lose going to California.

"Help you, sir?" the man asked while multitasking, stamping a travel log and waving Martin forward.

"One round-trip ticket to Lafayette, California, please," Martin said, handing over three twenty-dollar bills, plus three ones for a tip. It had only taken him two afternoons panhandling at the corner of Naito and Taylor, plus another timely donation from Eliza and Judith, to gather bus passage to the Bay Area and back. The downtown streets hadn't always been as mean as they were rumored to be.

Sweet sixteen: the right time and the perfect age for Martin to meet his younger daughter, the child he made with Mina. He had tracked down her adoptive parents investigative journalist-style, having retained a working knowledge about how to file successful public records requests. He called in a few favors, too, from old newspaper sources who still remembered him, bankers and politicians and a detective with connections down south.

"Thanks, Harry," Martin said to the retired cop who verified the address for him. "I owe you, buddy."

Mina had ignored Martin's efforts to reach her by email and phone. No matter; he would go it alone. He could nap on his way to the Golden State, or look out the window, enjoying the scenery as conifer forests morphed into redwoods. It would be a nice break from his apartment, old but adequate, the largest window of its beige walls overlooking other buildings, restaurants on the bottom and living spaces on the top. Having his own bed, after the toll sleeping in the back seat of Roger's car had taken on his broken-down body, was certain luxury.

**

Still waiting at the depot, Martin fingered the reporter's notebook he had purchased at the office supply store in his neighborhood, its silver spiral top jutting past the edge of his right coat pocket. He felt comforted by it, more like his old self. He patted the pocket and smiled. On the long bus ride, he would write down what he saw as the landscape rolled by. After meeting Greta, he would tell stories inside the notebook, returning to its pages whenever he needed reminding: how she stood, what she wore, the shape of her face, her first reaction to him. Her countenance, her way of being in the world.

**

The first thing Martin noticed when the cab stopped in front of Reg and Darla Sloan's brick two-story was the yellow-and-black Don't Tread on Me flag flying beneath the stars and stripes on a tall pole in the middle of their well-maintained front yard.

He couldn't help but stare.

Reg Sloan, an imposing six foot four, answered Martin's three solid knocks at the door.

"Yes?" he said, glancing backward, his wife hurrying up behind him and tying on an apron.

Martin made himself as tall as he could. He took out his notebook and flipped it open to the first page, where he had written what to say. He sucked in his gut, cleared his throat, and began.

"My name is Martin Donovan," he read, too loudly. "You don't know me, but I'm the biological father of your daughter, Greta. Her mother, Mina Breckenridge, gave her up for adoption when she was a baby."

The Sloans stared, fish mouthed, at their unexpected visitor. His faded shirt, his wild-man beard.

"This really isn't a good time . . ." Darla ventured, but Reg held up his hand to shush her. He stepped forward onto the stoop and planted a pair of XL-size hands on his hips.

"State your business," he said.

Martin felt slightly woozy but stood his ground.

"I'd just like to meet her," he said, reaching into his jacket pocket for the vital records proving the teen's paternity. "My daughter, I mean," he continued, shrinking back a step. "I've always thought about her, wanted to meet her. I've been ill and out of the country. I've made poor life choices. If only you'd let me meet her, so I can tell her she's been loved from afar. That's it. That's all. Nothing more."

Darla blanched. Reg's face went a dark shade of purple.

A young lady dressed in pink appeared in the doorway. She looked just like Mina, Mina from 1980.

"Who is it?"

Greta's parents parted like the Red Sea.

"I don't know yet, darling," said Reg, squaring up with Martin. "Not one of your party guests, that's for sure."

Martin flinched and addressed the girl. "You're beautiful," he said. "I hope you have a very happy birthday."

Greta raised dark eyebrows. Her eyes sparkled like Mina's. She smiled a thank-you, turned on white high-heeled pumps and disappeared back inside.

Reg Sloan had had enough. "All right, you've seen her," he said with spiraling energy. "You've met our Greta. Greta Hope Sloan. Not Breckenridge, not Donovan. *Sloan.* Now get off my property before I call the police."

Martin went. In the cab he thought about what he would say when Mina picked up his call. Someday. It wouldn't be never.

Part Three

MAYDAY:
2006–2022

Chapter Forty-Eight
Money for Obits Part of Paper's Financial Strategy
November 15, 2006

The day the *Juneau Tribune* started charging for obituaries was a tipping point for Mina, the lowest the newspaper had sunk in all the years she had been there. "Bread from the dead," she intoned when she informed her staff of the new policy, a flatly callous move to make money off the freshly grieving. Customers could still get a short death notice published in the B section for free, but if they wanted anything more than their loved one's name, birthdate, and expiration date, in addition to whatever funeral home was handling disposition arrangements, display ads started at fifty dollars a pop and went up from there.

Louise—lovely, efficient, front desk Louise, who always smelled of lilacs—was obliged to field the phone calls from angry subscribers whose elders in the greatest generation were dying off, only to leave their heirs an unwanted account payable from the newspaper's parent company. It was, after all, a remarkable shift in the *Tribune*'s decades-long custom of providing obituaries at no charge as a courtesy, a fitting way to express appreciation for a loyal—if in certain instances freshly interred—readership. To some, shuffle off this mortal coil and you get a free obit seemed an odd or insensitive gesture, but a fair number of folks were so upset over the change that they came to the office in person to express their objections. A few stood right there in the foyer and shouted at poor Louise.

"Do you mean to tell me you want fifty bucks to print a proper obituary for my uncle Mort?" one said, red-faced, his right hand squeezing and unsqueezing a fist. "He fought at the Battle of the Bulge, for cripes' sake!"

Louise nodded and murmured, "I understand," then handed him a flyer that laid out the specifics of the paper's about-face. "You can have a nice write-up with a black-and-white photo of your loved one. Fifty dollars for one hundred words," Louise said, but the man just grabbed the flyer and stormed out, so she didn't even get to tell him the money would buy five lines in eleven-point Times New Roman and that the ad staff would put a nice black frame around the whole shebang at no extra cost. "He could have said where Mort grew up, what his hobbies were, who he married," Louise said dejectedly. "He could have mentioned the Battle of the Bulge."

***

Mina knew it would have broken every rule Martin had about journalism to put a price on obits. At the *Cascadian* she had often heard him talking, chaplain-like, with someone who had lost a loved one and needed help writing their life story for the paper.

"I hear you saying your brother's pharmacist career was important to him, but what did he enjoy doing in his spare time?" Martin might ask, drawing the bereaved into a more intimate conversation that left them feeling cared for and affirmed. "Ah, bowling. Ned was in a bowling league! The Pinheads, you say? That's hilarious! Sounds like he was a really cool guy."

Ned would get a literary sendoff of sorts, with Martin as his ghostwriter, no charge. He was that invested in the life of the Yamhill community—*his* community.

"I think I know what your dad would say if he heard this bullshit was going down," Mina said to Eliza, who was busy drafting her own letter to management. "He'd march right into the publisher's office and argue with him until they reached a compromise. He wouldn't give in!"

Eliza nodded her emphatic agreement as she hit the Print key so Mina could read her draft on hard copy, ready for mark ups. That's the way they did it before email and digital pages. Before money for obits was a thing.

"It won't stand!" she insisted to Eliza, who knew exactly why she felt so strongly. It was Martin's standard, but one Mina had adopted as her own, another legacy he had left her.

***

The thing that bothered Mina most about charging for obits wasn't the fairly obvious inference that the *Juneau Tribune* was operating on thin financial ice. What bugged her more—much, much more—was that it suggested a certain desperation, a sleazy way of doing business that dipped deep into the reservoir of integrity and goodwill she always tried to maintain with people in her readership.

She wrote a scathing email to make her case:

Dear friends:

Yesterday morning I sat in a meeting with our advertising salespeople, our publisher, our associate publisher, and two newsroom colleagues. What transpired was so disconcerting it has prompted me to write this email.

It's no secret that the Juneau Tribune *has been searching for a financial model that allows it to remain true to its mission: covering the news in and around Alaska's capital city responsibly and objectively, while also turning a profit that satisfies our owners and investors. Recent years have seen the advent of new money-making tools—special sections with "advertorial" content, subscriber incentives, discount rates on display ads, various promotions on the internet—most of which appear to have had a limited positive effect on the bottom line.*

But I'm afraid that the strategy announced this week, a plan to charge for obituaries when, historically, we have provided them for free as a public service, will lead us down a very bad road.

I'm no economist, but I believe that in this instance the end completely fails to justify the means. It feels like a Hail Mary pass that compromises our organization's integrity—and for what? The outside possibility of a few more bucks, made off the backs of folks in mourning? I'm afraid it's a regretful precedent.

Please reconsider the plan discussed at the October 12 meeting. I'm going on record to oppose obit surcharges. If we pursue this course of action, in the long run we will lose subscribers, longtime loyal readers, and most importantly, our priceless respectability in exchange for short-term, dubious gain.

Thank you for reading this email and for taking my thoughts under advisement.

Sincerely,

Mina Breckenridge, managing editor

She drove her point home in the middle of the newsroom the day after the dictum came down.

"It's plain wrong," Mina said to no one in particular.

Max, his piehole full of Taco Bell burrito, mumbled, "Huh?" in case she was talking to him.

"I agree," Naomi said, furrowing her brows and crossing her arms. She thought for a moment. "What if we wrote a letter to management expressing our objections and all of us signed it? That might get their attention."

Max was tuned in by that time. Fletcher had gathered around as well. Tommy was off at the high school, covering the district wrestling meet.

"Slow down there, little lady," Max admonished Naomi, and she frowned harder. "I'm not sure we want to go that far. Sometimes it's best to stay under the radar."

Naomi and Mina looked at each other, unbelieving, retreating into a corner to kibbitz.

"He called me a 'little lady,'" Naomi fumed.

"What a chickenshit," Mina snarled. "It's time the people upstairs heard from us. Just grow a pair, Max."

Fortified, the two of them jumped back into the fray just as Tommy breezed back in from his assignment.

"What are we talking about?" He didn't want to miss anything.

"The *Tribune* has started charging for obits. Naomi wants to send management a letter of protest," said Fletcher, glad to be on top of things for once. He puffed up his chest as he stood next to Tommy. "It's kind of pathetic."

Tommy was still catching up.

"What is? Making money off obits or challenging the corner office brigade?" he asked. "I'm confused."

Mina bellied up to Tommy and laid it on the line. "Let me spell it out to you with an analogy you might understand," she spat, almost without taking a breath, in a thundering, stream-of-consciousness string of words. "You've been able to get a free cup of coffee and a bear claw in the company cafeteria every day since you came to work here, right? How long has that been?"

Tommy shifted from one foot to the other. "Six years, ma'am," he said, looking down at his size-twelve Nikes.

"Right! Six whole years. And what if, all of a sudden, the coffee is a buck and the pastries are two? No more freebies. How would you feel about that?"

Tommy took a step back and fell into a protective sideways stance he learned in karate class.

"I wouldn't like it, I guess," he said, chiseled cheeks flushing. "I'd feel ripped off, like the company was taking away something I'd been getting for nothing all along. It wouldn't be fair!"

Mina's mouth puckered, then opened into a triumphant smile. She gave Naomi a double thumbs-up and narrowed her eyes at Max.

"Thank you, Thomas Stanley Harwood II, for playing our game!" she said, whirling around and marching back to her desk.

"Eliza is already busy drafting a letter. A follow-up to my email," she called over her shoulder. "There'll be a hard copy on her desk soon. I want all of you to sign it before you clock out for the day."

Chapter Forty-Nine
"Bothsidesism" Popular in Wake of Historic Election
April 12, 2010

There were a lot of things to like about my newsroom, but day-after-deadline staff lunches at Mirador, margaritas included, were right at the top of my list. The word *mirador* translated to "lookout," and if there was one thing I had learned from Mina and the others, that was what we did at the *Tribune*: we looked out for our readers. Our stories took deep dives into the guts of the communities we covered and reflected that picture back to them, no matter what it showed—a crazy uncle or an adoring grandmother, a staunch supporter or an angry, embittered writer of letters to the editor.

"Give me the color!" Mina often admonished when any of us pitched her a story idea. She wouldn't accept a piece too heavy on jargon or too light on personality. I could be writing about the city planning commission's new director—yawn—and she wouldn't let me up off the mat until I had uncovered a scintillating nugget on which to hang my lede.

"Even the most boring person on the outside has a fascinating inside," she would say, and she was right. Half the fun was poking around until I discovered the fascinating bit. I would never describe the paper's readership as homogenous, but as sharp and plugged-in as they were, they deserved total transparency—with sprinkles on top.

Ever since Barack Obama's meteoric rise, a sizeable chunk of news junkies in the borough seemed to have gone batshit. That's what we talked about during those lunches at Mirador. Lately we had gotten way too many letters venting thinly veiled antipathy for Obama, and to her credit, Mina rejected a fair number of them. "Ash can that one," she would say to me when I was on opinion-page duty. "Lies upon lies. The bigots are coming out of the woodwork." If a letter contained misinformation or hyperbole, it got eighty-sixed. Mina had legit reasons for everything she did—at work, anyway.

"I don't believe in that old journalistic saw that you have to give both sides of an argument equal weight in service to 'fairness,'" she had said a couple weeks back at lunch, licking second-margarita salt from the back of her hand. "It's as rare as a spotted tiger in New Hampshire when the sides actually *are* equal, and as long as I'm at the *Tribune*, we're dealing in reality. No false equivalence stories in our paper. Remember that."

Me personally? I didn't much care for politics. Never had, even way back when my dad covered city council for the *Cascadian*. I had tagged along with him to a handful of meetings when Mom was working and they couldn't find a babysitter. I must've been only eight or nine, but I tried to pay attention. It had been a chore listening to a bunch of boring old men who liked to hear themselves talk, I thought at the time, and I still felt that way. All you had to do was take one look at Newt Gingrich, or Dick Cheney, or Bernie Sanders for that matter, the up-and-coming chatty Charlie senator from Vermont. Could you even imagine the words per minute issuing from those famously motorized mouths?

My mom did a lot of volunteering with activist groups in the '70s and '80s. Women's rights, equal pay for equal work, civil rights. "I'm marching for the cause," she would say when she left the house armed with cardboard signs, a sack lunch, and an ascendant tone of righteous determination. Throughout my growing-up years she kept me abreast of major political-cultural developments, eight years of Ronald Reagan's "shining city on a hill" and four more of George H. W. Bush's "read my lips." I was twenty-three when Bill Clinton's dalliance with a young White House intern came to light and his equivocation, "It depends upon what the meaning of the word 'is' is," delivered in front of a grand jury, became a monologue punchline for all the late-night cable TV comedians.

Five years later I had grown up, earned a college degree, and become a journalist, making politics an unavoidable, if unsavory, part of my professional landscape. I was twenty-eight and a reporter here in Juneau when Bush II invaded Iraq over weapons of mass destruction that didn't exist, then plastered a post-shock and awe banner on the side of an aircraft carrier falsely declaring Mission Accomplished in *Dewey Defeats Truman* style.

Mina always pointed out that hindsight was indeed twenty-twenty, and I was totally with her on that score. You would have to step into a time-travel machine to put a finger on where the big media-driven disconnect started, but that didn't stop Mina from trying to figure it out: after the Federal Communications Commission torpedoed the fairness doctrine in 1987—thanks for nothing, Ronnie—it was all downhill from there where the quality of US news coverage was concerned, with false-flag freedom of speech bloviations usurping respect for contextualized, fact-based reporting. Instead of *the* news—a summation of the day's top stories designed for general consumption—people started tuning in to *my* news and *your* news, each with its particular and persuasive bent, conservative or liberal, with barely an iota of ideological moderation in between. So began the catastrophic decline from trusted anchors and editors to the choice between Fox News and MSNBC, Hannity and Maddow, Limbaugh and Acosta, accelerating the conflict and confusion that had coarsened societal discourse ever since.

***

The intersection of politics and media was a topic Dad and I debated one out of five times we talked on the phone.

"It wasn't like this in the old days, before the FCC shut down the doctrine," he would say, and I would imagine him shaking his head in disgust. "People, average people and even presidents, used to be able to disagree without going for the jugular. And news folks mostly stayed out of the fray."

Back then, political rivals were opponents, not mortal enemies. Nowadays, I said to Dad—and here I was sure he would be grimacing—watching the TV news was like witnessing a car crash in slow motion, where neither driver gets out alive. That same acquiescence had trickled down to print journalism too.

"What we need is a journalistic renaissance," my dad mused, a note of finality in his voice. "Resistance hasn't worked. If newspapers are to survive, if they're to fulfill their mission, editors have to grow a backbone and stop pussyfooting around. Headlines should say it straight, never mind the political hacks or deep pockets. *Voter Fraud Is a Fever Dream* instead of *Ineligible Voters Show Up at Polls.* That kind of thing."

Sifting reportorial wheat from chaff was my father's strong suit, one that wasn't made of armor anymore.

***

Mina and I agreed that the fairness doctrine's demise was the single most damaging decision ever made during a modern US presidential administration, ushering in the post-truth era and the wholesale dumbing down of the American intellect. It made people less curious and more willfully ignorant, less likely to question leaders' motives and more open to latching on to dangerous conspiracy theories, even easily disprovable ones.

"It was crappy and destructive," Mina said at Mirador, downing the last quarter cup of her strawberry margarita. Naomi followed up with an early '70s song reference. "Bad juju," she hissed. "Leroy Brown bad, and that's an insult to Jim Croce."

***

The angry white man had both his genesis and his rebirth in the wide, fact-free wake left by those who worked hardest to forge a new, upside-down world path. By the middle of the aughts, spouting off about perceived grievances was in. Reading widely and intuitively to discern fact from fiction was out.

It had all been so perplexing and dispiriting.

"Eliza, there will always be people who lay traps, whose lives are self-involved," Dad used to say. "At the same time, there will always be far more good people—people who want to help, people who work to lift us all up—than there are bad." He was correct. The political pendulum took a huge swing when no drama Obama ran for president. Or, back the truck up, when he stood behind the lectern during the 2004 Democratic National Convention and delivered *that* speech—the one that rocketed him into the collective national consciousness. Democrats ate it up, and it positioned him as the next obvious occupant of the Oval Office. The handsome, eloquent first-term US senator from Chicago swooped in on a slogan of hope and change that hummed like humanity in his supporters' ears, hurtling a peace-parched nation back toward center left. When Obama won the White House in November 2008, there was dancing in the streets and at the neighborhood inaugural ball, where he swayed with his wife to Beyoncé's rendition of the Etta James ballad "At Last."

***

The atmosphere in the newsroom on election night had been electric and celebratory. Mina bought party hats and noisemakers. Naomi made chocolate cupcakes with Obama '08 written on the tops in white fondant. I made Dagwood-size sandwiches on sourdough French bread—salami, pepperoni, provolone, tomato, peppers, and lettuce—protein and carbs to see us through the evening. Fletcher contributed pretzels and Tommy brought beer, the good stuff, ales and IPAs. When the Republican nominee, John McCain, conceded at 8:15 p.m. Pacific time, we cheered and toasted Obama's victory. We guessed at the headlines that would lead the front pages the next morning.

Everything felt better then, in that one singular moment. *Obama Makes History*, the *Washington Post* trumpeted. The *New York Times* proclaimed Obama's achievement had swept away "the last racial barrier in American politics." It was like civil rights had come full circle, like the dream of Martin Luther King Jr. had finally, blessedly come true. Obama voters were euphoric, riding an electric blue wave from California to the Dakotas and straight down the Eastern seaboard. I loved what was happening, a power-to-the-people vibe with the potential to pull the country back from the economic brink and provide healthcare to millions who'd had to go without. Most of my journalist friends did too—but then again, we were on the same side.

Behind the scenes, though, Obama's detractors were already plotting to turn his skillful two-step into an utterly partisan tango, to devastating effect. Out there on the interwebs, bubbling up like molten lava inside the far right-wing media ecosystem, close to half the nation's citizens were aghast at what had transpired.

"Socialism!" some talking heads exploded, while others upped the ante with cries of "communism!" that struck a chord at the most extreme edge of the political panorama. Out of those exaggerations rose not an old party or a new party but the Tea Party, a movement whose followers were bent on slashing taxes for the wealthy and ensuring that Reagan's "nine most terrifying words in the English language"—*I'm from the government, and I'm here to help*—reverberated in red states and bled, uncauterized, into blue states as well.

***

Those were sobering times. Confusing too. The fairness doctrine was gone and it felt like everything was on the line. We had to act, right or wrong. At the *Juneau Tribune* a few reporters produced feverishly written, dripping-with-democracy columns and stories tinged either light blue or deep purple, to their everlasting shame. Others swerved right, caving to the publisher's demands that we post our stories online first and fact-check them later, opening ourselves up to criticism both deserved and undeserved. Many of us let phone calls from enraged readers go unanswered, communicating by email instead, at least partially insulated from the slings and arrows that gave us license to claim persecution. We hid. We obfuscated. We spent way too many on-the-clock hours with our heads down. We learned the meaning of implicit bias the hard way, some of us paying with our reputations when we were less than careful, when we let editorialized material slip into our exposés. At staff meetings the culpable cast furtive glances around the room to see if anyone had noticed, but to a person, we were slow to point an accusing finger that might eventually wind up pointing back at us.

***

I need to be honest, even after the fact. Most of us ended up falling into the cynicism trap at one point or another. Blame it on the starvation wages or the ridiculous hours, but it was true. The one shining exception was Mina. She of the old school, not the new media. She of classic pyramid writing—"the most important information always goes on top"—and ironclad sourcing. She of more than one voice in every story, of who, what, when, where, why, and how. She who pivoted to paraphrasing when a direct quote wouldn't do. She of no shortcuts, of one more phone call, of not a single inch going to waste. She of highest integrity, unrelenting work ethic, and heart. Mina wouldn't dream of filing a story that wasn't meticulously researched, with every question answered, something she was proud to attach her byline to, for all the world to see.

"It's not done yet," she would say, handing me back a story draft, the hard copy marked up in bright red, the next press deadline looming. "I've written some suggestions in the margins. Go back in there and make it better."

Chapter Fifty
Juneau Tribune *Joins National Newsroom Purge*
June 3, 2011

"Hey, Eliza. You get one of these?" Thomas Stanley Harwood II was waving a piece of paper with one hand and twiddling a carrot stick between the thumb and forefinger of the other, like Groucho Marx's cigar. The paper was Pepto-Bismol pink, twice the size of those While You Were Out notes no one wants to see on their desk when they get back from a two-hour lunch. But from what I could tell when his hand stopped waving, it wasn't nearly as innocuous as that.

It was a fucking layoff notice!

The guy with the longest name and the shortest active story list in the newsroom had been let go. He was still standing there, waiting for a reaction, crunching the carrot stick, his handsome face creased in consternation. He looked like he expected me to fix things for him.

Tommy was always on some kind of diet. He went in for the fads. Keto, Paleo, even that South Beach bunk. It showed, his commitment to keeping his weight low and his lean body mass high. He rode his bike to the office and worked out at the gym. He was in peak physical condition. But listening to him go on ad nauseum about all those infernal diets, "fueling plans," he called them, really got to me.

Naomi and I were sharing a plate of potato skins at lunch one day when Tommy leaned in and told us we were slowly killing ourselves.

"Criminy—do you two have any idea how many carbs are in those?" he asked, as if he really wanted to find out if we knew the answer, though his question was clearly rhetorical. Naomi had just taken a big bite, savoring the luscious alchemy of potato, cheddar, bacon bits, and scallions.

"No, Tommy," she said, sarcasm dripping from her lips along with the sour cream. "Care to enlighten us?" She put half of the potato skin down and arched one eyebrow in an unadulterated dare. He sat back, perching nine whole fingers on the rim of the table.

"Well, I'll tell you. Way more than your body needs in a day, that's for certain," he said, scripture-sure, his eyes trained on our half-finished meal. "You might consider some steamed veggies and brown rice next time. You'll be glad you did."

***

I looked up at Tommy and flipped the ends of my hair behind my shoulders. "No, man, I didn't get one," I said about the pink note and then, when he got twitchy, "at least not yet." He slapped the paper down on my desk blotter. Notice of Termination, it said on top, but it didn't give a reason. Libel risk? Plagiarism? Missed deadlines? Too many rewrites? That time Mina got after Max for the story about Officer Haas popped into my head, but that was *Max*, not our Tommy.

The note directed him to meet with human resources that very afternoon at four o'clock.

The sound of shuffling paper came from the direction of Max's desk. He had overheard us. "Glad I don't have to worry about getting the boot," he said, loudly, between keyboard strokes. God. He thought he was untouchable.

Tommy sighed, a whittled piece of carrot still poking out from between whitening-stripped teeth. "Guess this means I'll be clearing out my desk today," he said, resigned and unsmiling. "Of all the rotten luck."

The last bite of carrot vanished, and Tommy scooted back to his cubicle. I felt a weird impulse to get up and leave, walk right out the glass front doors and never look back. Newsrooms had been shedding jobs since 2008, since the height of the Great Recession. A third of US print journalism jobs had evaporated in the past five years. It was surprising we had been able to keep the people we still had.

Panic gurgled up inside my esophagus, and my throat tightened. Where would this end? I was the last hired—by Mina, no less, which gave me some insulation—but they were picking on Tommy, not me. As he walked I stared at his rippling triceps, his deltoids, his lats. My face flashed with heat. His shirt fit as well as any professional athlete's. Maybe after he left the paper he would get into some serious bicycle racing, or become a personal trainer. He could do that, couldn't he, even without that middle finger? There were lots of possibilities, I wanted to tell him, but he disappeared around an office divider.

***

The late-afternoon email from Mina was as succinct as it was revealing. "Our owners are unhappy with the paper's profit margin," it said, "and our newsroom is about to take a hit." Employees were "simultaneously the *Juneau Tribune*'s biggest asset and its biggest expense," she noted, but after exhausting other cost-saving measures—a blanket salary freeze, a halt to 401(k) matches, and monthly unpaid furlough days—the company had begun a targeted downsizing program that would touch every department. The newsroom would not be spared. The guillotine would fall on some of us. Tommy was only the first to go.

"It was bound to happen, you know." Max materialized at my desk less than a minute after Tommy departed for HR, his left thumb hitched inside his front pants pocket, his right hand clutching half a Snickers bar. He was chewing so hard his glasses shifted with every grind of his maw, right-left, right-left, his temples pulsing under the effort.

Why were the guys in the newsroom always eating?

Naomi hurried forward, her layered skirts swishing, her wrist bangles chiming. "Oh my gosh, have you heard?" she said, to me more than Max, as if what had gone down was some kind of state secret. I told her yes, I had already spoken to Tommy, and Max managed a raised-eyebrow acknowledgment, neither of which spoke to Naomi's existential dread. Her eyes darkened and she cleared her throat, then mumbled something about rent, and food, and her daughter's mounting college debt.

"I know I won't lose my job," she said doggedly, more question than comment.

Max's mind was elsewhere, on his own small sack of concerns, per usual. He stated the obvious: "We'll be down a man with Tommy gone," unable to resist a self-involved non sequitur. "I wonder whose plate his beat is gonna land on?"

He finished the last bite of his Snickers and harrumphed away just as Mina strode up in full damage-control fashion with Fletcher three paces behind.

"Okay, people, let's huddle," she barked, and all of us did, except Max, but she didn't bother waiting for him.

"Here's what I know. We had a newsroom of six, and now we have five." Mina pulled a loose thread from a button on the front of her jacket. She remained standing while the rest of us sat, a semicircle of dismay and raw nerves. "I'm going to fight like hell to keep it that way, so what I'd like you to do is come to work every day knowing I have your backs. I'll always tell you the truth, to the extent my bosses tell it to me."

Naomi raised her hand, her bangles dropping halfway to her elbow. "When did you know you had to let someone go?"

Mina paused, weighing her response. When her words came, they flowed like water. "The end of last month. I won't lie—I had a feeling it was coming. My newsroom budget's off 10 percent. It needed to be down to 5 percent by the end of the quarter.

We're close. I'm confident we can do 3 percent more with minor adjustments. I can practically guarantee you there'll be no more losses in the newsroom."

She used a knuckle to massage the sagging skin under each eye. "I had a rough night," she admitted and cleared her throat. Everyone looked skeptical, maybe me most of all.

"My job was to pick someone on the merits and tell them this morning. HR meets with people who get termed on Fridays, to help sort them out before the weekend. Tommy'll get COBRA and a few months' severance pay. But I think you'll all agree he was the logical choice."

We nodded concurrently, guiltily, like we were picking the bad guy out of a lineup. He hadn't been so awful, Thomas Stanley Harwood II. A little green, a lot unsophisticated, but sweet, too, in his own way. On the bright side, we would save a whole line of copy wherever his byline used to appear, and we wouldn't be subjected to his incessant health tips anymore. But damn, I was going to miss those muscles.

Chapter Fifty-One
Homeless Girl's Story Haunts Mina
August 6, 2013

Mina stood in the middle of the newsroom and took stock. Her eyes landed on Fletcher's desk, a veritable quandary of personal items including a small army of vintage Pez candy dispensers lined up against the divider, an eclectic collection featuring Goofy, Luke Skywalker, Dorothy from *The Wizard of Oz*, and Tweety Bird.

Aside from the items adorning his workspace, there were few indicators that Fletcher's everyday personality was anything but bland. He kept his head down and did his job without fanfare, exhibiting a practiced monotone whether he was chatting with Louise in the lunchroom or interviewing sources on the phone.

"Of course, sir. Yes. We can go over direct quotes, but I won't be providing you with my story draft," he might say, hunched over the dialing pad, the cord wound around an index finger. "That's against newspaper policy," he would add, his sandpaper voice rising not a single discernible decibel. Yelling and cajoling were Mina's territory. She was the one who practiced tough love on surly sources, explaining the way things worked so her staff didn't have to.

Fletch was big on rules. He followed them to the letter inside the office, never once straying from their strictures or questioning their intent. Fake a migraine to get out of covering a meeting for a vacationing colleague? Wouldn't happen with Fletcher. Leave the office early on a Friday afternoon? Unheard of in his world. Even his ready-to-wear fashion choices screamed conformity. He favored short-sleeved plaid cotton shirts with coordinating solid ties, worn under the same navy blazer and khaki pants every day of the week. Reliable, predictable, steady—that was Fletcher.

So it came as a bit of a surprise to everyone the day he hauled in a ten-inch-square cardboard sign, hand-lettered with the words *All I know is just what I read in the papers, and that's an alibi for my ignorance.* Everyone watched as he Scotch taped it to the edge of his cubicle divider, eraser-clapped his hands together, and stepped back to admire his handiwork.

"My buddy Steve at the model railroad club made it for me," he announced with a gleeful smile. "It's a Will Rogers quote. Pretty ironic, don't you think?"

Fletcher was the only newsroom employee who still had a Rolodex. Classic black plastic, the card tabs stained with ink and skin oil. "My secret weapon," he called it, our collective curiosity rising and falling with his words. His Rolodex probably just listed alphabetized names and phone numbers for everyone on the planning commission and the development review board, along with Domino's Pizza, under *D* for a quick lunch delivery. In a contemporary journalist's mind—which is to say, skeptical bordering on cynical—there was always room for curiosity.

Mina hadn't been aware of Fletcher's friend outside of work, this guy Steve, or that either of them were into model trains. And yeah, the idea that newspapers gave rise to ignorance was indeed kind of ironic. And funny. Reliable, steady Fletcher funny.

"When I die, my headstone is going to say, 'Here lies Fletcher. A guy you could count on,'" he announced to the entire newsroom once, with a Fletch-level flourish of dark humor, causing Naomi and Eliza to muse out loud about what messages might be chiseled onto their own grave markers.

"Mine would say, 'Not all those who wander are lost,'" Eliza said, quoting *The Lord of the Rings*.

Naomi played along. "My epitaph would be 'girl just wanted to have fun.'"

Depressing, Mina thought, but that's what her coworkers figured they deserved.

"What the hell was that?" she joked to Eliza when Naomi was out of earshot. "Have you ever known her to want to have fun?"

"Right," Eliza said, but didn't let Mina off the hook. "Well, what would yours say?"

"'She kept too many secrets,' maybe."

"Um, okay," Eliza replied, shifting from one foot to the other. "But what secrets are you keeping?"

***

It was Fletcher who took a first stab at talking Eliza down when she came back from her morning assignment in the suburbs, rattled and seething.

"Those kids!" she huffed, referring to the ones she had encountered not two hours before. They were not doing well in the foster care system administered by the Alaska Office of Children's Services. She was sure of it.

"It's supposed to protect them, to make their lives easier," she blurted as she stormed through the newsroom on the way to her desk. Fletcher stood near his cardboard sign, slurping his coffee, right in the line of fire.

He bit but likely wished he hadn't.

"What kids are you talking about? The foster parent story?" he asked, going directly to the point, very not-Fletcher. "Are they all right?"

Eliza stopped short, her body ricocheting off the wall, nearly knocking his mug from his hands. "Yes, the foster story! And they are most certainly *not* all right! Why else would I be so upset?" She looked over his shoulder, at his sign, then right past him to her next mark.

Mina was at the Xerox machine in the hallway, making copies, when Eliza blew by. "The system. I'm talking about the system!" she yelled. "How do these people sleep at night?"

Mina tried soothing Eliza with obvious platitudes. "It's unconscionable what folks try to get away with," she said, stretching her back, feeling her shoulder blades touch in the middle. "Plain fucking wrong, that's what it is." The copy machine wound down and stopped whirring altogether. Mina lifted the collated sheafs from the trays and started paper clipping them together in separate batches. Eliza moved closer. Mina turned to face her.

"Okay then," she said, "tell me what happened at your foster parent interview."

Mina knew better than to indulge Eliza's dramatic side. She slowed her speech in an effort to calm her. "I'm here, Eliza," she said. "It's me. Whatever it is, we can talk about it." Her altered tone didn't make any difference. Eliza detonated in a fit of angry indignation.

"That woman I interviewed is such a goddamn phony!" she shouted. "She's fostering six kids, and from what I could tell, none of them are properly cared for." Her eyes narrowed. "The youngest one was in diapers, crawling around on that beat-up old porch of hers. Probably got splinters in her knees."

Mina listened as Eliza carried on with her screed.

"She wouldn't even let me in the house, can you believe it? We stood outside the whole time, with those poor kids sitting there like trapped rats. She ordered them to hang around as props during the interview, no question."

Eliza had more on her mind.

"Did you know the system pays up to twenty-five dollars a day for each foster kid? That's a shit ton of coin on the monthly, even when you take out expenses. It's a no-brainer. She's doing it for the money."

Mina knew she had lost Eliza on this one. She would have to run interference, talk to the foster mom and social services herself, in order to save the story, a scheduled front-pager she was counting on. The system was admittedly overrun, with hundreds more kids needing placement than the number of available foster homes. But getting the green light to foster in the borough wasn't a slam dunk. Certain safeguards—background checks, home visits, personal references—had been built in to prevent fraud and the continued suffering of minors whose parents or guardians were unable to care for them.

Photos had been shot of all six kids draped across the steps with a bottle-blond Andrea Crowder hovering above them, looking benevolent. But photos or no photos, there was no talking Eliza out of her spider-sense conclusions. Mina asked her what had tipped her off to Crowder's mendacity.

"She said she'd prayed about it, that God told her to help those children," Eliza said, her nostrils flaring. "No way. They're captive to something they can't control. Social services is failing them, and even if it's on the opinion page instead of the front page, I'm going to write about that. I've never felt so blatantly lied to in my life."

***

Mina understood. She had reported her share of hard-luck stories over the years. The story of the homeless girl who washed her face in a gas station sink before school every morning would go down as one of the saddest and most troubling pieces she had written in her career, which by now spanned three decades. Sad, because Mina felt deep inside that the child was caught in a downward spiral not of her own making, a vortex from which she was unlikely to wrest herself. Troubling, because she never found out what happened to Desirée Joy, even after she reached the age of majority and Mina inquired about her welfare with all the usual agencies. It was as if she had simply vanished, as if she had never been.

"She was only in the third grade," she said of the girl, whose name she knew but wasn't allowed to mention in her story, a section anchor in the *Register* about a sharp increase in the homeless student population in Contra Costa County that year. Privacy concerns, school district officials said solemnly before giving Mina limited access to the eight-year-old, whom they had handpicked for the interview. A counselor sat nearby the entire time, listening in and later telling Mina what material she could and couldn't use—restrictions Mina normally would not have agreed to but did in this particular case, because she felt compelled to get the girl's story out in the world.

Sometimes—not very often, and never Fletcher—reporters broke their own rules.

They had sat on a park bench together that day in 1989. Mina gave Desirée a bag of Doritos, and she ate her way through their conversation, brown bangs falling in front of her eyes and cheese dust crusting her lips as she talked about dueling loyalties, shyly but forthrightly. She was far too rough and worldly for her age.

"My job is to help her stay clean," Desirée had said of her mother and her mother's drug addiction. She got up once, to deposit the empty chips bag in a garbage can whose lid was painted to resemble a purple monster's mouth. "Nom, nom," she joked when she dropped the bag in the mouth surrounded by giant white teeth. It was the only time Mina saw her smile.

She didn't care about the McKinney-Vento Homeless Assistance Act, a 1980s-era law that set aside federal funds for public school programs supporting students without stable housing. She didn't want to know what it was, and she didn't believe it could protect her, help her find food or a permanent home or a real shower in warm water, not cold. Her dad was in prison. Her grandparents were in Mexico.

What the girl cared about was keeping her last remaining lifeline alive. Otherwise, she said, "I'll be alone."

Desirée reacted to terms like *social services*, *child advocates*, and *temporary shelter* with clear irritation, shifting her waiflike body on the bench, responding succinctly to the questions Mina posed, as honestly as she was able.

How many schools had the girl attended in the past two years? Three.

Where did she sleep at night? Her friend's, mostly. Sometimes at her mom's boyfriend's place.

Were there adults at her school she could count on? Yes. Maybe. Not sure.

Only when Mina circled back to the topic of her mom did Desirée offer anything more substantive.

"She's really nice to me most of the time," she confided, her voice falling to a whisper. "She helps me with my math homework. Sometimes when there's money, we go to Burger King, or to the mall. She only gets mean when she's using."

How often was that? Mina ventured. Tapped her pen on her notepad, anxious, empathetic.

The girl's dewy eyes turned cold and blank. She had left the conversation.

"I don't know," Desirée said after too long. She picked up her backpack, a hot pink rabbit's foot fastened to one side, and put it on. One arm, then the other. She stood up, flicked her bangs off her forehead. She shook Mina's hand.

"It was nice to meet you," she said, "but I have to get to school now." She started walking east toward campus a block away, head up, shoulders squared, the rabbit's foot bouncing.

Chapter Fifty-Two
Eliza Pitches Adoption Story to No Avail
January 10, 2014

Work had been wearing me out more than usual. I barely had time to eat and sleep between deadlines. Everyone still had their usual stories to do, plus now we needed to handle everything Tommy used to cover. Mina said there was no use complaining, that he wouldn't be replaced, that his position was kaput, that there was no money, so we zipped our lips and did the best we could. We swallowed the extra hours, turned in the copy, and met our story quotas, but it took a toll. I wasn't exercising or meditating, and my primary relationship was halfway to dead. Oh, and I even started buying my own goddamn reporter's notebooks. Part of the 3 percent Mina needed to make up in the newsroom budget. Rat bastards!

About Abe. Abe Marsh was my boyfriend, the purported love of my life, but at that juncture he barely figured into my everyday routine, and there was no way one person could seriously connect with another if they hardly ever saw them, and if they weren't paying attention. Then there was the issue of whether you were with the person you should be with in the first place, if you were brave enough to face it. When I was alone with my conscience, it telegraphed the bare truth that I was just not that into Abe. He wouldn't be my soulmate even if I believed in that stuff. And my conscience was always right.

It was a fair question: Would I rather be by myself or with a crappy boyfriend? Ivy got right to the meat of it when we met for drinks after work at Café LaRoche, located on the hip side of the city, the west side, where we hadn't been before.

"Abe's trouble—I know it and you know it." Ivy craned her neck to check out the merchandise at the bar, adjusting her emerald-green silk blouse to highlight her *décolletage*. The place was decorated in shabby chic, more corner pub than fine dining, but Ivy had heard the pours were generous, and we found out they were. The café was packed, even on a weeknight. Ivy caught the eye of a twentysomething hardbody, smiled a Cheshire cat smile, plucked the maraschino cherry out of her Vodka Collins, and popped it into her mouth, tying the stem into a knot with her tongue and displaying it for his approval. It was one of her more bourgeois yet indisputably impressive talents.

"Yes! I've still got it!" she shouted, pumping both fists in the air. Mr. Hardbody and his friend had their heads together up at the bar, assessing Ivy's performance, but it was tough to tell whether they were a couple or looking to score. They turned around and slow clapped their appreciation. Ivy stood and took an exaggerated bow. I cringed and looked away, burying my head in my hands. Ivy turned away from the gawkers and nursed her drink, attempting to take things down a notch. She was a bit of a showboat sometimes, but she had a good heart.

"Why's Abe trouble?" I inquired innocently, a pretend ploy, a lead balloon. "Sounds like you think he's the wrong man for me."

I put on my sad face, lower lip way out, but Ivy wasn't buying it. I expected her to say I could do better, but also that she had seen worse.

Ivy spit a piece of ice back into her glass indelicately. She wound a lock of her hair, flat-ironed to oblivion, around two fingers and cleared her throat. "The first building block of any relationship is trust, and you can't trust that dude, Eliza," she said dispassionately. "Tell me I'm wrong."

She was correct, of course. I couldn't trust Abe. Not since he filched twenty bucks from my purse—to buy me a birthday present, he had said, what a worm—and definitely not since I found those text messages on his phone to his skanky former girlfriend in New Jersey, the ones I couldn't bring myself to insist he explain because I already knew what they meant.

One of my rules was never to ask a question if you didn't want to hear the answer.

"But he's a *musician*," I whined to Ivy, "and he's got a lot of other good qualities too," I insisted, though I knew I wouldn't be able to name a single convincing one if asked.

My friend from school was unmoved. She pressed me hard.

"Girl, you're just playing house with Abe. Get real—how many times have you seen him this week?"

Wrong question. How many times had I *wanted* to see him this week? Zero, that was how many. And work was a handy excuse. Maybe I was more of a one-month stand type of gal, not cut out for long-term relationships. I supposed I ought to do something about that, navel-gaze a while for starters, but it felt like too big an effort to make without disappearing into the woods, brooding and pity-partying inside a broken-down cabin over a long weekend with only me, myself, and I for company. Oh, and a tall stack of books, a bottle of Amaretto, and a bunch of scented candles. It would never happen though. I wasn't the kind of girl who ditched out. I had my reporting job to do.

Ivy was *exactly* that kind of girl but without the cabin, books, or a need for self-examination. For her, time between boyfriends was never long, one reason she wanted me to kick Abe to the curb and move on. Not so much with my life but to a different man.

"He's got to go," she declared and ordered another Vodka Collins as the clock above our booth ticked toward midnight. I looked up and noticed all the décor in the café was cat related. Shabby chic *and* cat related. Ick and double ick.

Ivy's gravitas was relentless and inescapable. "You know you deserve better, girlfriend," she said, but I knew no such thing. Lately, it seemed, I deserved exactly what I got, including all those niggling misgivings about the meaning of my career. What was I doing at the newspaper if my hard work wasn't advancing the cause of humanity? I would have to have a heart-to-heart with Mina about that.

***

"If one more thing lands on my plate, it'll push dessert right off the edge." That's how I started the conversation, first thing, when Mina and I were the only ones in the newsroom. The early birds, the stalwarts with the jittery nerves and bloodshot eyes to prove it. I thought it was clever, the play on words—the image of meatloaf, green beans, and potatoes supplanting a cherry-topped slice of cheesecake on my pretend Corelle.

"I'd hate that," I groused, swizzle sticking my coffee.

At first Mina's face was a blank slate, textbook phlegmatic. Then she squinched it in a perturbed sweet-baby-Jesus-I've-heard-this-a-hundred-times kind of way. She picked up a short pile of papers, shuffled them like playing cards, and handed me one that was dog-eared in the corner. From the suggestion box up front near Louise's desk, where readers could submit ideas for stories. A literal Pandora's box, and this one was a real doozy: *Please write about Jed Hames, who has volunteered at the Habitat for Humanity ReStore for more than ten years.*

"Are you kidding me?" My voice rose an octave higher and a number of decibels louder than I meant it to. "An old, retired guy who volunteers somewhere is hardly news! I'm so buried in work I can't even get to the story I want to do most." I looked at Mina with eyes that probably resembled a dying basset hound's.

"What story's that?" Mina asked with all the forbearance she could muster. I spoke with measured determination, like a teenager trying to convince their parents to turn them loose at the mall with questionable friends.

"The one about adoption." Mina shifted in her chair. "The lady at the park and rec who's trying to find her birth mother."

Mina's cheeks flushed. She took a sharp breath in.

"No," she said. "No way. That's absolutely not going to happen." She scooted her chair back and stood up, my signal to vamoose. She wouldn't give me a reason. She was adamantly, suspiciously obstructive. It didn't feel like Mina. It didn't feel like us.

Chapter Fifty-Three
Mina Files Freedom of Information Act Request
August 3, 2015

Mina logged off after filing her fourth story of the day, a monster investigative piece about downtown retail lease inequities in greater Juneau. She had worked on it for months. The property managers had tried stonewalling her, and when that didn't work, they sent the matter upline to legal, further delaying the inevitable. Mina called in a few favors with sources she had nurtured over the years and filed a Freedom of Information Act request for a raft of public documents, papers attorneys should've handed over in the first place. She wouldn't give up. Her tenacity paid off when she wrote that Jaris Limited was giving preferential treatment to some of its tenants based on personal relationships. Because of her dogged reporting, the company would be paying a hefty Alaska Department of Labor and Workforce Development fine, but the worst part was the beating its formerly peerless reputation was about to take. Jaris CEO Herb Dalrymple forced a meeting with Mina once he realized the jig was up. This was a man who had never lowered himself to pay a call to a newsroom. Before that story, he hadn't needed to.

"You really don't want to do this," Dalrymple growled to Mina after marching into her office like he owned the place. "You could ruin me." He had no appointment. He had gotten past Louise by telling her he was there to buy advertising, the lying sack.

Mina met him standing up. "Oh, but I do," she said, inviting him to sit, which he begrudgingly did. Dalrymple proceeded to lay out his case in thou-dost-protest-too-much detail, presenting her with a two-inch stack of lawyerly papers in a pitifully misguided effort to dissuade her. It was a losing gambit.

"In fact," Mina said as she shook his hand and ushered him out of the building, "it's what I was hired to do."

***

Mina had used the afternoon to greatest effect, beating the newspaper's deadline like a dirty, dusty carpet.

"Reminds me of the time that slimy realtor tried to pressure me into writing my story his way, not mine," she said, posed mannequin still against the west-facing windows of the office, her right palm pressed against the glass, her long legs crossed at the ankles. The look on her face was distant, wistful, reflective of some other time and place. She drew her left hand up and placed it on the window, too, uncrossed her legs and stretched her long back. "But I told him what was what," she said, turning her head a quarter turn. "He wasn't going to get preferential treatment from me, no matter what a big shot he thought he was."

Naomi, Eliza, and Fletcher had all stopped typing and started listening. Max, as usual, was oblivious.

"Dorsey," Mina said, nodding to herself, extracting information from the recesses of her memory. "The Herb Dalrymple of the '80s. His name was Patrick Dorsey."

Chapter Fifty-Four
Eliza Finds Out about Secret Baby
August 6, 2015

Even after a year and a half, my speculative adoption feature still burned hot as a viable story. I had met with Sandra the swimming aficionado—who came to Alaska in a past life, when she was married to an army captain stationed at Fort Wainwright—three times already. Once for coffee, twice at the pool. I imagined a complete feature package: the main story, first-person from Sandra's point of view with photos of her as a child and teenager in the home where she grew up. A sidebar interview with her adoptive parents, Polish nationals who immigrated to California in the late 1980s, where they opened a coin-operated laundry. To top it off, a second sidebar about the legal and emotional intricacies of undoing a closed adoption.

Today was the day I would push the envelope. I wasn't going to let Mina leave the office before I got an answer. She was at her desk when I rushed around the divider.

"I can't stop thinking about that poor woman," I said, offering Mina a look at my copious reporting notes. "She wants to find her bio mom more than anything." I reminded her I met Sandra after a parks board meeting, that she had approached me about a story on the new swim center.

"Are you a swimmer yourself?" I asked Sandra then. "Will you use the new pool?"

"Oh, definitely," Sandra replied. "I've been swimming since my adoptive parents gave me lessons for my sixth birthday in 1994. Great cardiovascular exercise, and it's good for people of any age. No stress on the joints."

I recalled to Mina that at the time, my source had appeared suddenly nervous, as if she had confessed a terrible secret.

"It's not that I don't appreciate what my folks did for me," Sandra said, "but I'm determined to find my birth mother. I'm on a quest, you might say. I know it's silly after so many years, but I can't seem to let it go."

I had assured Sandra her aspirations were anything but silly. That I could fully, completely relate.

"I closed my notebook and put my hand on her shoulder," I said. "I told her the next part of our interview would be off the record. I told her, 'I know how you feel. My dad left us when I was ten.'"

I drew a bead on Mina, looking for a reaction. A confession, even. Surely she remembered the kiss, the mistletoe moment. Surely she recalled her part in what had gone down. Her arms were crossed and her eyes were fixed, a mountain that couldn't be moved.

"So what do you think?" I asked anyway.

She laid her markup pen on the desk. "I can't rationalize the resources," she said flatly. Her response seemed rehearsed. "We can barely put out a paper as it is. I need you on your regular beat."

A dam burst inside me. I felt myself start to unspool.

"That's *so* not fair! You abandoned me, Mina!" I yelped. "All of a sudden, you were just *gone*. Not even a note to say where you were going or why you left. First you, and then my dad! I totally get how Sandra feels. Don't keep this story from me."

The blood left Mina's face and returned a few seconds later, her cheeks as red as a bad sunburn. "It's not the same thing, Eliza! Sandra was adopted. You weren't. You had two parents who knew you, loved you, from the beginning. Trust me, you don't want to open this door." She started gathering her things. I stepped into the side aisle and blocked her path to the exit.

"That's exactly what my dad said, Mina. 'Trust me.'" My words vibrated with righteous anger, with a young child's hurt.

Mina swept close to me, almost menacing. "I'm going to tell you something," she said. She nudged me into an empty office and proceeded to unravel a mystery that was more than two decades old.

"I didn't have a choice back then." Mina's upper body went rigid, her speech percussive. "At least I felt like I didn't." Her stoicism faltered. Words tumbled out. "I was pregnant, Eliza. It was your dad's. Raising a child would have ruined everything for me, and for you and your parents. That's why I left Oregon. It wasn't about you."

Finally, the truth was out. I had one question to begin with. "Did my dad know?"

"Not at first," Mina answered guardedly.

"Wait, you got pregnant with Dad's baby and didn't tell him?"

My old mentor looked cornered. She took a big breath. "When I was ready, I called your dad about the baby, Eliza. I told him she was his. He asked if he could help, but I didn't want him to."

I recoiled. I staggered back two paces.

"After she was born I had to let her go," Mina continued. "A nice couple adopted her. I made the best decision I could."

I went wobbly as Mina's appalling story sank in. She plucked three tissues from a box on the conference table and handed them to me as my tears flowed, hot and bitter. She must have rendered this moment in her mind a hundred times.

"So you're telling me I have a half sister? Out there somewhere?" I gestured and stammered and spluttered. My eyes burned and shot daggers Mina's way. "She was Daddy's, and you gave her up? Oh my fucking God, I can't believe this."

I felt the enormity of Mina's confession all at once. The lies, the obfuscations, the betrayals. I screamed at her: "All this time, and my father *knew*?"

I made a mental note: call Dad and excoriate him.

Mina coughed a couple of times. Her eyes went as dark as Max's on his worst day. She turned around, and with a stage performer's bluster, strode out of the room, leaving the door ajar. I heard her inform the remainder of the newsroom that for her, the day represented a production record.

"I've got three twenty-plus inchers in the queue along with the Dalrymple caper," she announced. My coworkers had all aimed their chairs, like orienting arms on a compass, to take in Mina's words.

"That's almost an entire page of copy without ads. Can I get an amen?"

It was a huge brag, perfect cover for her abominable revelations to me. Still, it wasn't out of line, given the circumstances at the *Juneau Tribune*. Things were getting crazier by the day: the head-spinning velocity of the news cycle, the expectations, the 24-7 responsibility. Day or night, it didn't matter. Our staff covered it all and then some.

I wiped my face and walked back to the newsroom in time to see Mina stride up to a wooden sign hanging in the hallway with EVERY DAY'S A WORKDAY carved into it, a gift from the publisher, who sincerely believed he had come up with the phrase, that it was original thought. She parked herself underneath it and pointed upward.

"They never let up. Remember that," she barked, looping her bag's faux-leather strap over her head and smoothing it across her cable-knit-sweatered torso. "They never will. It's going to drive me to an early grave."

She wagged a warning finger at the group. "And all of you, too, if you let it."

As Mina exited the building my constitution crumbled and my heart went kerflooey. *So Dad knows about my half sister. Does Mom?*

Chapter Fifty-Five
Judith Castigates Mina for Confession
August 25, 2015

Judith wound a hand-knitted scarf around her neck and gave Harold a peck on the cheek as she prepared to drive the short distance from their house to the *Juneau Tribune*, where she intended to tell Mina off. It had taken her two weeks to gin up the courage, but she was ready. Mina had no right to spill the beans about her affair with Martin to Eliza, let alone tell her about their love child. It was a clear breach.

"When something's broken, you take steps to fix it. At least you try," Judith said to her husband as she turned the knob and opened the door, chilly air entering as she exited.

***

"Do you have an appointment?" Louise went into full gatekeeping mode when Judith showed up and asked to see Mina. "I believe she's on deadline."

Judith knew a thing or two about the *Tribune*'s press schedule. She willed her face to go soft. It caught Louise off guard.

"Today's publication day, isn't it?" she said, sugar sweet, aware Louise couldn't argue the point. "I'd like a few minutes of Mina's time."

Mina was reapplying lipstick, squinting into a small oval mirror wedged between the *AP Stylebook* and a beat-up copy of *Webster's Dictionary* on her bookshelf, her back to her desk. The mirror caught Judith's approach. Mina snapped to and turned around, a feeble smile complementing freshly glossed lips. She checked her watch. She had a lunch date. "Why, Judith! To what do I owe the pleasure?"

Judith's heart and mind were fury machines. "I think you can figure that out." She pressed ample hips against the edge of Mina's desk, her flowing skirt bunching over the top. Her quilted vest stretched across her bosom as she made herself as tall as she could, long strands of wavy gray hair catching on the vest's large decorative buttons. Mina's manicured bob remained stubbornly in place, her fitted knit dress accentuating well-defined, pantyhose-clad legs. *Control top, Barely There by Hanes*, Judith thought.

"Back to dresses for the office, I see." She looked her nemesis up and down. "Good move."

Mina deflected. "If you were hoping to catch Eliza, she's on deadline right now," she said coolly.

Judith scowled, deepening the lines on her face. "I'm aware of that." Her words bit. "It's you I wanted to see."

Mina started to explain that she had a midday engagement, but Judith wasn't budging.

"I can give you until eleven thirty," Mina said. She glanced again. Her watch said eleven twenty.

It was all the time they would need. Mina walked them across a corridor into the office where she had come clean to Eliza about her dalliance with Martin and about the baby. The women sat across from each other, the table between them a formidable physical barrier.

Mina smiled pertly, staying quiet. Judith began.

"It's no secret that there's never been any love lost between the two of us," she said, "and that's all right with me. But what's *not* all right is your interfering—yet again—in my family's life."

Mina started to say she hadn't done any such thing. Judith stopped her cold.

"I'm over your affair with my ex-husband. Ancient history. But you had no right to tell Eliza about Martin's other child!"

Judith watched the cogs inside Mina's brain turn and catch. An anger balloon expanded inside her chest. "In case you're wondering, Mina, yes, she told me." Judith donned a self-satisfied look. "She came to my house right after you spilled the beans because she was worried I didn't know."

Mina stayed steady, staring right back at her. "You can't blame me for this, Judith. You had a hundred chances to talk to Eliza, and you didn't do it. She asked me point-blank, so I told her. It's not my fault your relationship with your daughter is in shambles."

Judith sat in stunned silence. Mina kept after it.

"Why didn't you tell her? Who were you protecting? Martin,

maybe? Or yourself? Certainly not Eliza!"

Mina huffed, her breaths coming fast and loud, like the chug of a freight train.

Judith tried to calm herself. She had no immediate rejoinder. Her mind and body went boggy. All the old emotional wounds gaped at once. This whore had slept with her husband! How could she speak to her like this? But also, whose responsibility had it been to inform Eliza?

Fuck. Mina was right.

"All right, Mina. You've got me there." Judith wasn't getting anywhere. Her voice went from shrill and fast to low and slow. "Could we come to terms? I'm so tired of all this. Can we please just stop arguing?"

Mina looked eager to assent. "Taking this discussion down a notch is a good idea."

Judith nodded.

"I'm sure you can imagine how hard it was for me to give up my baby."

Judith nodded again. Her mother's heart felt the agony Mina's had endured.

She sighed and said her piece. Gently, insistently. "Neither of us can change what happened at the *Cascadian*. It was a long time ago. And the decision to let go of your child must have been wrenching. But no matter how old she gets, Eliza will always be *my* baby. I know she's in journalism for the duration, and that's your territory. But I'm begging you not to influence her personal life any more than you already have."

Ten minutes were up. Mina stood, a tower of power. She needed to make her appointment. The next arrow in her quiver was sharp, ready to meet its target.

"You don't know shit about what I went through, Judith!" she spat, taking two steps toward the door. "I never got a chance to raise my own daughter. But I can assure you that if I had, I would've told her everything. We would have been honest with each other."

***

Judith was watering her parched summer garden when the phone erupted with her preferred ringtone, a mechanical-sounding version of "Hava Nagila." She had left her cell on the kitchen counter to keep it from getting wet. She ran into the house, almost tripping over the unfurled hose, to reach it before it went to voicemail.

"Hello?" she puffed, regaining her footing. "Eliza?"

"I hear you went to see Mina," Eliza said accusatorily, her voice dry and icy. "I really wish you hadn't. I'm a big girl. I can handle my own stuff."

Judith would never stop being surprised at the way her daughter perceived her best intentions. She had only been trying to help.

"It was enough to find out you knew about Dad and Mina's baby for years, Mom. Years! The whole newsroom didn't have to hear about it."

Wait, Judith thought, wiping her soil-stained right hand on her gardening apron. She and Mina had been discreet, hadn't they? They had taken their conversation into an office to keep it private. Perhaps their voices had carried? Judith remembered there had been some shouting.

"Naomi told Fletcher, who told Max, who told me," Eliza complained. "Do you know how embarrassing that was, Mom?"

The worry lines on Judith's face got deeper just listening to her daughter's harangue.

"I had to explain the whole thing to them. It was humiliating. They're my colleagues, Mom, the people I work with every day. And Mina! She's our leader. Because of you, she lost so much face . . ."

Mina. Judith didn't give a hoot about her. The only one she cared about was Eliza. Her apology came swiftly. "Please, sweetheart," she said, fatigue and pain garbling her words. "I'm sorry. It's been hard enough on you, learning the truth after so many years." She used a phrase she got from her therapist, long ago in Portland. "Your betrayal trauma is yours alone. I had no right to intervene."

She felt Eliza seethe all the way across town.

"You're damn right about that, Mama," she said and slammed down the phone.

Chapter Fifty-Six
Eliza Confronts Martin about Baby with Mina
September 2, 2015

Eliza left a message when Martin didn't pick up. She wasn't sure she had the right number until she heard his recording.

"You've reached Martin Donovan, former newshound, current advocate for the homeless. If you're a bill collector, I can't help you. If you're anyone else, talk to me."

Beeeeeeeeeep.

That sense of humor. The Martin Eliza loved.

"Dad," she said, her voice porridge-thick with emotion. "Call me back. I need to talk to you about Greta."

It's your Sunshine Girl, she wanted to add but didn't. He didn't fucking deserve it.

***

Fresh off a long shift at Dignity Village, all Martin wanted to do was go home and veg out. Flop on the couch, turn on the tube, get lost in one of the old classics. *Casablanca*, maybe. Bogart and Bergman. Here's looking at you, kid.

He emptied his pants pockets and checked his phone. Eliza. She had called. She had his number. Got it from Mina, probably. He would have to call her back. He rummaged in the pantry for a snack and found the free bag of popcorn city officials had passed out to folks lining the village's periphery. He sat down, staring at the phone on the coffee table. Like he could make it evaporate, worried it might ring again.

He listened to his daughter's voicemail. Once, twice. He needed to have this conversation with her. There was nothing else to do. He girded himself and called her back.

***

"Dad!" There was Eliza. His little girl, his grown-up daughter. Martin could hear the *tap-tap-tap* of keyboards, reporters composing stories in a busy newsroom.

Right. Thursday. Deadline day.

"Sunshine," Martin said tentatively, having lost his appetite for stale popcorn. "Do you have a minute? I want to tell you how sorry I am."

She didn't miss a beat. Her words hit him rapid-fire. "You're *sorry*, Dad? That's seriously all you've got?"

Martin didn't have a handy comeback.

"This is going to take way more than a minute," Eliza hissed. "And you're going to have to do better than sorry."

There was nothing Martin could say, nothing he *should* say to pacify her, to assuage her anger and disappointment.

Eliza, three steps ahead of him, had a proposal. "Monday's Labor Day. I'm off work because Naomi is on breaking news duty. I'll have all day to talk. Can we make that happen? Can you call me at nine o'clock your time?"

***

Thank God Eliza hadn't demanded to see him. He looked and felt like hell. But she was up in Juneau, a thousand miles away, so that wasn't going to happen on the fly. Martin took a holiday break from the village, screwed up his courage, and called her at the prearranged time. He clasped the handle of his favorite emotional-support coffee mug as he tried to make amends.

"I didn't know what to do," Martin said, mealy-mouthed. "You were only thirteen."

Eliza wasn't buying what he was selling. "And a half," she countered. "I could have handled it, Dad. I would have preferred you'd trusted me."

That was a mistake, Martin admitted. Even as a young teen, Eliza had been smart and resilient. "It wasn't you," he assured her. "And it wasn't Mina either. The problem was me. I didn't trust myself."

Martin went on to enumerate the reasons: His dystonia, not knowing if he would get better, feeling that if he didn't, his second baby was best left a secret. His fears, his recklessness, his impulsiveness, his overwhelming guilt. Besides, Mina hadn't wanted to keep the baby. She had already decided.

"I was so ashamed, Eliza," he said then. "I couldn't face you with my failure."

"Oh—so you just *left me!*" Eliza couldn't help herself. "You up and went to Mexico after Mina went to California! Do you know how hard that was on me, Dad?"

Martin claimed he didn't know at the time. "I just kept thinking you'd be better off without me," he said, "and that your mother would be too." They both began to cry. The conversation went quiet until Martin spoke again.

"I know how wrong I was, Sunshine. Can you ever forgive me?"

Those five words were the bridge Eliza would walk across in order to return to her father. When she was ready.

Chapter Fifty-Seven
Mina's Revelation, Max's Bravado Last Straws for Eliza
November 11, 2015

I felt the familiar rush of deadline pressure as I ran the cursor down my main education story, a whopper about the school district's annual test scores. Mina was waiting on it for the front page. I had read that sixty-two-incher so many times I had probably made it worse, the price one can pay for perfectionism. I finger combed greasy hair. The snarls were starting to turn into dreadlocks. I hadn't washed it since the weekend, when I went out with my friends. What a bunch of live wires! I dug my thumbs into my temples to stop my head from pounding. Tried to untangle my feelings. I wanted to face them straight on, to take responsibility.

I was almost forty-one, and everything about this place bugged me. Absolutely everything. I scanned the newsroom and my stomach tightened. These people didn't know what it was like, covering news back when real news mattered. Before facts were fake and truth was dispensable.

Before working as a professional reporter took a nosedive in esteem from writerly white-collar crusader to unscrupulous used car salesman.

I had been popping melatonin to get to sleep at night, it had gotten that bad. I felt resentful and anxious, skeptical bordering on cynical. That was it in a nutshell. I had become extremely apathetic, but not about journalism—I could never feel that way about the First Amendment, about the people's right to know. In my book freedom of the press was the last bastion of accountability for the rich and far too powerful.

But tired? Hell yes, I was tired.

Tired of pushing these newbies to dig deeper instead of whining like petulant toddlers whenever they hit an obstacle in their reporting. Tired of half-hidden eyerolls in response to my coaching efforts. *Get a sit-down interview, or at least call your source on the phone. Email doesn't cut it. Show some enterprise, people. Use your training!*

I was sick of feeling like a washed-up dinosaur in a room full of Millennial Twitter fanatics. Thank God Max boosted the age quotient here into the solid early forties. He was bad for my ego, but at least he was good for *something*.

A wiseacre voice drifted above the next divider. "Ed Begley Jr. says the Clean Air Pledge is the key to combatting climate change."

Ryan, the company's latest history major turned journalist, was scrolling through tweets with an iPhone in his left hand and a sesame-seed bagel in his right, a napkin protecting his red striped tie. His deskmate, who sported a man bun and an earring, had brought in a whole sack of the treats. I watched man-bun guy smear way too much cream cheese on his bagel, cinnamon raisin.

There were so many eleven-dollar-an-hour interns in the newsroom.

"Maybe we could work some of it into an op-ed about local airport emissions," Ryan said, his tongue swiping a plastic knife. "Begley Jr. is hella smart. I've been following him on Twitter for a while now."

I seriously thought I might barf.

***

When Mina asked, and only because it was her, I agreed to post links to my stories on Facebook and Instagram, but that was the high-water mark. After that I stepped off the social media merry-go-round. I drew the line at tweeting. I only checked my accounts a couple times a day for news tips. They were too much of a distraction from real life, real journalism, the way I had learned it. The right way. From my dad, who threw in the towel when he was just a couple years older than I was now. He blamed his dystonia. And his pipe, that nasty pipe. Whenever he wrote a story he was smoking it.

He had so much more writing in him.

"Bagel, Eliza?" Ryan had planted himself in front of me, licking his fingers. His tie swung forward as he thrust the half-empty sack my way.

I told him no thanks as politely as I could and returned to my story, tweaking the sentence construction to assuage my feelings. They were huge, so huge. Ryan wouldn't understand.

Dad's illness had been a factor, sure. But after he knocked Mina up, he decided all on his own to exit stage left. That part wasn't her fault. I didn't think I would ever stop being mad at him for leaving, despite our working through it. We lost all that time together.

My neck muscles were cramping into the shallows of my shoulders. I got up to work out the kinks and glanced toward the corner. Max was clicking through the competition's news feed, bent over what used to be Tommy's desk. Max, with his tiny eyes and duplicitous demeanor, was news editor now. Unbelievable. I could hardly stand to think about it. He had boomeranged back after leaving the *Tribune* for the *Ketchikan Dispatch*, in Alaska's First City at the state's southeastern tip. The *Dispatch* was an old paper but not nearly as ancient as the *Juneau Tribune*. And the *Dispatch* was a better-paying place by far, as Max loved to point out.

I had to admit he had played his hand well, parlaying his cops and court gig into the top news job in Ketchikan. At the going-away party the *Tribune* threw for him, he telegraphed his new salary, "five figures—a four and four zeroes," to anyone who would listen. He was more than happy to.

But like a bad penny, Max was back. Water-cooler talk was he had left the *Dispatch* after a knock-down, drag-out with a female superior. No surprise there. But wagging tongues also put his prodigal-son compensation at $45,000, a third higher than mine. That stung so bad. He was driving a red Camaro now. Talk about in your face.

I accosted Mina on her way down the hall. I was still pissed at her after twenty-seven years. The hasty move, the baby, the subterfuge. All of it. But I was even angrier at Max.

"I've been here fifteen goddamn years!" I seethed. "How is it fair that he makes so much more money than I do?"

Mina put on the brakes and stared at me with weary, boy-do-I-get-you-girl eyes. She was fifty-six years old, had been in the biz for thirty-five. She had seen it all. She was a survivor, and I gave her props for that. Not that it would ever make things totally copacetic between us. Trust was a two-way street.

"If you're looking for satisfaction, you're never going to find it here," she said, slumping back against the wall. "You've got to adjust your expectations. Get on board or get out."

In that instant I knew she was right. No matter how much I wanted it to be different, equity in the newsroom was a losing battle. But I also blamed Mina for ruining what little pleasure I used to get out of being there. Every time I looked at her, I felt gratitude and contempt in equal measures. How could she have been so selfish? And how could my dad?

My eyes zeroed in on the ridiculous poster above Max's laptop. That effing poster pushpinned to his cubicle divider. It showed a large penguin striding forth, six smaller ones behind it, backs to bellies. *The leader always sets the trail for others to follow*, read the caption. I felt like one of the six. I wanted to kick the biggest bird in the nuts.

I wondered if penguins even *had* nuts.

I needed it to be Friday already.

But it was only Wednesday, and I willed myself to greet Max, to be the bigger person. I covered the five feet between our desks in two seconds flat.

Mouse clicks muted my approach. Max smelled of corn nuts and Polo Sport. My boyfriend Abe wore that cologne. I was sick and tired of both.

"Um, there are bagels over there—Ryan brought 'em in." I lingered behind him, out of the scent cloud. "Good to see you," I added, though it wasn't.

Max's body didn't move, but his comb-over flinched.

"Oh. Eliza. Didn't notice you there. You still working the trenches, old-school style?" He kept clicking away, the jerk. "Education editor now, right?" He whirled his chair around, khaki knees jutting into my personal space. "Bet you're having fun chasing stories about rogue administrators and the like."

Sarcasm dripped from his salty lips onto a sparsely whiskered chin that used to have a small dimple. He had gained weight, so the cleft was deeper.

I played it cool.

"You got it," I said, clenching my teeth. "I'm a regular Christiane

Amanpour, shining a light on all kinds of official misconduct. Nothing new there."

Max popped another corn nut and smiled a taunt of a smile.

I paused, then pounced. "The *Tribune* should be so lucky as to keep me on staff. I've thought about pulling a Max too. I know where the bodies are buried on the peninsula."

It was a trap I wasn't proud of setting.

Max's rat eyes narrowed to slits behind rimless glasses. He couldn't help himself. "Speaking of payroll." Max glanced left and right. No bigwigs around. He leaned in and cupped fat fingers around his mouth.

"I seriously can't believe this place can afford me," he gloated. "They sprang for five grand more than I was making at the *Dispatch*. Max for the win, right?"

It made me crazy when he referred to himself in third person. He had to know how his boasting made people feel. Or maybe not. He wasn't the most conscious crayon in the box, but he was definitely the most arrogant.

My gut churned. I had confirmation: the good old boys club was alive and well. Like I preached to my protégés, face-to-face interviews always worked. My dad's journalism lessons, particularly that one, had stuck with me.

I grinned as sincerely as I could. "Good for you, Max. Seriously. Good for you."

***

I filed the test scores story and consulted my online calendar. Girls at Lengua, it said in the seven o'clock block. I slid my phone forward, picked up the receiver, and dialed nine to get out.

My voice echoed over the line. I sounded much younger than I felt deep inside. "I'd like to make a reservation for six people," I said to the hostess. "Can we get your back room? It's a celebration."

Chapter Fifty-Eight
Eliza Leaves Alaska Behind, Returns to Oregon
January 20, 2017

What was left for me in Juneau? Zilch, nada, nothing. Except the job, which I had mostly grown to hate, and also my mom, whom I would miss only sometimes given the tension between us. She was getting older, but she had staying power. She could take care of herself with a little help from Harold. The house was too much for them to manage by themselves though. It needed a fresh coat of paint and someone to regularly clear the driveway of snow. The gutters were full to overflowing. Harold had promised me neither of them would attempt the ladder. I was glad they had each other and Boo Two, every bit as good a dog as Boo One had been in my opinion.

It made sense for me to take control, to leave the *Juneau Tribune* before I got fired. It was only a matter of time, given my rotten attitude. I needed to make a move before I completely lost my nerve.

***

That ladies' night out in Juneau did it, gave me the courage to make a sea change. I took the leap and moved back to Oregon. Closer to my roots. Closer to my dad. Now I was sitting in another cool bar in an even cooler town, the Rose City, with a different group of longtime gal-pals, back where I belonged. My friends were great about Dad. "Don't give up on him, Eliza," they told me. "Call him once a week until he agrees to see you." I would follow their advice. I would keep inviting him to meet with me—coffee, lunch, dinner, whatever—and I lit a candle every night, hoping for that to happen.

We would see each other again. No way we wouldn't.

Even before resigning from the *Juneau Tribune*—it was torture leaving Mina, despite our falling out—I had applied for a job at an organic market on Sauvie Island and got it. That was most of my life now. Tuesday through Saturday I sorted pumpkins by size, separated the white corn from the yellow, stocked shelves, and swept up. It was deliciously mindless, perfect for me.

"I'm decompressing like a boss," I told Ivy over the phone. "It's so freeing! I never take my work home anymore. I don't miss the paper." I could live with the money—not much less than what I had made in Alaska—and I loved the peace and quiet.

Thank the goddesses for my Beaver State girlfriends. They had survived multiple address-book evolutions when I lived up north. I didn't forget them, and they didn't forget me. Those women were true-blue. And now here we were, out on the town, back together again.

"Hey Eliza. Pass me the margarita salt, would ya?"

I hadn't expected my second cousin Sonja, on Midge's side, to show up with the rest of them, but she did, and she was a great addition. Sonja's middle name was mischief. I slid the bowl her way and she spooned some of the salt onto her plate. Licked her finger, dipped it in, brought it to her dark pink lips.

"Mmm," she said, closing her eyes and taking a long sip of her drink. Sixty years old and a silver-haired grandma, Sonja was rocking faded denim jeggings, her butt cheeks bedecked with rhinestones, her cell phone peeking out above her right back pocket. "In case my prince charming calls," she joked, tapping the phone with a fresh gel manicure, flamingo-pink with tiny white dots. "Ringer's on so I won't miss it." A humongous plate of nachos centerpieced the table. Every bite belonged to a torchbearer for a different social justice cause: affordable housing, LGBTQ+ rights, voter rights, equal pay for equal work. Sonja's thing was reproductive healthcare, preserving a woman's right to choose.

The vibes were totally, intoxicatingly real.

"I'm going to meet Mr. Right at a pro-choice rally," Sonja predicted, a disc of jalapeño escaping her mouth and falling onto the table, splatting sour cream. "Wouldn't that just be the most ironic thing?"

"Sure would," echoed one of my buddies. "One of those emotionally conscious dudes! You know, the ones who get that our bodies belong to us."

Four heads nodded around the table. Halfway into a second plate, stories of love lost and found having reached their inevitable end, talk turned to making a living. I told my companions what happened at the *Juneau Tribune*, how the systemic inequities had grated on me, how the gig hadn't been what I wanted anymore, how I had loathed those know-it-all hipsters posing as actual journalists, how I resented having to put up with their constant complaining.

How I was working at a produce market, enjoying the break from the pressure cooker at the paper.

Sonja drained her margarita. She appeared unpersuaded. "As long as I've known you, you've lived for a challenge," she said, and I wriggled in my seat. Sonja saw through my crap. Always had. "What are you doing sorting pumpkins?" The others shifted, too, their body language confirming they agreed with Sonja.

Sonja was right. I was bored out of my gourd at the market. I needed something more. I had been obsessing about what happened with me and Mina, how she had round filed the one story I was absolutely excited about, the one about adoption. How her baby revelation had broken things between us. The pain, with all of its twists and tentacles, burned so bad.

Someone asked about my mom. I often thought about calling her, I confessed, but most of the time I didn't, and then I felt guilty. Especially because I *was* making the effort to call my dad. Not that he picked up.

"We're . . . distant." The women in the circle were on a second round of drinks. "But of course I'll always love her. I mean *them*. All of them. My mom. And Mina. And Harold."

I felt better, saying out loud that I loved Harold. He was a good man.

Chapter Fifty-Nine
Mina Tells Journalism Students:
"Truth Isn't Dead Unless We Kill It"
February 5, 2017

The week Eliza backed out of her driveway in Haines Borough for the last time, Portland or bust, Mina did the only thing she could do in the midst of actual, physical grief. Grief for the loss of Eliza and for the loss of what might have been if the 2016 election had gone her way.

She accepted an invitation to fill in as a guest lecturer in a beginning journalism class at City University, Eliza's alma mater, at the request of a source turned friend who needed a break.

Not long after she got to the *Tribune*, Mina had done a story on the number of full professors at City, breaking it down into male and female. How long it had taken each of them to achieve that status and under what circumstances they had arrived. The first thing Professor Aponi Bylilly of the English and Literature Department told Mina after agreeing to an interview was that her first name, according to her Navajo mother, meant *transformation*. "That's what I've been doing my whole career," she asserted with not a hint of modesty. "Transforming. Changing. Relying on intuition and determination." It hadn't been easy, but it had been rewarding, going from graduate teaching assistant to assistant professor to associate professor over too many years, then finally, "belatedly yet mercifully," Aponi emphasized, her promotion to full professor just after 9/11. "It was as if it were preordained, that I'd risen from the ashes of those three thousand souls," she said, a faraway look on her well-lined face, which carried the bone structure of a warrior. "My mother knew exactly what she was doing when she christened me," Aponi said. "I'm still evolving." She was proud to call the Cochiti Pueblo home. Deep-toned drums and storytelling figurines lived like fire in her belly. The Eastern Keres dialect rang sweet in her ears.

Thirty years in, Aponi remained steadfast in her passion for supporting women who loved to teach, who wanted to be recognized for their talents, who wished to hold the title of professor. "Many of the men are fine instructors," she said, "but the women have to work much harder for the same recognition. And even then, sometimes they get passed over." Her advice to female aspirants— Mina reported a 65/35 percentage split in a story headlined *University Employs Lopsided Number of Male Professors*—could be summed up in a single word: *perseverance.*

"You just can't quit," she said. "You can get mad, you can get discouraged, but your best defense against the patriarchy is to stand your ground. Do the work, make it count, show your mettle. Then when you get there, it's all the sweeter."

Growing up in northern New Mexico in a modest house with a single mother, Aponi played kickball with the boys and demonstrated her athletic prowess early. "I wore a dress, but I didn't give an inch," she told Mina. "I could run as fast as they did, and I was better at the boot. Some of them were jealous, but mostly they admired me for it." She learned not to hold back, to never give up or give in. That way, she said, "you can round the bases for home."

***

"Whatever you want" was what Mina should talk about, Aponi said over speakerphone while packing for her getaway to Gustavus on Glacier Bay. "Anything journalism related. Source development, *New York Times Co. v. Sullivan*, how to fact-check, where to find trustworthy news sources. You'll have thirty minutes in front of the class. They're totally going to love you. I'm sure you'll be brilliant."

Mina stood before the mirror at home, practicing. She began over and over. She wanted to get it right. This speech was about something everyone needed to know, at a time when people didn't respect news sources. Didn't respect educated society. Why was that? She planned to explore the topic with them, the young people, whose brains were still malleable. Their motherboards weren't yet full.

She would admonish them. *Now isn't the time to distrust journalists. Now is the time to appreciate your local news. Go to school board meetings and city council meetings. Subscribe to your community newspaper. Read what trained reporters have to say. Contrast and compare. Forty-five years ago, thanks to Woodward and Bernstein, coverage of the Watergate break-in had a huge impact. Nixon got his hand caught in the cookie jar, and he ended up resigning. Freedom of the press in action. Others have died for their pursuit of the truth. Don Bolles, the* Arizona Republic, *in 1976. Chauncey Bailey, the* Oakland Post, *in 2007. Alison Parker and Adam Ward of CBS in 2015. The* Capital Gazette *five in 2018. But you can't kill a story by killing a journalist. This critical work continues today.*

She would school them. *Imagine a person in power telling you to disbelieve your own eyes and ears and instead listen only to them. That's called gaslighting. And while it might be tempting to check your curiosity at the door—information-gathering isn't for the lazy or indiscriminate—resist taking the easy route. Some in the media have a habit of relying on soundbites and volume to carry the day. But credible sources are still out there. My favorites are the AP (of course), BBC News, ProPublica, NPR, Reuters, the* Guardian, *and RealClearPolitics. I can show you how to find others. And don't forget FactCheck.org and PolitiFact. They do the heavy lifting for you.*

She would encourage them. *My old news editor Martin, a wonderful, visionary mentor, used to say this: "When we have the facts, we have everything. But when we squander opportunities to seek out, internalize, and elevate those facts, we have nothing." Remember, kids—truth isn't dead unless we kill it with our complacency.*

Mina tucked a printed outline into her purse, but as she rumbled toward campus in her green Subaru Forester, she wasn't at all convinced she would follow her own script. When she stood at the lectern and sipped from a water bottle provided by someone tasked with such details, looking out at a sea of unfamiliar undergrad faces—some eager and expectant, others distracted or sleepy—a lightbulb went on inside her head. She knew what she had to say and said it, in a lecture so powerful her professor friend later asked if she could incorporate it as part of a TED Talk featuring every single faculty member in the English Department.

"Mina! I told you you'd be wonderful," Aponi gushed in a follow-up phone call. "My voicemail's full of thank-you messages from my students. You're the best substitute ever."

***

It had been an address for the ages, an oration loaded with emotional urgency. When it was over Mina remained behind the lectern and accepted several rounds of enthusiastic applause, then stayed to field questions. It took a while for her to answer them all. Some of the students in the rows nearest the stage were taking notes; "pure gold," one young man characterized her words while grinning his appreciation through a few days' worth of red-brown stubble.

"Thank you," he said, clasping her right hand in both of his and vigorously shaking it. "I'm going to remember this day forever."

His effusiveness felt good to Mina. It was twilight when she found her car in the parking lot, light from the descending sun glinting off its hood. She made her way home, the radio playing bluegrass, her thoughts wandering far from the *Juneau Tribune*, back to her first job at the *Cascadian* and to a fantasy future in a classroom. Back to one Martin Donovan. For a few heady moments, she was every inch a bona fide professor.

Chapter Sixty
Martin Saves Man from Tent City Blaze
February 14, 2017

It would be a frosty Valentine's Day night in Portland, down to a forecasted twenty-eight degrees. Puffy-parka weather. Martin was on volunteer duty at Dignity Village, a public service that would continue for as long as Martin was able to perform it. He had made the commitment to his friend Pete back when the two of them bonded over cups of stale coffee in the waiting room at HUD, and he intended to keep it. He proactively layered his clothing: wool socks, long underwear, flannel shirt, and fleece-lined hat with ear flaps. It had taken him a while to accumulate this specific couture, mostly at Harbor Light, which offered a wide array of donated clothing the last Friday of every month along with the usual free lunch. Being a man's size petite worked in Martin's favor, as he could have his pick from the far left side of the table.

"Extra small," he would say to the volunteer watching over the merchandise, who would approve his selections and wave him along with the bored detachment of a crossing guard. It was in Martin's best interest to choose items that could see him through an entire Oregon winter. He had gone from his car to a Section 8 apartment long before Donald Trump rode down that golden escalator in New York and announced his bid for the presidency, Goliath against David. There were no jobs that paid livable wages to people like Martin, guys with gimpy arms, guys born in the '50s. For him there would be no more journalism, or pretty much any other kind of career. The Great Recession had compounded income inequality and heralded a protracted downturn for all but the wealthiest, most ivory-tower Americans. That wasn't Martin, not by a long shot.

"God bless America," he mumbled to himself one day while attempting to fix a leaky pipe under his kitchen sink with a rusted wrench and a disease-weakened wrist. The world could be a cruel and frustrating place. Yet he was thankful. For his apartment, for free winter clothing, for the dried-up roll of plumber's tape he found in a drawer. For regular monetary gifts from Eliza and Judith—so kind, so generous, so unexpected—now that his jobless, service-forward future was set in cement.

***

It was Harold who had paved the way for Martin to receive that support from his ex-wife and his daughter. He took time over President's Day to fly down from Alaska, meet Martin, and help him open a bank account at People's First Credit Union on Northeast Lombard.

Martin felt sheepish—his driver's license had lapsed and his credit score was in the toilet—but Judith's husband had been good enough to understand the reasons behind her generosity and kind enough to make the long trip to Oregon, so he was grateful.

"Is there a beneficiary?" the personal banker asked, to which Harold and Martin exchanged wry smiles. Eliza was the obvious choice, should Martin predecease her, but it would be circuitous to give her back her own money.

"None at this time," Martin said, and the banker handed him a temporary debit card. There would be separate deposits of seventy-five and twenty-five dollars, Harold noted, going into the account every month.

A tidy sum, a nest egg that would see Martin through. He tucked the bank card into his wallet before he and Harold shook hands.

"I'm off to the airport," Harold said, releasing Martin's hand. He adjusted his plaid scarf and zipped up his wool jacket. He would be returning to subfreezing temps. Portland's winter weather was mild in comparison.

"Thank you," Martin said. "I appreciate it. So long, Harold. Please give my regards to Judith."

***

Pete had made up his mind to make the best of things at the village, given the clear signs he would never succeed in his bid for government housing. "You can't outrun your transgressions," he had said to Martin more than once, a statement that rang as truth.

After years of knocking at the door and wooing Zelda with his lively banter and entertaining stories, the answer Pete still and always got from Zelda was "Sorry again, sweetie," as she handed back his paperwork stamped REJECTED in the upper-right corner.

"Writing's on the wall, man." He clapped a ski-gloved hand on Martin's shoulder and the two of them man-hugged, a quick in and out so as not to court curiosity among the denizens of Tent City. "You know how it is."

Martin did know. And didn't. After all, he had slipped past the gatekeepers at HUD, no criminality to his name. But the word *transgression* echoed as code for his own malfeasances, and the lightning rod of his soul vibrated with remorse.

***

The village gig was easy enough, and infrequent enough, for Martin to keep faith with it even after Pete had gone "back to the dust I used to kick up," as he had said with droll self-deprecation just days before his death. Martin made sure his buddy got the burial he deserved at Willamette, the military cemetery on top of Mount Scott. Pete had always been proud of his short stint in the army, an honorable discharge among his few lasting sources of pride.

Whatever he had done afterward hadn't obscured what he did before, Martin figured, "for love of country and my fellow man," Pete had said when he was still mostly healthy, his riding days over, his mission to help on full tilt. Keeping occasional tabs on Pete's brethren at the village seemed the least Martin could do for someone who had taken an interest in him at his lowest ebb. Some of those brothers didn't make it easy, though.

***

Making his rounds, Martin made a mental note to call Eliza. She had left him a breathless voicemail about the *Caller*, how they had been invited to report a story on homelessness together.

"It'd be like old times, Dad!" she said.

It would.

***

"Hey dude! Can you keep it down?" Martin said in a yip of a voice. "Your neighbors are trying to sleep!" It was getting close to midnight and his eyes could no longer focus on the small print of the newspaper he had scabbed from the corner stand, Trump's Muslim ban dominating the headlines. There was always someone blasting the blues in Tent City. Martin was a tolerant man and accepting of tastes not his own—he much preferred jazz or soft rock—but the lateness of the hour tried his patience.

His neighbor's music had reached atomic-level volume. Martin rolled over, unfurled himself from his blankets, and stepped out of the volunteers' tent. He peeked around a cement divider and saw a man curled up in a fetal position, unmoving, the flames from his firepit ominously high.

"You okay, buddy?" Martin screamed above the racket, but the man didn't flinch. A bottle of rotgut lay beside him, an unidentifiable dinner burned to black inside an iron skillet. Martin used one foot to nudge the man's leg just as a small propane canister sputtered and exploded. Flames shot up the side of the tent. Embers spilled onto the street.

"GET UP! NOW! FIRE!"

The man woke, angry and disoriented. He spewed vomit as Martin tackled him with a tarp and dragged him from the inferno. It was only after the hapless fellow was in the care of emergency personnel that Martin realized flames had scorched his own face and neck. His jaw throbbed and stung. When he touched it, the top layer sloughed off like snakeskin.

"Shit," he breathed and reached for his phone to call 911, an automatic response.

A strapping young paramedic rushed over to Martin as he made efforts to dial, his shaking hand hitting the wrong buttons. "We're already here, man," the paramedic soothed before his second patient lost consciousness.

***

Martin came to in the burn unit at Legacy Emanuel, both hands bandaged, his head throbbing as if it were still on fire. A nurse stood on the left side of his bed, checking monitors and taking notes. "You've been in an accident," she said, leaning down so he could hear her. "You're in a safe place, Mr. Donovan."

The first thing Martin asked about was his poor inebriated charge, whom he had pulled from a nightmare of his own making. "He's stable," the nurse told him and smiled. "He's in the next room. He's going to be all right, thanks to you."

The next thing Martin asked for was a mirror.

"Let's put that off for a bit, shall we?" the nurse suggested, her fresh face turning tense and nervous. "The doctor's out on morning rounds. She'll come talk with you soon."

***

"Eliza?" Martin said, lifting the phone to his ear with his left hand, working around the IV line. He caught his daughter on her way to work. "There was a fire at the village. I'm okay. I'm in the hospital. They're taking good care of me."

He was scared. He wanted so badly to see Eliza. But now, after the accident, that was out of the question. Martin got ahead of that curve.

"I can't see you right now, Sunshine," he said. "My face. It got burned."

"Oh my God, Daddy!" his daughter returned. "What hospital are you in?"

Martin assured her there was no need for her to come, that he would be discharged in short order. He would be able to manage. He put Eliza off.

"The folks at Dignity Village have my back," he said. "But I'm also calling with good news. I'd love to do the homelessness story with you. After I get back on my feet, I mean. For the *Caller*. And for us."

***

Once he got out of the burn unit, Martin figured his new scars would help him fit in better than ever among the tent-community denizens under the Burnside Bridge, a living revenant honoring his pledge to Pete. "A face only a mother could love" was how he planned to reintroduce himself to folks at the village, including Homeless Scotty, that lucky son of a gun who had left Emanuel before him, no skin grafts required. There would be no more propane canisters heating up Scotty's food. Only rides to Blanchet House on the west side of the river, where he would take all his meals from now until the end.

Martin, who hadn't been so fortunate, would make sure of that.

Chapter Sixty-One
Doctor's Diagnosis Consigns Judith to Hospice
April 18, 2018

First signs sure can fool a person, Judith breathed as she dropped back against her feather pillow, too sapped to start the day. She arched her back and pressed her chest toward the ceiling, running her palms from her latissimus dorsi to her glutes. She dug her thumbs and fingertips into sore muscles, the mattress giving her arthritic knuckles a gentle massage. Two days before, in a rare burst of energy, she had gone out to the porch and split a quarter cord of oak herself, carried the kindling inside, and stacked it neatly on the living room hearth. Maybe that was why she felt so punk.

She had overdone things. Harold had placed her green terry cloth bathrobe on her side of the bed where she could reach it. He was such a thoughtful man. It made up for all the hours he disappeared into his own world, inside his study, alone. She wrapped herself up in it, rolled onto her side, and sat up slowly, sliding frigid feet into fleece-lined clogs. Her circulation had gone haywire again. She rose to walk across the room to the master bathroom, glimpsing her reflection in the vanity mirror as she went. Every inch of her body showed its age and the experience of her years, curse and comfort both. She splashed water on her face, dried it with a hand towel, and smiled herself fully awake. Harold had been up for hours, she knew, holding court in the largest room of their creaky old Victorian, the one that held all his books. He would have already eaten his breakfast, a single lightly poached egg on sourdough toast and decaf coffee with cream. Stepping on the scale, Judith found she had dropped another half pound and felt simultaneously pleased and alarmed at the number flashing red on the digital display.

Martin had lost weight both times he was sick.

"How will I tell Eliza?" she asked herself out loud. Physical fatigue explained things for her just as facial spasms had for her former spouse. "She'll freak."

As on other recent mornings, Judith had little appetite. When she reached the bottom of the stairs, entered the kitchen, and opened the refrigerator door, nothing appealed. She stood there contemplating, tightening the belt on her robe, the light inside the fridge blinking like the bulb was going out. She wrote a note reminding herself to change it, then poured a small glass of orange juice and swallowed an assemblage of herbal supplements recommended by her naturopath. The capsules burned on their way down. The thought that she might need to switch to a different doctor went in and out of her head, as did any inclination to bother her daughter about her symptoms. Eliza was busy starting over in Oregon.

"Good morning, my love." Harold's strong voice echoed behind his study's French doors, sturdy eight-footers made from hand-hewn knotty alder. He opened the doors just a crack, so only his nose and part of his lips showed, in an attempt at humor. Noting Judith's nonreaction, he poked out his head, already adorned in a wool herringbone cap. "I'm almost finished with the fisher poets section," he said. "Five minutes to our walk?" Judith felt heat prickle up her neck to her hairline. Harold was always tinkering with his bookshelves, endlessly arranging and rearranging them, obsessing over the placement of the titles and only occasionally culling them like cast-aside friends, making somber, grudging pilgrimages to the Goodwill donation bin.

Harold's head remained in the breach, inviting her answer.

"Would you mind very much taking Boo by yourself today?"

Her husband's face registered a slight frown, but he said yes, it was okay, she might feel better if she stayed back. Boo Two sat expectantly, his head cocked slightly to the right. Harold slid the doors all the way open, bent down, and hooked up the leash. He tucked a poop bag into the front of his canvas vest, where it stuck out like a comical black plastic pocket square. Judith chuckled. A moment later after a short, solicitous hug, man and dog were off.

***

It occurred to Judith, on nights when sleep didn't come, that she needed to update her will if she was going to leave ongoing money for Martin. Not a lot but enough to keep him on beans and rice at least. She and Eliza had already agreed that continuing to support him was the right thing to do. And the fire at the village had made that all the more critical. Judith bore Martin no ill will. He had suffered enough. She would meet with her lawyer the next week, on a day she felt up to the task. Harold supported her decision.

"Absolutely, my love," he'd said, patting her hand, kind eyes twinkling. "It's what you want, and that's good enough for me."

She hadn't yet told Eliza she was dying. Ironic that it was she, and not her ex-husband, facing imminent demise.

***

"Mama!" Eliza gushed, already well into her morning when she called. Judith deduced her daughter had something exciting to share. She never phoned this early, and she never called her *mama* these days, only *mom*.

"I just got off the phone with the *Neighborhood Caller*. The editor approved me as part of their freelance staff. Isn't that fantastic?" It took Judith a minute to catch up. Her meds hadn't kicked in yet.

"The *Caller*? Isn't that an alternative paper?"

Eliza was ready with an answer. "Yes, Mom, it is. Competes with *Willamette Week*. New paper, quite edgy. But I really like the editor. A woman. Super smart, super savvy." She went on to say she had received Veronica's blessing to do a piece about Portland's homelessness crisis.

"And here's the best part! Dad finally called me! Himself, without me initiating!" Eliza sounded triumphant. "We're going to do the story together! There's no big rush. We can take our time. I'll add the extra money to my 401(k)."

Martin would handle the in-person interviews as a trusted volunteer at Dignity Village, Eliza told Judith, and she would do the research, digging into documents at City Housing Concern and Multnomah County Cares.

"Well, that's just wonderful," Judith said softly and meant it. Eliza and her dad, back together again.

"I can't wait for you to read the story," Eliza said then. "This is the best thing that's happened to me in a while, Mama."

Back to *mama*, Judith noted. Things were way better between them.

***

The pain had been manageable at first, something Judith could ignore easily enough after a couple ibuprofen and a sit-down with the morning newspaper, always a potent distraction. Seeing Mina's byline no longer triggered her. She had largely let go of that resentment. It no longer burned hot for her. Probably the organic effects of getting older, she reasoned as she rubbed a specific spot on the lower right side of her abdomen, a spot that felt rigid sometimes and malleable others. She was nearly sixty-six now, her system stubbornly averse to spicy foods, a likely culprit in her present circumstance. Between chores and pastimes—knitting or reading or walking—the confusing constellation of symptoms troubled and frightened her, though not enough for her to get on the phone to Dr. Marks, at least not yet, and not enough to confide her fears to Harold. "I'm sure I'll be fine," she said to him, fingers pressed deep in her belly, as though she was working out a stitch.

When the phone on the nook table rang, she had answered it herself to keep her husband's head buried in the newspaper.

She was glad to have a few minutes alone with Eliza, just the two of them, hearing about her story prospects for the *Caller*.

"Well, that's my big news," Eliza said, summing up. "What's happening up there in the Land of the Midnight Sun?"

Judith took a sip of air. "Nothing much yet. It's only seven here," she reminded Eliza. She swallowed the last of her orange juice.

"Oh, right, an hour's time difference. I keep forgetting," Eliza said. "But you're already up and at 'em, I suppose. Going out for a walk soon, with Harold and the new Boo? How is that furry guy?"

They laughed about which furry being Eliza was referring to, human or canine, their chitchat inevitably hitting dead air. Despite their relational gains, conversation still came hard. Martin had always been an open book. Why couldn't mother and daughter be that way with each other? From separate homes in separate cities, each woman waited for the other to fill the gap.

"Boo's fine. Harold too," Judith said, making sure her voice was even.

"That's good to hear." Eliza had picked up a watering can and started sprinkling the half-dead marigolds in planter boxes lining the deck. "I miss that silly old dog like crazy."

Silly. Old. That was how Judith felt nearly every day now, a notion that grew with every week, every long, dark day. Eliza must realize she needed her here, in Juneau, bearing witness to her increasing frailty. To sit beside her, like the two of them had for Martin years before. Where she could follow in her father's and grandfather's footsteps, where she could venture out into the wild world but still have a safe place to land at night. Where Judith could keep tabs on her only child and make sure nothing bad happened to her. Judith shook her head in a stop thought. It wasn't right, grasping at something *she* wanted, not Eliza. Her daughter needed to claim her own life, even if it meant moving to Oregon and finding a new boyfriend, one who would treat her better than Abe had.

Judith tightened her grip on the phone, worried Eliza would hang up before anything more passed between them. "Thank you for calling and for telling me the good news," she said, each word quieter than the last. "Harold and I love you very much. Take care of yourself, Eliza, won't you?"

***

Bile duct cancer wasn't something mortals typically came back from, the doctor behind the big desk said to Judith and Harold, not in those words exactly, but the meaning was clear to them anyway. "Late-stage cholangiocarcinoma," he pronounced with a physician's detachment, a sucker punch to the spirit. Dr. Marks still had a stethoscope looped around the collar of his lab coat from a visit with his last patient, the frequent glances at his watch indicating he would soon be leaving to see the next one despite Judith and Harold's long list of questions, despite their early grief.

"I'm sorry, but your tumor is inoperable, Mrs. Dixon," the doctor observed with death sentence-level surety. "The disease is far too advanced for it to respond to further treatment," he added, lowering his glasses to scan Judith's chart notes, not bothering to meet their eyes. Harold said a quiet thank you and helped his wife into her overcoat.

Judith had but one question on the walk back to the parking lot. "Will we?" she asked Harold.

"Will we what?"

Her arm was hooked in his, same as the evening he invited her to join him in Alaska, to join him for life.

"Will we be able to handle my illness at home?" Judith said. "With additional help from hospice?"

Harold leaned over and kissed the side of her face, at a loss for words.

Chapter Sixty-Two
Eliza Forgives Her Mother for Keeping Baby Secret
May 23, 2018

Alone in my kitchen, the counter littered with evidence of my new man—his brand of organic coffee in the canister, an Oregon Zoo mug shaped like a hippopotamus head—I sifted through my recipe cards, most of them handwritten by my mom.

Matzah. Yes, that's what I would make. Mom and I used to have fun making matzah together for Passover.

I had flour, kosher salt, and olive oil on hand. Running water and eighteen minutes of time. Easy peasy. Mom would be proud.

Mom.

I thought of her as I lifted the ceramic bowl from the cupboard and set the oven to 500.

Was she in pain? Was Harold remembering her meds? Would she feel good enough to take a short walk today? Ever since Harold told me the news—that Mom was in hospice—I had been a wreck.

Spotify was playing *NPR News Now*. A federal judge had decided the President couldn't block people on his Twitter feed for disagreeing with him. Public forum and First Amendment, duh. Served him right.

Oven preheated, timer set. I got to mixing and rolling out the dough. Tears came. I wiped my eyes with a hot pad. Good thing I had the recipe memorized. Just like Mom's challah. Ten more minutes to baking time.

I have to go see her.

***

In my post-Abe period it would never have occurred to me to look for a new boyfriend on the web. But things had moved stratospherically fast technology-wise. All of us in our forties were finding love online. I went on Bumble one particularly lonesome night and created an account. Poof! There was Bruce. *Likes adventure (not the risky kind). Loves opera (mostly Tchaikovsky).*

Hippo aficionado, endangered animal supporter. Would treat a like-minded lady well, read his profile. And he wasn't bad looking. Red hair, blue eyes, clean-shaven. I swiped right.

***

Mom was still ambulatory and lucid the first time I visited Alaska during the longest, shortest weeks of her decline, before the catheter and the feeding tube. I brought her warm chamomile tea and read to her from Kerouac's *On the Road*, regaled her with stories about heron and beaver sightings along the riverbank in Oregon as night fell on late-spring Alaskan afternoons.

One momentous morning, careful not to startle her, I tempered my elation and woke my mother gently, sliding the newspaper's front page into her fading line of sight.

"Mama," I said, one hand on her scrawny shoulder. "I have something amazing to show you."

She stirred and yawned, blinking her eyes open, rejoining the world. She clutched the issue of the *Caller* that contained my story with Dad.

Officials Say Portland Homeless Numbers Reach "Crisis" Point, read the two-deck headline, featured prominently in the righthand gutter, along with a photo of Homeless Scotty. Mom ran her fingers over the double byline, *by Martin Donovan and Eliza D. Dixon,* no extraneous syllables, no Thomas Stover Harwood III machismo. She smiled and looked up at me.

"I'm so proud of you, Eliza," she whispered, nodding off again. "Happy for you and your dad. Leave it with me, won't you? I'll read the story later today."

The second time I returned to Alaska, it was impossible to ignore Mom's shallow breathing and her noisy groans when she attempted to turn over in bed. Because of the drugs, I had to explain over and over what was happening around her, visual, olfactory, and auditory: the odor of an egg salad sandwich sitting too long on her nightstand, its crust going hard. The bleats of song lyrics she used to know, Karen Carpenter and Judy Collins on constant loop.

Mom was actively dying. I knew that now. It was really hard to take.

After all we had been through, I was still angry with her. And yet I loved her like crazy. Both those things were true, but one was fading as the other came into sharp relief.

My tardiness in getting to Juneau had been a sore spot with Harold, a place he drew a line. "She needs you, Eliza, in ways I can't address," he pleaded, often and with increasing alarm, before I took time off from work and went up. "Thank you," he said simply when I finally showed up at their door. I sat at my mother's bedside, stroking her hand as she withered away, as she forswore this still-spinning planet. I hadn't realized how soon the end would come. I hurt so much inside, below the layers, the scar tissue thick and impossibly tangled, like Pacific madrone in the damp Northwest woods.

Dad. Mom was going, but he was still here. He had told me about his injuries from the fire, that his face had been burned, that we could see each other when he felt comfortable, after he healed all the way. Mama would like that, knowing we had reunited.

She even said so, one rare afternoon when her energy surged. She had a book in her lap, Boo Two snoozing beside her on the sofa.

"Eliza, don't give up on your dad," Mama encouraged. "He's always been so hard on himself. He needs you to tell him he's all right with you. That you love him no matter what."

***

Mom laid everything out in her advance directive, down to the tiniest element, as organized as she had always been. The doctors and nurses fell in line, administering drug doses that kept her pain levels just short of intolerable so she could remain clearheaded for the duration. "No heroic measures and no machines," she told Harold—explicitly, her expression dead serious—and cremation, not burial. For the service she requested a single simple song, specific readings from ancient scripture, and private inurnment afterward, just me and Harold.

And then there was the instruction to keep sending Martin the seventy-five dollars a month after she was gone, a directive Harold had embraced.

***

Mom looked small under the quilted coverlet when she brought the topic up, her face chalky, her parched lips forming a determined arch.

"So, your half sister," she said, a skipped stone across water. She wove her fingers together, rings hanging loose on their bones. "You knew about Greta because Mina told you."

I nodded my yes as she summoned strength. I hoped for an explanation. My mother did not disappoint.

"I wanted to tell you. I wish I had." Inside me, something broke in two. We both started to cry.

"You kept it to yourself for so long," I soothed. "It must have been difficult."

Mom squeezed dry eyes and reached for my hand. "The thing about secrets," she said, her lids fluttering open and closed, "is they waste so much time."

***

We were lucky we had each other, Mom and I. That was what everyone said about us after Dad went to Mexico. I was only a kid then, but I knew what it meant. I would have to hang on to her, and she to me, even in the shrunken spaces that couldn't be filled by anyone other than Dad, the places inside me that would pine for his presence forever. It was an impossible thing for her to be both mother and father to me—and new wife to Harold. I hadn't given her any credit, not one tiny little bit.

Mom tried. But as I grew older, I blamed her for everything, including the spare attic room I had to live in. Its hand-me-down appointments, its emotional disassemblage, its never-enoughness. As a girl, standing in the moonlight streaming through my one small window, I wove dreams that Dad would come home and put everything right again. The next morning, I would descend the staircase and wave my magical thinking right in Mom's anxious, defeated face. As the years went by, whenever she tried to help, whenever she tried to talk to me about almost anything—a dress for the high school dance, taking up a musical instrument, which reliable used car I might consider buying and from where—I would devise yet another way to sabotage her efforts to give me the support I was missing with Dad gone from my life.

"I hate you!" Over the never-ending roller-coaster ride, at the top and the bottom and in the middle, I spat those horrible words out at Mom far more often than she deserved, with far more frequency than I generally felt comfortable admitting, though I did acknowledge my wrongdoing that one Sunday afternoon after she passed when I called Mina back.

"Whenever my mom spoke, no matter what she said, she was like a mirror held up to me," I said, sipping in short breaths. "She was a reflection that triggered all my worst inclinations, my most ghastly behaviors."

My mom *was* me, and I detested that.

"Thou shalt honor thy father and thy mother," Mina said then, though she didn't believe in the Ten Commandments any more than I did. But she did believe in empathy and kindness and in the right thing to do, whenever and wherever she understood what that was. I felt the cool breeze of her counsel in the nudge of her next provocative question.

"If you could do one thing to settle things with your mother, posthumously, what would that be?"

The answer was as simple and as complicated as things had always been between Mom and me, ever since everything I never asked for happened anyway, in the years after my family of origin splintered and split, when our lives bifurcated into two stark columns, before and after, the in-between ceasing to exist. The answer was I needed to forgive. My parents and myself.

***

It was an uncommonly warm, dry morning when a small party of mourners gathered at the Abernethy Cemetery to say farewell. Joshua the apprentice glassblower, Mom's scopophobic nephew, came all the way from eastern Oregon to kick things off. Perched on a stool at the far edge of the columbarium, he strummed his guitar, long beard quivering, and warbled Donovan's "Catch the Wind," the melody drifting across the grass and over the gravestones, dispatching its lilting rhymes to the universe. The black-clad bereaved formed an untidy circle and held hands, per written encouragement from Mom. Harold stood stiffly, bleary-eyed, his face a puffy crimson. My heart went out to him. The British singer's folk tune had been one of my dad's favorites.

"Shalom," intoned the rabbi, and the circle-makers *shalom*ed him back. We bowed our heads and went silent for the Mourner's Kaddish, recited by Harold in a trembling voice. He had snuck in the prayer without his wife's approval "to put parentheses on things," he rationalized after recovering his usual baritone.

Readings from the Didache felt like a head fake from Mom, an immutable punctuation mark at the end of a lifetime of seeking. She had carried a heavy mixed bag of religiosity, her devotion to matters of the spirit hitting its zenith in meditative practice only after I was grown. Dad's equivocations in that arena had always crowded hers. What she had embraced was the idea that all people were on equal footing when it came to matters reserved for Judgment Day. "The left and the right," she had often said. "Only God finally decides."

***

I kept the small key to the niche that held Mom's ashes inside a jewelry box in the sock and underwear drawer of my dresser—a reminder, whenever I saw it, that I had a place to visit her if I wanted to. There was one other good reason to go back to Alaska— Harold—and he would be pleased to accompany me to the columbarium. It had all happened so fast, light years faster than my dad's illness and leave-taking. Sometimes I took the key out and turned it over in my fingers, felt its bumpy brass face, something tangible that made me remember even when I would rather not.

Chapter Sixty-Three
Eliza, Mina Reconnect over
Tangled Maternal Relationships
October 15, 2018

With Mom's funeral over, I prepared to fly back to Oregon. I closed the door to the attic room that used to be mine. Downstairs, I gave Harold a see-you-later hug and patted Boo Two's head.

"Well," I said, and Harold hugged me again.

Mina was the last detail I needed to tie up. She had agreed to meet me at the Juneau airport for coffee. Starbucks it was, though I much preferred the independent espresso shops dotted around the city, which had gone bananas for best-bean status as demand for such indulgences increased. As if "coffee sommelier" was a real job.

Mina arrived with a copy of the *Juneau Tribune* sticking out of her bag. I was curious about the headlines but pretended I wasn't. "So," she said, stirring her mocha and mixing in the extra pump of chocolate. She put her lips to the edge of the cup but drew back. "Too hot," she assessed and set it down.

She reached for my hands. I wasn't ready for that, not ready to admit we were saying goodbye.

I reached under the table, opened the top of my carry-on and located Mom's cremation niche key, turning it over in my fingers as we talked. About Alaska, about the state of the news, about not much of anything. Mina hadn't attended the funeral. She knew what this coffee date meant to me.

"It must be so tough," she said. Sincerely, I thought. "I'm sorry she's gone."

The key felt small and cold in my palm. I gripped it tighter and placed both my hands on top of Mina's, the key in between. It seemed right.

"Me too," I said, our hands still clasped. "Thank you, Mina. For helping me understand her. For everything."

I paused, considering what I was about to tell her and deciding to continue.

"You can do that, you know. You can care deeply for someone, and they you, even if you don't understand each other most of the time. You can say the words and mean them. You can come to terms."

There was an extended silence as Mina processed my words. We had fought so bitterly the last time we were together. But my friend had an uncanny ability to fill in the blanks with emotional-intellectual viscera that tempered and preserved our connection.

Mina ahemmed and jumped in.

"How would you characterize your relationship with your mom?" she asked. "In an overarching kind of way, from beginning to end, with the middle years, I suspect, feeling kind of fuzzy by now?"

Another pause settled in the air, followed by a chronological zinger.

"Since you're over forty and she's dead now, I mean."

Mina had never, ever been shy. She got right to it, ever the quintessential reporter. I checked my cell for the time, three forty-five already. I still had to get through security. I needed to be on my way. "I'll think about your question," I promised. "Maybe we can check in with each other once I'm home?"

"Give me a ring Saturday or Sunday," Mina suggested, "or on a weekday after the paper's out." And then, before our quick embrace: "I'm here for you, Eliza. I always will be. Trust me on that."

***

Back in Portland, back on the island, my spiraling mind kept me in bed all morning. Half the day was gone by the time I slid out from under the sheets—flannel, with bright yellow sunflowers blooming behind white picket fences. I yanked on a pair of sweatpants, thick and dark as the sky outside my window, and headed downstairs to the kitchen. The wall thermometer read fifty-two degrees, chilly for mid-October, but I wasn't about to start a fire in the woodstove so early in the season. Too messy, too much work. I zipped up my favorite nubby cardigan—the one from four boyfriends ago, the one that gave me an odd kind of comfort when I was down—unlocked the floating home's main door and pushed the screen door open. A northeast wind blew my hair into my face and forced the sweater from my shoulders, exposing my bony chest and my stone-cold mood.

I counted four creaky wooden steps from the kitchen down to the head dock, leading to a concrete ramp and up to the graveled parking lot and the marina's entry behind an electric gate. My head felt heavy and my back was in knots after a long, sleepless night. No wonder. I had hoovered up preprogramming on the Supreme Court confirmation hearings every day the previous week.

I stepped over the oldest cedar boards, the most obviously rotten ones, and shuffled my feet to keep from slipping on a thin layer of moss, barely perceptible in the shadows cast by the midday light of early fall. I wasn't eager to break an ankle, but then again, what if I did? There were worse things than compulsory recuperation in a cozy cabin on the river.

Sweet, opera-loving, animal-adoring Bruce had moved out. The man who had made me a perfect, expertly foamed cappuccino every morning and baked me vegan banana muffins on weekends. The guy who always smelled nice and kissed me goodnight. He had returned to his home state of Montana, back to his cowboy roots. No more Tchaikovsky overtures in the house. Hippo mug gone. I couldn't blame him. Another sabotage job by yours truly. When would I learn to love myself enough to fully love someone else?

The long marina ramp, nearly horizontal to the river, was easy to ascend. Winter had been mild, with only a few days below freezing. Spring had been unusually wet. Summer gave the island days of blistering heat. Now it was fall, and the birds were beginning to migrate. At the top of the ramp I stopped and looked up. A small flock of Canada geese flew in a tidy V formation directly above my head, honking their good afternoons.

I reached my car and retrieved my backpack, damp and in need of laundering, lest it succumb to mildew. A couple more days in the trunk would do that. Since Hillary's Electoral College loss, I had followed the news more closely than ever, Facebook and Instagram included. My old friend Stephanie posted an invitation on social media to "join a movement of, by, and for the people that protests dishonesty and greed at the highest levels of government, scourges that promote inequality and undermine democracy." She was talking about a protest.

"You *have* to come," Stephanie begged me over the phone from Seattle. "We can do a Thelma and Louise thing—two downtrodden ex-journos rubbing elbows with the masses, bitching about the sorry-ass turn our lives have taken." She had been eighty-sixed from the *Seattle Times*, collateral damage during the paper's third round of staff layoffs in as many years. She took the small buyout and packed up her cubicle, holding both middle fingers aloft as she left the building for the last time. A gaggle of gray heads had hovered over her on the totem pole, "seniority," her boss had said with a shrug as he handed her a final paycheck. She tried to keep things in perspective in the months since going on unemployment. But like me, Stephanie was no coffee jockey—she was a journalist through and through.

"I'll be a one-woman antidote to Fox News and Breitbart," she had bragged after joining the *Seattle Times*' breaking news team. Before the layoffs, before the Green River Killer. Before her newspaper prospects started circling the drain.

Stephanie and I were two peas in a pod, a couple of feisty middle-aged women who wanted to do good in the world. Something lasting, something significant. I bought a train ticket from Portland to Seattle, saying yes to the protest, saying you bet to Stephanie. We both said hell yeah to ourselves. All it cost me was time in the rain up in the Evergreen State and a break from stocking shelves at the produce market, no real loss at all.

Chapter Sixty-Four
Martin Spies Eliza at Cooperative Grocery
March 21, 2019

Martin adored Portland. All its weirdness, the buskers and unicycle riders, the themed mom-and-pop coffee shops, the satellite libraries. And the cooperative grocery on Northwest Thurman Street that had been bustling since opening hour, according to the chatty, green-aproned checker who rang up his box of Earl Grey tea bags and handed him a half-dollar back from his five.

As he wrestled the too-big parcel into his too-small coat pocket, she started scanning the next customer's items: a pint of grapefruit juice, some bulk figs, a small bag of pecans, and an organic chocolate bar. "Receipt for you?" she inquired, grinning, adjusting her silver nose ring.

"No, thank you," the woman answered breezily as she angled her debit card into the machine. Early forties, maybe, with wavy red hair. She chewed gum that smelled of cloves. The aroma seized Martin's attention. The timbre of her voice struck him like a thunderbolt from heaven.

It was Eliza!

Martin moved toward the market's exit sign, his heart a snare drum, gooseflesh overtaking his body. He lingered inside the automatic doors as Eliza approached. She smiled at him through lips that opened like flower petals, revealing a matched set of dimples. Raising his good arm, he waved his newsboy bag back and forth in an inelegant salute. She gave him a quick nod and shifted the weight of her own bag from one side to the other, placing the handle of her umbrella in the crook of her elbow.

"Try to stay dry out there!" the checker called after her, waving a friendly goodbye. A Celtic cross tattoo shimmered aquamarine on her wrist.

Martin motioned toward the glass doors. "Please, after you," he said to his daughter, his speech rushed, an unfamiliar baritone. Eliza smiled again and raised an eyebrow, but still did not seem to recognize him. *It's the scars from the fire*, Martin thought, his heart sinking, his mind relieved.

He hadn't seen his daughter in person, even back when they reported that homelessness story together. They had only talked on the phone. His excuses—*I have to heal first; I'm afraid my appearance will repel you*—had worn thin though. Even now, he wasn't prepared to meet her face-to-face. But this was his chance!

Eliza exited the building, opened her umbrella, and started up Northwest Thurman. When she looked back to thank Martin for his courtesy, he was gone.

It was an overcast Portland day, but darkening skies still threatened rain. The thoroughfare was so clogged with shoppers that Eliza nearly tripped over a figure crouching beside a newspaper box a block up the street. The box dispensed the *Oregonian* for seventy-five cents on weekdays, one dollar for the Sunday edition, according to the sign. The man had ducked under a crude shelter made of cracked plastic sheeting and crooked poles. He was moving copies of a tabloid-size paper from his bag onto a large tarp spread out on the asphalt. He wore his hood up, partially obscuring his face.

"I didn't mean to startle you," Eliza said. Martin was on his knees, facing the street. Blond-gray curls strayed out from the sides of his hood. She stayed a minute, observing him. Rain began to fall and despite his best efforts, tiny rivulets of water started making their way through channels in the tarp's brittle folds.

The Neighborhood Caller! The man peddling papers mesmerized Eliza. *Could this scruffy guy be my father?*

Using his functional hand, Martin swiped some of the rainwater away and spread the tarp's corners as far as they could go, as if rolling out cookie dough, then swiped again, his efforts protecting most of the papers from calamitous damage.

"I'll take one of those," Eliza told him, peering over his shoulder at the masthead. "How much?" A gold locket swung on its chain from under her sweater.

Martin selected a dry copy from the middle of the pile and rose slowly, one foot and then the other. He turned toward her, his face a spray of brown-red freckles across pale skin, his cheeks smudged with newsprint. Burned-flesh striations—raised and long healed over—marred the left side of his jaw from his earlobe to his chin.

He looked up at her tremulously, with eyes the color of the sea, eyes that seemed to see right through her, eyes that knew everything. Eliza took a step forward.

"Dad! It's me, Eliza!" She half shouted the greeting. She wanted to scream at him for leaving her, for going to Mexico, for staying away from her since she returned to Portland. Press him about why he hadn't told her about Mina's baby, also *his* baby, her half sister. Why she'd had to hear it from Mina. To confront him with all the ways his decisions, his behavior, had affected her life.

His scars shimmered, pearly white abalone. There was nothing written under My Name Is on the ID card clipped to his jacket. Dimples showed between the scars. Martin wore his struggles like Jacob Marley's chain. Now was not the moment for more conflict.

"I see you, my Sunshine Girl," he said and looked at her, begging forgiveness. "The paper's only a dollar." He exchanged a copy for a crisp George Washington.

"Thank you," he said and winked. "At the *Caller*, what we write is hope."

***

The best thing that had happened to Martin since the old days, since the years back in Yamhill at the *Cascadian*, was working with Eliza on that double-bylined feature for the *Caller* about the Portland homelessness crisis. It felt critically important, and it gave them a way to share something they hadn't shared in decades: purposeful professional collaboration.

For her part, Eliza met with a half dozen county officials to get all the information she needed to back the story up records-wise. Martin, ever the color man, went solo to do his interviews.

Homeless Scotty's tent, two doors down from the first aid pavilion, had been his first stop. The pavilion, a better-than-average tent made of high-quality canvas, was erected after the fire that had nearly taken both their lives, a good use of taxpayer dollars.

Scotty had cleaned up a bit. Cut his hair, tidied his beard. Martin greeted his old acquaintance with a half hug, the way men do. He wondered if he had spruced up anticipating their interview.

"Looking good, Scotty," Martin's comment drew a shy smile from his subject. "Ready to talk?" The freelance photographer from the *Caller* started snapping away. Nursing a mug of coffee, Scotty began telling Martin about his drug use, the thing that had landed him on the street.

Before Dignity Village. Before the fire.

Martin recorded their exchange on his cell phone. Eliza would transcribe the interview later with strong, capable hands and an open heart.

"Meth," Scotty told Martin with contrition and shame. "It was my fault. I didn't curb my habit. I let it get out of hand."

Scotty reached up and scratched his face. Without thinking, through force of habit. The sores had healed over, faded, since he had gotten out of rehab. It would take him a while to regain the weight.

After the story came out—Portland's streets buzzed about it for weeks—the next obvious thing had been for Martin and Eliza to see each other again, in the flesh, as both the same and different people, as father and daughter, as proud reporter colleagues, but Martin had still been too stubborn to agree. Chance, eventually, intervened. Neither of them imagined the co-op market would serve as the surprise backdrop. Both of them were eternally grateful it did.

Chapter Sixty-Five
Eliza Meets Half Sister Greta
September 13, 2019

It was time I met my sibling, the product of my father's fling with Mina. It was almost too convenient that Greta lived across the Willamette in the Lents neighborhood, forty-five minutes from my place on Sauvie Island.

We had arranged to meet in Northwest Portland, a halfway point for each of us. "I'm Eliza Donovan Dixon," I said to the young woman across from me at Haven Coffee. Her heart-shaped face, bathed in sunlight from a far corner window, was a near mirror image of her mother's. She looked nervous. I reached out my hand and our palms touched. "My dad—your dad—is Martin Donovan, the newspaperman."

Greta wore a headband with flannel stars, fingerless gloves, and a flowing vintage dress in a floral print, making me feel a bit stodgy in my sweater, jeans, and ankle boots.

"How old are you now?" I asked, blowing on my coffee, an opening salvo.

"Thirty-one."

"I'm forty-four, so that adds up."

I tried not to let this grown-up Greta know I was sizing her up, but I couldn't help noticing that all of her fingers, and even her thumbs, were adorned with rings. Some had faux gems, others were plain rose gold. There was even a silver one carved with a pair of hands holding a heart. Again, so totally Mina. I felt resentment rising up inside me. She had already taken so much from me and now, it seemed, she had coopted my sister too.

"So, you really like rings," I said, emptying a packet of Stevia into my coffee and jabbing at the mixture, too hard, with a stir stick.

***

It had required most of my skill set as a reporter to get to this point, starting with that come-to-Jesus conversation with Mina, the one that pieced together the real story of her carnal relationship with my dad. Turned out the reindeer journal wonderings of my eight-year-old self hadn't been more than a skip away from the truth: the two of them had shared far more than that one moment under the mistletoe.

"My apartment in Yamhill. My bedroom," Mina disclosed, her eyes meeting mine in an anxious yet unapologetic stare. "We'd been on assignment that night. I was intoxicated. Your dad wasn't."

Mina made it clear she didn't wish to find their daughter. She waved her hand dismissively. "Too much pain and too much regret," she said. "Plus, I don't deserve her." I took her at her word and pursued Greta solo, looking for answers. Public records requests to Contra Costa County were a no go. The 1988 adoption had been a closed one. Ditto an online search for the baby's birth certificate. I googled and called and wrote to Lutheran Family Services, the outfit that arranged the appointment with Caring Connections, exactly the way I had done my research for the adoption story Mina refused to greenlight at the *Juneau Tribune*.

***

"What was your midwife's last name?" I had asked Mina, unsure she would give me an answer. "Erica-Lee what?"

"Merchant," Mina told me. "I'll never forget that woman. She was an angel, manna from heaven."

I called the clinic where Mina received her prenatal care, but Erica-Lee had moved on "some time ago," according to the man who answered the phone. "I heard she's an addiction therapist in LA now. Sorry, no forwarding address." Caring Connections was a dead end too.

"We never reveal our clients' names," the young manager said with a whiff of condescension. "Especially to a reporter."

Social media had never been my go-to as a reportage tool, but sometimes a hunch was even better than a solid source interview. Facebook, of all places, was where I located Greta Hope Sloan, *Adoptee. California native. Lover of the Pacific Ocean, Mary Oliver's poetry, and coconut cream pie.*

Adoptee! I private-messaged her. Two days later she messaged me back.

"I grew up without siblings," Greta wrote. "I'd be happy to meet you. I live in Portland now. I work for a newspaper called the *Propagandist*." Like me, like our dad.

"In fact," Greta continued, a bit more forward than I expected her to be, "I think my boss is one of your former colleagues. "His name is Max. Max Medlin."

***

Greta said it would be best for her if we talked about her birth mother before going any further; would that be okay? She tapped her index fingers together, the rings making a soft clanking noise, and bit her lower lip just like Mina did when she was concentrating. Her eyes were the same blue as Dad's.

"It's fine," I told Greta. "I've known your mom since I was in kindergarten. You'd love Mina. You really would."

Her next two questions came rapid-fire, hitting me right between the eyes.

"If she's so great, why'd she give me up?" Greta wanted to know. She brought her gloved hands up to her face, rubbing her temples with her fingertips. "And what happened to my father?"

She was asking about Dad, but all I could think of was my poor, dead mama. She tried to protect me all those years by keeping Greta a secret. Now Greta was a grown-up, sitting right here in front of me. My mom was only human.

A string of words rushed from my mouth.

"How crazy is it that all of us work for newspapers? Or *worked*, anyway. Dad had so much journo talent. Those things run deep." My sister smiled an amused, knowing smile.

***

Our second meeting took place at a park on the east side. I could see it from my perch on the park's swing set, that hideous red baseball cap with the white capital letters. As Greta approached,

291

wearing a smirk not even her perfect dimples could atone for, I got ready to let her have it.

She snatched the MAGA hat from her head and tossed it into a recycling bin. "Just kidding!" she sang. "Maybe someone can make something useful out of that crappy bit of cloth."

I swallowed the harsh words that bubbled at the top of my throat. "I seriously doubt it," I frowned, "but we've got bigger fish to fry, Greta. Today's the first day of the rest of your life." I slid off the swing and the two of us strolled toward the west end of Grant Park, past dormant fountains and splash pads, stopping where the three main characters from Klickitat Street—Ramona Quimby, Henry Huggins, and Henry's dog Ribsy—formed a trio of magnificent, life-size statues. I grasped Ramona's hand and Greta sat astride Ribsy. Both of us whipped out our cell phones for selfies.

I mimed a hug. "Show him some love!"

My half sister pretend smooched the pup's bronzed head. "Beverly Cleary lived to be 104. This is good karma."

Greta promised to gin up the courage to contact her bio mom and ask for a meeting. "You'll have to convince Mina you're not one of *them*," I cautioned, striding away from Ramona's likeness and handing Greta my phone. "One of those QAnon nuts. I mean—the MAGA hat you were wearing."

The hat was a joke, Greta said, "but I definitely grew up politically conservative. My parents were pretty right-wing."

She dutifully transferred Mina's cell number, work number, and email address into her contacts. "Gotcha, sister," Greta said. "I hear you loud and clear."

She was trying to make sense of her upbringing, square it with what was happening in the country. All the lies, all the posturing, all the division. "My parents think Trump's a hero," she said. "For a while I did too."

I listened impatiently, wanting to save Greta from herself. She did it on her own, without an intervention.

"I'm over that now." Greta's eyes were fixed on my locket. "Look at his insane call to Zelensky in Ukraine. He said it was 'perfect.' The guy should've been impeached and convicted the first time around."

Chapter Sixty-Six
Max Starts Underground Paper
October 2, 2020

How do facts become lies and lies become facts? I would wager Max Medlin had a pretty good idea when he gave himself that phony title and started up his wrong-way paper at the east end of Providence Park in a rent-free basement room he wrangled from an old sportswriter buddy with dubious connections.

From the outset, the *Propagandist* was meant to appeal to a particular, narrow demographic. "Niche marketing," was how Max, the paper's executive editor, couched it in a series of texts, letting me know he was moving from Juneau to Portland to put what he called the "next big thing in digital media" into motion.

I had deleted Max's number from my phone as soon as I left the *Juneau Tribune*. Good riddance. So when it popped up on my screen, at first I didn't recognize it was him.

"INVEST IN THE BEST," read one message, all caps, vintage Max. No mistaking that kind of hubris. "You're invited to get in on the ground floor of a spectacular opportunity. The *Propagandist* will cater to the affiliation needs of dittoheads and disrupters, offering a sumptuous monthly buffet of news articles fit for true patriots only."

Ironic, considering Max had worked for a respectable newspaper all those years. What had happened to make him go 100 percent rogue? Even at the *Tribune* he had been a walking, talking antithesis to the "liberal media," slanting his news stories to the right and thinking he had gotten away with it. Such a sly dog. But we noticed, all the rest of us. Max had the publisher's ear and the newsroom's second-highest salary, so we kept our own counsels, a counterpoint to his surreptitious, neoconservative nonsense.

When I didn't respond to his robo-texts, Max called me out personally.

"Eliza! Don't be shy!" he wrote. "I hope you'll support my new venture. I know you've always been a fan of the Medlin Man!"

It still confounded me that Max and I managed to get along at a real live newspaper in a real live newsroom up in Juneau. Once he took up residence in Portland, he shattered every unspoken caveat I ever thought we had agreed on, beginning with the way he took other people's money to finance his stupid vanity paper instead of doing the harder work of making the case for paid subscriptions himself. I could only imagine the kind of people who would want to read that rag, the sort who thought Black and Hispanic and Asian humans should know their places—the same for women, the same for those working two jobs, or living on the streets. Folks who would sooner sign on to kooky conspiracy theories than reach for reasonable solutions to society's problems, solutions that engaged peoples' whole brains, not just the parts that craved a return to the good old days, a time when fill-in-the-blank had made life worth living.

And that masthead: the *Propagandist*. Come on. Yuck to the max, no pun intended.

It was astonishing how much damage a small splash in a large pool could do to a community on the cusp of redefining itself. That was the situation Stumptown found itself in during the summer of 2020, a decade after TV's *Portlandia* poked fun at over-caffeinated hipsters who insisted that the eggs at their favorite brunch spot in the Pearl come from free-range chickens and the milk in their coffee be squeezed from oats. It was before BLM and the Proud Boys clashed on the streets surrounding the Park Blocks but after that officer knelt on George Floyd's neck and murdered him as he called to his mother, the scene caught on video for the world to consider, all over a counterfeit twenty-dollar bill.

According to the *Propagandist*, every single person who set fires outside federal buildings or chucked projectiles at police officers that July and August were automatically antifa, sworn enemies of counterprotesters carrying Back the Blue signs and waving Thin Blue Line flags, as if anyone joining the nightly melees could fit neatly into those two boxes.

Shame on any publication that deployed the written word to incite people in such crass and destructive ways. I would have loved it if that sorry, slimy scandal sheet had died a slow, tortured death, but it was all over so quickly it was almost as if it had never blighted the streets of Portland at all, as if the six paper-thin issues defining its short little life had been anything more than a self-serving wet dream, Max's own nightmare on Morrison Street.

***

It had been "a terribly embarrassing episode," Greta said, one she was glad to have put in the history books. The way she told the story of her brief, ill-fated employment at the *Propagandist*, Max had been quite the ill-tempered, abrasive boss. Why was I not surprised?

"I need the main op-ed—*now!*" he had often shouted as he manhandled the keyboard and checked to make sure he hadn't ash canned any hard copy, in case a power surge made his rehabbed laptop go berserk. Night classes at Bridge City Community College had turned Greta into an accomplished proofreader, but Max always insisted on being the last person to go over his poison-pen pieces, the latest about a Portland commissioner who hated cops. "Trust no one" had become his personal motto since his clunky exit from the *Tribune*.

"Give me a minute!" she would answer, with proper aplomb. "I'm just finishing up."

Greta threw in with the *Propagandist* on a whim, eager to plunge into the communications profession and taking the first job in the field she was offered. Max wooed her from the moment they bumped into each other in line at Rip City Roasters, exhibiting a faux bonhomie while spinning his new paper as "cutting-edge radical" and coaxing her to jump on board.

"He was convincing," Greta told me later. "I was gullible. And stupid. Should have known better."

As soon as she handed Max her first hundred-dollar donation, part of a monthly stipend from her parents back in California, he'd had her in his clutches.

"I look at this as an investment in our constitution," she said to Max, who believed her because he needed to. Groveling for dollars hadn't turned out to be his forte. Greta—and a few others given to lining the pockets of TV preachers—were all he had.

***

Ten years was a long-ass time for a person to stew over their life's intentions. Two years at Bridge City left Greta with an associate degree and an outsized estimation of her employment potential. She pinballed from waitressing to retail sales, both of which failed to bolster her wispy self-image. She returned to campus to edit copy for the student newspaper for minimum wage, a step down from nowhere.

That was before she met Max, before her adult-size awakening.

She'd had it by her third week on staff. *We can't go back*, she thought while editing his column, calling out misogyny in the margins. *Women can't go back.*

"Why the hell are you slamming *Black Panther* in your piece?" she thundered, exiting out of the document, staring Max down. "Why are you saying it's dangerous for Hollywood to depict women as warriors?"

Max munched his Italian hoagie, his rat eyes gleaming, and told her he stood by every word. Then he said something she had known for quite a while.

"This is a man's world, Greta," he said. "Always has been, always will be. You should get used to that."

Repudiation and disgust roiled Greta's gut. Her friend Aisha's lovely moonbeam face flashed in her mind. What a lucky stroke it had been for Greta to meet her in high school! None of Reg and Darla Sloan's fears about Muslims had come true. And Aisha was a doctor of jurisprudence now! Cal Berkeley School of Law, class of 2014. Plus, she had qualified to run the Boston Marathon. She would toe the starting line that April. Greta was so proud of her.

Words rushed from her mouth like lava down a volcano.

"Let me tell you something, Max," she said evenly, unflinchingly. "Girls don't just want to have fun anymore. We won't stop until we smash the patriarchy."

Max wiped pepperoncini juice off his face.

"*You* get used to it," Greta added and meant it. Her fangirl flirtations with Max's ill-fated publishing project were over.

"I'm done with this place," she said to him seven days before he locked the front door one last time. "Now I know I can do anything if I stay away from people who drag me down. I have you to thank for that." His weak white chin quivered.

"Good luck to you, Max. I really hope you get the help you need."

***

Back in Juneau, it didn't surprise Mina one iota when I told her what Max had been up to.

"Poor guy went completely off the rails this time," I said when she had a minute to take my call. "Word is he got so depressed when the *Propagandist* went belly-up that he canceled his subscription to the *Daily Wire* and grew a long beard. A friend of mine saw him shuffling down Salmon Street, muttering to himself. Said he looked awful."

Mina was unsurprised by the whole sordid mess. What did surprise her was Greta's involvement. She couldn't fathom being taken in by Max.

"Such a small world," she sighed, telegraphing her relief that their alliance was over. "I trust Greta learned a valuable lesson."

Mina still hadn't heard from her daughter, the way she wanted it. But in that moment curiosity overtook caution.

"Is she . . . well?" Mina asked Eliza. "What's she like?"

"To tell you the truth, Mina, she's a lot like you. Tall, beautiful, wicked smart. She's all grown up, you know?"

Eliza wanted to get them together so badly. Now that her own mother was gone, she knew Mina would regret it if she kept pretending her own daughter didn't exist, if she didn't ever meet her.

"I gave Greta your contact information," she blurted, then waited for an angry avalanche that never came.

Chapter Sixty-Seven
Martin's Satchel Reveals Unmailed Letters
October 25, 2020

The diminutive man was perched on the wide, flat edge of a concrete trash can near the public water fountain and the porta-potty, a stack of newspapers in his lap and a coffee can between his knees, waiting for his next customer. His head moved studiously from side to side as runners and walkers streamed by, checking their watches and inhaling the crisp fall air before taking off up the rocky trail and disappearing around the first bend leading to Forest Park. He didn't seem to mind that no one stopped to chat with him, denying him anything more than a passing glance or an asymmetrical smile.

He was the same person I had encountered outside the co-op grocery on Northwest Thurman Street the year before. *My dad.*

***

By the time I saw him at the fountain, that slip of a character with ruddy cheeks and rumpled hair, I was completely out of the journalism game and the natural foods world, wholeheartedly in love with my new pursuit, a nonprofit dedicated to advocating for the homeless. I walked right up to him and started telling him about my life, all the trifling details, like I used to do after a day at grade school, bursting into his *Cascadian* office, delivering breathless accounts of decisive playground victories over the boys who always expected to win at dodgeball.

I smiled to myself at the memory and leaned over to tie my running shoes in double knots. I adjusted my CamelBak and stretched my calves and quads, getting set for eight miles up the Leif Erickson trail and back.

"I'd love it if you'd watch me race sometime, Dad," I said. "I'm thinking of doing a half-marathon." He grinned a grin as wide as the sky.

"I'll swing back to see you after my run. If you'll still be here?"

"Yes," he said, and I smiled back. A few more hamstring stretches and I shoved off.

Dad's words reached my ears as lyrics not three seconds later.

"Like the wind, Eliza," he called after me. "Run like the wind."

***

Community Partners for Alternative Housing was a too-long name for a small organization with a lionhearted purpose: to help unhoused people find permanent shelter, or as the motto went, A Place Where Hope Is Built. Stephanie turned me on to it when I needed it most, when I was alone and adrift in my being, when I didn't know who I was anymore after quitting the *Juneau Tribune* and moving away from Alaska. After leaving my chosen profession for a gig on Sauvie Island stocking shelves at the market. After Abe the babe and Bruce the boring. It was something to hang on to, something meaningful.

The housing crisis had displaced so many people, rent chewing up half their pay or more. It was an untenable situation.

"I have a friend on the board of directors," Stephanie had said on the train ride back from the government corruption rally in Seattle, between drinks in the lounge car and lunch in the café car. "They're looking for an events coordinator. My friend could get you an interview." I must have looked skeptical or uninterested, possibly both. I remember the window, fogged up on the inside, streaks of rain making abstract patterns on the outside as I fretted about the in-between.

"If the Northwest protest circuit doesn't turn out to be your thing, I mean." Stephanie studied me like she needed to understand who I was—different from the person she had known in the journalism world, the self-assured, take-charge me. That woman didn't exist anymore, and Stephanie knew that frightened me, so she reached out like a good friend does.

"Wherever you are or whatever you decide to do with your life," she had said, her hand resting on my forearm, "you'll always be okay with me."

***

The blue nylon satchel, secured with a brass snap at the bottom of the front flap and a long, buckled strap worn across the body, made its first appearance as morning at the trailhead warmed to just below toasty. Dad was still there when I returned from my run an hour after starting. He had doffed his outer layer. The pile of papers was still in his lap, the coin can undisturbed. I marveled at his ability to balance it all with the agility of a circus performer. I wanted so badly to know what was in that bag. Part of me worried he would bolt if I said something, but I wiped the sweat from my face with my shirtsleeve and asked him anyway. People do that sort of thing, inquire after each other's lives, and Dad and I were getting to know each other again.

I went the lighthearted, humorous route.

"Whatcha got hidden in your man purse?" I teased, and he smiled and looked down, his good hand grasping the newspapers, making sure they didn't scatter, his shrunken right hand patting the satchel. Carefully, lovingly, he patted it. He ran his fingers around its front edge, lifted the magnetic snap and closed it. He didn't say anything at first.

"No problem if you don't want to tell me what's in there," I said, giving him an out. I pointed at his hip. "I mean, if it's a secret." My father shifted his position, his body language broadcasting discomfort. I was starting to feel sheepish when he surprised me by switching hands—right hand on the pile of papers and left hand on the satchel—and lifted the flap to display its contents.

"They're letters," he said, reaching in and producing a lone envelope that had seen better days: corners bent, paper yellowed, faded writing on the front. It carried no postage stamp. He let out a sad sigh. "Letters I wrote but never sent."

I strained to see who they were addressed to, who might have received them had he mailed them out. I tried to be discreet, but my companion was a keen observer. Nothing got past him. He nudged the envelope back into the bag and closed the snap. My curiosity would have to wait for another day, when he was ready.

Chapter Sixty-Eight

White House Lies a "Clear and Present Danger"

In the first year of the pandemic, as American deaths from COVID-19 piled up, the flagrant lies coming from 1600 Pennsylvania Avenue had snowballed, too, at one point averaging more than sixty a day, two or three per hour. Even if she made a concerted effort, Mina doubted she could come up with more than a handful of fibs to tell in any one twenty-four-hour period.

"Un-fucking-believable," she said to Naomi, her closest ally in the newsroom.

It was interesting to Mina, the way it felt so personal. She had been lied to before, most egregiously by Martin, back in the day at the *Cascadian*. He had said he cared, that he would be there for her. But he hadn't and wasn't, and though she had forgiven him, she couldn't forget. She would never get past his wholesale rejection, however predictable or inevitable it may have been. She wouldn't put up with more lies. Not from him, not from anyone.

So it hit her hard, the megalomaniacal tendencies of the man who had gasbagged his way into the national consciousness and somehow into the presidency itself, telling whopper after whopper until minds turned to mush, beaten down by an unrelenting firehose of falsehoods. Repeat a lie often enough and people will believe it. Some people, anyway, the ones who love a cult of personality.

Not Mina. But Max was a different animal. A year after the inauguration, before he left the *Juneau Tribune* and moved to Portland with his beady eyes and his delusions of grandeur, he had shown himself to be one of those hook, line and sinker folks. The day Mina heard him tell Fletcher that forty-five "really wasn't so bad" and that he "had some good qualities," Mina fled into the bathroom, lest she be tempted to box his ears or find a reason to fire him. And when he defended those straitjacket-level assertions from the Oval Office that the press couldn't be trusted—"we journalists need to get our act together," he scolded, with an expression as serious as a funeral director's—Mina still held her tongue, but barely. She had never forgotten that.

"Folks like Max and Trump are so sure of themselves," she said to Naomi one Throwback Thursday, speaking of newsrooms past. "Funny, because listening to them makes the rest of us less sure about everything."

***

It was all going to come home to roost, this new blood sport of trashing "the media," lumping all reporters together as if tabloid tittle-tattle were the same thing as solid investigative reporting. If Mina and her colleagues looked the other way when powerful people dodged or diminished the truth, everything they worked for would be lost. It was the stuff of nightmares, but did it need to be the zeitgeist of their era? It made her shiver to think about it.

"Clear and present danger," Mina remarked to Naomi after editing her latest story.

Naomi donned her glasses squarely, a piece of armor. "It's our job to keep fighting," she asserted from behind her mask, and she and Mina bumped elbows on it.

Defending facts, they knew, was the same thing as defending the commons.

***

A few weeks into 2017 Naomi had hammered out a column about the fabulist nascent politician who had promised to be a president for all Americans in his postelection victory speech. "These observations are less about the man," she wrote, "and more about his reliance on disorienting speech that dilutes our trust in one another, a tactic that has the potential to fracture our society so thoroughly that it dooms the American experiment." The column got thousands of clicks, more than any other op-ed the *Juneau Tribune* had published in years. The publisher was so pleased with the numbers he paid a rare visit to the newsroom.

"Your column mattered," he said to Naomi, shaking her hand

and placing an Olive Garden gift card—with his own business card attached—inside it. "We've had several new subscriptions already."

A fortified Naomi had a few more words, uttered in Ogles's presence. "That pledge was complete and utter hogwash," she snarled, her voice registering off-the-charts acrimony. "It was his first bald-faced lie as POTUS-elect, and I was happy to say so. Running for office was always only about his ego."

Journalists had to stick together and resist complacency, Naomi said, tucking the gift card into a pocket inside her purse and continuing. She had the publisher's ear. "If we don't persevere— write this down and quote me verbatim if you want to—as Lincoln warned, we will not be able to keep our republic."

***

America made it six whole days into 2021 before a violent mob attacked the halls of Congress to try and overturn the 2020 election, when Joe Biden shellacked Donald Trump by seven million votes. Everyone knew it was coming because it was all over social media. "Big protest in DC on Jan. 6th," the almost-ex-president tweeted. "Be there, will be wild!" The only thing left was the execution.

The clown-car attempted coup was the last straw for Mina. She was fed up with post-truthers and their dangerous nonsense, she told Eliza over the phone, the line burning hot from Juneau to Portland.

"I did a deep purge of my Facebook 'friends' over the weekend," she said, her raw alto unrepentant. "I won't miss any of them. You can't fix stupid."

When the library doors swung open promptly at nine o'clock, Martin was third in line to access the free computers. He was used to waiting and practiced patience, a discipline he owed to the example of his amigo Pedro. That morning, though, his fingers— the five on his healthy hand, anyway—were itching to peck out a message to Mina he had already composed in his head. An apology of sorts, along with an entreaty.

Multnomah County Library had reopened five of its branches in summer 2021, after the Alpha and Beta variants but before Delta. The last big covid surge had quieted somewhat, enough for the Centers for Disease Control to say it was safe for vaccinated people to gather indoors, masks on and socially distanced. Restauranteurs were welcoming diners again but limiting the number allowed inside. Theaters and sports arenas required patrons to show their I Got My Shot cards.

The public was learning to contend with the virus, confusing though it was. "No other choice," Martin shrugged to the man next to him in line, from behind an N95, its multiple white paper layers muting his speech. "We gotta keep living, right?"

On the *Juneau Tribune*'s website, the Contact Us page listed Mina's email address second, just after the publisher's. *Easy peasy*, Martin thought as he brought up the Compose page and started writing. It took him twice as long to navigate the right side of the keyboard as it did the left, stabbing those letters painstakingly. He hoped he would be able to finish and push send before his fifteen minutes were up.

"Dear Mina," his message began. "It's high time I explained why I left Oregon all those years ago. Why I went to Mexico after you left for California. I know Judith felt totally abandoned. Maybe you felt the same way. Maybe you wondered why I never looked you up."

He told her about the progression of his hemidystonia, how it had denied him the use of his dominant right hand. "I couldn't write stories," Martin said. "I couldn't provide for my family. I wouldn't have been good for any of you, given my affliction." Eventually, he disclosed, "after pushing my pride and vanity aside," he made the wrenching decision to return to Oregon, away from his "oasis in the sun," back to a reality that included joblessness, the spiraling housing crisis, and hours upon hours by himself each day.

"Things are better for me now," he told her in the final paragraph. "I'm making my way. But like anyone I guess—perhaps like you— I'll never be whole. Truth is, I never really was."

Living without his daughter had broken his heart in two, he wrote before signing off. "I'll spend the rest of my life trying to make up for lost time," he wrote, wistfulness permeating the page. "I wish you well, Mina. Whatever you think of me, I hope you'll forgive my thoughtless indiscretion when I was your boss."

***

Two thousand miles away in Juneau, Mina stared at Martin's message in her inbox, masterfully crafted and punctuated just so. As she read it, over and over, she felt a weight lift and fly away. After all the time that had gone by, here he was, owning his part in what had transpired.

Her fingers rested on the middle row of her keyboard as she sipped her coffee. "Dear Martin," she wrote, then went blank. It took quite a while for the right words to come to her.

"I'm glad to hear you're doing all right. Our night together was a beautiful, one-time thing. All is forgiven. Eliza told me you two are back in touch. That makes me happy."

He hadn't asked, so she made no mention of Greta. Or of her own deep regret, burnished in the crucible of her own understanding.

Chapter Seventy
Mina Puts In Remote Work Request amid COVID-19
December 21, 2021

Mina drummed her fingers against a half-empty can of Coke, its fizz all gone, its contents at room temperature. Her longer-than-normal nails were getting in the way of her typing and her Coke can drumming. Her hair had split ends. Her legs had gone unshaven. She had made certain promises to herself, exercise and clean eating among them, promises she wasn't keeping.

Still and all, everything was new again that could be new, and that would have to be enough.

The *tink, tink, tink* of her fingernails kept time with the clicking of the newsroom clock affixed to the wall above the big metal file cabinet full of folders containing reporters' research, sources and public documents and story timelines. Mina had been staring at that clock all afternoon. She had tried, many times, to give up the habit—the Coke drinking, not the clock watching—but ultimately resigned herself to its dubious benefits. Caffeine and sugar had seen her through many a deadline, like a friend who wasn't good for her but was always there anyway, ready to party. Besides, the publisher was addicted to the stuff, and even though it had turned his teeth a dingy yellow, Mina made believe that if she threw in with him, if she let him know she was a Coca-Cola girl all the way—Pepsi could go to hell—he might be amenable to giving her a nice severance when she retired. They would clink their cans together and he would write the check.

Right. When pigs fly, she groused.

A final tick turned the time to five o'clock, jolting Mina from her reverie. She was more than ready for the long weekend. She had taken Friday off. Three days stretched in front of her, like a white-sand beach in the Pacific Islands. She needed a place to retreat to, away from the carnival barker who had vacated the White House but continued his delusional rantings. Away from Alaska and the *Tribune*, away from her regrets and from everyone but herself. Airbnb showed a one-room log cabin for rent on Lake Washington's

Mercer Island, east of Seattle, a two-hour hop from Juneau. Perfect. She planned to stop by home, stuff three paperbacks into her carry-on—two period novels and a thin volume of Mary Oliver poetry—and off she would go.

She planned to be the last one out of the office. With a turn of the key in the front-door lock, she would emancipate herself.

***

In forty years, from aol.com to juneautribunenewsroom.net to the current m.breckenridge@co.juneautribune Mina hadn't changed her mind about email, its very nature oppressive, its constant flow as suffocating as laundry. Out of every ten messages, she found value in only one or two. She would delete five, and a dozen more would take their place.

"Trifling," she said as she ditched message after message, drawing little reaction from the rest of the newsroom. "That's what they are, trifling," she repeated, but none of the younger reporters paid her any mind. Mina felt dejected. She thought about ratcheting up her depression meds, which she had started before Trump took office. She thought about asking her coworkers if they knew what *trifling* meant. She considered getting up and walking right out the door, but it was only nine. Would anyone even notice?

Ever since Eliza left, and especially since the scourge, the newsroom had taken on all the luster of a county jail cell: colorless, soulless, uninspiring. Naomi was still there, hanging on, but even she was losing her spark, beaten down by the culture wars. Mina actively sought out places to hide: the old editions morgue, the picnic table out back. When that tactic failed, she marched into the publisher's office and made her case for working remotely.

"I got vaccinated as soon as my age group was eligible," Mina said, "and I've had both boosters. Dr. Fauci would be proud," she added, looking for an inflection point.

Jiles Ogles didn't crack a smile.

"But as one of the company's senior workers, I have to take more precautions. I'm still worried about getting covid."

To Mina's surprise Jiles—five years her junior—granted her

request with the caveat that she show up once a week, online, for the newsroom staff meeting.

"I'm hardly here either." He turned his computer screen toward her, showing off the Zoom icon he used at home, a cartoon Jiles with a Fu Manchu, holding a martini glass. "I get where you're coming from."

***

Friday was waning. Mina took a last look at her email before shutting down her laptop in case one of the twentysomething slackers had sent a zinger she needed to handle. The name *Greta* jumped from her screen, giving her an instant pounding migraine. She clicked on it.

"Our mutual friend Eliza suggested that we meet and get to know one another," the message read, "but I'm not sure that's a good idea. What do you think, Mom?"

Mom. God. Mina couldn't move, as if her butt was glued to her chair.

Fletcher passed by her desk. "So long, compatriot," he said, delivering a crisp salute. She sat there, mute and befuddled. What was she going to do about this?

Chapter Seventy-One
Chance Meeting Occurs at Mill Ends Park
June 5, 2022

Afternoon errands brought me downtown. I parked my car near Mill Ends Park and tapped my license plate number into the meter. It wouldn't take long to reach the library and return the books I had borrowed. I hurried along, dodging dog walkers and shoppers with bags from the Apple store and Marios. To my right, not more than five yards away, a man's familiar silhouette entered my peripheral vision. I came to an abrupt halt. The red ten-second light counted down, beeping its warnings, but I stopped short of the crosswalk.

I squinted and stared. The man was squatting inside a traffic median in the middle of the thoroughfare. He sat cross-legged, like the Buddha, his countenance serene and open. He looked like my dad!

Cars approached the intersection. Stopped, idled, proceeded forward. The Buddha man retained his posture, still as a statue. A wispy beard fanned out beneath his mustache, thick in some places and thin in others, revealing Etch A Sketch scars on his cheek and jaw. Ruddy lips poked through the jungle of hair and skin. A cardboard sign was propped against his knees, its bottom edge cresting Crocs-clad feet. Scrawled across the sign were six words in three lines, written in a cursive-print hybrid. Seven words, counting the signature. "Everything was beautiful and nothing hurt." I knew that phrase. The great Kurt Vonnegut. And the handwriting. There was no mistaking it.

A pile of newspapers sat at his side, a rock on top securing them. "Daddy!"

He grinned and pointed at the sign, rising from the cushion, beckoning me forward. I rushed into his embrace, feeling the warmth of his strong arm, the tragic blight of the other.

I pressed my head into his shoulder and imagined a place beyond knowing, that thin space between right and wrong, between here and there, where acceptance and understanding shimmered and hovered, as perfect as things could ever be.

It was him. My dad. Again.

Chapter Seventy-Two
Eliza Brings Greta to Meet Martin
June 6, 2022

I was on a mission when I returned to the same spot in the downtown core the following day. The median where I encountered Dad. I marched up to my father and side hugged him. I spoke to him with a sternness that said I was not playing.

"No more cat and mouse, Dad. I brought Greta with me. She's waiting a few streets from here. I'm going to bring her over to see you," I said, breathless. "She's thirty-four now. An advocate, like us."

Dad gaped. His pitted face turned ashen. He arched his small back defensively. "Okay," he said. "Let's do this, Eliza."

I charged off, around the block where he couldn't see me. I wanted him to feel the enormity of this moment, not just for him but for me and for Greta. My shoulders were wound as tight as springs. Blood pulsed behind my eyes.

I opened my car door to fetch Greta. "C'mon, let's go," I demanded, almost changing my mind, but this wasn't just about me. In a blink the two of us were back at the median, standing in front of our dad. Not *my* dad, *our* dad. He greeted us with his chin up, ready to face the music.

"Well, here she is." *Again,* I thought, still pissed that Dad had found her first, when she was a teenager. I could have picked his brain when I was looking for her, mimicked his process. It would have saved me so much goddamn time.

Greta stepped forward awkwardly, like a beauty pageant contestant whose turn for a twirl in front of the judges had arrived.

Dad studied adult Greta: Her sleek dark hair. Her long legs. Her five-foot-eight frame. Totally Mina from three decades past. He shook his head, recalling their first meeting when Greta was sweet sixteen, about to entertain guests at her birthday party.

Poetic justice that Greta didn't remember him.

"I'm very pleased to meet you, Martin," Greta smiled with one side of her mouth. Her family-trait dimple popped out. "I honestly never thought I would."

She kept beaming. Finally she had a visual.

Dad's elf face exulted. Not just one daughter. *Two* daughters. Eliza and Greta. In the same space, not one and then the other. What a trip.

"Thank you for coming," he said to Greta, nodding his shaggy head. He gave me a look of affection that turned me five again, waiting for him to finish his work at the *Cascadian*, my small hand clutching a piece of hard candy.

He turned toward me, grateful. "I can't tell you what it means to me that you made this happen, Sunshine. I wrote to Mina, asked her about Greta, whether she'd told you about her. But she never wrote me back."

EPILOGUE
Eliza Gets News from Greta in Alaska
Portland, Oregon: October 8, 2022

By all measures, today's rally supporting journalists was a rousing success. Attendance in the thousands, and no one arrested or thrown into vans, even with those flag-waving counterprotesters in full riot gear trying to rattle everyone's cages. Biden and company have worked hard to claw back a modicum of respect for ethical reporters and editors, countering the last administration's "fake news" bullshit, but they still have a long way to go. I was happy to be part of it, doing my bit for a more enlightened world.

There have been other demonstrations—Black Lives Matter, police brutality, *Roe v. Wade*—with opposing factions showing up and scrambling the signal. I've never seen the citizenry so divided. As long as they aren't hurting someone else, people should be able to live and work and express themselves however and wherever they want. And that goes for all of us First Amendment fans too.

"Back off, cops," I snarl to myself. "We know our rights."

Voices in the scattering crowd fade to echoes. "NOT THE ENEMY!" One person is still yelling. They don't realize the rally is over.

"For the *Juneau Tribune*!" whoops another, and then another, a mixed chorus trailing off in the atmosphere.

A pink-pussy-hatted woman tosses a pro-journalist sign into the trunk of her SUV, shakes the rain off her umbrella, closes it up, and gets in. Her left turn signal blinks and she enters the roadway. A power fist emerges from the driver's side window.

Everyone is leaving after a job well done, making separate journeys home.

***

As I walk to my car my phone lights up, buzzes for the hundredth time. Another text pops up on the screen.

"Eliza, I'm up in Alaska."

It's Greta. She actually went! She's in Juneau with Mina. All will be well.

I text her back, fat-fingering the display. "Greta! What's going on?"

"Mina got shot at the *Tribune*."

Pause.

"She was leaving the office for the weekend."

Pause.

"Eliza, she didn't make it."

Holy shit, no!

I type the only obvious question: "Are you sure?"

"Yes, I am. She's dead. And Fletcher got shot too."

Pause.

"In the leg. He'll be OK."

***

For hours I've been trying to keep up with the news in Juneau. Who's okay, who's injured. Who's alive, who's dead. Names, locations, statuses. The reporting is infuriatingly spotty. Everything's happening in real time. Gathering facts in a crisis isn't easy. No one had reported a threat from the shooter. No warning, not a peep. Why had this happened?

I know what I need to do. Drive to PDX, catch the first flight to SeaTac, then on to Juneau. I have to get to Greta. I have to see Mina one last time.

I locate my Subaru, fumble for the keys. Click the fob, open the door, drop into the driver's seat. I steer my car over the Marquam Bridge in a fog. My phone lights up again. I engage my Bluetooth and point my car toward I-84.

"I'm so sorry, Eliza." Greta texts. "Mina knew you loved her. Enough to send me to meet her."

I take a sharp breath in. Fletch will be all right. He's tough under that soft exterior. But Mina? Dead? It can't be. She's the most alive person I've ever known! Did I misinterpret Greta's messages? Of course I didn't. Mina's gone, just when I'm back together with my dad. None of it makes any sense.

I call Greta. Leave a voicemail. "I'm on my way, sis," I say, my voice catching, my nose a faucet. "You're not alone."

Sis. Who would have ever thought?

***

I stow my carry-on bag and take a window seat halfway down the aisle in exit row sixteen. My hand trembles as I cradle my phone and search for Mina in my contacts. I start reading back through our text messages. Hundreds of them, some short and succinct, others long and involved, a few arguments containing curse words and exclamation points. Photos of the two of us together. A couple of the *Tribune* crew.

The flight attendant leans into my row, asks me to put my phone in airplane mode. A last message from Greta beeps through as the plane starts to taxi. A picture of Mina and Daddy on the steps of the *Cascadian*, arm in arm, smiling the smiles of intrepid journalists. Greta must be in possession of Mina's phone, all that remains of her.

My chest collapses, my heart a giant, black-and-blue bruise.

The plane lurches and shudders, its engines near maximum thrust. "I trust you, Mina," I say out loud, to no one, as the wheels leave the runway. "And you too, Mom." Now I know trust equals love. I blow a kiss to the black outside the window. To destiny, to wherever they are.

ACKNOWLEDGMENTS

So many big-hearted humans shared their superpowers with me during the making of this book. When I first dreamed the dream, they saw promise in it. When I floundered in the middle, they took my hand and helped me fix things. When I thought about stopping, they pushed me forward with love.

They are the kernel of truth in my story, the nut graph, the beginning and ending, the lifeblood.

From West Coast to East Coast, fragrant colorful bouquets to my splendid publisher Naomi Rosenblatt, who grasped my intent with this novel, embraced the narrative, improved the storyline, and took a chance on me as a debut author. Working with Heliotrope Books has been the best reason ever to finally visit The Big Apple.

A tip of the fedora to Howard "Lefty" Page, my friend Lisa's father, who nicknamed me "Scoop" in 1980, my first year as a newspaper reporter. I embodied that moniker and tried to live up to its promise. I hope I did journalism proud.

A boldface 60-point thank you headline to my community newspaper colleagues over the years for inspiring this story and conjuring these amalgamated characters. Janie, Sharon, Mikel, Kevin, Jim, Christina, Jessie, Jaime, Laura, Tracy, Shasta, John, Jill, and Michael, we did excellent work together. We had fun doing it. I couldn't have asked for more.

Suzy Vitello Soulé for her deft developmental edits, her pitch-perfect feel for the narrative, and her smart "But what if you did this?" ideas that made so much sense.

Natalie Hirt for her incisive micro-level editing, her effusive enthusiasm, and our multiple come-to-Jesus conversations over chocolate-banana muffins and strong coffee.

Abiding appreciation to the inimitable Laura Stanfill for believing in this story and my unique ability to tell it. For cheering me on with phone calls and sparkly handmade gifts. For her steadfast friendship since our newsroom days, when we sat side-by-side in "the dungeon" and wrote stories together on deadline. For her generous guidance throughout the publishing process. For saying yes to a last-minute editing pass. For being the light she is, for me and so many others.

Crackerjack copy editor Gina Walter, who caught things both big and little in my manuscript.

Jackie Shannon Hollis for her gentle presence, humor, and sage writerly advice.

Kathlene Postma for her generosity, empathy, and humanity.

Dian Greenwood for our walks and talks about writing and books and aging and not ever giving up.

Cindy Sullivan for her whimsical original *Sunshine Girl* art. I blew kisses to that painting every morning until the magic happened.

Wonderful, visionary Portland book designer Gigi Little for creating the cover of my dreams. Seeing it still gives me goosebumps.

Miriam Gershow for her careful read and face-saving suggestions.

Uber-talented, fairy dust-sprinkled, meet-cute creative couples Gigi Little and Stephen O'Donnell and Carmel Breathnach and Parag Shah, who always greet me at book events with warmth and genuine interest in my life. Ditto the amazing author Rene Denfeld, whose novel *The Enchanted* blew my hair back when I read it for the first time, and whose praises I'll continue to sing loudly at every opportunity.

To Steve Arndt, the Portland literary community's ambassador and biggest cheerleader, for reminding all of us that art is life.

Women of The Dugout 2018-2020 — Mary, Laura, Dian, Natalie, Kirsten, Suzy, and Suzanne — who read first chapters of this novel and gave me essential feedback. Your kindness and collective intelligence nourished me and propelled me onward.

Brilliant beta readers Steve, Mike, Christina, Tracy, and Kristen for commenting on early drafts of the manuscript with honesty, intelligence, and open hearts. You are all rock stars.

Gratitude to creative dynamo Jen Knox and Unleash Lit for publishing an early excerpt from this book.

Mad respect to Letty Owings, my high school Honors English teacher, whose perfect cursive note on my report card, "You have a flair for writing," set me firmly on the journalist path. Her spirit, wisdom, and verve live on.

Thanks and appreciation to all the indie booksellers and bookstores out there. You're the tops.

To my children and their children, without whom this book would mean nothing. Lindsey, Kelly, Tim, Tommy, Ezra, Calvin, and Saul, you are my reasons. I love you all forever.

To my sweet husband Gregg for traveling with me on this crazy-quilt ride called life. You have my heart. We're lucky ducks.

And to the dedicated professional journalists out there, still doing the hard work of preserving democracy, which does indeed die in darkness: Thank you.

BOOK CLUB/DISCUSSION QUESTIONS

1. Author Nancy Townsley spent almost four decades in newsrooms in Oregon. How does her novel about a family of journalists impact your understanding of the media? What's something you didn't know about newspaper journalism before reading the book?

2. Eliza's relationship with her father is at the core of the novel. Why do you think she follows in his footsteps? What's one difference between how she approaches news stories and how her father did during his time as an editor? How is her experience as a female journalist different from Martin's experience?

3. What role do you feel journalism played in the outcome of the 2024 election? How did that compare to previous elections?

4. In the novel, both Mina and Eliza have to deal with newsroom sexism: Mina at The Cascadian in the 1980s, butting heads with the football coach and the realtor—even her well-meaning boss, Ed McKee. Eliza at the Juneau Tribune in the 2000s, overhearing a sexist conversation between male colleagues and getting paid less than Max for doing the same job. Do you think women are more widely accepted and respected nowadays in the field of journalism? Or less?

5. The journalists in Sunshine Girl—Martin, Mina, and Eliza—grapple with the human temptation to shade the truth. Is there ever a good or noble reason to skew the news?

6. How do you think the media as a whole has changed over the course of your lifetime? How have the lines between truth and opinion been blurred? Is objectivity still a goal in a media landscape that prioritizes hot takes and controversy?

7. After the rise of the internet, do you think Eliza's job as a reporter got easier, or harder? Why? When looking for information about politics, culture, or current affairs, what are your go-to news sources? How does social media fit into that scenario?

8. The novel includes scenes about the Challenger explosion, the 9/11 attacks, and the coronavirus pandemic. Could journalists have done a more effective job covering those crises? What about mass shootings? Do media stories related to gun violence and firearms control contribute to or detract from your understanding of those issues?

9. Sunshine Girl outlines the role of journalism in a supposedly free society, and the challenges to it in an increasingly unfree one. What specific steps should journalists take to preserve and protect democracy?

10. What do you think the result would be if members of the press were banned from covering US political news altogether? Would society be better off? Worse off?

11. How did you feel about Martin at the end of the novel? Was he a good father to Eliza? Would you say Eliza was a good daughter? Why or why not?

12. What were the differences in the bond between Eliza and Mina versus Eliza and Judith? What woman (or women) in your own youth had the greatest or most lasting impact on you?

13. Which character did you as a reader most relate to, and why?

14. For those interested in maintaining a free press in America—in elevating truth over lies in the public square—what's one step you can take to support journalists today?

AUTHOR BIO

Nancy Townsley lives in a floating home along the Multnomah Channel near Portland, Oregon, with her husband Gregg and their golden retriever Bernie. Her debut novel, *Sunshine Girl*, was inspired by her long career as a newspaper journalist. She continues to have a keen interest in the cultural and political changes altering the media landscape, channeling that fascination into writing fiction and nonfiction. Her creative work has appeared in *Hippocampus, The Big Smoke, Nailed* magazine, the *Timberline Review*, *Elephant Journal, Mountain Bluebird Magazine*, and several anthologies. "Leaving Tulum," an excerpt from her first novel, can be found at unleashcreatives.com.

Photo © Brian McDonnell, Bmac Studio